RAVENSDALE'S DEFIANT CAPTIVE

BY
MELANIE MILBURNE

Harlequin (UK) Limited's policy is to use papers that are natural, renewable and recyclable products and made from wood grown in sustainable forests. The logging and manufacturing processes conform to the legal environmental regulations of the country of origin.

Printed and bound in Spain
by [...], Barcelona

MILLS
BOON

Published in Great Britain 2015
by Mills & Boon, an imprint of Harlequin (UK) Limited,
Eton House, 18-24 Paradise Road, Richmond, Surrey, TW9 1SR

© 2015 Melanie Milburne

ISBN: 978-0-263-24941-5

Harle
renew
sustai
to the

Printe
by CP

An avid romance reader, **Melanie Milburne** loves writing the kind of books that gave her so much joy as she was busy getting married to her own hero and raising a family. Now a *USA TODAY* bestselling author, she has won several awards—including The Australian Readers' Association most popular category/series romance in 2008 and the prestigious Romance Writers of Australia R*BY award in 2011.

She loves to hear from readers!

MelanieMilburne.com.au
Facebook.com/Melanie.Milburne
Twitter @MelanieMilburn1

Books by Melanie Milburne

Mills & Boon Modern Romance

At No Man's Command
His Final Bargain
Uncovering the Silveri Secret
Surrendering All But Her Heart
His Poor Little Rich Girl

The Chatsfield

Chatsfield's Ultimate Acquisition

The Playboys of Argentina

The Valquez Bride
The Valquez Seduction

Those Scandalous Caffarellis

Never Say No to a Caffarelli
Never Underestimate a Caffarelli
Never Gamble with a Caffarelli

The Outrageous Sisters

Deserving of His Diamonds?
Enemies at the Altar

Visit the Author Profile page at
millsandboon.co.uk for more titles.

To Ella Carey,
a talented writer, a dear friend and a wonderful person.
I love our writing chats! xxx

CHAPTER ONE

JULIUS RAVENSDALE KNEW his housekeeper was up to something as soon as she brought in his favourite dessert. 'Queen's pudding?' He raised one of his brows. 'I never have dessert at lunch unless it's a special occasion.'

'It *is* a special occasion,' Sophia said as she put the meringue-topped dessert in front of him.

He narrowed his gaze. 'Okay, tell me. What's going on?'

Sophia's expression was sheepish. 'I'm bringing in a girl to help me run the house. It's only for a month until this wretched tendonitis settles. The extra pair of hands will be so helpful and I'll be doing my bit for society. It's a win-win.'

Julius glanced at the wrist brace Sophia had been wearing for the past couple of weeks. He knew she worked far too hard and could do with the extra help but he liked to keep the staff numbers down in the villa. Not because he was mean about paying them. He would pay them triple to stay away and let him get on with his work. 'Who is it?'

'Just a girl who's in need of a bit of direction.'

Julius mentally rolled his eyes. Of all the housekeepers he could have chosen, he had employed the Argentinian reincarnation of Mother Teresa. 'I thought we agreed your lame ducks were restricted to the stables or the gardens?'

'I know, but this girl will go to prison if—'

'Prison?' he said. 'You're bringing a convicted criminal here?'

'She's only been in trouble a couple of times,' Sophia said. 'Anyway, maybe the guy deserved it.'

'What did she do to him?'

'She keyed his brand-new sports car.'

Julius's gut clenched at the thought of his showroom-perfect Aston Martin housed in the garage. 'I suppose she said it was an accident?'

'No, she admitted to it,' Sophia said. 'She was proud of it. That and the message she sprayed on his lawn with weed killer.'

'She sounds delightful.'

'So you'll agree to have her?'

Julius took in his housekeeper's hopeful expression. His sarcasm was lost on her. Sophia was the most charitable person he knew. Always doing things for others. Always looking for a way to make a difference in someone's life. He knew she was lonely since both her adult children had moved abroad for work. What would it hurt to indulge her just this once? He would be busy with fine-tuning his space software. He had less than a month to iron out the kinks in the programming before he presented it to the research team for funding approval.

He let out a long breath. 'I don't suppose you've ever thought of taking up knitting or cross-stitch instead?'

Sophia beamed at him. 'Just wait until you meet her. You're going to love her.'

* * *

Holly considered making a run for it when the van stopped but the size of the villa and its surrounds made her pause. It was big. Way big. Massive. It probably had its own area code. Maybe its own political party. It was four storeys high, built in a neo-classical style with spectacular gardens and lush, rolling fields fringed by thick forest. It didn't look anything like the detention centre she'd envisaged. There was no twelve-foot-high fence with electrified barbed wire at the top. There was no surveillance tower and no uniformed, rifle-toting guards—or, at least, none she could see—casing the joint. It looked like a top-end hotel—a luxurious and very private resort for the rich and famous. Which kind of made her wonder why she'd been sent here. Not that she'd been expecting chains and bread and water or anything, but still. This was seriously over the top.

'It's only for a month,' Natalia Varela, her case-worker, said as the decorative wrought-iron gates opened electronically, allowing them access to the long, sweeping limestone driveway leading to the immaculately maintained villa. 'You got off lightly considering your rap sheet. I know a few people who'd happily swap places with you.'

Holly grunted. Folded her arms across her breasts. Crossed her right leg over her left. Jerked her ankle up and down. Pouted. Why should she look happy? Why should she act *grateful* that she was being sent to live with some man she'd never heard of in his big, old fancy villa?

A month.

Thirty-one days of living with some stranger who

had magnanimously volunteered to 'reform' her. Ha-ha. Like that was going to work. Who was this guy anyway? All she'd been told was he was some hotshot techie nerd from England who had made the big time in Argentina designing software for space telescopes used in the Atacama Desert in neighbouring Chile. Oh, and he was apparently single. Holly rolled her eyes. He'd agreed to take on a troubled young woman for altruistic reasons? And the correctional authorities had actually *fallen* for that?

Yeah, right. She knew all about men and their dodgy motivations.

After being given the all clear from the security intercom device, Natalia drove through the gates before they whispered shut behind the car. 'Julius Ravensdale is doing you a big favour,' she said. 'He's only agreed to this—and very reluctantly at that—because his housekeeper has tendonitis in her wrist. You'll be her right-hand helper. It's an amazing opportunity. This place is like a five-star resort. It'll be great vocational training for you. I hope you'll make the most of it.'

Vocational training for what? Holly thought with a cynical curl of her lip. No one was going to make a housekeeper out of her just because she'd made a few mistakes, which weren't even really mistakes, because her pond-scum stepfather had seriously had it coming to him. It was just a dumb old sports car, for pity's sake. So what if he had to have it re-sprayed and his precious lawn re-sown after the weedkiller incident?

Holly was not going to be some rich man's lowly slave scrubbing floors until her knees grew callouses as big as cabbages. Her days of being pushed around were long over. Julius Ravens-whatever-his-name-was would be in for a big shock if he thought he could exploit her to suit his nefarious needs.

What if it wasn't the kitchen he planned to have her slaving in? What if he had more salacious plans? In her experience, men with money thought they could have anything and anyone they wanted. All that nonsense about him 'reluctantly' agreeing to take her on was just a ruse. Of course he would say that. He wouldn't want to look *too* eager to take in a prison statistic waiting to happen. He would be 'doing his bit for society' by trying to *do her*.

Bring it on, she thought. *Let's see how far you get.*

'Oh, I'll make the most of it, all right,' Holly said as she sent the caseworker a guileless smile. 'You can be sure of that.'

Natalia let out a world-weary sigh as she put her foot back on the accelerator. 'Yeah, that's what I'm afraid of.'

The housekeeper whom she had met a few days before greeted Holly at the door of the villa while Natalia took an urgent call from one of her other charges.

'It's lovely to have you here, Holly,' Sophia said. 'Come in. Señor Ravensdale is busy just now so I'll show you to your suite so you can settle in.'

Holly wasn't expecting a welcoming committee with banners and balloons and a brass band or anything but surely the very least her host could do was make an appearance? If he'd agreed to have her here then he could at least do the polite thing and greet her face to face. 'Where is he?' she asked.

'He's not to be disturbed,' Sofia said. 'I'll show you to the suite I've pre—'

'Disturb him, please,' Holly said. *'Now.'*

Sophia looked a little taken aback. 'He doesn't like to be interrupted while he's working. He doesn't allow anyone into his office unless it's an emergency.'

Holly gently elbowed her way past to the door she took to be the study. It was the only door that was closed along the long, wide corridor. She didn't knock. She turned the handle and barged in.

A man looked up from behind a desk where he was tapping at a computer keyboard. His fingers stalled as she came in, the last click echoing in the silence as his gaze met with hers.

Holly drew in a breath to speak but for some reason her voice wasn't on active duty. It had locked behind her shock at how different he was from her expectations. He was nothing like she had envisaged. He wasn't old or even middle-aged. He was in his early thirties and movie-star handsome, athletically lean and tanned. His hair was a rich dark brown with light waves running through it. It looked as if it had been recently styled with his fingers, for she could see the roughly spaced plough marks that gave him a sexily tousled look, as if he'd just tumbled out of bed after vigorous sex. He had a determined looking jaw, a straight nose and a firm but sensually sculptured mouth that for some reason made the ligaments at the backs of her knees weaken alarmingly.

He pushed back his chair, and the room instantly shrank as he stood. 'Can I help you?' he said with the sort of tone that suggested he was not in the least motivated to do so.

Holly had never been one to beat about the bush. Her tactic was to get in there with a verbal weed-whacker. 'Don't you know it's impolite to ignore your guests when they arrive?'

His eyes held hers with steely focus. 'Strictly speaking, you're not my guest. You're Sophia's.'

Holly hitched up her chin, flashing him an I-know-what-you're-up-to glare. 'I want to let you know straight from the outset I'm not here to be your sex toy.'

His dark brows rose in twin arcs over his impossibly dark blue eyes. With his black hair and olive-skinned complexion, she had been expecting them to be brown. But they were an astonishing sapphire-blue fringed with thick black lashes. He seemed to measure her for a moment; his gaze taking in the tiny diamond nose piercing and the pink streaks in her hair with a tilt of his mouth that was unmistakably mocking.

A knot of bitterness inside Holly tightened. If there was one thing she loathed, it was being made fun of. Belittled. Mocked.

'How do you do, Miss, er…?' He glanced at his housekeeper, who had come in behind Holly, for a prompt.

'Miss Perez,' Sophia said. 'Hollyanne.'

'Holly,' Holly said with a black look.

Julius offered his hand. 'How do you do, Holly?'

She glared at his hand as if he'd just offered her a viper. 'Keep your hands to yourself.'

Natalia entered his office sounding a little flustered. 'I'm terribly sorry, Dr Ravensdale, but I had to take an urgent call about another client—'

Holly swung around and frowned at Natalia. '*Doctor*? You didn't tell me he was a doctor. You said he was a computer geek.'

The caseworker gave Julius a pained smile before addressing Holly. 'Dr Ravensdale has a PhD in astrophysics. It's polite to call him by his correct title, if that's what he prefers.'

Holly swung back to look at Julius. 'What do you want me to call you? Sir? Master? Oh Mighty Learned One? Your Royal Tightness?'

His lips twitched as if he was fighting back a reluctant smile. 'Julius will be fine.'

'As in Caesar?'

'As it turns out, yes.'

'You're into Shakespeare?' Holly said it as if it was a noxious disease from which she had so far managed to escape contamination. No point letting him think she was anything but what he had already judged her as: uneducated and unsophisticated. Trailer trash.

'No, but my parents are.'

'Why'd you agree to have me here?' she said, eyeballing him.

'I didn't want you here,' he said. 'But my current domestic circumstances made it impossible for me to refuse.'

Holly folded her arms across her chest. 'I can't cook,' she said with an obdurate 'so what are you going to do about *that*?' look.

'I'm sure you can learn.'

'And I hate housework,' she said. 'It's sexist expecting women to clean up after you. Just because I've got boobs and ovaries doesn't mean I—'

'Point taken,' he said quickly. So quickly Holly wondered if he was worried she was going to list all of her feminine assets. 'However, you need to do your stint of community service,' he continued. 'I need some help around the house until Sophia gets better. It's win-win.'

Holly made a harrumphing noise and unwound her locked arms, turning her gaze to the caseworker. 'Have you done a police check on him to make sure he's the real deal?'

'I can assure you, Holly, Dr Ravensdale is a totally trustworthy guardian,' the caseworker said.

Holly pushed her bottom lip out like a drawer as she swung back to size Julius up. 'Do you drink?'

'Socially.'

'Smoke?'

'No.'

'Drugs?'

'No.'

Holly upped her brazenness another notch. 'Sex?'

'Holly…' the caseworker began.

'What?' Holly asked with a petulant scowl.

'You're embarrassing Dr Ravensdale.'

'I'm not embarrassed,' Julius said. 'But I'm also not going to answer such an impertinent question.'

Holly coughed out a laugh. 'Which means you're not getting any, right?'

He stared her down with a look that made her insides feel wobbly. He didn't look the type of man to go too long between drinks. He looked the type of man who could take his pick of women. She could feel his sensual allure like a force field. Her mind ran wild with images of him getting down to business. He wouldn't be one for a quick, sleazy grope. He would take his time. He would know his way around a woman's body. He would know how to send female senses spinning into the stratosphere. She could see it in the darkly confident glint of his gaze. 'While we're on the topic,' he said, 'I would appreciate it if you would abstain from bringing men here for the purpose of having intimate relations with them.'

'So…you get to have sex but I don't? That is…' Holly dropped her voice to a deliberately husky purr '…unless we have it with each other?'

'I have to get going,' the caseworker said as her phone buzzed with an incoming message. 'Holly, I hope you'll behave yourself while you're here. This is your last chance, don't forget. If this fails you know where you'll be going.'

'Yeah, yeah, yeah,' Holly said with a bored flicker of her eyelids as she turned to look at the view from one of the windows next to a wall of bookshelves. She didn't want to go to prison but neither did she want to be exploited by yet another man who assumed he had some sort of power over her. If Julius Ravensdale wanted a plaything, why hadn't he cut one from the herd? The herd he belonged to—the 'beautiful people' herd. She wasn't even his type. How could she be, with her cheap chain-store clothes? Not to mention her background. The background she was still trying to escape. It clung to her like thick axle grease. No amount of washing and cleansing and sanitising would remove it.

Julius Ravensdale came from money. She could see it in the way he dressed, in the way he held himself with supreme confidence, with cool and collected authority. She could see it in the furnishings he surrounded himself with: the priceless paintings, the books and the hand-woven floor coverings. He hadn't lived his childhood in sweat-soaked fear. He hadn't had to fight for survival. He'd had everything handed to him on a gilt-edged platter. Why was he agreeing to have her here if not to make use of her? She clenched her back teeth in determination. He would *not* use her.

She would use *him* first.

* * *

'I'll call each day to see how she's getting on,' the case-worker said to Julius as she shook his hand. 'It's very good of you to commit to this programme. It's helped many people turn their lives around.'

'I'm sure everything will be fine,' Julius assured her. 'Sophia will do most of the mentoring.'

'All the same, it's very kind of you to open your home like this.'

'It's a big house,' he said. *Maybe not big enough.*

Julius turned once Sophia had escorted the case-worker out of his office to find Holly looking at him with a flinty gaze. 'How much are they paying you to have me?' she said.

'I've told them to donate the fee to charity.'

'Big of you.'

He leaned against the windowsill behind his desk with his hands balanced either side of his hips to study her. It was a casual pose that belied the havoc her presence caused to his senses. He could feel the blood humming through his veins in a way it hadn't since he'd been a teenager. He looked down at her upturned, defiant face with its flashing caramel-brown gaze and sulky cherry-red mouth. A tiny diamond winked from the side of her right nostril. The bridge of her retroussé nose was dusted with freckles that reminded him of nutmeg sprinkled on top of a dessert. But that was about as far as he could go with the sweetness description. She looked sour and bitter and ready for a fight.

Something about her blatant rudeness made everything that was cultured in Julius stiffen. *Not, perhaps, the best choice of word*, he thought wryly as he scanned her impudent features. But her rudeness wasn't the only

thing that was blatant about her. She had an earthy, raw
sensuality about her. The way she moved her body. The
way she inhabited her body. *His* body recognised it like
a stallion scenting a potential mate.

He forced his mind out of the gutter. Clearly he
needed to get some work-life balance if this little up-
start was attracting his attention.

Her face was not what one would call classically
beautiful but there was an arresting quality to it that
made him want to study her for longer than was socially
polite. He noted the high and haughty cheekbones you
could slice a Christmas ham on. Eyelashes that were
thick and long without the boost of mascara. Her skin—
apart from the freckles and the diamond piercing—
was creamy and make-up-free. Her hair was a mass of
springy shoulder-length curls and was a mid shade of
brown, apart from some rather vivid streaks of pink.

Julius was still waiting for her to make the connection between him and his parents. It didn't usually take
this long. He had got used to it over the years. Well, almost: the wide-eyed wonder. The delighted shock that
produced a sickening number of gushing comments:
*Oh, you're the son of the famous London West End ac-
tors Richard Ravensdale and Elisabetta Albertini! Can
you get me their autographs? An invitation to opening
night? Front-row seats? A back-stage pass? An audi-
tion?*

But Miss Holly Perez had either never heard of his
parents or was not impressed by his lineage.

Julius had to admit he found her forthrightness
strangely appealing. It was such a refreshing change.
He'd had his share of sycophants. People who only
wanted to be associated with him because of his connec-

tion with London theatre royalty. Women who wanted to be squired by him on the red carpet in the hope of catching the eye of a casting agent. It was refreshing to be in the presence of someone who didn't give a toss for the shallowness of his parents' celebrity.

Julius didn't care too much for the word 'guardian' the caseworker had used in reference to him. It made him sound decades older than his thirty-three years. Holly was younger than him certainly but only by about seven or eight years at the most. Twenty-five, but hardened by her experiences. He could see it in her eyes. There was no sheen of innocence in that thickly fringed brown gaze. It was full of cold, hard cynicism. A mess-with-me-at-your-peril gleam. What had led her to a life of petty crime? He'd seen the list of her offences: theft; wilful damage to property; graffiti; vandalism.

Sophia's rescue mission was perhaps going to be a little more challenging than he'd bargained for. He'd agreed to it because he trusted his housekeeper's judgement. But Sophia's judgement was clearly not what it used to be. Holly had come striding in like a denim-and-cheap-cotton-clad whirlwind—asking him about his sex life, for God's sake..

He knew he was acting and sounding like a stern schoolmaster. But he figured it was best to get the ground rules in early. He wasn't going to stand by while Holly conducted drunken parties or all-night orgies under his roof.

Julius didn't care how many impertinent questions she asked, he wasn't going to admit to his current sex drought. He'd been busy. He was working on some new top-secret software. He wasn't like his twin brother, Jake, who had sex as if he were training for the Olympics. Nor was he like his father, who had a reputation as a womaniser that was regrettably well deserved.

Julius enjoyed the company of women. He dated from time to time. He enjoyed the physicality of sex but he didn't care for the politics of it. The agenda women brought to the bedroom irked him. If he wanted to marry and settle down, then he would make the decision when he was good and ready. Although he seriously wondered if he would ever be ready. Having witnessed his parents' turbulent marriage, acrimonious divorce, remarriage and ongoing drama-filled relationship, he wasn't sure he wanted to sign up for the potential for so much disruption and chaos.

'I know why you've agreed to have me here, so don't bother pretending otherwise.' Holly's look had a bad-girl gleam to it that messed with his hormones. He felt a stirring in his groin. A lightning flash of unbidden lust that made his blood throb and pound in his veins. He was surprised—and deeply annoyed—by his reaction to her. She was obviously well aware of her effect on the male gaze, exploiting it for all it was worth. Her unusual beauty, even though it was currently downplayed, was the sort that could stop a bullet train in its tracks. She had a sensual air about her. A way of moving her body that made him ache to see what she looked like naked. He kept his expression masked but he wondered if she sensed the impact she had on him.

How had he got himself into this? Julius thought. He should have called an agency. Employed someone who had credentials. Someone who had training. Manners. Decorum. Why had he allowed Sophia to talk him into taking on someone as cheeky and wilful as Holly Perez? She was going to be living under his roof. For a month!

'You are mistaken, Miss Perez,' he said coolly. 'My taste in women is far more sophisticated.'

She adopted a femme fatale pose, all slinky hips and shoulders, her mouth in a come-and-get-me moue. 'Of course it is,' she said with a devilish little twinkle that matched the diamond in her nose.

Julius felt the swell of his flesh at her brazen sexuality. The pounding and purring of his blood drove every rational thought out of his brain. Sex was suddenly all he could think about. Hot, sweaty, bed-wrecking sex. Mind-blowing caveman sex. Driving himself into her tight, wet warmth and exploding like a bomb. How long had it been? Clearly too long if he was getting jumpy at this outrageous little flirt. Holly Perez was a troublemaker. It might as well be branded across her forehead. He wasn't going to fall for it. He was not at the mercy of his hormones…or at least he hadn't been before now.

Holly moved around his office with cat-like grace. Slinky, silent, sensuous. Dangerous, if stroked the wrong way. Although when he checked he noticed she didn't have claws. Her fingernails were bitten down to the quick. When she lifted her hand to push her hair back off her face he noticed a long white scar on the fine blue-veined skin of her wrist. 'How did you get that scar?' he asked.

A mask came down over her features as she pushed down her sleeve. 'I broke my arm when I was a kid. I had to have it pinned and plated.'

Julius let a silence slip past. He watched as she fiddled with the hem of her sleeve, her fingertips tugging and twisting the light cotton fabric as if it irritated her skin. Her eyebrows were drawn together, her forehead pleated, her expression broody. It intrigued him how quickly she had switched from impudent vamp to bad-tempered brat.

'Would you like to look around the villa?'

She gave an indifferent shrug. 'Whatever.'

Julius had intended to get Sophia to give Holly a guided tour but he decided he would do it. He told himself it was so he could check she didn't pilfer any of his belongings or carve her initials or a curse word into one of his antiques. Why on earth had he agreed to this? God knew what she would get up to once out of his sight.

He led the way out of his office. 'I detect a trace of an English accent,' he said as they walked along the hall. 'Are you originally from the UK?'

'Yes,' she said. 'We moved out here when I was young. My father was Argentinian.'

'Was?'

'He died when I was three. I don't remember him, so there's no need to get all soppy and sentimental and feel sorry for me.'

Julius glanced down at her walking beside him. She barely came up to his shoulder. 'Is your mother still alive?'

'No.'

'What happened?'

'She died.'

'How?'

Holly threw him a hardened look. 'Didn't Natalia show you my file?'

Julius was a little ashamed he hadn't read it in more detail. But then he hadn't planned on having anything to do with her. Apart from Sophia, he didn't have much to do with his staff on a personal level. They did their job. He did his. He'd focussed on Holly's rap sheet without looking at the story behind the miscreant behaviour. Some people were born bad, others had bad things happen to them and they turned bad as a result. Where did Holly fit on the spectrum? 'I'd like you to tell me.'

'She killed herself when I was seventeen.'

'I'm sorry.'

She gave another careless shrug. 'So what about your parents?'

'They're both alive and well.' And driving him nuts as usual.

Holly stopped in front of a painting. It was a landscape he'd bought at an auction his sister, Miranda, had given him the heads-up on. Miranda was an art restorer, yet another Ravensdale sibling who had disappointed their parents by not treading the boards.

Holly resumed walking, idly picking up objects he had on display, turning them over in her hands and putting them down again. Julius hoped she wasn't sizing them up for later theft.

'You got any brothers or sisters?' she asked after a long silence.

Julius was finding it a novel experience, meeting someone who knew nothing about his family. Didn't the girl have a smartphone? Internet access? Read newspapers or gossip magazines? 'I have a twin brother and a sister ten years younger.'

She stopped walking to look up at him. 'Are you identical?'

'Yes.'

Her eyes suddenly danced with impish mischief, dimples appearing either side of her mouth, completely transforming her features. 'Ever swapped places with him?'

He put on what his kid sister called his 'I'm too old for all that nonsense' face. 'Not for a very long time.'

'Can your parents tell you apart?'

'They can now but not when we were younger,' he said. Mostly because they hadn't been around enough. Their fame was far more important to them than their family. Not that he was bitter. Much. 'What about you? Do you have any siblings?'

'No.' Her dimpled smile faded and the frown reinstated itself on her forehead as she resumed walking along the corridor. 'There's just me…'

Julius heard something in her tone that suggested a resigned sense of profound aloneness. He hadn't expected to feel sorry for her. He had strong values on what constituted good and bad behaviour. The law was the law. Breaking it just because you'd had a difficult childhood wasn't a good enough excuse, in his opinion. But something about her intrigued him. She was light and dark. Moon shadows and bright sunlight. She reminded him of a complicated puzzle that would need more than one attempt to solve it.

Maybe his housekeeper's mission would prove far more interesting than he'd first thought.

Holly stopped in front of the windows overlooking the formal gardens. 'Do you live here alone?' she asked.

'Apart from my staff, yes, but they have separate quarters. Sophia is the exception. She has a suite on the top floor.'

Holly turned and looked at him with a direct gaze. 'Seems a pretty big place for a single guy.'

'I like my own space.'

'Must cost a ton to keep this place ticking over.'

'I manage.'

'Yeah, well, money and possessions don't impress me,' she said, turning to look at the gardens again.

'What does?'

She swivelled to face him and tilted one of her hips, lowering one shoulder lower than the other so her thin chain-store sweater slipped to reveal the creamy cap of her shoulder. She looked at him through eyes half-shielded by the thick dark fans of her lashes. 'Let's see...' She pursed her full lips in thought before releasing them on a breath of air. 'I'm impressed by a man who knows his way around a woman's body.'

Julius was doing his darnedest not even to think about her luscious little body. Or that full-lipped mouth and the mayhem it could cause if it came too close to his. He had a feeling she was testing him. Testing his motives. Seeing if he was going to exploit her. Had she been exploited before? Was that how she viewed all men? As manipulators and bullies who forced their will on her?

He might be a man who liked his own way but there was no way he would ever describe himself as a bully. He could be arrogant at times—stubborn, even—but he was a firm believer in treating women with respect. Having a shy and reserved much younger sister had instilled in him the importance of men taking a stand against all forms of violence against women and girls.

'That's it?' he said. 'Just whether he can perform?'

'Sure,' she said, eyes gleaming with pertness. 'How a man has sex tells you a lot about them as a person. Whether they're selfish or not. Whether they're uptight or casual.' She tapped two of her fingertips against her mouth in a musing manner. 'Let's take you, for instance.'

Let's not, he thought. 'This theory of yours is imminently fascinating but I think—'

'You're a man who likes to be in control,' she said. 'You like order and predictability. You don't do things on impulse. Your life is planned, timetabled, scheduled to the nth degree. Am I right?'

Julius didn't feel too comfortable at being so rapidly written off as a boring stereotype, as nothing more than a cliché. He liked to think he wasn't *that* predictable. He had nuances; sure he did. Layers to his personality that were there if you took the time to find them. He might spend a lot of time in the land of logic and reason but it didn't mean he couldn't use the right side of his brain. Well…occasionally.

He stepped towards the nearest door. 'This is the library,' he said. 'You're welcome to help yourself to books as long as you don't dog-ear them or leave them outside.'

'See?' She gave a bell-like laugh. 'I was spot-on.'

He gave her a look before he moved to the next door farther down the corridor. 'This is the music room.'

'Let me guess,' she said with another one of her impish smiles. 'You don't mind if I play the piano as long as my fingers aren't sticky or I don't drop crumbs between the keys. Correct?'

Julius found the picture she was painting of him increasingly annoying. What gave her the right to sum him up in such disparaging terms? She made him sound like some sort of house-proud obsessive. 'Do you play an instrument?' he asked.

'No.'

'Would you like to learn?' Music was supposed to tame wild things, wasn't it? He could engage a tutor for her. What was that saying about the devil and idle hands? Piano lessons would at least keep her out of his way.

'What?' she said, the cynical glint back in her gaze. 'You think you can teach me the piano in a month?'

'I have other instruments.'

'I just bet you do.'

He gave her a droll look. 'Flute. Tenor recorder. Saxophone.'

She looked at him, one side of her plump mouth curved in a mocking arc. 'Impressive. Gotta love a man who's good with his mouth *and* his hands.'

Julius put his hands deep in his trouser pockets in case he was tempted to show her just how good he was. Why was she being so damn brazen? Winding him up for what reason? To prove he was as predictable as all the other men she'd dealt with? What did she hope to gain? Would he be just another male trophy for her to gloat over? Another man she had slayed with her sensual allure? He wasn't going to fall for it. He had no time for vacuous game playing. She might think him predictable and a walking, talking cliché but he was not when it came to this. She could flirt and tease and taunt him as much as she wanted but he wasn't going to fall into her honey trap. He might be his father's son by blood, name and looks but he wasn't like him by nature.

'I'll leave Sophia to show you around the rest of the house,' he said, his tone formal, clipped. Dismissive.

Her mischievous gaze danced. 'Aren't you going to show me where I'll be sleeping?'

'I'm not sure where Sophia has put you.'

But I hope to God it's nowhere near me, Julius thought as he turned and strode briskly away.

CHAPTER TWO

HOLLY WATCHED AS Julius Ravensdale made his way down the lengthy and wide corridor with long, purposeful strides. She felt strangely breathless after their encounter. Her pulse was thrumming too hard and too fast. It felt as if something small and scared was scrabbling inside the valves of her heart.

Her reaction to him confounded her. Confused her.

Men didn't usually have that effect on her. Even good-looking ones. And they didn't come much better looking than Julius Ravensdale. She'd been expecting some long-haired, bushy-bearded, shoulder-hunched computer geek and instead had found a man who looked as if he could fill in for a European male model in an aftershave or designer watch advertisement. His tall, broad-shouldered athletic build gave him an air of authority that was compelling. There was something about his looks that rang a faint bell of recognition in her head. Had she seen a picture of him somewhere? Or was his twin famous? Even his name struck a chord of familiarity but she couldn't remember where she'd heard it before.

His thick, wavy dark brown hair was tousled in a mad professor sort of way she found intensely attractive.

He was clean-shaven but with just enough regrowth to confirm he hadn't been holding the door for everyone else while the testosterone was being handed out. She had felt the impact of his male hormones as soon as she'd entered his office. It was like a collision against her flesh. Potent. Powerful. Primal. Making her aware of her body in a way she hadn't been in years. Maybe had never been.

He triggered something in her, something deeply instinctive. Something rebellious. She felt an irresistible desire to dismantle his façade of cool civility. To unpick the lock on the brooding passion she could sense was under lockdown. She wanted to tease out the primitive man behind the aristocratic manners. He was so rigidly controlled with an aloof and haughty air. There was an invisible wall around him warning her not to come close. But what if she did? What if she dared to come so close he wouldn't be able to keep that iron control in place? She gave a secret smile. *Tempting thought*.

Holly couldn't get over his incredible eyes. Dark as navy fringed with thick lashes and strong eyebrows. Intelligent eyes. Observant. Intuitive. He had a straight nose and a jaw that hinted at a streak of stubbornness. He looked like he lived in his head a lot. Thoughts and logic were his currency. Action would come later after due consideration.

If nothing else it would make a change from the men she'd been forced to share quarters with—her low-life stepfather being a perfect case in point.

Maybe this month wouldn't be such a hardship after all. It was exhilarating, winding Julius up. It amused her to see him act all schoolmasterish and stern in the face of her brazen behaviour. She was picky when it came to whom she shared her body with but that didn't mean she couldn't have a bit of fun rattling his chain. He was starchy and formal in that 'stiff upper lip' way the well-born English male was known for. Maybe it would fill in the time to try and loosen him up a bit. Show him a top-notch university degree didn't make him any different from any other man she'd met. Men driven by hormones. Greedy to have their lust slaked with whomever was available. She'd prove to him he had no right to look down his nose at her.

Holly gave a little smile. Yep, this period of house arrest could prove to be the best fun she'd had in years.

The housekeeper appeared at the end of the corridor and came towards Holly with her wrist supported in a brace. It brought back memories of the time her step-father had snapped her wrist when she'd been eleven and then told her he would kill her or her mother if she told anyone how she'd got injured. She'd had to pretend she'd fallen off her bike. A bike she hadn't even pos-sessed. The plates and screws in her wrist weren't the only scars her stepfather had left her with.

Her issues with authority, her rebellious streak, her distrust of men and her cold sweat nightmares were the hoofmarks of a childhood and adolescence spent at the mercy of a madman. She wouldn't have had to be here doing this ridiculous programme if it hadn't been for the way her stepfather and his bullying lawyer had made it seem as if *she* was the criminal.

'Come this way, Holly,' Sophia said as she led the way to the next floor. 'So, what do you think of the place so far?'

'It's okay, I guess.' Holly didn't see the point in get-ting too friendly with the natives. Sophia seemed nice enough but it would be a waste of energy striking up a friendship when in a matter of weeks—if not before—she'd be gone.

'I had to twist Señor Ravensdale's arm to agree to having you here,' Sophia said as they came to the first-floor landing. 'It's not that he doesn't want to do his bit for charity. He's incredibly generous and supports lots of causes. He just likes to be left alone to get on with his work.'

'Has he got any lady friends?' Holly asked.

Sophia's expression closed down. 'Señor Ravensdale's privacy is of paramount importance to him.'

'Come on, there must be someone in his life,' Holly said.

Sophia's mouth tightened as if she were physically restraining herself from being indiscreet about her employer. 'I value my job too much to reveal such personal information.'

Holly gave a lip shrug. 'He sounds pretty boring, if you ask me. All work and no play.'

'He's a wonderful employer,' Sophia said. 'And a decent man with honour and sound principles. You're very lucky I was able to talk him into having you stay here. It's not something he would normally do.'

'Lucky me.'

Sophia gave her a warning look. 'I hope you're not going to cause trouble for him.'

Who, me? Holly thought with another private smile. Julius Ravensdale's loyal housekeeper thought he had sound principles, did she? How long before his honourable motives were exposed for what they were? She'd seen the way he'd run his gaze over her. He might be clever and sophisticated but he had the same needs as any man his age. He was healthy and fit and in the prime of his life. Why wouldn't he take advantage of the situation? She wasn't vain but she knew the power she had at her disposal. It was the only power she had. She didn't have money or prestige or a pedigree. She had her body and she knew how to use it.

'How'd you injure your wrist?' Holly asked to fill the silence.

'It's just a bit of tendonitis,' Sophia said. 'I get it now and again. It will settle if I rest up. All part of getting old, I'm afraid.'

Holly followed the housekeeper to the third floor of the villa. The Persian carpet was as thick as velvet, the luxurious décor showing French and Italian influences. Gorgeous artworks decorated the walls, portraits and landscapes of various sizes, and marble busts and statues were positioned along the gallery-wide corridor. Chandeliers hung like crystal fountains above and the wall lights sparkled with the same top-quality glitter.

Holly had never been in such an opulent place. It was like a palace. A showcase of every fine thing a sophisticated and wealthy person could acquire. But there were no personal items scattered about. No family photographs or memorabilia. Not a thing out of place and everything in its place. It looked more like a museum than a home.

'This is your room,' Sophia said, opening a door to a suite a third of the way along the corridor. 'It has its own bathroom and balcony.'

Balcony?

Holly stopped dead. Her heart tripped. Fear sent a shiver through the hairs of her scalp. The silk curtains at the French doors leading onto the balcony billowed with the afternoon breeze like the ball gown of a ghost.

How many times had she been dragged to the rickety balcony of her childhood? Locked out there in all types of weather. Forced to watch helplessly as her mother had been knocked around on the other side of the glass. Holly had learned not to react because when she had it had made her mother suffer all the more. Holly's distress revved up her stepfather so she taught herself not to show it.

But she felt it.

Oh, dear God, she felt it now.

Her chest was tight, heavy. Every breath she took felt like she was trying to lift a bookcase. She couldn't speak. Her throat was closed with a stranglehold of panic.

'It's breath-taking, isn't it?' Sophia said. 'It's only been recently renovated. You can probably still smell the fresh paint.'

A shudder passed through Holly's body like an earth-quake. Her legs went cold and then weak as if the ligaments had been severed with the swing of a sword. Beads of perspiration trickled down between her shoulder blades, as warm and as sticky as blood. Her stomach was a crowded fishbowl of nausea. Churning. Rising in a bloated tide to her blocked throat.

'I—I don't need such a big room,' she said. 'Just put me in one of the downstairs rooms. We passed a nice one on the second floor. That blue one back there. That'll do me. I don't need my own balcony.'

'But there are nice views all over the estate and you'll have much more privacy. It's one of the nicest rooms in the—'

'I don't care about the view,' Holly said, stepping back from the door to stand near a marble statue that felt as cold as her body. 'It's not as if I'm an honoured guest, is it? I'm here under sufferance. Your employer's and mine. I just need a bed and a blanket.' Which was far more than she'd had in the not-so-distant past.

'But Señor Ravensdale insisted you—'

'Yeah, yeah, I know—be put as far away from his room as possible,' Holly said, hugging her arms across her body. 'Why? Doesn't he trust himself?'

The housekeeper's mouth pulled tight like the strings of an old-fashioned evening purse. 'Señor Ravensdale is a gentleman.'

'Yeah, well, even gentlemen have hormones.'

Sophia let out a frustrated breath. 'Will you at least look at the suite? You might change your mind once you see how—'

'No.' Holly swung away and went back down the stairs, one flight after another, her feet barely landing long enough on each step before it clipped the next one. She didn't draw breath until she got to the nearest exit. She stopped once out in the sunshine, bending forward, hands on her knees, her lungs all but exploding as she gasped in the warm summer air.

There was no way she was going to sleep in a room with a balcony.

No way.

Julius was standing at his office window when he saw Holly striding off towards the lake past the formal part of the gardens. Was she running away already? Absconding as soon as she saw an opportunity? He was supposed to call her caseworker if there was an issue.

He glanced at his phone and then back at Holly's slight figure as she stopped in front of the lake. If she'd wanted to escape she surely would have gone in the other direction. The wide, deep lake and the thick forest fringing it behind were as good a barrier as any. He watched as she bent down and picked up a pebble and skimmed it across the surface of the water. It skipped several times before sinking, leaving a ring of concentric circles in its wake. There was something poignant and sad about her slim figure standing there alone.

There was a tap on his door. 'Señor? Can I have a word?'

Julius opened the door to Sophia. 'Is everything all right?'

'Holly won't have the room I prepared for her,' Sophia said.

He tilted his mouth in a sardonic arc. 'Not good enough for her?'

'Too big for her.'

He frowned. 'Is that what she said?'

Sophia nodded. 'I made it all nice for her and she won't have it. She stalked off as if I'd told her she'd be sleeping in the stables.'

'Whose idea was it to bring her here again?' he said with mock rancour.

'I'm sure she'll grow on you,' Sophia said. 'She's a spirited little thing, isn't she?'

'Indeed.'

'Will you talk to her?'

'I just spent the last half hour with her.'

'Please?' Sophia, for all that she was close to retirement, had a tendency to look like a pleading three-year-old child when she wanted him to do things her way.

'What do you want me to say to her?'

'Insist she take the room I prepared for her,' Sophia said. 'Otherwise where will I put her? You told me you didn't want her on your floor.'

'All right.' Julius let out a long breath of resignation. 'I'll talk to her. But you'd better get the first aid kit out.'

'Come, now. You wouldn't hurt a fly.'

He gave her a wry look as he shouldered open the door. 'No, but our little guest looks as if she could stick a knife in you and laugh while she's doing it.'

Julius found her still skimming rocks across the surface of the lake. She was damn good at it, too. The most he could get was thirteen skips. Her last one had been fourteen. She must have heard him approach as his feet made plenty of noise on the pebbles at the edge of the lake but she didn't turn around. She kept skimming pebble after pebble with a focussed, almost fierce concentration.

'I believe you have an issue with the accommodation I've provided,' he said.

She threw another pebble but not as a skimmer. It went sailing overhead and landed with a loud *plop* in the centre of the lake. 'I don't need a suite in first class. I belong in steerage,' she said.

'Surely that's up to me to decide?'

She turned and faced him. It unnerved him a little to see she had a stone rather than a pebble clutched in her fist. Her eyes flashed at him. 'What are you trying to do? Conduct your own Pygmalion experiment? Well, guess what, Mr Higgins? I'm no fair lady.'

'No; you're a bad tempered little miss who seems intent on biting the hand that's generously offered to feed you.'

She glowered at him with her chest rising and falling as if she was only just managing to control her fury. 'You didn't offer me anything,' she shot back. 'You don't want me here any more than I want to be here.'

'True, but you're here now and it seems mature and sensible to make the best of the situation.'

Holly turned and flung the stone at the lake but it hit a tree on the left-hand side with a loud thwack. 'How are you going to explain me to your fancy friends or family?' she said.

'I don't feel the necessity to explain myself to anyone.'

'Lucky you.'

Where was the cheeky little flirt now? he wondered. In her place was a woman brooding with anger. Anger so thick he could feel it in the air like the humidity before a violent storm.

Julius picked up a pebble and sent it skimming across the surface of the lake. 'That's a personal best,' he said as he counted fifteen skips. 'Think you can match it?'

She turned and looked at him with a watchful gaze. 'What about your girlfriend? What's she going to say when she hears you've got me living with you?'

He bent down and picked up another pebble, rolling it over to check its suitability. 'I don't have a current girlfriend.'

'When was your last one?'

He glanced at her before he skimmed the pebble. 'You ask a lot of questions, don't you?'

'I know you're not gay because no gay man would look at me the way you did back in your office,' she said. 'You fancy me, don't you?'

Julius tightened his mouth as he reached down for another pebble. 'Your ego is as appalling as your manners.'

She gave a cynical laugh as she threw another pebble, even farther this time, as if all her pent up energy went into the throw. 'I suppose no one without a university degree with honours need apply. So what do you talk about in bed? Quantum physics? Einstein's theory of relativity?'

He looked down at her upturned face with its mocking smile and impossibly cute dimples. What was it about her that made him feel this was all a front? He was all too familiar with theatrical talent. His parents were some of the best in the theatre. Even he had to acknowledge that. But this defiant tearaway was putting on an award-winning performance. 'Why don't you want the room Sophia prepared for you?' he asked.

Her eyes lost their cheeky sparkle and her expression became sulky again. 'I don't want to be shoved at the top of your grand old house like some freak you want to hide in case she does the wrong thing in front of your fancy guests. I suppose you'll insist on me taking my meals in there or with the servants in the kitchen.'

'I don't have servants,' Julius said. 'I have staff. And, yes, they make their own arrangements over dining but that's more out of convenience than convention.' He paused for a beat before adding. 'I expect you to dine with me each evening.' *Are you out of your mind? The less time you spend with her the better.*

'Why?' she said with a surly look. 'So you can criticise me when I use the wrong fork or knife?'

'Why do you think everyone you meet is automatically against you?'

She turned and looked at the lake rather than meet his gaze. He could see the flicker of a tiny muscle in her cheek as if she was grinding down on her molars.

It was a while before she spoke and when she did it was with a voice that was pitched slightly lower than normal with a distinctly husky edge. 'I don't want *that* room.'

'Why not?'

'It's…too posh.'

'Fine,' Julius said, mentally rolling his eyes. 'You can choose your own room. God knows there are plenty to choose from.'

'Thank you.' It was not much more than a whisper of sound and she still wasn't looking at him but there was something in her posture that suggested enormous relief. Her shoulders had lost their tense, bunched-up-to-her-ears look. Her spine was no longer ramrod straight. Her hands were not curled into tight fists or clutching pebbles but hanging loosely by her sides.

He had a strong urge to reach out, take one of her hands and give it a reassuring squeeze but somehow refrained from doing so. Just. 'Do you want to walk back with me or hang around down here for a little bit?' he said.

She turned her head to look at him. 'Aren't you worried I might run away when your back is turned?'

He studied her for a moment, taking in her shuttered gaze and the pouty set to her mouth. 'You'd be running towards prison if you do. Hardly something to look forward to, is it?'

She bit down on her lower lip and turned to look at a water bird that had flown in to land in the centre of the lake, its paddling feet sending out concentric circles of disturbance. He watched as a slight breeze played with some loose tendrils of her hair and she absently brushed them back with one of her hands. His chest gave a sharp little squeeze when he saw her hand was shaking. There was no sign of the tough, angry girl. No sign of the brash guttersnipe. Right then she looked like your average girl next door who had suddenly found herself at an anxiety-inducing crossroads.

Julius bent down, picked up a pebble and handed it to her. 'My brother Jake holds the record down here. Seventeen skips.'

She took the pebble from him but as her fingers touched his he felt an electric shock run up along his arm. She slowly raised her gaze to mesh with his. A pulsing moment passed when he lost all sense of time and place. It could have been seconds or minutes or even days.

His eyes kept tracking to her mouth, the shape of it, the fullness of it that suggested passion and heat, and yet a strange sense of untouched innocence. He felt like a magnet was pulling his head down towards it. He had to fight every muscle and sinew and throbbing cell in his body to counter its force.

He watched as the tip of her tongue slipped out between her lips and moistened the top lip, then the bottom one, leaving each one glistening with a tempting sheen. Blood rushed to his groin, thickening him with a rocket blast of lust.

He had a sudden feeling he had been asleep all of his life until this moment. It was like coming out of cold storage. A slow melt was moving through his body; he could feel it all the way to his fingertips, the urge, the compulsion to touch, to feel her soft skin, sliding, stroking, moving against his own.

His mind was not following its usual logical pathways. It was short-circuiting with erotic images, hot fantasies of him burying himself inside her body, bringing them both to completion in a matter of seconds.

Could she sense the turmoil in him? Had she any idea of the effect she was having on him? He tried to read her expression but her eyelids were lowered over her eyes as she focussed on his mouth.

He lifted his hand to her cheek, barely aware he was doing it until he felt the creamy softness of her skin against his palm, tilting her face so she had to meet his gaze. Those bewitching eyes made his pulse pound all the harder. Every beat of his heart felt like a hammer blow, each one sending a deep, resounding echo to his pelvis. Her skin felt like silk against his palm and fingers. Warm. Smooth. Sensuous. Her eyes contained a glint of anticipation, of expectation. Of triumph.

He moved the pad of his thumb over the small, neat circle of her chin, watching as her pupils flared like pools of ink. Her lips were slightly apart, just enough for him to feel the soft waft of her vanilla-scented breath. How easy would it be to close the distance and touch his lips to hers? The urge to do so was strong, perhaps stronger than at any other time in his life, but he knew if he did it he would be crossing a line. Breaking a boundary. Inviting trouble.

'I'm not going to do it,' he said, dropping his hand from her face.

Her look was all innocence. 'What?'

'You know what.'

She met his eyes with a hard gleam in her own. 'I could make you disregard those principles you're clinging to. I could do it in a heartbeat.'

Julius frowned until his eyebrows met. 'Why are

you trying to ruin your one chance of getting your life in order?'

She glared at him. 'I don't need you to get my life in order. I don't need anyone.'

'How's that been working out for you so far?'

Her eyes were twin flashpoints of heat. 'You know what I hate about men like you? You think just because you have it all, you can have it all.'

'Look,' Julius said. 'I get this is a tough gig for you. You don't want to be here. But what's your alternative?'

She pressed her lips together and looked at him mulishly. 'I'm not the one who should be threatened with going to prison.'

'Yes, well, apparently most prisons are full of innocent people,' he said. 'But according to our current laws you can't steal or damage property or whatever else you did and not be punished for it.'

She swung away. 'I don't have to listen to this.'

'Holly.' Julius caught her by the arm and turned her to face him. 'I want to help you. Can't you see that?'

She gave him a disdainful look as she tested his hold. 'How? By making me get used to all this luxury, only to be tossed back out on the streets as soon as the month is up?'

Julius's frown deepened. 'Don't you have a home to go to?'

Her eyes skittered away from his. 'Let go of my arm.'

He loosened his hold but kept her tethered to him with the bracelet of his fingers. 'No one is going to toss you anywhere,' he said. *What are you going to do with her once the month is up?* The thoughts were like popup signs in his head. If she didn't have a home to go to, then where would she go? Where did his responsibility towards her begin and end?

Did he have a responsibility towards her?

'Is that where you've been living?' he asked. 'Out on the streets?'

She slipped her wrist out of his hold and folded her arms across her body, shooting him a fiery glare. 'What would *you* care? People like you don't even notice people like me.'

Julius noticed her all right. A little too much. His hand was tingling where he'd been holding her wrist. It was as if his blood was bubbling through his veins like boiling soda. He noticed the way her brown eyes sparked with venom one minute, glittering with an erotic come-on the next. He noticed the way she moved her body like a sleek pedigree cat, only to turn around, spit and hiss at him like a cornered feral one.

He had no idea how to handle her. He wasn't supposed to *be* the one handling her. This was his housekeeper's mission, not his. He was supposed to be getting on with his work while Sophia did her bit for society by taking in a stray and reforming her.

But Holly Perez was no ordinary stray.

She was a feisty little firebrand who seemed determined to cause trouble with everyone who dared to come too close.

'While you're under my roof I'm responsible for you,' Julius said. 'But that means you have responsibilities, too.'

Her chin came up. 'Like what? Servicing you in the bedroom?'

He set his mouth. 'No. Definitely not.'

Her look said it all. Cynicism on steroids. 'Sure and I believe you.'

'I mean it, Holly,' Julius said. 'I'm not in the habit of bedding young women who have no manners, no respect and no sense of propriety.'

She gave a musical sounding laugh. 'I am *so* going to make you eat your words.'

He stoically ignored the throb of lust that charged through his pelvis. 'I'll see you at dinner,' he said. 'I expect you to dress for the occasion. That means no jeans, no flip-flops and no plunging necklines or bare midriff. Sophia will organise suitable attire if you have none with you.'

Holly gave him a mock salute and a deep, obsequious bow. 'Aye-aye, Captain.'

Julius strode about thirty or so paces before he swung back to look at her but she had already turned back to face the lake. He watched as she hurled a rock as far as she could. It landed in the middle of the water and sank with a loud *plop,* but not before it created tsunami-like ripples over the surface.

CHAPTER THREE

HOLLY WAITED UNTIL Julius was out of sight before she left the lakeside. What right did he have to tell her how to dress? No man was going to tell her what she could and couldn't do. If she wanted to wear jeans, she would wear them. She'd wear high-cut denim shorts and trashy high heels to his stuck-up dinner table if she wanted to. He couldn't force her to dress up like one of his posh girlfriends. He might deny having a current lady friend but no man with his sort of looks went long between hook-ups.

He had *so* been going to kiss her. She had been waiting for him to do it. Silently egging him on. Waiting for him to break. What a triumph it was going to be when he finally did. She would get the biggest kick out of seeing him topple from his high horse. He had no right to lecture her as if she were ten years old. She would show him just how grown up she was. He wasn't dealing with a wilful child. He was dealing with a woman who knew how to make a man weaken at the knees. She would *do* him before he could do her. Although, the thought of having him do her was strangely appealing. He wasn't her type, with his control freak ways, but he was so darn attractive it almost hurt her eyeballs to look at him.

What was it about him that seemed vaguely familiar? His surname kept ringing a faint bell of recognition in her head. Where had she heard the name Ravensdale before?

And then it finally dawned on her.

He was the son—one of the twin sons—of the famous Shakespearean actors Richard Ravensdale and Elisabetta Albertini. They were London theatre royalty; Holly had seen articles about them in gossip magazines. Not that she ever had the money to buy such magazines but occasionally one of the shelters she had stayed in had them lying about.

Julius's parents had married thirty-four years ago after an affair during a London season of *Much Ado About Nothing* and celebrated their first wedding anniversary with the birth of identical twin boys. Seven turbulent years later, they had had a very public and acrimonious divorce. Then, three years later, they'd reunited in a whirlwind of publicity, remarried in a big celebrity-attended wedding service, and exactly nine months later Elisabetta had given birth to a daughter called Miranda.

Holly wondered if Julius had chosen to work and live in Argentina as a way of putting some distance between himself and his famous parents. The attention they attracted would be difficult to deal with, especially since what she had read indicated neither he nor his siblings had any aspirations to be on the stage. He hadn't once mentioned his parents' fame, although he'd had plenty of opportunity to do so.

Was that why he had initially been so reluctant to

have her here? Would her presence draw press attention his way he would rather avoid? If the press got a whiff of her chequered background it might cause all sorts of speculation. Holly could imagine the headlines: *Celebrities' Son Living with Trailer Trash with Criminal Record.* How would that go down with Julius's sense of propriety?

Holly pursed her lips as she thought about her next move. If she called the press it would draw too much attention to herself just now. She didn't want her creep-aholic stepfather to know where she currently was, although, given the friends in high places he had, she wouldn't put it past him to know already or to make it his business to find out.

Franco Morales had influence that had already stretched further and wider than she had planned and prepared for. No sooner would she get herself back on her feet in a new job and a new place than something would go wrong. Her last employer had accused her of stealing from the till. Holly might have a rebellious streak that got her into trouble now and again but she was no thief. But the money had been found in her purse and she'd had no way of explaining how it had got there. Even the shop's security cameras had 'mysteriously' been switched off at the alleged time of the theft.

Holly had been evicted from her last three flats due to property damage that had been wrongfully levelled at her. But she knew her stepfather had staged it, along with the shop theft. He had set her up by sending in a mole to do his dirty work. That was why she had keyed his brand-new sports car and sprayed that message in weed killer on his perfectly manicured front lawn right where his neighbours would see it: *wife beater.*

Holly believed her mother would never have killed herself if it hadn't been for the long years of physical, emotional and financial abuse dished out to her by a man who had insisted on total obedience. Slavish obedience. Demeaning obedience that had left her mother a shadow of her former self. Franco had kept Holly and her mother oscillating between grinding poverty and occasional, large cash hand-outs that he'd never explained where they were sourced from. It was feast or famine. One minute the fridge was full of food. The next it was empty. Or sold. Furniture and appliances would be bought and then they would be sold to solve a 'cash-flow problem'. Things Holly had saved up for and bought with her meagre and hard-earned pocket money would be tossed out in the garbage or disappear without any explanation.

Holly vowed she would *never* break under Franco's tyranny. Even as a young child she had suffered his slaps and back-handers and put-downs without shedding a tear. Not even a whimper had escaped her lips. Not even her 'time-outs' on the balcony had made her give in. Even if her mother hadn't been abused on the other side, Holly would have locked off her feelings; cemented them deep inside. Hardened herself so she could withstand the abuse without giving him the satisfaction of breaking her spirit.

But unfortunately her mother had not been as strong, or maybe it had just become too hard for her to try to protect Holly as well as herself. Holly had never doubted her mother's love for her. Her mother had done everything she could to protect Holly from her stepfather but eventually it had become too much for her. She had become drug- and alcohol-dependent as a way to anaesthetise herself against the prison of her marriage to a beast of a man who had exploited her from the moment he'd met her.

Even though she had only been four at the time, Holly remembered the way Franco Morales had charmed her poor, grieving mother a few months after Holly's father had been killed in a work-place accident. He had taken control of her mother as soon as he'd married her.

At first he had been supportive, taking care of everything so she no longer had to worry about keeping a roof over their heads. He'd even been kind to Holly, buying her toys and sweets. But then things had started to change. He'd begun subjecting her mother to physical and verbal punishment. It had started with the occasional blow-out at first. One-off losses of temper that he would profusely apologise for and then everything would return to normal. Then a week or two would pass and it would happen again. Then it was every week. Then it was every day—twice a day, even.

And then he'd started in on Holly. Insisting she be brought up according to his rules. His regulations. The slaps had begun for supposed disobedience. The backhanders for insolence or often for no reason at all. Holly had got so stressed and wound up by the anticipation of his abuse she would often trigger it so it was out of the way for that day.

Although he'd no longer smacked her once she got a little older, his verbal sprays had worsened as she'd got to her teens. He'd called her filthy names, taunting her with how unattractive she was, how unintelligent she was, how no one would ever want her. All of which had been confirmed when her mother had died. Holly hadn't known what to do, where to go, how to manage her life.

During that awful, anchorless time she had done things she wished she hadn't and not done things she wished she had. She had mixed with the wrong people for the right reasons and mixed with the right people for the wrong reasons.

But things were going to be different now.

Holly was determined to get her life heading in the right direction. Once this community service was over, she was going to go to England, as far away as possible from her stepfather, back to the country of her mother's birth.

Then, and only then, would she be free.

Holly walked back towards the villa via the gardens. There were hectares of them, both formal and informal. There was even a swimming pool set on a sun-drenched terrace that overlooked the fields where some glossy-backed horses were grazing. The summer sun was fiercer now than earlier. The clouds had shifted and the bright light sparkled off the swimming pool like thousands of brilliant diamonds scattered over the surface. She bent down and trailed her fingers in the water to test the temperature. It was deliciously, temptingly cool. Not that she was much of a swimmer, but the thought of cooling off was irresistible.

She glanced at the villa to see if anyone was watching. Not that she cared. If she wanted to have a dip in her underwear who was going to stop her? She kicked off her sandals and shimmied out of her jeans, dropping them in a heap by the pool. She hauled her cotton sweater and the vest top she was wearing under it over her head and sent it in the same direction as her jeans.

Holly stood for a moment as the sun's rays soaked

into her all but naked flesh. She pushed all her thoughts about her bleak childhood out of her head. They were like toxic poison if she allowed them to stay with her too long. Instead, she pretended she was on holiday at an exclusive resort where she had total freedom to do what she wanted.

And then, taking a deep breath, she slipped into the water and let it swallow her into its refreshingly cool and cleansing embrace.

Julius heard a splash and pushed his chair back from the computer to check who was using the pool. He should've guessed and he *definitely* shouldn't have looked. Holly was swimming, wearing nothing but what looked like a transparent bikini. Or was it a bikini or just her bra and knickers? He knew he should get away from the window. He even heard the left side of his brain issue the order. But the right side wilfully drank in the sight of her. Lustfully feasted on the vision of her playing like a water sprite. Her lithe limbs and pert breasts with their pink-tipped nipples showing through the thin cotton of her bra tantalised his senses and drove his blood at breakneck speed to his groin. Her wet hair was slicked back and looked as dark as the pelt of a seal. She did a duck dive, and he caught a delicious glimpse of her neat bottom, long legs and thoroughbred-slim ankles. She kicked herself to the bottom of the pool before re-surfacing like a dolphin at play. He heard the sound of her tinkling laughter just as she went back down for another dive.

When she came up she had her back to him. He saw the neat play of the muscles of her back and shoulders as she lifted her hair off her neck, using its length to tie it in a makeshift knot on top of her head. She went back under the surface with a splash of her legs and ballerina-like feet.

The agility of her firm young body drove his stunned senses into overdrive. She could have been a model showcasing a new line of swimwear. She was athletically slim but with just the right amount of curves to make his blood pound with heightened awareness.

He couldn't take his eyes off her. He was mesmerised by the vision of her. The way she moved as if she had no care for whoever might be watching. The way she played like a fun-loving child and yet her body was all sensual woman.

When she came up the next time she turned her body so she was facing his window. As if she had some internal tracking device, her gaze honed in on his office window. She raised one of her brows before her mouth slanted in a knowing smile as she gave him a cheeky little fingertip wave.

Julius let out a stiff curse and turned away. He raked a hand through his hair, hating himself for the way his body reacted to her of its own volition. He had no control over it.

He saw. He ached. He throbbed. He *lusted*.

It shocked him how easily she reduced him to the level of an animal looking for a chance to mate. Surely he had more taste than to have his tongue hanging out for an outrageous tease? How was he going to survive a month of this? With her flaunting herself at every available opportunity? What was she doing, playing in the pool? This wasn't a holiday resort, for God's sake. She was here to work.

And, God damn it, he would make sure she did.

* * *

Holly heard the tread of firm footsteps coming along the flagstones as she sat on the top step of the pool idly kicking her feet just under the water. She stopped kicking and looked over her shoulder to see Julius striding towards her with a brooding expression on his face.

'Having fun, are we?' he said.

'Sure.' She gave him a breezy smile. 'Why don't you join me? You look like you could do with a little cooling off.'

Something dark and glittering flashed in his navy-blue gaze as it collided with hers. 'You're not here on holiday.' His tone was terse. Curt.

Holly felt a little thrill course through her body at the way he was trying not to look at her wet breasts. Her well-worn cheap bra was practically as sheer as cling film. His jaw had a tight clench to it as if his teeth were being ground together like chalk. She could see the tiny in-out movement of a muscle near the side of his flattened mouth. *Go on*, she silently dared him. *Have a good old look*. She arched back against the pool steps so that her breasts were above the water line. She watched as his eyes dipped to her curves, where the water was lapping her erect nipples, before he dragged his gaze back to hers, his mouth a flat line of disapproval.

'I don't see why I shouldn't be allowed to make use of what's on offer,' she said with a sultry smile.

'Get out,' he said with a jerk of his head.

Holly arched one brow at him. 'I would've thought those posh celebrity parents of yours would've taught you better manners than that. Say the magic word.'

He said a word but it had nothing to do with magic. It was a colourful swear word with distinctly sexual connotations that made the atmosphere between them even more electric.

Holly felt an unexpected frisson deep in her core, a flicker of arousal that licked along her flesh like the tail of a soft leather whip. Julius's nostrils were wide, flaring like a stallion about to rear up to take charge of its selected mate. She had never seen a man look so magnificently stirred by her. The sense of power it gave her was tempered only by the fact he stirred her in equal measure. He *aroused* her. He turned her on to the point where she could feel her body contracting with want. It was a new experience for her. She was usually the object of desire while feeling nothing herself. But this was different. She felt urges and cravings that were overpowering to say the least.

'You either get out on your own or I'll get you out,' he said through clenched teeth.

Holly gave a mock shudder. 'Ooh! Do you promise? I love it when a man gets all macho with me.'

His jaw clamped down so hard she heard his back teeth connect. 'Firstly, you're not dressed appropriately,' he said. 'I have staff members about the property— both young and old—who would be offended by your lack of modesty.'

Holly laughed at his priggishness. He wasn't worried about his staff. He was worried about himself. How she made him feel—out of control and unsettled by it. *What fun this was turning out to be.* 'Are you in some sort of time warp?' she said. 'This is the twenty-first century. Women can dress how they want, especially on private property.'

'Secondly, you're not here to party,' he said as if she hadn't spoken. 'You're here to work. W-O-R-K. Maybe you haven't heard that word before. But by the time you leave I swear you'll know it intimately or I'll die trying. Sophia is waiting for you in the kitchen. There's a meal to prepare.'

'Go help her yourself,' she said with playful splash of her toes that sent a spray of water over his crisply ironed trousers. 'You've got two arms.'

Those two strongly muscled arms suddenly reached down into the water and hauled her to her feet to stand dripping in front of him. Close to him. So close she could feel his body heat radiating towards her. Any second now she thought she would hear the hissing of steam.

'I gave you an order,' he said, breathing hard, eyes glittering darkly.

Holly stood her ground even though his hands gripping the tops of her arms were searing through her flesh like scorching-hot brands. The proximity of his hard body was doing strange things to hers. She could feel a pulse of excitement roaring through her flesh, a zinging awareness of all that was different between them: his maleness, her femaleness, his determination to keep control and her determination to dismantle it.

It crackled in the air they shared like a current set on too high a voltage.

She looked at his grimly set mouth and the dark shadow of sexy stubble that surrounded it. The clench of his jaw that suggested he was only just holding on to his temper. Her heart began to thump, but not out of fear. It wasn't him she was afraid of but her reaction to him. She had never felt her body react in this way. His touch triggered something raw and primal in her. She had never felt her body *ache*. Pulse and contract

with a longing she couldn't describe because she had
never felt it quite like this before. She wasn't a virgin
but none of her few sexual encounters had made her
flesh sing like this. He hadn't even kissed her and yet
she felt as if she was on a knife-edge. Every nerve in
her body was standing up and waiting. Anticipating.
Wanting. *Hungering.*

But then he suddenly dropped his hands from her
arms. The movement was so unexpected she nearly
toppled backwards into the pool but somehow managed to regain her balance. She maintained her composure—*just*—with a cool look cast his way. 'One thing
you should note,' she said. 'I *don't* take orders. Not from
you or from anyone.'

His jaw worked for a moment. She saw the way his
eyes went to her heaving chest as if he couldn't stop
himself. When his gaze re-engaged with hers it burned
with heat as hot as a blacksmith's fire. 'Then you will
learn how to do so,' he said with a thread of steel in his
voice. 'If I achieve nothing else out of this month, I *will*
achieve that. You will do as I say and not question my
authority. Not for a moment.'

Holly inched up her chin. 'Game on.'

Julius paced the floor of his office a short time later.
How could he have let Holly get under his skin like
that? He had gone down there to draw a line with her
but she had flipped things so swiftly he had ended up
acting like a caveman. He had never felt more like slak-
ing his lust just for the heck of it and to hell with the
consequences. His body was still thrumming with the
thunderous need she had stirred in him.

Holly was doing her best to break him, to reduce

him to the level of a wild animal. She was taunting him with every trick she had in her repertoire. She was in his house, in his private sanctuary, for the next four weeks. *Four weeks!* How was he going to withstand the assault on his senses?

She was so determined, so devious, so...*distracting.* His flesh still tingled with the aftershocks of touching her. Her skin against his had felt hot. Scorching hot. Blistering. He could still feel the sensation firing through his body. Touching her had unleashed something frighteningly primal in him. It roared through his blood like a wild fire. He had been knocked sideways by the sensation of holding her so close to the throbbing need of his body. It had been all he could do to keep himself from ripping that ridiculous see-through underwear away, driving himself into her and thrusting madly until he exploded.

Was he so sex-deprived that her teasing come-on had reduced him to the behaviour of a wild beast? The temptation of her, the thrill of touching her, of smelling that intoxicating scent of jasmine, musk and something else he couldn't pin down had wiped out the motherboard of his morality like a lightning strike.

What was it about her that caused him to react this way? She was wilful, wild, unpredictable and wanton. Being anywhere near her was like fighting an addiction he hadn't even known he possessed. He wanted her. He ached to have her. He pulsed with the need to feel her surround him with her hot little body. He could feel it rippling through him: lust let loose taking charge of him, demanding, dictating, directing. Dismantling all of his efforts to resist it.

He *would* resist it.

He would resist her.

He was not a hedonist. He wasn't a knuckle-dragging Neanderthal who could only respond to primal urges. He had intellect, discipline and self-control. A moral compass. A conscience.

Julius sat down heavily on his Chesterfield office chair, rotating it from side to side as he gathered his fevered thoughts. What was that crack Holly had made about his celebrity parents? So she knew exactly who he was, did she? Had she known all along or had someone told her? Sophia wouldn't have said anything. He trusted his housekeeper to take a bullet for the sake of his privacy. Had Holly somehow stumbled on his identity? No doubt that was why she was playing her seduction game. She wanted a celebrity trophy to hang on her belt. A show business shag to boast about to her friends. Could there be anything more nauseatingly vacuous?

He was lucky the press left him alone here in Argentina. He was able to walk around without the paparazzi documenting his every move. In England it was different. As a child he had found the intrusion terrifying. As an adult it was nothing less than sickening. Being chased down the street, cameras shoved in his face, when he was coming and going to lectures at university. Hounded while he was trying to go on a date with someone. It had got to the point where he had stopped dating. It wasn't worth the effort.

He was often mistaken for his brother, Jake, and that caused heaps of trouble, the sort of trouble for which he had no time or patience. Jake had no issues with the press. Jake accepted it as part of being related to famous people, but then, he had always been the more outgoing twin. Although Jake had no aspirations to be on the stage, he loved being the centre of attention and used their parents' fame to get what he wanted—a constant stream of beautiful women in and out of his bedroom. Jake didn't mind being compared to their father. He wore it like a badge of honour.

Julius would rather poke a skewer in his eye.

He would *not* have people compare him to his father. It wasn't that he didn't love his father. He loved both of his parents in a hands-off sort of way. He had never been one to wear his emotions on the outside. Even as a child he had never been the sort of person who was comfortable with over-the-top displays of emotion. His parents' loud arguments, their torrid displays of temper and their passionate and very public reunions had always made Julius cringe with embarrassment. He was glad he'd spent most of his childhood and adolescence at boarding school. He had found study an escape from the unpredictability of his home life. He had found the structure, order and strictly timetabled life a natural fit for his personality.

Jake, on the other hand, loved spontaneity. Jake hadn't enjoyed the discipline of school and had always found ways to buck the system. He was like their father in that he lapped up the attention and if it wasn't shining his way he found a way to make it do so.

Julius hated the limelight. He liked to work quietly in the background without the world's eye honed on him. His success as an astrophysicist had drawn far more attention to him than he would have liked but he comforted himself with the fact that he was successful in his own right, that he hadn't used his parents' fame as a way of opening any doors. He took a great deal of satisfaction in his work and, although the hours and the responsibility of heading a software company, along with his regular work came with its own set of problems, he enjoyed the flexibility of working from home, flying in and out as necessary.

The fact that the sanctuary of his home was now occupied by a mischievous hoyden was a state of affairs he would have to address, and soon. How was he supposed to concentrate with her flouncing around his villa?

The way she had challenged him as if fighting a duel. *Game on.* What exactly was she trying to prove? Hadn't she done enough by that little strip show in the pool? She was supposed to be making a new start. Reforming her bad ways. But from the moment she'd arrived she'd been playing him like a puppet master. Tugging on his strings until he was so churned up with lust he couldn't think straight. That was no doubt why she wouldn't accept the room Sophia had prepared for her on the third floor. Of course that room wouldn't suit Miss Bedroom Eyes. It was too far away from his. What did she have in mind? A midnight foray into his suite?

He would *not* allow her to win this. She would *not* get the better of him. She might think he was just like any other man she had lured into her sensual web in the past. She might think he was weak and spineless and driven by hormones—but she would soon find she had underestimated him. Big time.

He was putting an end to this before it got started.

Holly Perez was going straight to jail and he was making damn certain she wasn't collecting two hundred pounds—or anything else of his—on the way past.

CHAPTER FOUR

HOLLY WAS HELPING Sophia by preparing the vegetables for dinner while the housekeeper had a lie-down. Not because Julius had *commanded* her to get to work but because Sophia clearly couldn't do much with her wrist in a restrictive brace. Holly remembered all too well how painful a damaged limb could be. The simplest tasks were a nightmare and if you did too much it could compromise the healing process.

Besides, she quite liked cooking, for all that she'd told Julius she couldn't boil an egg, or words to that effect. She even liked cleaning. The repetitive nature of it was somehow soothing. It had helped her many a time as a child and teenager to put some order into the chaos of her home life. Her mother had got to the point of not being able to cope with the running of the home so Holly had taken it over. From a young age she knew how to cook, clean, tidy cupboards, fold washing and iron. It had also been a way to keep her stepfather from criticising her mother for not doing things properly around the house. If the house was as perfect as Holly could make it then a day or two might pass without a showdown.

What Holly didn't like was being ordered about. *Con-*

trolled. No one was going to command her like a serf. If she chose to do something, then she would do it because it was the decent thing to do, or she wanted to do it, not because someone was trying to lord it over her.

As if Holly had summoned him with her thoughts, Julius came striding into the kitchen. 'I want a word,' he said. 'In my office. Now.'

She blithely continued peeling the potato she was holding. 'I'll be there in ten minutes. I've still got the tomatoes and the courgettes to do.'

He came to the opposite side of the island bench to where she was standing and slammed his hands down on the surface, nailing her with his gaze. 'When I issue you an order, I expect you to obey it immediately.'

Holly held his intensely sapphire gaze with an arch look. 'Why can't you talk to me here?' She lowered her voice to a husky drawl. 'Or are you worried your housekeeper will come in and catch us at it on the kitchen bench?'

His eyes went to her mouth for the briefest moment before flashing back to hers, twin flags of dull red riding high on his cheekbones. 'I want you out of here by morning,' he said. 'I'm withdrawing my support for the scheme. You can find some other fool to take you on or you can go straight to jail where you belong. I don't care.'

'Fine.' Holly put down the peeler, untied the apron Sophia had given her and tossed it on the bench. 'I'll go and pack my things. Sophia can take over here. I'll just go and wake her from her nap and tell her. Her wrist was giving her a lot of discomfort earlier so she took a stronger painkiller. I reckon she's been doing too much because she doesn't want to let you down. But, hey, that's what she's paid for, right?'

He glanced at the half-prepared meal before reconnecting with Holly's gaze. 'You—' he bit out. 'This is one big game to you, isn't it?'

Holly leaned over the bench so her cleavage was on show. He reared back as if the backdraft of a fire had hit him in the face. 'You know what your trouble is, Julius? You don't mind if I call you that, do you? It makes things a little less formal between us since we're living together and all, don't you think?' She heard his teeth audibly grind together as she fluttered her eyelashes at him but she carried on regardless. 'Your problem is you're sexually frustrated. All that pent-up energy's gotta have an outlet. You're tearing strips off me when what you really want to do is tear my clothes off.'

His expression was thunderous. 'I have *never* met a more audaciously wanton woman than you. You have zero shame.'

Holly gave him an impish smile. 'Aw, how sweet of you to say so. Such flattery is music to my ears.'

He muttered a savage swear word and pushed his hair back from his forehead. It looked as if it wasn't the first time he'd done it that evening. The thick, glossy strands were in a rumpled state of disorder. His whole body was taut, rippling with tension. He reminded her of a tightly coiled spring about to snap.

'Here's what you've got wrong about me,' he said, facing her again with a hardened glare. 'I *can* resist you. You might think all those come-on looks will make me fall on you like some hormone-driven teenager, but you're wrong.'

Holly held out her hand, palm up. 'Want to lay a bet on it?'

He eyed her hand as if it were something poisonous. 'I don't gamble.'

She laughed. 'You're even more boring than I thought. What are you afraid of, Julius? Losing money or compromising one of your starchy old principles?'

He gave her a black look. 'At least I have some, unlike some other people I could mention.'

'Like your father?' Holly wasn't sure why she thought immediately of his father. But she'd heard enough about Richard Ravensdale's reputation to wonder how Julius could possibly be his son. Julius was an apple that had rolled so far away from the tree it was in another orchard. He was so uptight and conservative. His brother, Jake, was another story, however. Jake's exploits were plastered over the internet. It made for very entertaining reading.

Julius's brows snapped together in a single black bar. 'What do you know about my father?'

'He's a ladies' man,' Holly said. 'He's what I'd call a triple-D kind of guy: dine them, do them, dump them is his credo, isn't it? A bit like your twin brother's.'

'You didn't let on that you knew who my family was earlier,' he said. 'Why not?'

Holly gave him a cheeky smile. 'Fame doesn't impress me, remember?'

His mouth tightened until his lips almost disappeared. 'This is a bloody nightmare.'

'Hey, I'm not judging you because of your parents,' Holly said as she resumed preparing the vegetables. 'I reckon it would totally suck to have famous parents. You'd never know who your friends were. They might only be hanging out with you because of your connection with celebrity.' She looked up to find Julius staring at her with a frown between his brows. 'What's wrong?'

He gave his head a little shake, walked over to the fridge and opened it to take out a bottle of wine. 'Do you want one?' He held up the bottle and a glass.

'I don't drink.'

His gaze narrowed a fraction. 'Why not?'

Holly shrugged. 'I figure I've got enough vices without adding any more.'

He leaned back against the counter at the back of the kitchen as he poured a glass and took a deep draught of his wine. And another. And another.

Holly shifted her lips from side to side. 'You keep going like that and Sophia won't be the only one around here needing strong painkillers.'

'Tell me about your background,' Julius said suddenly.

Holly washed her hands at the sink. 'I expect it's pretty boring compared to yours.'

'I'd still like to know.'

'Why?'

'Humour me,' he said. 'I'm feeling sorry for myself for having a triple-D dad.'

'Aww. All those silver spoons stuffed in your mouth giving you toothache, are they? My heart bleeds. It really does.'

He screwed up his mouth but it wasn't a smile. More of a musing gesture, as if he were trying to figure her out. 'I know I come from a privileged background,' he said. 'I'm grateful for the opportunities it's afforded me.'

'Are you?' Holly asked with an elevated eyebrow.

His frown carved a V into his forehead. 'Of course I am.'

'So that's why your housekeeper had to twist your arm to do your bit for charity?' she said. 'To convince you to help someone a little less fortunate than yourself? Yeah, I can totally see how grateful you are.'

He had the grace to look a little uncomfortable. 'Okay, so you weren't my first choice as a charity, but I give to other causes. Generously, too.'

'Anyone can sign a cheque,' Holly said. 'It takes guts to get your hands dirty. To actually physically help someone out of the gutter.'

'Is that where you were?'

She challenged him with her gaze. 'What do you think?'

He held her look for another pulsing moment. 'Look, I'm sorry we got off to a bad start. Maybe we could start over.'

'I don't think so,' Holly said. 'You've already made your mind up about me. It's what people like you do. You make snap judgements. You judge people on appearances without taking the time to get to know them.'

'I'm taking the time now,' Julius said. 'Tell me about you.'

'Why should I?'

'Because I'm interested.'

'You're not interested in me as a person,' Holly said as she checked the oven where she had put the galantine of chicken earlier. 'You just want me out of here because I make you feel uncomfortable.'

'That was your intention, wasn't it?'

Holly closed the oven door and faced him. 'You want to know about me? I'm twenty-five years old. I had my first kiss at thirteen and my first sex partner at sixteen. I left school at seventeen without finishing my education. I have no qualifications. I speak two languages, English and Spanish—three, if you count sarcasm. I don't drink. I don't do drugs. I hate controlling men and I have issues with authority. That's about it.'

He glanced at the vegetable dish she had prepared. 'You told me you couldn't cook.'

'So I lied.'

'Why?'

Holly gave a lip-shrug. 'Felt like it.'

He came over to where she was standing. He stopped within touching distance but kept his hands by his sides. Even so, she could feel the magnetic pull of his body against hers. It was like a force field of energy. Strong. Powerful. Irresistible.

She glanced at his mouth, wondering if he was going to lean in to kiss her. She suddenly realised how much she wanted him to. Not to prove her point; somehow that agenda had taken a back seat, so far back it was now in the boot. No, she wanted him to kiss her because she really wanted to know what his mouth felt like. How it would feel as it moved over hers. How it would taste. How his tongue would feel as it stroked along hers. *Mated* with hers.

Then he did touch her. It was a fleeting stroke of two of his fingers down the slope of her cheek in a movement as soft as an artist's sable brush. It sent a shockwave through her senses. Every nerve in her face began tingling, spiralling in dizzy delight. She moistened her lips, barely aware she was doing it until she saw the way his sexily hooded gaze followed the pathway of her tongue.

Holly slowly brought her gaze back up to the midnight-sky-dark intensity of his. His expression was unfathomable. She didn't know what he was thinking. What he was feeling. She was scarcely able to think clearly herself. And as to her feelings… She didn't allow her feelings to get involved when she got physical with a man. *Never.*

'Who are you, Holly Perez, and what do you want?'

'I really should've made you lay down some money,' she said.

'You think I'm going to kiss you?'

'You're thinking about it—that much I *do* know.'

Why am I speaking in such a husky whisper? Holly thought. Anyone would think she was falling under some sort of crazy spell. Sure, he was handsome and he smelled good. Way too good, compared to some of the men she'd been up close and personal with. But he was a man who wanted to tame her and that she could never allow. Not in a million years.

His mouth tilted in a half smile. 'You think you can read my mind?'

'I don't know about your mind but your body's giving off one heck of a signal,' she said.

'So is yours.'

Tell me something I don't already know, Holly thought, sneaking in a hitching breath. Somehow the power base between them had shifted. She was no longer in charge of her body. It was reacting according to its own schedule, a schedule she had no control over. Her senses were scrambled. Caught up in a maelstrom of feelings she had never encountered before. Desire was running like a hot fever in her blood. She could feel her own wetness between her legs. She wondered if he could smell the musk of her arousal. She could feel the tingling of her breasts in anticipation of him reaching for them. As it was, his chest was barely half an inch away from hers.

In the past her breasts had felt nothing when a man stood close to her. They were just there—part of her anatomy. Now they were deeply sensitive erogenous zones that craved contact. They pushed against the fabric of her bra, swelling in need, her nipples peaking in response to his presence.

She could even sense the swell of his erection close to where her pelvis pulsed with need. The hot, hard, swollen heat of him was sending out a signal like sonar to her body, making her ache and throb with want.

'I would only sleep with you to prove a point,' Holly said in a way she hoped sounded offhand. 'Sorry if that offends your ego.'

He picked up one of her curls and wound it around his index finger. The gentle tug on her scalp sent a shot of lust between her legs, turning her core to molten fire. His eyes were so dark they reminded her of deep outer space. Limitless. Fathomless. 'It doesn't, because we're not going to sleep together.' His voice was only slightly less husky than hers.

'Could've fooled me.'

He pressed the pad of his thumb against her lower lip, holding it there for a moment before lifting it away. But still he didn't move away from her. His body was toe to toe with hers. If she leaned forward a fraction, their thighs would touch. The temptation to do so was like an invisible hand pushing her from behind. She brushed against the unmistakable hardness of him. Felt the shock through her flesh like a powerful current. It shot through her body in an arc of erotic energy that left no part of her unaffected. She saw the way his pupils flared, his eyes darkening, pulsing and glinting with want.

'You want me so bad I bet all it would take is one little kitten-lick of my tongue to send you over the edge,' Holly said, shocking herself at her wanton goading of him. Why was she being so utterly brazen? He had the edge on her here. He had already told her he would evict her from the programme. That had been his intention when he'd come down to speak to her. She would be sent to prison. She had no second chances. If she pushed him too far, he would get rid of her. Wasn't that what *everyone* did to her? She knew what was at risk but even so she couldn't stop herself. She was driven by the urges of her body—her traitorous body—which seemed to have developed an agenda of its own.

Julius sent a fingertip from the top of her cleavage, down the length of her sternum, over her quivering belly and then down to the zip of her jeans. He outlined the seam of her body through the denim and metal teeth of her zip, all the while holding her gaze with the smouldering blaze of his own. 'I bet I could make you come first,' he said in a two-parts gravel, one-part honey tone.

Holly almost came on the spot. She felt the flickering of her nerve endings, the swelling of her body as it ached and throbbed for more stimulation. She had to get away from him before he won this. He had far more self-control than she had bargained for and certainly far more than she had. What was he…made of steel?

'I could be faking it and how would you know?' she said.

His mouth slanted again in a cynical smile. 'I would know.'

Holly let out a breath that caught at her throat like a tiny fishhook. 'In my book, sexual confidence in men is arrogance in disguise.'

He outlined her mouth with that same lazy, tantalising glide of his finger. Tracing, touching, teasing her lips until she wanted to suck his fingertip into her mouth and draw on it as if she was drawing on him intimately. Not that she ever did that. Not for anyone. She hated it. It was gross and so were the men who insisted on it. But something about Julius made her want to step outside her boundaries. He triggered all sorts of forbidden urges in her. Was it because he was so conservative? Or was it because he was the first man she had ever felt this raging, red-hot passion for?

'You think I'm arrogant because I can pleasure you like you've never been pleasured before?' he asked.

'Promises, promises,' Holly said in a singsong voice.

He upped her chin between his finger and thumb so her gaze had nowhere to go but to mesh with his. The burn of his touch moved through her body like a trail of fire. The scorching circle of his thumb beneath her chin sent her pulse into overload.

His eyes moved between hers, back and forth, like the beam of a searchlight. She felt the magnetism of him, the sheer power he had over her with his laserlike touch. The touch she craved in every pore of her body. Her flesh ached to feel his hands move all over her. To shape and caress her breasts, her thighs and what pulsed and fizzed with longing between them. The need was thrumming inside her like the twang of a cello string plucked too hard. It reverberated through her racing blood, tripled her heartbeat and sent her already scudding pulse haywire.

'You're beautiful, but you know that, don't you?' Julius said in a deep, rough baritone that sent another tremor of want through her core. 'You know the power you have over men and you use it every chance you get.'

'A girl's gotta do what a girl's gotta do,' Holly said, trying to keep her gaze from skittering away from his probing one, trying to keep the fragile hold on her equilibrium disguised. Never had she felt such a compulsion to indulge her senses, to lose herself in a feast of the flesh, to allow herself to be consumed by the power and force of attraction and lust.

He threaded his fingers through her hair, lifting it away from her scalp, only to let it fall in a bouncing cascade against her neck and shoulders. 'That's why you were cavorting out in the pool,' he said. 'You wanted my attention. How better to get it than to strip off and parade that beautiful, tempting body beneath my office window?'

'You didn't have to look,' Holly said. 'You could have drawn the curtains or pulled the blind.'

He gave a little sound of sardonic amusement. 'You're not going to pull my strings like I'm some spineless puppet. I'm made of much sterner stuff.'

That goading little devil was back on Holly's shoulder, urging her to push Julius as far as she could. 'So that's why you came stomping out to the pool and manhandled me out of the water, was it? Just to show how stern and disciplined you are? Don't make me laugh.'

His eyes flashed with a flicker of anger. The same beat of anger she could see in a muscle beside his mouth, flicking on and off like a faulty switch.

The tug of war between his gaze and hers went on for endless seconds.

The air bristled with static.

But then he suddenly stepped back from her with

a muttered expletive. Holly hadn't realised she'd been holding her breath until he walked out of the kitchen without a backward glance.

She expelled the banked-up air in a long, jagged stream.

Round one a draw, she thought. *You'll win the next.*

But a nagging doubt tapped her lightly on the shoulder... *Maybe you won't.*

CHAPTER FIVE

JULIUS STRODE OUT of the villa in search of fresh air. Of common sense. *Control.* Where the hell was his control? He was furious with himself for allowing that toffee-eyed little temptress to trigger his hormones. Why hadn't he kept to his plan? He owed her nothing. What did he care if she went to prison? It was where she belonged. Why had he allowed her to manipulate his conscience?

Or maybe it wasn't his conscience she'd manipulated...

He was disgusted with himself for wanting her like he had wanted no other woman. He was annoyed he had allowed her to needle him to the point where he was as close to breaking as never before. How could he have allowed that to happen? He wasn't the sort of man who put sex before sense. This was nothing but a game to her.

She could tease and taunt him all she liked. She could walk around his villa scantily clad. She could flash her delectable cleavage at him. She could wiggle her hips and pert bottom. She could pout her sexy little mouth at him all day long. She could swim in his pool stark naked for all he cared.

He would *not* let her win this.

He had been tricked by her chameleon-like behaviour. The way she'd fooled him by her charitable act of taking over the cooking while Sophia had rested, after she'd been so adamant she wasn't going to take orders from him or anyone.

What was true about her and what were lies?

She was a smart-mouthed, streetwise siren. Flirting with him, teasing him, daring him, goading him until his blood ran so hot and fast through his veins it scorched him. He was burning for her. Throbbing with the ache to have her. He had never felt desire like it. It was like a storm in his body. A powerful combustion of energy that built each time he was near her. It was brooding inside him even now. The pressure of high arousal. The ache of unreleased desire was a burning ache he couldn't tame or dismiss. It consumed his thoughts as well as his flesh. Wicked, damning thoughts of what he would like to do to her—*craved* to do to her.

His brain was racing with a constant loop of hot images of them having sex like jungle animals. No 'finesse' sex. Hard and fast sex. 'Any position' sex.

Holly Perez was the most dangerous woman he had ever met. With her bedroom eyes and wily ways, she threatened everything he stood for. She made him feel things he had trained himself not to feel. Emotions were things he controlled. Desires were something he properly channelled. He did not rush into mad flings and one-nighters with strangers, especially ones with a criminal past.

He had standards. Principles. He was a good citizen who paid his taxes on time. He never coloured outside the lines. Damn it, he didn't even park outside of them.

Call him conservative, or even obsessive, but rules were things he respected because for most of his life his parents had disregarded them. Rules provided structure in a disordered world. He liked order. He liked predictability. Planning was his forte. He didn't do things on the fly. He wasn't spontaneous. He wasn't a risk taker. He left that sort of thing to his brother, Jake, who loved to live life in the fast lane. Julius was only happy in the fast lane if he knew exactly how fast it was, how long, how wide and how long he would have to be in it.

He did the calculations and *then* he acted.

And right now his calculations told him in big neon flashing letters: Holly Perez was danger personified.

But for all that something about her got to him...not just physically, but on an entirely different level. He felt something for her. Something he hadn't expected to feel. He was drawn to her. He couldn't get her out of his mind. He couldn't forget her touch. The way she moved. Even the sound of her laughter—the tinkling-bell sound that made his spine shiver. She was blatant, brazen and in-your-face, yet beguiling. He'd seen a glimpse of vulnerability down at the lake. And when he'd asked her about the scar on her arm. For just a moment he had seen a flicker of something behind the mask she wore. He couldn't help feeling there was more to her than met the eye. Yes, she made him uncomfortable. Yes, she was a flirt. But he had some sort of responsibility towards her, didn't he?

It was only for a month. He would be away for part of that with work. He would hardly have to have contact with her if he chose not to.

And right now the less contact he had with her the better.

Julius was back in his office trying to work when his phone rang. He was in two minds to ignore it when he saw it was his brother calling. 'Jake,' he said heavily.

'Whoa, bro, you sound a little tense there, man,' Jake said. 'So I take it you've already heard the news?'

Julius sat upright in his chair. 'Heard *what* news?'

A list of possibilities went through his head in the nanosecond that followed. His father had had another heart scare. His parents were splitting up. Again. His sister was finally going on a date after losing her child-hood sweetheart to cancer when she was sixteen. *No*, he thought; Miranda was too intent on martyrdom. Jake was getting married... *No*. That would *never* happen.

'A skeleton has come out of Dad's closet,' Jake said.

'Another one?' Julius asked, thinking of the veri-table cast of mistresses and hook-ups his father had dallied with over the years in spite of 'working at his marriage'. Not that his mother, Elisabetta, could stand in judgement. She'd had a fling or two herself. 'How old is she this time?'

'Twenty-three.'

'God, the same age as Miranda,' Julius said.

'It gets worse,' Jake said.

'Go on, ruin my day,' Julius said.

'She's not his mistress.'

Julius's heart stopped as if a horse had kicked him in the chest. 'He's not a bigamist? Tell me he's not got a secret wife?' *Please, God, spare us all that shame.*

'She's his daughter.'

'His *daughter*?'

'Yep,' Jake said in a grim tone. 'He's sired himself a love child. Katherine Winwood.'

'Dear God, what does Elisabetta think of this?' Julius said. 'How's she taking it?'

'How do you think?' Jake said wryly. 'Hysterically.'

Julius groaned at the thought of the temper tantrums, door slamming and object throwing that would be going on in his parents' hotel suite in New York. He couldn't face another divorce. The last one had been bad enough. The press. The publicity. All of their private lives exposed. 'Is it in the papers?'

'Papers, internet, every social media platform you can poke a finger at,' Jake said. 'It's gone viral. And that's not all.'

Julius's stomach pitched. 'It gets worse?'

'Way worse,' Jake said. 'Kat Winwood was born two months after Miranda.'

Julius did the maths. 'So that means Dad was still seeing this woman's mother when he reconciled with Mum?'

'Got it in one.'

Julius let out a colourful curse. 'What's Dad got to say for himself? Or is he denying it?'

'You can't deny the results of a paternity test.'

'How did this Kat girl get one done?' Julius said. 'Who is she? Where did she come from? Why's she revealed herself now? Why didn't her mother tell Dad she was pregnant, or has he always known?'

'He knew all right,' Jake said. 'He paid the woman to have an abortion. Handsomely, too.'

Julius swallowed a mouthful of bile. Just when he thought his father couldn't shock him any more, he raised it to a whole new level of indecency. 'But she didn't go through with it,' he said unnecessarily.

'Nope,' Jake said. 'She had the kid and kept the father's identity a secret. Even the birth certificate says "father unknown".'

'So why come forward now?' Julius asked.

'She died recently of a terminal illness,' Jake said. 'She told Kat on her death bed who her father was.'

'So this girl Kat is after money.'

'What else?'

Julius scored a hand through his hair. 'How many more like her could there be out there? Why can't Dad keep it in his trousers? He's nudging seventy, for God's sake.'

'I just thought I'd give you the heads up on it in case the press come sniffing around you for an exclusive,' Jake said. 'They've been parked outside my place since the first Tweet went out.'

His brother's words sent an army of invisible ants across Julius's scalp. A drumbeat of panic started up in his chest. His blood ran hot and cold. He felt beads of sweat break out across his brow. If the press came here they would find Holly—*living with him*. A girl not much older than his father's love child. In fact, Holly looked younger than twenty-five. What would the press make of her holed up here with him? Especially if they caught a glimpse of her flaunting her flesh at every available opportunity. They wouldn't wait for the truth. They would jump to sensational conclusions to razz up a storm of scandal.

He had to keep her away from the press. God knew what she would say to them to stir up trouble for him. One look at her and they would assume he was indulging in a lust fest and was no different from his Lothario father. With her sexy little body and her cheeky personality, why wouldn't they assume he was making the most of the situation? Why, oh, why, had he agreed to have her here? It was a disaster of monumental proportions.

'You okay, bro?' Jake cut through Julius's racing thoughts. 'I know it's a shock but think how Miranda's taking it.'

That was enough to snap Julius back into protective big-brother mode. 'How *is* she taking it?'

'I haven't spoken to her yet,' Jake said. 'She wasn't answering her phone. Probably switched it off to keep the press off her back. But think about it. She's always been the baby of the family. How's it going to feel to know there's a new half-sister who's now the youngest?'

'I'll call her as soon as I finish with you,' Julius said, expelling a long ragged breath. 'Poor kid. You know how embarrassed she gets by Mum and Dad's behaviour. This will be hardest on her. We've already been through one divorce with them so we know what we're in for. She has no idea of how ugly this could get.'

'Yeah, tell me about it,' Jake said. 'But it might not come to that.'

'You seriously think Mum won't want a divorce after Dad produces a secret love child out of the woodwork?' Julius said. 'Come on, Jake. This is our mother we're talking about. Any chance for a scene and she's right there in full costume and make-up.'

'I know, but Flynn's trying to smooth things over,' Jake said. 'Another divorce will be costly to both of them, and not just financially. Their popularity could rise or fall according to how they handle this scandal. You know how fickle the fans are. Flynn's hoping he can silence the girl with a one-off payment. Something big enough to keep her mouth shut and go away. Preferably both.'

Julius was relieved to hear it was all in good hands. Flynn Carlyon was the family lawyer; he'd been a year ahead of them at school. He handled Julius's parents' legal affairs as well as run offices in London. Flynn wasn't just a solicitor to the stars. He had won several high-profile property settlement cases that had given him the tagline around the courts: *Flynn equals win.* He had a sharp mind, an even sharper tongue and a cutting wit.

'Have you met this girl?' Julius asked.

'Not yet,' Jake said. 'You might want to drop by next time you're in town and say hello. After all, she's your new baby sister.'

How could I possibly forget? Julius thought with a despairing groan.

Holly put the finishing touches to dinner before she went up to her room on the second floor to have a shower. The room she had chosen was four doors down from Julius's suite but on the opposite side of the wide corridor. It didn't have a balcony—*thank God*—but it did have a nice view over the front gardens and the tree-lined driveway. It had its own en suite, which was decorated in a Parisian style with lovely ceramic-and-brass tap handles and a claw-footed bath that was centred in the middle of the floor, with a telephone-handle fitting as well as taps. There was a separate shower stall big enough for a football team and lots of gorgeous, fluffy white towels, fragrant French soaps and expensive hair products. A gilt-framed oval mirror hung over the ped-

estal washbasin and there was another full-length one
in the bedroom.

The only issue Holly had was with her clothes. They
didn't feel right for her surroundings. All this high-
end luxury made the clothes she'd brought with her
look even dowdier than usual. She had never been financially stable enough to follow fashion. Fashion was
something other people followed. Shopping was a pas-
time other people indulged in. Rich people, people who
had money, security and the safety net of family. Holly
had taught herself not to want things she could never
afford. She had deadened her desire for nice feminine
things. It was pointless to wish she could dress like the
women she saw about town. Smart women; educated,
sophisticated, polished and poised, with hair, make-up
and nails done like models and movie stars. She could
never compete with that. It was so far out of her reach,
she didn't bother trying.

But right now she would have loved a nice dress to
put on and some high heels to go with it. Some classy
underwear—not cheap, faded cotton but some slinky,
cobwebby lace. She would have liked some make-up—
not much, just enough to highlight her features, to put
some colour on her eyelids and some tinted gloss on her
lips. She would have liked to get a decent haircut, perhaps get some professional foils done to cover the pink
streaks she'd done with a home kit that hadn't turned
out quite the way she'd planned. Maybe a bit of jewel-
lery—pearls, perhaps—to give her a touch of elegance.

But what was the point of wishing she could dress
like a glamour girl when all her life she had been the
girl with the charity shop clothes? The girl with the bad
haircut, the bitten nails and the cheap shoes with the

soles worn through? She had always felt like a donkey showing up at a posh dressage event.

Why should now be any different?

After her shower Holly slipped off her towel in front of the mirror. At least she had a good figure. It was her only asset. Good bones; long, slim limbs; a neat waist; nicely shaped breasts; mostly clear skin, apart from that ridiculously childish patch of freckles over the bridge of her nose.

Her gaze went to a pattern of damson-coloured marks around the tops of her arms. She reached up and touched them, her stomach doing a funny little dip and dive when she realised what they were. Julius's fingerprints had branded her flesh with light but unmistakable bruises.

She bit her lip, looking at the grey cotton tank top she had been planning to wear with another pair of jeans—her only pair without holes in them, although they did have a frayed hem. She put on the tank top and picked up a green cardigan, even though the evening was warm, and slipped it on. It wasn't the nicest weave—the acrylic in it always made her skin feel itchy. But it was either that or a denim jacket or a pilled woollen sweater that would have her sweating within seconds. Finally, she bunched up her hair and secured it with an elastic tie in a makeshift knot at the back of her head.

Holly drew in a breath and let it out in a long, slow sigh. Why she was trying to look half-decent for Julius Ravensdale wasn't something she wanted to examine too closely. It wouldn't matter if she'd been dressed in the finest designer wear; he would still look down his imperious nose at her.

Just like everyone else.

CHAPTER SIX

JULIUS HADN'T BEEN able to track down Miranda or his father. But he had fielded several calls from his mother, who was beyond hysterical. He did what he always did. He listened, he stayed calm, he bit his tongue. His mother vented, raged and fumed so much that he began to wonder if she was actually enjoying herself. It was an opportunity to play the victim, one of her favourite roles. His parents' relationship was toxic. He hated the way they were madly in love one minute then hated each other the next. When one did something out of line, the other went into payback mode. It was childish and puerile.

The press was having a ball with this latest bombshell. He'd clicked on a couple of links Jake had sent him. The girl in question was stunning. If her mother had looked anything like Katherine Winwood, Julius could see why his father's head had been turned. Julius only hoped no one would track him down for a comment. His life here in Argentina was his way of flying under the radar. Over here hardly anyone knew who he was and he wanted it to stay that way. But what was he going to do if the press came sniffing around? Holly was a loose cannon. There was a possibility she would deliberately mislead the press if given half a chance. Should he send her away? He looked at his phone. He had the number of her caseworker on speed dial. His finger hovered over it…but then he pushed his phone away.

For all her feistiness and brazen behaviour, there was something about Holly that mystified him. She seemed so determined to challenge him, yet he had seen that glimpse of touching vulnerability down at the lake. He had never met anyone quite like her before. He found her…interesting. Stimulating, and not just because of his overactive hormones. There was a hint of the lost waif about her. Or was he completely hoodwinked by her? Was it his rescue complex in overdrive? He wasn't the sort of person to walk away from a person in need. Holly was difficult and disruptive but if he sent her away now she would have no choice but to go into detention. He knew enough about the penal system to know it was not the place he would want anyone under his care and protection to go. Sophia had been so keen to take Holly on. He would be letting her down if he quit now. The least he could do was talk to Sophia about it. Get her perspective on things.

It was Julius's routine to go to the sitting room before dinner each evening to have a quiet drink with Sophia before she served the meal. It was a pattern they had fallen into over the past few months. He enjoyed hearing about Sophia's extended family and her interesting childhood as the daughter of Italian immigrants. They often spoke in Italian, as he was fluent, given his mother was from Florence.

He wanted to use this time to inform her of his father's latest peccadillo so she could put steps in place to maintain Julius's privacy.

His parents—most particularly his mother—would be appalled at Julius for being so familiar with his housekeeper or, indeed, any of his staff. When he'd been growing up, his parents' housekeeping staff had not been considered part of the family. There'd been strict codes of behaviour forbidding anything but the strictest formality from the staff towards family members. One did not discuss one's private affairs with the staff. One did not fraternise with or consider them as friends. They were employees. They were kept at arm's length. They were taught to know their place and never stray from the boundaries of it.

The only exception had been Jasmine Connolly, the daughter of Hugh Connolly, the gardener at the family property in Buckinghamshire called Ravensdene. Jasmine had come to live with her father after her mother had dropped her at Ravensdene on a visit and was never seen or heard from again. Julius's parents had taken pity on Hugh Connolly—unusual for them, considering their almost pathological self-centredness—and had offered to pay for Jasmine's education. Jasmine was like a surrogate sister to Julius, and certainly to Miranda, as they were much the same age.

Jake, however, had a tricky relationship with Jasmine after an incident when she'd been sixteen. Both blamed the other and as a result they were sworn enemies, which made for some rather interesting dynamics at family gatherings.

But this time it wasn't Sophia who joined Julius for a drink. In walked Holly, carrying a tray with savouries on it, which she put down on the table in front of him, but not before he got a tantalising glimpse of her cleavage as she leaned over.

'Sophia sends her apologies,' Holly said. 'She's having an early night.'

Julius frowned. 'Is she all right? I haven't seen her all day.'

'She's fine. Just needs a rest, is all.'

He watched as Holly poured him a glass of white wine. Clearly Sophia had filled her in on his preferences. She handed it to him with a tight-lipped smile. 'Two standard drinks is all I'll serve. Just so you know.'

He took the glass, only just restraining himself from draining it dry. Mixing one glass of wine with Holly Perez was like drinking five tequilas and expecting to remain sober. It was impossible to remain sober and sensible in her company. He could already feel the tightening of his groin; the stirring of lust her presence triggered was like someone flicking a switch inside him.

For all that he'd wanted to get rid of her, she had turned things around with her concern for Sophia. But was it concern…or conniving behaviour to serve her own ends? He wanted to know more about her. He wanted to know why she was so determined to make trouble for him. It didn't add up. If she made too much trouble, she would be sent to jail. Why then sabotage her last chance at making something of her life? She seemed intent on destroying any hope of a positive future. If he sent in a bad report to her caseworker, it would be disastrous for her. She knew that. He knew that. Why then was she so determined to ruin everything for herself? It didn't make sense. It wasn't logical.

If there was one thing in life Julius demanded, it was sense and logic.

'I thought I told you not to wear jeans to dinner,' he said.

A flash of defiance—or was it pride?—sparked in her caramel-brown gaze. 'I don't have any dresses. I could've come in shorts or my underwear. I can go upstairs and change or I could strip off here. You choose. I'm easy.'

'Undoubtedly.'

She gave him a withering look. 'Not as easy as your old man, according to the news I heard just now.' She sat on the edge of the sofa opposite him. 'He's quite a cad, isn't he? Nothing like you, or so you say.'

Julius forcibly had to relax his hold on the stem of his glass in case he snapped it. 'I would appreciate it if you would refrain from discussing my father's affairs with anyone. If you say one word to the press, I'll send you packing so fast you won't know what hit you.'

'Are you going to fly home to England to meet your new sister?'

He tightened his jaw. 'I'm not planning to.'

'It's not her fault your old man's her father,' Holly said. 'You shouldn't judge her for something she had no control over.'

Julius took another mouthful of wine. She was right and he wanted to hate her for pointing it out to him. But he needed time to get used to the idea of having a half-sibling. He thought he was used to his father's scandals but this one took the prize. The press had been still banging on about it last time he'd looked. Katherine Winwood might be gorgeous to look at but who knew what her motives were in coming forward? Money, most probably. That she might be entitled to some compensation for how his father had treated her mother was not something he wanted to comment on. He was sick to the stomach over his family's dramas. What or who would turn up next?

Julius decided a change of subject was called for. 'I'll order some clothes for you. Let me know your size and I'll make sure you have what you need.'

Holly's eyes danced. 'So you're going to be like a sugar daddy to me or something?'

He ground his teeth until his jaw ached. 'No.'

She picked up a canapé and bit into it. 'Pity.'

'It's rude to speak with your mouth full.'

'I'll make sure I remember that when we're in the bedroom,' she said with a naughty smile.

Julius kept his gaze locked on hers but he wondered if she could sense the fireball of lust that hit him. He was suddenly so erect he could feel it pressing against his trouser zip. The thought of her hot little mouth on him made his blood pound in excitement.

He distracted himself by leaning forward to take one of the canapés off the platter. 'Where did you learn to cook?'

'Picked it up along the way.'

He sat back and crossed his right ankle over his left thigh in the most casual and relaxed pose he could manage while his erection still throbbed. Painfully. 'Along the way where?'

'Here and there and everywhere.'

It seemed he wasn't the only one keen to avoid discussing family issues, Julius thought. 'What are your plans once you leave here?'

She gave a loose little shrug before taking another appetiser. 'I want to get a job and save up enough money to go to England.'

'To holiday?'

'To live.' She took a noisy bite and munched away, like a bunny rabbit chewing a crunchy carrot.

Julius knew she was doing it to annoy him. Her rebellious streak was kind of cute, when he thought about it. It reminded him a bit of Jasmine Connolly, the gardener's daughter, who liked to have a bit of fun at times—mostly with Jake, who for some reason didn't see the funny side.

Cute?

What was he thinking? Holly wasn't cute. She was as cunning as a vixen. She was out to prove he was unable to resist her. He was out to prove he could. He had the edge on her. She might be doing all she could to get thrown out of his house but without him as her guardian she would find herself doing time. Why then was she pushing him to evict her? Was it deliberate or a knee-jerk thing? Was her behaviour a pattern she had developed in order to survive? From the scant details she'd given him, her childhood clearly hadn't been a picnic. Did she push people away before they pushed her?

And why did *he* give a damn?

'Do you have relatives in England?' Julius asked.

'My mum was an orphan. My dad was, too. An English couple adopted him, which is how he met my mum over there. It's why they hit it off so well. They were two lonely people who found true love.' Her mouth took a sudden downturn and she looked at the remaining piece of her canapé as if it had personally offended her. 'Pity they didn't get the happy ending they deserved.'

'How did your father die?'

'He was killed in an accident at work.'

'What sort of accident?' Julius pressed a little further.

'A fatal one.'

He gave her a look. 'I realise it's probably painful to talk about but I—'

'It happened a long time ago,' Holly said, interrupting. 'Anyway, I only remember what I've been told.'

'What were you told?'

'That he died in a work-place accident.'

She was a stubborn little thing, Julius thought. She would only reveal what she wanted to reveal. 'Did your mother ever remarry?'

Holly got up abruptly from the corner of the sofa and dusted her fingers on the front of her jeans. 'You want to make your way to the dining room? I'll only be a minute or two. I promised I'd take Sophia's meal up to her.'

Julius sat back and sipped his wine, a thoughtful frown pulling at his brow. So it wasn't his imagination after all. There was definitely something about Holly's background that made her reluctant to speak of it. Could he get her to trust him enough to reveal it?

He pulled himself up short. Why on earth was he even *trying* to understand her?

He was supposed to be keeping his distance. He wasn't the type of guy to let his emotions get the better of him. It was fine to care about her welfare—perfectly fine. Any decent person would do that. But if he thought *too* much about her cute dimples, and pert manner and that far away look she sometimes got in her eyes when she didn't know he was looking, he would be feeling stuff he had no right to be feeling. It was bad enough being attracted to her physically. God forbid he should start liking her as a person. Feeling affection. Holly was a temporary inconvenience and he couldn't wait to get rid of her so he could get his life back into its neat, ordered groove.

Even if at times—he reluctantly conceded—it was a little boring.

* * *

Holly made sure Sophia was settled in her suite with her meal, a drink and the television remote handy. She had cut up the chicken and the vegetables so Sophia could eat with her left hand using a fork. 'I'll be back in half an hour to bring up dessert and to clear your dishes,' she said.

'Muchas gracias,' Sophia said with a soft smile. 'You're a good girl.'

Holly gave a little grunt of a laugh. 'Try telling your boss that.'

Sophia looked at her thoughtfully for a moment. 'You don't need to be bad to be noticed. There are other ways to get his attention.'

Holly frowned. 'I'm not trying to get anyone's attention.'

Sophia gave her a sage look. 'Earning someone's respect takes time. It also takes honesty.'

Holly fiddled with a loose button on her cardigan. 'Why should I bother trying to earn someone's respect when I'm not going to be here long enough to reap the benefits?'

'Señor Ravensdale could help you get on your feet,' Sophia said. 'He could give you a good reference. Find employment for you. Recommend you to someone.'

Holly snorted. 'Recommend me for what? Scrubbing someone's dirty floors? No thanks.'

Sophia released a sigh. 'Do you think someone who's in charge of maintaining the upkeep of a house is not worthy of respect? If so, then you're not the person I thought you were. People are people. Jobs are jobs. Some people get the good ones, others the bad ones— sometimes because of luck, other times because of opportunity. But as long as each person is doing the best job they can where they can, then what's the difference between being a CEO and a cleaner?'

'Money. Status. Power.'

'Money will buy you nice things but it won't make you happy.'

'I'd at least like the chance to test that theory,' Holly said.

Sophia shook her head at her. 'You're young and angry at the world. You want to hit out at anyone who dares to come close in case they let you down. Not everyone will do that, *querida*. There are some people you can trust with your love.'

Holly swallowed a golf ball-sized lump of sudden emotion. Her father had called her *querida*. She still remembered his smiling face as he'd reached for her and held her high up in his arms, swinging her around until she got dizzy. His eyes had been full of love for her and for her mother. They had been a happy family, not wealthy by any means, but secure and happy.

But then he had died and everything had changed.

It was as though that life had happened to another person. Holly *felt* like a different person. She was no longer that sweet, contented child who embraced love and gave it unquestionably in return. She was a hardened cynic who knew how to live on her wits and by the use of her sharp tongue. She didn't feel love for anyone.

And she was darn certain no one felt it for her.

'I'd better go serve His High and Mightiness his dinner,' Holly said. 'I'll see you later.'

'Holly?'

She stopped at the door to look back at the housekeeper. 'What?'

'Don't make things worse for him by speaking to the press if they come here. He doesn't deserve that. He's trying to help you, in his way. Don't bite the hand that's reached out to help you.'

'Okay, okay, already. I won't speak to the press,' Holly said. 'Why would I want to? They'll only twist things and make me look bad.'

'Can I trust you?'

'Yes.'

'He won't let you win, you know.'

Holly kept her expression innocent. 'Win what?'

Sophia gave her a knowing look. 'I know what you're trying to do but it won't work. Not with him. If he wants to get involved with you then it will be on his terms, not yours. He won't be manipulated or tricked into it.'

'That's quite some pedestal you've got him on,' Holly said. 'But then, he pays you good money. You'd say anything to keep your job.'

'He's a good man,' Sophia said. 'And deep down I know you're a good woman.'

You don't know me, Holly thought as she closed the door. *No one does.*

I won't let them.

CHAPTER SEVEN

JULIUS WAS STANDING at the windows of the dining room when Holly came in with the food. She unloaded the tray on the table and then turned briskly to leave.

'Aren't you joining me?' he asked.

Her chin came up. 'Apparently I'm not dressed for the occasion.'

There was a bite to her tone that made him wonder if he had upset her. Embarrassed her. Hurt her, even. She always acted so defiant and in-your-face feisty that to hear that slightly wounded note to her voice faintly disturbed him. There was so much about her that intrigued him. The more time he spent with her, the more he wanted to uncover her secrets. The secrets he caught a glimpse of in her eyes. The shifting shadows on her face he witnessed when she didn't think he was looking at her.

She was an enigma. A mystery he wanted to solve. She played the bad girl so well, yet he saw elements to her that showed her vulnerability, her kindness. Like the way she had taken over the kitchen so Sophia could rest. That showed sensitivity and kindness, didn't it? Or was he being the biggest sucker out to fall for it? Was it all an act? A charade? How could she be as bad as she made out? What was her motive to make him think she was out to seduce him? Was it because he wasn't taking her up on it? Did his refusal to succumb to the temptation she offered make her see him as even more of a challenge?

'It's not a formal dinner,' Julius said. 'If I had guests, then, yes, I would insist on you dressing appropriately. I'm sorry I didn't realise you haven't the suitable attire in which to do so but that will be rectified as soon as possible tomorrow.'

Her small, neat chin came up. 'Once you've coughed up that dictionary you've swallowed, maybe you'll have room for the dinner I've prepared. *Bon appetit.*'

He let out an exasperated breath. 'Look, if I've upset you I'm sorry. But things are a little crazy for me just now.'

Her eyes flashed with unbridled disdain. 'Why would I be upset by someone like you? I don't care about your opinion of me or my clothes. It means nothing to me. *You* mean nothing to me.'

Julius pulled out the chair to the left of his. 'Please join me for dinner.'

Her mouth took on a mutinous pout. 'Why? So you can train me like a pet monkey?' She put her hands on her hips, deepened her voice and did a surprisingly credible imitation of his British accent. 'Don't hold your knife like a dagger. That's the wrong fork. Don't cut your bread. Break it. No, don't call it a serviette, call it a napkin.'

Julius couldn't stop his mouth from twitching. She had definitely missed her calling. She could tread the boards as well as anyone. 'I promise not to criticise you.'

She narrowed her gaze in scepticism. 'Promise?'

He didn't know which Holly he preferred—the snarky challenger or the hot little seductress. Both, he realised with a jolt of surprise, were vastly entertaining. 'Promise.'

She made a little huffing noise. 'Fine.'

He seated her then came around to his own chair and took his place. He spread his napkin out across his lap and watched as Holly expertly served the vegetable dish with silver-service expertise. Then she served the herbed chicken galantine with the same level of competence. She sent him a look from beneath half-mast lashes that made him realise how much he had underestimated her. How much he had misjudged her. She might come across as a bad girl from the wrong side of the tracks but underneath that don't-mess-with-me attitude was a young woman with surprising dignity and class. And pride.

During the course of their meal he made desultory conversation: stuff about the weather, movies and the state of the economy but she didn't seem inclined to talk. The questions he asked her were greeted with monosyllabic responses. He tried using open-ended questions but she just shrugged in a bored manner and mumbled something noncommittal in reply. She didn't eat much, either. She just moved the food around her plate, only taking the occasional mouthful. Was she doing it to punish him? To make him regret his all-too-quick summation of her character and seeming lack of abilities? She was more than capable of holding her own in sophisticated company. Why had she let him believe otherwise? Or was she just contrary for the heck of it? Thumbing her nose up at anyone who judged her without getting to know her?

'Are you not feeling well?' Julius asked.

'I'm fine.'

He studied her for a beat or two. 'You're sweating.'

She gave him a haughty look. 'Ladies don't sweat. They perspire.'

He felt another smile tug at his mouth at the way she so expertly parodied his accent. 'Take off your cardigan if you're hot.'

Her eyes skittered away from his. 'I'm not hot.'

He watched as she made another attempt at her meal but every now and again she would shift in her seat or wriggle her neck and shoulders as if her clothing was making her itchy.

'Holly.'

'What?'

'Take it off. You're clearly uncomfortable.'

'I'm not.'

'Would you like me to adjust the air-conditioning?'

'I told you, I'm fine.'

He shook his head at her in disbelief. 'This afternoon you were parading around half-naked and now you're acting like a nun. What is it with you? Take it off, for God's sake, or I'll take it off for you.'

Her eyes were narrowed as thin as twin hairpins. 'You wouldn't dare.'

'Wouldn't I?'

She shot up from the table and spun around to leave but Julius was too quick and intercepted her. He caught her by the back of her cardigan but when she pulled away from him it peeled off her like sloughed skin.

His heart came to a scudding stop when he saw what was on her upper arms before her hands tried to cover it. The cardigan he was holding slipped out of his hand

and fell to the floor. His mouth went completely dry. His stomach dropped as if it had been booted from the top of a skyscraper.

'Did *I* do that?' His voice came out rusty, shocked. He was ashamed. Mortified.

'It's nothing. I can't even feel it.'

His stomach churned in disgust. 'I hurt you.'

'I bruise easily, that's all.'

Julius scraped a distracted hand through his hair. Dragged the same hand over his face. How could he have *done* this? How could he have been so…so *brutish* to mark her flesh? For what? To prove a point? What point was worth proving if a woman was hurt in the process? It was against everything he believed in. It was against everything that defined him as a man—as a civilised human being. Real men did not use violence. It was the lowest of the low to inflict physical hurt on another person, particularly a woman or a child. How could he have lost control of his emotions to such a point that he would do something like that? He had grabbed her on impulse. He had been so het up about her goading behaviour it had overridden all that was decent and respectful in him.

'Don't make excuses for me,' he said. 'I'm appalled I did that to you. I can only say I'm deeply, unreservedly sorry and assure you it will never, *ever* happen again.'

'Apology accepted.' Her chin came up again, her gaze as hard and brittle as shellac. 'Now, may I get on with serving the rest of the meal?'

Julius had never felt less like eating. His stomach was a roiling pit of anguish. Shame and self-loathing were curdling the contents like acid. He'd thought his father's scandal was bad. This was even worse. *He* was worse.

His behaviour was reprehensible. He had hurt Holly like a thug. 'I think I'll give dessert a miss. Thanks all the same.'

'Fine.' She made a move towards the table. 'I'll just clear these plates.'

'No. Let me,' he said, but stopped short of putting a hand on her arm to stop her. He curled his fingers into his palms. Put his hands stiffly by his sides. 'You see to Sophia. I'll clear away.'

Her eyebrows rose ever so slightly as if she found the thought of him doing anything remotely domestic in nature totally incongruous to her opinion of his personality and station. 'As you wish.'

Julius bent down, picked up her cardigan from the floor and handed it to her. 'I'm sorry.'

'So you said.'

'Do you believe me?' It was so terribly important she believed him. He could think of nothing more important. He couldn't bear it if she didn't believe him— if she didn't trust him. If she didn't feel safe with him. Sure, they could flirt and banter with each other, try to outwit each other with smart come-backs, but there was no way he could bear it if she didn't feel physically safe under his roof—under his protection.

She held his gaze for a long beat, searching his features as if peeling back the skin to the heart of the man he was inside.

'Yes,' she said at last. 'I do. You don't strike me as the sort of man to take his frustration out on a woman.'

'You have experience of those who do?'

Her eyes fell away from his to focus on his top shirt button. 'None I care to recall in any detail.'

Julius wanted to push her chin up so she had to meet

his gaze but he was wary of touching her. He *longed* to touch her. To *hold* her. To reassure her. To remove the stain of his careless fingerprints with a caress as soft as a feather. To press his mouth to her and kiss away those horrible marks; to make her feel secure and safe under his protection.

But instead he stood silently, woodenly, feeling strangely, achingly hollow as she turned and walked out of the room.

Holly had finished seeing to Sophia and tidying up the kitchen. Not that she'd had to do much, as Julius had loaded the dishwasher and washed up by hand the baking dish she'd cooked the chicken in. It surprised her he knew how to do such mundane stuff. He was from such a wealthy, privileged background. He'd had servants waiting on him all of his life. He wouldn't have had to lift a finger before some servant would have come running and seen to his needs and that of his siblings. And yet he had left the kitchen and the dining room absolutely spotless. The uneaten food was packaged away with cling film in the fridge. The benches had been wiped. The lights were turned down. The blinds were drawn.

Holly was too restless to go to bed. She thought about going for another swim but didn't want to encounter Julius. Well, that was only partly true. She could face him when he was stern and headmaster-ish but, when he got all caring and concerned and…*protective*, it did strange things to her insides. She had never had anyone to protect her. Not since her father had died. No one had ever stood up for her. Everyone was so quick to judge her. They never waited to get to know her, to try and understand the dynamics of her personality and what had formed it. Tragedy, abuse, maltreatment and neglect did not a happy person make. She knew she should try harder to be nicer to people. She knew she should learn to trust people because not everyone was an exploitative creep.

The news of his father's love child was clearly a terrible shock to Julius. Finding out he had a half-sister would have rocked him to the core. He hadn't wanted to discuss it, which she could understand, given his personality. He didn't like surprises. He liked time to think things over. She suspected he would eventually come round to wanting to meet his half-sister. He was too principled simply to pretend she didn't exist.

But the news of the existence of a love child certainly did raise the chance of the press hounding him. He was obviously worried Holly would exploit the situation—dish the dirt on him or make things look salacious between him and her. She might like to rattle his chain for a bit of fun but there was no way she would take her games into the public sphere. She didn't want her stepfather to know where she was. If she drew attention to herself by speaking to the press, who knew what would happen.

Holly wandered along the corridor past the library on her way to her room. The door was slightly ajar and the room was in darkness except for the moonlight shining through the waist-high window. One of the windows must have been mistakenly left open for she could see one of the sheer curtains fluttering on the light breeze coming from outside. She considered leaving it but then remembered Sophia was tucked up in bed upstairs. It would be a shame if it rained overnight and some of those precious books nearest the window were damaged.

Holly moved over to the window without bothering to turn on the light, as the moonlight was like a silver beam across the floor. She closed the window and straightened the breeze-ruffled curtain. She stood there for a long moment looking out at the moonlit gardens and fields beyond. It was such a beautiful property. So peaceful and isolated. There wasn't a neighbour for miles. No wonder Julius loved working and living here. She had spent most of her life in cramped flats in multi-storey buildings with the roar of traffic below and the sound of neighbours packed in on every side. But here it was so serene and peaceful she could hear frogs croaking and owls hooting. It was like listening to a night orchestra. The moonlight cast everything in an opalescent glow that gave the gardens a magical, storybook quality.

It was only when Holly turned around to leave that she saw the silent, seated figure behind the large mahogany leather-topped desk. 'Oh, sorry,' she said, somehow managing to smother her startled gasp. 'I didn't see you there. The light wasn't on so I thought someone must've left the window open. It looks like we could get a storm so I thought I'd better shut it since Sophia's gone to bed.' *Shut up. You're gabbling.*

Julius's leather chair creaked in protest as he rose from behind the desk. 'I'm sorry for giving you a fright.'

'You didn't,' Holly said then, seeing the wry lift of one of his eyebrows added, 'well, maybe a little. Why didn't you say something? Why are you sitting here in the dark?'

'I was thinking.'

'About your family…um…situation?'

'I was thinking about you, actually.'

Her heart gave a stumble. 'Me?' His eyes went to her arms. 'Oh. Well, you said sorry, so it's all good.'

His frowning gaze meshed with hers. 'How can you be so casual about something so serious? I hurt you, Holly. I physically hurt you.'

'You didn't mean to,' Holly said. 'Anyway, it was probably my fault for stirring you up.'

'That's no excuse,' he said. 'It shouldn't matter how much provocation a man receives. No man should ever use physical force. I can never forgive myself for that. I'm disgusted with myself. Truly disgusted.'

Holly rolled her lips together for a moment. 'I've not been the easiest house guest.'

A host of emotions flickered over his face. Emotions she suspected he wasn't used to feeling. It was there in the dark blue of his eyes. It was in the thinned-out line of his sculptured mouth. 'You don't have to be anything but yourself,' he said in a husky tone. 'You're fine just the way you are.'

No one had ever accepted her for who she was. Why would they? She wasn't the sort of person people found acceptable. If it wasn't her background, then it was her behaviour. She rubbed people up the wrong way. How could he say she was fine the way she was? *She* wasn't fine with the way she was.

'So, how are things with your family?' Holly said to fill the heavy silence.

He turned away as he pushed a hand through his hair. 'I haven't been able to contact my sister. The legitimate one, I mean.'

'You're worried about her?'

'A little.'

Holly couldn't help feeling a little envious of Miranda Ravensdale. How wonderful to have a big brother to watch out for you. Two, in fact. Not that she knew if Julius's twin brother, Jake, had the same protective qualities as Julius. She got the impression Jake was a bit of a lad about town.

'Maybe her phone is flat, or she's turned it off or something,' she said.

'Maybe.'

Another silence ticked past.

'Oh, well, then,' Holly said, making a step towards the door. 'I'd better let you get on with it.'

'Holly.'

She turned and looked at him. 'Would you like me to get you a coffee? A night cap or something? Since Sophia's off-duty you'll have to put up with me doing the housekeeper stuff.'

His dark eyes moved over her face, centred on her mouth and then came back to her gaze. 'Only if you'll have one with me.'

Holly chewed the inside of her mouth. She didn't trust herself around him. He was dangerous in this gentle and reflective mood. Keeping her game face on was easy when he was being sarcastic and cynical towards her. But this was different. 'It's a bit late at night for me to drink coffee, and since I don't drink alcohol I'd be pretty boring company...'

His mouth twisted ruefully. 'I suppose I deserve that brush off, don't I?'

'I'm not brushing you off. If I were brushing you off then you'd know about it, let me tell you,' she said.

'I'm not the sort of person to hand out a parachute for anyone's ego.'

He gave a soft laugh, the low, deep sound doing something odd and ticklish to the base of Holly's spine. 'That I can believe.'

There was another beat of silence.

'What would you do if you found out you had a half-sibling?' he asked.

Holly shifted her lips from side to side as she thought about it. 'I would definitely want to meet him or her. I've always wanted a sister or brother. It would've come in handy to have someone to stick up for me.'

He studied her for a long moment. The low light didn't take anything away from his handsome features. If anything, it highlighted them. The aristocratic land-scape of his face reminded her of a hero out of a nine-teenth-century novel. Dark and brooding; aloof and unknowable.

'Things were pretty tough for you as a kid, weren't they?'

Holly moved her gaze out of reach of his. 'I don't like talking about it.'

'Talking sometimes helps people to understand you a little better.'

'Yeah, well, if people don't like me at "hello" then how is telling them all about my messed-up childhood going to change their opinion?'

'Perhaps if you worked on your first impressions you might win a few friends on your side.'

Holly thought of how she'd stomped into his office that morning—had it really only been a day?—with her verbal artillery blazing. She'd put him on the back foot at the outset. But she'd been angry and churned up over everything. Her forthrightness had been automatic. She liked to get in first before people took advantage. 'I could've come in and been polite as anything but you'd already made up your mind about me. You'd heard about my criminal behaviour. Nothing I could've said or done would've changed your opinion.'

Julius took a step that brought him close to where she was standing. Holly held her breath as he sent a fingertip down the length of her arm, from the top of her shoulder to her wrist. The nerves fluttered like moths beneath her skin. Her heart skipped a beat. Her stomach tilted. 'Are you sure I didn't hurt you?' His voice was low, a deep burr of sound that made the base of her spine fizz.

'I'm sure.'

He sent the same fingertip down the curve of her cheek, outlining her face from just behind her ear to the base of her chin. 'I think underneath that brash exterior is a very frightened little girl.'

Holly quickly disguised a knotty swallow. 'Keep your day job, Julius. You'd make a rubbish therapist.'

His eyes held hers for another long moment. 'I'll see to the rest of the windows,' he said. 'You go on up to bed. Sleep well.'

Like that's going to happen, Holly thought as she turned and slipped out of the room.

Holly didn't see Julius for over a week. He hadn't informed her he was leaving at all. She heard it from Sophia, who told her he was working on some important software and had to attend meetings in Buenos Aires, as well as flying to Santiago in Chile. It annoyed Holly he hadn't bothered to tell her what his schedule was. He could have done so that night in the library, especially as she'd heard him leave the very next morning. But then, she reminded herself, she was just a temporary hindrance for him. The more time away from the villa—*away from her*—the better. The bruises on her arms had faded but the bruise to her ego had not. Why couldn't he have talked to her in person? Told her his plans?

The fact was, it was dead boring without him. Sophia was kind and sweet and did her best to make sure Holly had plenty to do without exploiting her. But spending hours with a middle-aged woman who reminded her too much of the mother she no longer had was not Holly's idea of fun. The more time she spent with the gentle and kind housekeeper, the more she ached for what she had lost. Sophia had a tendency to mother her, to treat her like a surrogate daughter. Holly appreciated the gesture on one level but on another it made her feel unutterably sad.

Which was all the more reason she missed the verbal sparring she'd done with Julius. She missed his tall figure striding down the corridors with a dark frown on his handsome face. She missed the sound of his cultured accent in that mellifluous baritone that did such strange things to her spine. She missed the excitement in her body, the buzzing, thrilling sensation of female desire he triggered every time he looked at her. Her body felt flat and listless without him around to charge it up with energy.

The days dragged with an interminable slowness that made Holly's restlessness close to unbearable. Although she enjoyed the tasks Sophia set her, as the villa was beautiful and full of exquisite works of art and priceless collector's pieces, it just wasn't the same without

Julius there. The nights were even worse. Sophia usually went to bed early, which meant there was no one to talk to. The rest of the villa staff—the gardener and the man who looked after the horses on the property—lived in accommodation separate from the villa. There was only so much television Holly could watch and, even though she enjoyed reading, the evenings were particularly tiresome.

The one thing Julius had done for her since he'd gone away, however, was have some clothes delivered to the villa for her. They were mostly smart-casual separates, as well as a couple of dresses, including a long, slinky formal one made of navy blue silk. There were shoes and underwear the likes of which she had never seen before: cobweb-fine lace, some with fancy little bows and embroidered rosebuds or daisies. There were bathing suits as well, a one-piece black one and a fuchsia-pink bikini.

Make-up and perfume arrived in neat little packages. A hairdresser arrived at the villa and worked on Holly's hair until she barely recognised herself in the mirror. Gone were the pink streaks and split ends. Her wild curls were toned, tamed and cut in a shoulder-length style that could be worn up or down, depending on her mood or the occasion.

But for all the finery Holly felt dissatisfied. What was the point of all these gorgeous clothes if she had no one to see her in them? She didn't even have anywhere to go because she wasn't allowed to leave the premises unless Julius accompanied her as her official guardian. It was part of the diversionary programme's fine print.

Late on Sunday, well after Sophia had retired for the night, Holly turned off the show she had been only half-watching on television and made her way to her room. But on the way past Julius's suite she stopped. She had been in a couple of days ago with Sophia to do a light clean. His suite had a balcony but the doors had been closed and Holly had kept her back to it. She had worked briskly and efficiently with the minimum of talk, desperate to stave off a panic attack if Sophia asked her to dust or sweep out there. If Sophia had sensed anything was amiss, she hadn't said, although Holly suspected there was not much that would escape the housekeeper's attention.

Before Holly could change her mind she turned the handle on the door of the suite and stepped inside. The balcony doors were closed and locked, the gauzy curtains pulled across the windows. Even though the room had been empty for days, Holly could still smell the lemon and lime notes of Julius's aftershave. She turned on one of the bedside lamps rather than the top light in case Sophia saw the spill of light from her room on the top floor.

The forbidden nature of what Holly was doing made a frisson of excitement shiver over her flesh. This was where Julius slept. This was where Julius made love with his occasional lovers. The lovers Sophia stalwartly, stubbornly, refused to comment on or reveal any information about. Holly had looked on the internet on the library's computer for any press items on him but there was virtually nothing about his private life. There was stuff about Julius's work in astrophysics and about his software company that had come about after he had designed a special computer programme used on the space telescopes in the Atacama Desert and which had turned him into a multi-millionaire overnight.

There was plenty of stuff about his father's love-child scandal. Every newsfeed was running with it. There was also plenty of information on Julius's twin, Jake. Jake was the epitome of the 'love them and leave them' playboy: the 'Prince of Pickups' as one article described him. It was uncanny seeing the likeness to Julius. They were mirror images of each other. She wondered if she met them together if she would be able to tell them apart. The only slight difference she could see was in every photo Jake was smiling as if that was his default position. Julius, on the other hand, was not one to smile so readily. He was serious in demeanour and nature. He was conservative where, from what some of the photos suggested, his twin was a boundary-pusher—a born risk-taker.

Holly wandered about Julius's suite, stopping to check out a photo of his younger sister on his dressing table. Miranda was pretty in a pixyish, girl-next-door sort of way. She was petite with porcelain-white skin and auburn hair. Nothing like her extraordinarily beautiful mother, Elisabetta Albertini, Holly duly noted. She put the photo down and stepped over to the walk-in wardrobe, hesitating for a nanosecond before she slid the door back and walked inside.

All of his shirts, suits and jackets were in neat rows. His sweaters were folded in symmetrical colour-coordinated stacks. His shoes were all polished and paired and perfectly aligned on the tiered shoe rack.

She picked a pair of cufflinks up from the waist-high shelf above a bank of drawers. The cufflinks were a designer brand with diamonds in the shape of a J. She wondered if he had bought them for himself or whether they had been a gift from a member of his family. Miranda, perhaps? The photo of her in his room suggested he adored her. It was the only photo she had seen of any of his family in the villa.

The sound of a footfall in the bedroom startled Holly so much she felt her flesh shrink away from her skeleton. She slipped into the shadows of Julius's suits, using them as a shield to hide behind. Her heart hammered. Her breath halted. She couldn't allow Julius to find her in here. But how on earth was she going to get out? Why hadn't he told her and Sophia he was coming home tonight? Why turn up unannounced? What if he went to bed while she was stuck here, hiding in his wardrobe? She would have to hope and pray he'd go to the en suite and have a shower or something so she could sneak out without being detected. Hopefully the fact his bedside lamp was on wouldn't make him suspicious. He might think Sophia had left it on in anticipation of him coming home…or something.

The thoughts were a tumbling mess inside her head. Round and round they went until she felt dizzy. Her skin was breaking out in a sweat. She could feel beads of it rolling down between her breasts, under her arms, across her top lip.

'Holly?' Sophia's voice called out. 'Is that you?'

The relief Holly felt was so great it was as if her legs were going to fold beneath her as the tension washed out of her. Even her arms felt boneless, her shoulders dropping as if had just been relieved of carrying a tremendous weight. She took a steadying breath and walked out of the wardrobe with what she hoped was a calm, collected and innocent look on her face. 'Sorry,' she said. 'Did I give you a scare?'

Sophia was frowning. 'What were you doing in Señor Ravensdale's wardrobe?'

'I was just…checking to see if I'd put his shirts I ironed the other day in the right place,' Holly said, mentally marvelling at her ability to construct a credible excuse at such short notice. 'You know how fussy he is. I didn't want him to come home and get antsy about the blue shirts mixed up with the white ones. Oh, and I straightened his ties. One was hanging half a millimetre lower than the others.'

Sophia's frown lessened slightly but didn't completely disappear. 'You don't have to work at this time of night. You're entitled to time off.'

'I know, but I was bored, so I thought I'd double-check stuff.'

'You've worked hard this week,' Sophia said. 'Much harder than I thought you would.'

'Yeah, well, I'm not afraid of hard work,' Holly said. 'So, why are you up? I thought you were in bed.'

'My wrist is giving me a bit of pain,' Sophia said, wincing as she cradled her arm against her body. 'I was coming past to go downstairs to make a hot drink when I heard a sound.'

'Weren't you worried it might be a burglar?'

'No, I knew it was you.'

'How?'

'I could smell your perfume,' Sophia said. 'The one Señor Ravensdale bought for you. It was a good choice. It suits you.'

Holly gave the housekeeper a quick stretch of her lips as a smile. 'That man has serious class. Does he always buy women such expensive gifts?'

Sophia gave her the sort of reproachful look a parent would give to a persistently naughty child. 'Come and make me a hot chocolate,' she said. 'Then it's time, young lady, for bed.'

'When is Julius coming home?' Holly asked as they walked down to the kitchen together. 'Have you heard from him?'

'He sent a text a couple of hours ago,' Sophia said. 'His plane was delayed in Santiago.'

'Maybe he's catching up with a lady friend.'

Sophia pursed her lips without responding.

'Why do you call him "Señor" instead of Julius?' Holly asked.

'He's my employer.'

'I know but you and he seem to be pretty chummy,' Holly said. 'How long have you worked for him?'

'Since he moved to Argentina eight years ago.'

'So you would've seen quite a few girlfriends come and go in his life, huh?'

Sophia cast her a glance. 'Why are you so interested in his private life? Do you have designs on him?'

Holly coughed out a laugh. 'Me? Interested in him? Are you joking? He's the last person I would fall for. The very last.'

Sophia released a soft sigh. 'That's probably a good thing.'

'Because I'm too far below his station?'

Sophia shook her head. 'No. He wouldn't let something like that be an issue. I think he wouldn't fall in love too easily, that's all.'

'Like we have a choice in these things,' Holly said, then quickly added, 'not that I'm speaking from experience or anything.'

'So you haven't lost your heart to anyone yet?' Sophia asked with another sideways glance.

The word *yet* seemed to hang in the air. It was like a gauntlet being thrown down. Fate issuing a challenge. A dare.

Holly laughed again. 'Not yet.' *Not ever. Not going to happen.*

Not in a million years.

CHAPTER EIGHT

JULIUS HADN'T PLANNED to drive home so late but his flight back to Buenos Aires from Santiago had been delayed several hours due to a storm. A solid week of work, long hours of meetings and field research had done little to quell the errant feelings he had for Holly. Feelings he hadn't expected to feel. Didn't want to feel. She occupied his thoughts whenever his mind drifted away from work. She filled his brain. She filled his body with forbidden desires and wicked urges. She filled his every waking moment—and even his dreams—with visions of her lithe body, her pert breasts, her cheeky smile and the way she upped her chin in a challenge or twinkled her brown eyes in a dare.

He could not remember a time when he had been more obsessed with a woman. She was as far from an ideal partner as any he could imagine. Her wilfulness, her defiance and her rebellious nature made every-thing that was rational, logical and intellectual inside him shrink away in abject horror. But everything that was male and primal in him wanted to possess her. He ached and pulsed to feel her body, to be surrounded by her. Every hormone in his body twanged with longing. Every nerve-ending craved the stroke or glide of her touch. He had X-rated dreams about her pouty little mouth on him, drawing on him, pleasuring...

Julius was disgusted with himself. Not just because of his uncontrollable desire for her but because he still couldn't forgive himself for the way he had hurt her. What had he been thinking, hauling her bodily from the pool like that? There was *no* excuse. So what if she had goaded him? So what if she had defied him? Disobeyed him? He was an adult. He was a civilised, educated man. What had he hoped his action would achieve?

Or had he secretly—*unconsciously*—wanted to touch her? To hold her sexy, wet body against the throbbing heat of his...

He had wanted to kiss her so badly it had tortured him not to. Her mouth had been so close he'd felt the breeze of her sweet breath. It had taken every ounce of self-control he possessed and then some to drop his hold on her and step back. He could still feel the silk of her skin against his fingers. He could still feel the magnetic force of her body drawing his closer. It was stronger, way more powerful than anything he had ever felt before. How he had not slammed his mouth down on hers and thrust his tongue through her lush lips still surprised him.

He had been so close.

So terrifyingly, shamefully close.

Work had legitimately called him away, thankfully. He hadn't trusted himself to be around her. He still didn't trust himself, which was even more worrying.

But it wasn't just the physical attraction that was so troubling to him. There were other feelings he was experiencing that were far more dangerous. Tiny sprouts of affection were popping up inside him. He actually *liked* her. He admired her spirit. Her edginess. Her blatant disregard for the rules. For propriety. He found himself missing her teasing playfulness. He missed her dimpled smile and the way her eyes danced with mischief.

He had no business missing her. He wasn't supposed to get attached to her. She wasn't his type. And he clearly wasn't hers. She only wanted to sleep with him to prove a point. It was nothing but a game to her.

He was nothing but a game to her.

Another bonus of being called away to work was that the press had stayed away from his villa. He had been intercepted at the airport and issued his usual 'no comment' response to the media. The last thing he wanted was the press sniffing around his home and finding a young woman in residence, especially as he didn't trust Holly to behave herself. He'd left strict instructions with Sophia on monitoring Holly's movements and making sure she didn't speak to anyone if they should turn up at the villa. No one had, which gave him some measure of comfort, but how long before someone did?

Julius parked in the garage and walked into the villa as quietly as he could so as not to disturb anyone. It was two in the morning so he hoped his little house guest was tucked away safely in bed.

She wasn't.

Holly came out of the kitchen as he came in the back door. She was wearing one of the outfits he'd bought her. The cashmere separates looked far slinkier on her than it had in the online catalogue. But then she would make a bin liner look like a designer gown, he thought. The fabric draped her slim curves like the skin of an evening glove.

'How was your trip?' she asked.

Julius wasn't in the mood for trite conversation. Not with her looking good enough to eat and swallow whole. How did she manage to stir him up so easily? 'Tiring.'

She moved towards him with catlike grace. 'Fancy a snack?'

'What's on the menu?' *Bad choice of words.*

Her eyes glinted. 'What do you fancy?'

He tried not to look at her mouth but a force far more powerful than his resolve pulled his gaze to its lush ripeness. 'What's on offer?' What was it with him and the double entendres? He was acting like Jake, for God's sake.

'Whatever you want,' she said. 'Your wish is my command.'

'I thought you didn't take too kindly to commands?'

She tiptoed her fingers along the corded muscles of his arm. 'Maybe I'll make an exception tonight.'

He suppressed a shiver as her fingers lit every nerve under his skin with red-hot fire. Need pulsed in his groin. Lust growled, roared. 'Why?'

'Because I've missed you.'

Julius barked out a laugh and gently pushed her arm away as he moved past. 'Go to bed.'

'Why didn't you tell me you were going away?'

He turned back to look at her. 'You're answerable to me. Not me to you. Or has that somehow slipped your attention?'

Her caramel-brown eyes ran over him like a lick of flame. 'Were you with a lover?'

He gritted his teeth until his jaw ground together like two tectonic plates. 'No. I was working. Remember that word you seem to have so much difficulty with?'

She leaned one shoulder against the door jamb. 'I've been working. Go ask Sophia.'

'I will, but not at this time in the morning.'

Her eyes did another scan of his body, her chin coming to rest at a haughty height. 'I even cleaned your room.'

Julius didn't like the thought of her in his room. Actually, he liked the thought way too much. His mind filled with images of her laid out on his bed, her gorgeous, luscious body as hungry for him as he was for her. His flesh crawled with lust. It was like a fever in his blood. Raging. Taking him. Taking over his control like a shot of a powerful drug. 'I'd prefer it if you'd stay out of there.'

'Why?' she said. 'You let Sophia change your bed. Why shouldn't I?'

Because I want you in it, not changing it, he thought with a savage wave of self-disgust. 'I trust you left everything as you found it?' he said.

Her brows drew together. 'What's that supposed to mean?'

'I seem to recall your rap sheet includes theft.'

'So?'

'So I want you to keep your hands clean.'

Her top lip curved up on one side. 'Don't worry,' she said. 'You have nothing I want.'

'Only my body.'

A dark, triumphant glint shone in her gaze. 'Not as much as you want mine.'

'You think?'

'I know.'

Julius wanted to prove he could resist her. He *needed* to prove it, if not to her then to himself. He reached for her, encircling her wrists with his fingers. Holding her. Securing her. Her eyes widened but not in fear. He could read her signals as easily as she read his. Mutual desire ran between them like the shock of an electric current. He could feel it through her flesh where it was in contact with his. He looked at her mouth and watched as she ran the tip of her tongue over her lips, leaving a glistening sheen.

Her eyelashes came down over her eyes, her breath dancing over his lips as she rose on tiptoe. He felt the brush of her body against his just before her mouth touched his. He didn't move. Didn't respond. Willed himself not to respond. Her tongue licked his top lip and then his lower one. The tantalising friction set his nerves screaming for more but still he stayed statue-still.

She came at him again, her tongue sweeping over his lower lip in a drugging caress that made his groin tighten to the point of pain. The need to taste her, to take control of the kiss, was like an unstoppable tide. He let out a muttered swear word as he splayed his hands through her hair and covered her mouth with his.

Her lips were soft and full, her mouth tasting of chocolate, milk and temptation. He drove his tongue through her parted lips, plundering her mouth, seeking her tongue to tangle with it in a duel that made the blood pump all the harder in his veins. She made a sexy little sound of approval as he pulled her closer to his body, letting her feel his hardness, the need he couldn't hide even if he'd wanted to.

Julius succoured on her mouth as if it was his only source of sustenance. She was a drug he hadn't known he had a taste for until now. He was lethally addicted to her. His body craved hers. Ached for hers. He pulled at her lower lip with his teeth, taking little nips and bites before using his tongue to salve where he had been. She responded with her own little series of playful bites, not just on his mouth, but also on his neck, and his earlobes, sucking on them until he thought he was going to disgrace himself. He shivered as her tongue came back to play with his, in and outside of their mouths in little flicks and thrusts of lust.

He took charge again by backing her up against the wall, his hands shaping her curves as his mouth crushed hers. She made a little whimpering sound as one of his hands cupped her breast. She moved against him, a gesture of encouragement he was in no state to resist. He shoved aside her top and bra to access her naked flesh. He brought his mouth down to suckle on her erect nipple before he swirled his tongue around her areole. He kissed his way over her breast, lingering on the underside when he heard her gasp as if he had found a particularly sensitive erogenous zone.

The skin there was as soft and smooth as silk. He trailed his tongue like a rasp along that scented curve, his senses in overload as he thought of how much he wanted to possess her. It was a driving force in his body. A primal urge he had no hope of controlling. His desire was a wild, primitive beast that had broken free of its chains and was now on the rampage.

Julius uncovered her other breast and subjected it to the same sensual assault, breathing in the fragrance of her body—a mixture of the flowery perfume he had bought her and her own bewitching female scent. The scent that was filling his nostrils, making him crazy, making him want her more than he had wanted anyone.

He left her breasts to come back to her mouth, driving his tongue through the seam of her lips, as he wanted to drive through the seam of her body. She gave a breathless whimper and reached between their hard-pressed bodies to uncover him. Her hands were on his belt buckle and then his zip, but he didn't do anything to stop her. It was too intoxicating to feel those wicked little hands moving over him, releasing him, stroking him, pleasuring him.

He smothered a rough curse as her thumb caressed the sensitive head of his erection while her mouth played with his. He had never had a more exciting encounter. He wanted to feel her mouth on him, to have her submit to his wildest fantasies.

And, as if she was acting a role scripted right from his imagination, she sank to her knees in front of him, cupping him, breathing over him with her dancing breath, her moist tongue poised.

He put a hand on the top of her head and pulled back. 'No,' he said. 'You don't have to do that.'

She looked up at him questioningly. 'But I thought all guys…?'

'It's not safe without a condom,' Julius said.

She got to her feet, pushing a strand of her hair back behind one of her ears as she did so. 'That's a first.'

He frowned as he thought of all the men who had been with her. How many? Did it matter? Who was he to judge? He'd had his share of sexual encounters. Not as many as his brother, but enough to forget times, places and, yes, even some names.

But there would be no forgetting Holly Perez, he thought. The taste of her was still fizzing on his tongue.

The feel of her was still tingling in his fingertips. His need of her was still firing in his blood.

'Holly.'

She rounded on him with a combative look. 'So who won that round, do you think? I kissed you but you took it to another level.'

Julius blew out a jagged breath. 'That should never have happened.'

Her chin inched up, her eyes flashing at him. 'You want me but you hate yourself for it, don't you?'

'I don't want to complicate my life, or indeed yours.'

'That wasn't the message I was getting a few minutes ago when you had your mouth on my breast—'

'Will you stop it, for God's sake?' Julius said. 'This is not going to happen, okay?'

Her brown eyes shone with a victorious gleam. 'It already did,' she said, moving up so close he could feel her breasts against his chest. 'You're not going to get that wild animal back in its cage any time soon, are you, Julius?'

He looked down at the tempting curve of her sinful mouth. The mouth he had savaged, pillaged and supped on like a starving man. The luscious and deliciously ripe mouth that had offered to pleasure him. *God strike him down for wanting her to.* He put his hands on her hips to gently push her back from him but then his right hand felt a cube-shaped ridge against her hip. 'What's that in your pocket?'

Her expression faltered for a moment before she tried to move away. 'What? Oh…nothing.'

Julius held her steady, his hands anchoring her so she had to face him. 'Empty your pockets.'

Her eyes flickered with something that looked sus-
piciously like panic. 'Why?'

'Because I asked you to.'

'Just because you asked me doesn't mean I'll—'

Julius held her left hip with one hand while he dug
in her right pocket with the other. He pulled out the
cufflinks Miranda had bought him for his last birthday, holding them right in front of Holly's defiant face.
'Want to tell me how they got in there?'

Her teeth sank into her bottom lip. Her eyes skittered
away from his. 'I—I can explain…'

He dropped his hands from her as if she was burning him. Which she was. Burning him. Exploiting him.
Stealing from him while his back was turned. How
could he have thought she might not be as bad as she
acted? How could he have been so stupid as to feel *affection* for her? What an idiot he was. How could he
have let her fool him into believing she was worthy of a
second chance? She wasn't just deceitful—she was dangerous. He was nuts to have let her get under his guard.
She was a liar and a thief and he'd been too damn close
to getting caught in her sugar-coated web.

'I want you out of here by morning,' he said. 'I don't
want to hear your explanation. There isn't an explanation you could give that would satisfy me.'

'I was in your walk-in wardrobe earlier tonight.'

'Doing what?'

'Straightening your ties.'

Julius laughed. 'What? You can't do better than
that?'

Her chin came up to a pugnacious height. 'I got
caught off-guard when Sophia came in unexpectedly.
I panicked. I hid in your wardrobe as I thought it was

you. I didn't realise I'd put the cufflinks into my pocket until just now. I honestly don't remember doing it. It must've been an impulse or…or something…'

He rolled his eyes. 'Do you really think I'm *that* stupid?'

She bit her lower lip again. 'I know it looks bad…'

'Why were you in my room?'

She shrugged one of her shoulders. 'I was having a look around.'

'For what?' he said. 'Loose change?'

She gave him a gimlet glare. 'I know you think I'm nothing but a petty thief but I didn't take them on purpose. It was an…an accident.'

Julius gave another cynical laugh. 'Yes, Officer,' he said in a parody of her voice. 'I was just walking past Mr Ravensdale's wardrobe and the diamond cufflinks fell into my pocket *by accident.*'

Holly set her mouth. 'I don't care what you think. I know I didn't steal them and that's all that matters.'

'Actually,' Julius said. 'It's not all that matters. Your caseworker will ask me when she calls in the morning and I'll have to tell her you've been stealing.'

Her eyes blazed as they met his. 'Tell her. See if I care.'

She did care. Julius was sure of it. He came to stand in front of her, close enough to feel the heat of her body emanating towards his. He picked up a handful of her hair close to her scalp, making her feel each strand pulling as he brought her mouth close to his. He let his breath mingle with hers, teasing her with the promise of what was to come. 'Here's where your little game backfires, *querida,*' he said. 'You want me just as much as I want you. You weren't expecting that, were you? You thought this would be a one-sided game but it's not.'

Her body brushed against his, by intention or chance he couldn't quite tell. But he saw the reaction on her face—the flicker of want that flashed across her features. The way her pupils dilated, the way her tongue sneaked out to moisten her lips. 'Get your hands off me,' she said.

'When I'm good and ready.' He brought his mouth even closer, breathing in the scent of her, bumping noses with her, nudging her with his chin, rasping his tongue along the seam of her mouth. Teasing her the way she had teased him. He heard her sharp intake of breath as his tongue stroked harder, more insistently. He could feel the struggle in her. The will she had to resist him was faltering just as his had faltered in him. She leaned towards him, her mouth open, her hands on his chest, not flat in the effort of pushing him away, but her fingers curling into the front of his shirt as if she never wanted to let him go.

He allowed himself one touchdown on her mouth. But one wasn't enough. How could he have thought it would ever be enough? Her mouth flowered open even further beneath the light pressure of his until he was suddenly swept up in a passionate exchange that had his blood thundering all over again.

Her tongue entwined with his, her arms looped around his neck, drawing him closer. His hands went to her neat behind, holding her against his throbbing heat. Her breasts were pushed against his chest so hard he could feel her pert nipples through the layers of their clothes.

Her hand reached between their bodies and stroked the hardened length of him, inciting his lust to fever pitch. He did the same to her, outlining her feminine form with the stroke of his fingers until she was breathing as hard as him. He took it one step further, driven by an urge he couldn't control. He tugged her trousers down past her hips so he could access her naked skin. He slipped one finger inside her, his control almost blowing when he felt how hot and wet and tight she was. She gasped and moved against his hand in a plea that needed no language other than the one their bodies were speaking. He stroked the bud of her core with the pad of his thumb, feeling it swell and peak under the pressure of his touch.

She suddenly gripped his shoulders and arched up as she convulsed. Violently. Repeatedly. He felt every contraction of her orgasm. Watched as the pleasure rose in a tidal glow over her face.

He kissed her mouth. Hard. Passionately. Swallowing the last of her breathless gasps as the aftermath of release flowed through her.

But then she slipped out of his hold, not quite able to hold his gaze. Her hands pulled up her trousers and fixed her gaping shirt before going across her body in a defensive, keep-away-from-me pose.

'Holly…'

She gave him a tight smile that didn't reach her eyes. 'What's the protocol here? Should I say thanks? Or offer to do you in return?'

He let out a long breath. 'That won't be necessary.'

'Well, thanks anyway,' she said. 'I didn't know I had it in me to get off like that. That's quite some technique you've got there.'

Julius scraped a hand through his hair. 'I shouldn't have taken things that far.'

'No problemo,' she said. 'I enjoyed it, as you could probably tell. Which is another first.'

He frowned. 'What do you mean?'

'I've never had an orgasm with a guy before.'

'Never?'

'No, but don't tell any of my ex-partners that,' she said. 'You know how fragile the male ego is.'

'How many partners have you had?'

'Four. Five, if you count yourself,' she said. 'But does that count, since you didn't actually put your...?'

'No,' Julius said. 'It doesn't.'

She shifted her lips from side to side. 'So, are we done here?'

He moved far enough away from her so he wouldn't be tempted to touch her. 'I'll see you in the morning. Goodnight.'

'You mean you're not sending me on my way to prison after all?'

Julius clenched his jaw. 'I'm giving you one more chance.' He hoped he wouldn't regret it.

She walked to the door to leave but at the last moment turned and looked at him. 'If I'd wanted to pinch your cufflinks, do you think I'd be carrying them around in my pocket?'

'Maybe you haven't had time to hide them in your room.'

Her eyes held his without shame. Without flinching. 'I had time to do lots of things. I could've called the press, for instance. I could've given them an exclusive.'

'Why didn't you?'

She gave one of her cute little lip-shrugs. 'I don't like it when people say stuff about me that isn't true, so why would I do that to someone else?'

Julius had measured the risks when he'd left to go away for work. But he'd figured Sophia would keep things in check. His housekeeper guarded his privacy almost more zealously than he did himself. But it was true Holly could have made things difficult for him. She could have made herself a small fortune. All it would have taken was a phone call. Why hadn't she? It wouldn't even have broken her probation conditions. Had he misjudged her? Or was this a clever ploy of hers, to get him to trust her before she went for broke? 'Thank you for acting so...honourably,' he said.

Her features took on a cynical cast. 'Haven't you heard there's honour amongst thieves?'

'But you keep insisting you're not a thief.'

'I'm not.'

Julius wanted to believe her. He wasn't sure why. Maybe to reassure himself he wasn't harbouring a criminal under his roof. Maybe so he could justify his growing affection for her. Something about the way she held herself, the stubborn pride he could see glittering in her gaze as it held his, made him wonder if he wasn't the only one to have misjudged her. He knew enough about the legal system to know the courts did not always serve justice. Attack-dog lawyers could swing a case. Evidence could be planted. Reputations ruined by innuendo. Holly had no money, no way of defending herself against a powerful lawyer. She had already hinted about the bleakness of her background. What chance would someone like her have against a system that favoured those with unlimited money and power at their disposal?

'It's late,' he said. 'You should've been in bed hours ago.'

'By the way, thanks for the clothes and make-up and stuff.'

'You're welcome,' he said. 'Your hair looks nice, by the way.'

'Much more acceptable, huh?'

'It was fine the way it was, but I thought—'

'It's fine, Julius,' she said with another stiff smile. 'Do you airbrush all of your girlfriends?'

'You are not my girlfriend. And, no, I do not.'

There was an odd little silence.

Julius watched as she sank her teeth into her lower lip as if she had suddenly found herself out of her depth. Had he offended her by organising a hairdresser? Sophia had suggested it, but now that he thought about it, maybe it had sent the wrong message. Had the clothes also been too much? Had he made her feel she wasn't acceptable without fine feathers? He thought he'd been helping her. She'd been bathing in her underwear. Surely it was the decent thing to do, to buy her appropriate clothing? The make-up and perfume... Well, didn't all girls enjoy that sort of stuff? She had come with so little luggage. Just a beaten-up backpack that hardly looked big enough to carry anything. Surely it hadn't been wrong to give her a few things to make her feel better about herself...or was he trying to make himself feel better about those fingerprints on her arms?

His gut clenched sickeningly as he thought of how easily she could have exploited him. All it would have taken was a photo of those bruises and a call to a nosy journalist and his reputation would have been shot. She'd had the perfect opportunity to get back at him, yet she hadn't. The week had passed without incident. Sophia had informed him Holly had been a perfect house guest, going out of her way to be helpful.

A good girl...

Not a moment's trouble...

'If you say you didn't intend to steal the cufflinks, then I believe you.' It was only once Julius said the words that he believed they were true. Her explanation was perfectly reasonable. She could have been startled and slipped them into her pocket without realising. How many times had he done the same with his keys when something or someone distracted him?

Or was he looking for a way to keep her with him?

It was a shock to think his motives were perhaps not as altruistic as they ought to be. The energy he felt with Holly, the electric buzz of sensation and thrill of her, overrode everything that was logical and responsible in him.

Her eyes widened momentarily before narrowing. 'Why?'

'I just do.'

She dropped her gaze from his. 'Thank you.' Her voice was just a thread of sound. Then she seemed to gather herself and brought her eyes back to his for a brief moment. 'Well, goodnight, then,' she said and left him with just the lingering scent of her fragrance to haunt his senses.

CHAPTER NINE

HOLLY CLOSED THE door to her bedroom and leaned back against it as she let out a long, shuddering breath. Julius *believed* her. He actually believed she hadn't tried to steal those wretched cufflinks. She hadn't registered she'd put them there, or at least not consciously. It had been a knee-jerk reaction to being discovered in his room. She must have slipped them into her pocket when she'd first heard Sophia and forgotten about them.

But Julius said he believed her.

How could he? She would never have believed him if the tables had been turned. But then, she was cynical. She didn't trust anyone. She was always on guard, always watching out for someone to take advantage, to rip her off or exploit her.

Was Julius different? Was he the sort of person to suspend judgement until reliable evidence came in?

Holly wondered if she had done herself a disservice by antagonising him so much. He might turn out to be the best ally she had ever had. But from the moment she had met him she had put him off-side. Winding him up, needling him, making him believe things about her that weren't true.

Was it too late to turn things around? Could she even

bother? She would only be here another couple of weeks and then she'd be gone. It had never worked for her to get too attached to anyone or any place. They always changed. People changed. Circumstances changed. One minute she would feel marginally secure and then the rug would be ripped out from beneath her and she would hit the hard, cold floor. This time with Julius in his flash villa was a temporary thing. There would be no point in getting too comfortable. He hadn't even wanted her here in the first place. She was a burden he had to bear.

Why was she always a burden?

Why couldn't someone want her in spite of all her faults? In spite of all her failings? In spite of all her stupid impulses that caused her more trouble than she wanted?

Her body was still firing with the sensations Julius had made her feel. Cataclysmic sensations she had never felt before. He had barely touched her and she had gone off like a firecracker. But he had remained in control. She had even offered to pleasure him and he'd held back. She still couldn't understand why she had done that. Why she had felt such an urgent desire to take him in her mouth bewildered her. She loathed oral sex. The musky, stale scent of a man usually nauseated her.

But with him it was different.

He wasn't musky and stale. He was fresh and intoxicating in his maleness. She had wanted to explore him, to pleasure him, to make him buckle at the knees in the same way he had done to her. But he hadn't insisted on her doing it. He hadn't pressured her.

He'd *protected* her by his restraint.

He'd pleasured her without wanting or insisting on anything in return. Even now she could feel the aftershock tremors moving through her body, awakening more news: new needs, needs that wanted—craved and hungered—to be assuaged. Maybe that was his power trip. Maybe that was his way of keeping a step in front of her. Maybe his self-control was superior after all. Far more superior than she'd thought.

Something had changed in their relationship…something she couldn't quite put her finger on. No one had given her the benefit of the doubt before. No one.

No one had made her feel the things Julius made her feel. No one.

No one had seen behind the mask she wore to the person she wanted to be.

No one.

When Holly came downstairs to organise breakfast the following morning, Sophia was already up and about. 'I'm going to spend a few days with my sister,' Sophia said. 'You're doing so well managing things here I thought I'd make the most of it by having some time off. Maria's picking me up in a few minutes.'

Holly frowned. 'Is Julius okay with that? I mean, leaving me in charge?'

'He's the one who suggested it.'

Holly's frown deepened. 'Really?'

Sophia nodded. 'He's also worried I might be tempted to do too much. I think he's right. I have been overdoing it. But this little break will help.'

'But what will Natalia have to say?' Holly said. 'Aren't you supposed to be the one mentoring me?'

Sophia's expression turned to one of concern. 'Would you rather I didn't go? I can cancel if you like. I'm sure my sister won't mind.'

'No, don't do that. I'm just wondering about the programme.' *And being left alone in the villa with Julius without a chaperone.*

'Señor Ravensdale is the one who is ultimately responsible for you,' Sophia said. 'I'm here as a guide but you don't need me. In many ways you're more competent than me. Your cooking is restaurant standard. I'm the one who should be taking lessons off you.'

'Yeah, well, it's easy to cook nice things when you have access to top quality ingredients,' Holly said.

Sophia smiled. 'Would you mind taking Señor Ravensdale's breakfast to him? He's in the morning room upstairs.'

'Sure.'

'Ah, that's Maria's car now.' Sofia gave her one last smile and left.

Holly waited for the coffee to percolate before she put it on the tray to take upstairs. The morning room was on the second level of the villa, which wasn't convenient to the kitchen in terms of serving breakfast, but it had a lovely easterly aspect overlooking the gardens and the lake. She had been in a couple of times to dust and vacuum. It was decorated in soft yellows and cream with a touch of blue, giving it a fresh energetic look perfect for the start of the day.

When Holly shouldered open the door, a quake of dread moved through her. The French doors leading to the balcony were wide open. Julius was sitting in a patch of sunlight at the wrought-iron table with some papers set in front of him. The slight breeze was ruffling the pages, and she watched as one of his hands reached out to anchor them.

He must have sensed her presence, or maybe he heard

the slight rattle of the cup in the saucer on the tray she was carrying, for he looked up. 'Good morning.'

Holly swallowed a bird's nest of panic. Fear crawled over her scalp. Her blood chilled, freezing in her veins until she was certain her heart would stop. Her feet were nailed to the floor. She couldn't move. She was frozen.

Julius frowned. 'What's wrong?'

'Nothing.' Holly took a step forward but couldn't go any farther. 'Um, would you come and get this? I've left something on the hob downstairs.'

'Why don't you come back and join me?' he said as he took the tray from her and placed it on the table on the balcony.

'No thanks.'

'Got out of the wrong side of the bed, did we?'

'Wasn't in it long enough,' she said with a little scowl.

He surveyed her features for a beat or two. 'Come on and join me once you've turned off the hob. It's a lovely morning. There's enough food and coffee here for both of us. Just get another cup and saucer.'

'I said no.'

Julius shrugged as if he didn't care either way. 'Suit yourself.'

'Could you bring the tray back down when you're done?' Holly said as she got to the door.

He turned around to look at her. 'Isn't that your job?'

She held his penetrating look. 'Is that why you've sent Sophia away? What is it about having someone wait on you that gives you such a thrill? Is it the power? The authority? The ego trip?'

A frown tugged at his brow. 'Doesn't the fact I asked

you to join me for breakfast demonstrate I'm not on
any power trip?'

She crossed her arms and sent him a hard glare. 'So
what was last night all about, then?'

He let out a rough-sounding breath. 'Last night
was... I was wrong to let things get to that point,' he
said. 'I'm sorry.'

Holly wasn't ready to be mollified. She was still feeling annoyed he'd been able to prove his point so easily. He had won that round. She had responded to him
like a sex-starved fool. Which was basically what she
was, but still...

He came to where she was standing. He didn't touch
her but was close enough for her to feel the tempting
warmth of his body. His dark-blue eyes held hers in a
gentle lock that made her wonder if he was seeing much
more than she wanted him to see. She tried to keep her
expression blank but she wasn't quite able to stop her
tongue from quickly moistening her lips. She watched
as his gaze dipped to follow the movement before coming back to reconnect with hers.

'This thing we have...' he began.

'What thing?'

'I've never met someone who's got my attention quite
the way you have,' he said.

'Well, they wouldn't have a chance with you locked
away in your mansion with no social life to speak of,
now, would they?'

He gave her a wry hint of a smile. 'I get out when
I need to.'

'When was the last time you—' Holly put her fingers up in air-quotation-marks '—got out?'

'I had a brief relationship a few months back.'

'Who was she? What was she like?'

'Someone I met at a conference in Santiago,' he said. 'She was beautiful, well educated, came from a good family. She had a nice personality…'

'I'm hearing a big "but".'

'No chemistry.'

'Not good.'

'Definitely not good.' He brushed a stray strand of hair back from her forehead. It was the lightest touch but it made every nerve in her body shudder in delight. Had anyone ever touched her as gently? Had anyone ever looked at her so intently? As if they wanted to see right into the very heart of her?

'So who broke it off?' Holly said. 'You or her?'

'Me.'

'Was she disappointed?'

'If she was, it can't have lasted long as she got engaged a few weeks later to a guy she'd been dating before me.'

'You win some, you lose some.'

His eyes did that back-and-forth searching thing with each of hers. 'It would be highly inappropriate for me to get involved with you,' he said. 'You do understand that, don't you?'

'We're both consenting adults.'

His finger traced the underside of her jaw in a feather-light touch. 'It's not a matter of consent. It's a matter of convention.'

Holly twisted her mouth in a cynical manner. 'Oh, right—the upstairs, downstairs thing.'

He frowned. 'That's not what I meant at all. It wouldn't reflect well on me if I were to engage in a relationship with you. It would look like I'm exploiting you.'

'But making me fetch and carry and ordering me about doesn't?'

He dropped his hand from her face. 'You really suit your name. I don't think I've ever met anyone more prickly.'

'Your breakfast is getting cold,' Holly said, nodding towards his abandoned tray out on the balcony.

Julius narrowed his gaze in thoughtful contemplation. His forehead was lined like tidemarks on the seashore. She could almost hear the cogs of his brain going around. 'You don't have anything on the hob, do you?'

Holly tried to disguise a swallow. His dark blue gaze was probing. Like a strong light shining into the outer limits of her soul. 'No…'

'So unless it's my company there's some other reason you don't want to have breakfast with me on the balcony,' he said in a tone that sounded as if he was thinking out loud.

A loaded silence passed.

Holly let out a shaky sigh. 'I have a…a thing about balconies.'

'You're scared of heights?' He didn't say it in a mocking way. He simply stated it as if it was perfectly reasonable for her to be scared and he wouldn't judge her for it.

Holly felt something hard and tight slip away from her heart. As if a rigid band had come undone. 'Not heights, specifically. Just balconies.'

He took one of her hands and held it in the shelter of his. His thumb stroked the back of her hand in a slow, soothing motion. 'That's why you didn't want the room Sophia prepared for you, isn't it?'

Holly pressed her lips together. Hard. She never spoke to anyone about this stuff. It was stuff she had locked away. But for some reason Julius's gentle tone picked the lock of her determination. He had unravelled the tightly bound knot of her stubborn pride. She released another sigh. 'I got locked out on the balcony when I was a kid,' she said. 'It was something my stepfather thought was entertaining. Seeing me out there in all sorts of weather. He wouldn't let me come in until I said sorry for whatever I'd supposedly done. Not that I ever did much; I only had to look at him a certain way and he'd shove me out there.'

Julius's frown was so deep it was like a trench between his eyes. 'You poor little kid. What about your mother? Didn't she stand up for you?'

'My mum was unable to stand up for herself, let alone me,' Holly said. 'He'd done such a good job of eroding her self-esteem, she chose death instead of life. He drove her to it. He hates me because I didn't cave in to him. That's why he keeps making trouble for me. He follows me wherever I go. He has ways and means of reminding me I can't escape. But I *will* escape. I'm determined to get away and make a new life for myself.'

Julius took both of her hands in his, holding them gently but securely. 'He can't touch you while you're with me. I'll make sure of it.'

Holly's chest swelled with hope at his implacable tone. How long had it been since she'd felt safe? Truly safe? 'Thank you…'

He touched her face with a barely there brush stroke of his bent knuckles. His eyes had a tender look that made the base of her spine hum. 'I can't imagine how difficult your life must've been compared to mine,' he said. 'No wonder you came in that first day with your fists up.'

'Yeah, well, sorry about that, but I like to get in first in case things turn out nasty, which they invariably do,' she said. 'Maybe it's my fault. I attract trouble. I can't seem to help myself. It's automatic.'

'No.' His hands took hers again in a firm but gentle hold. 'You shouldn't blame yourself. Your stepfather sounds like a creep. He belongs in jail, not you.'

Holly looked at their joined hands. Hers were so small compared to his. She slowly brought her gaze up to his. His eyes meshed with hers in a look that made her legs feel fizzy. 'Why are you looking at me like that?' she said.

'How am I looking at you?' His voice was a deep, resonant rumble.

'Like you're going to kiss me.'

He brushed an imaginary strand of hair away from her face. 'What gives you the idea I'm going to kiss you?' His mouth was half an inch from hers, his breath a warm, minty breeze against her lips.

'Just a feeling.'

His lips nudged hers in a playful manner. 'Do you always trust your feelings?'

Holly slipped her arms around his neck and pressed herself closer. 'Mostly.'

His mouth brushed hers, once, twice, three times. 'This is crazy. I shouldn't be doing this.'

'*This* being…?'

He rested his forehead against hers. 'Tell me to stop.'

'No.'

'Tell me, Holly. I *need* you to tell me.'

'I want you to kiss me,' Holly said. 'I want you to make love to me.' As soon as she said the words, she realised how much she meant them. How from the moment she'd met him she'd been drawn to him like a moth to a bright streetlight on a hot summer's night. The desire he triggered in her was unlike anything she'd ever felt before. She wanted him. She ached for him. She burned for him.

He looked at her with darkened eyes, the pupils wide with desire. 'Why?'

'Because we're attracted to each other and we might as well make the most of it.'

One of his hands cupped her face, the other rested in the small of her back. 'Why me?'

'Why not you?' she said. 'You're single. I'm single. What's the problem?'

He was still frowning. 'Is once going to be enough?'

Holly stroked the side of his jaw. 'Do you have to think about everything before you act? Don't you ever just go with the flow?'

He turned her palm towards his mouth and kissed it, all the while holding her gaze. 'Do you ever stop and think before you act?'

She shivered as his kiss travelled all the way to her core. 'I'm thinking we should make the most of the fact that Sophia's away with her sister.' Is that why he'd sent his housekeeper away? Perhaps it was unconscious on his part but he had cleared the way for them to indulge in an affair without an audience.

He framed her face with his hands, his expression darkly serious. 'I want you like I've never wanted anyone else.'

'Same.'

His head came down, and his mouth sealed hers in a kiss as hot as a flashpoint. Heat pooled between her legs as his tongue drove through the seam of her mouth to find hers. Lust raced through her blood as he stroked and thrust and cajoled her tongue into play. His body crushed hers to his, every hard contour of his enticing every softer one of hers. Her breasts peaked against his chest, her pelvis thrumming with want as she felt the thickened ridge of him.

His hands moved over her lightly, touching, exploring, discovering. He came to her breasts, lifting her top out of the way so he could access them. He swirled his tongue over and around her nipple, making her ache with longing as his teeth gently nipped and tugged at her flesh.

His hands skimmed down the sides of her body to grasp her hips, holding her tightly against the throb of his need. He made a deep sound at the back of his throat as she moved against him. A sound of approval, of want, of raw, primal lust.

'Not here,' he said as he swept her up in his arms and carried her towards his suite.

Holly noticed the balcony doors were open as she pulled him down with her on the mattress, but she pushed her fear away, not willing to be separated for a second in case he changed his mind. Her whole body was on fire. Pulsating with a longing so intense it was mind-blowing. Every part of her body was alive and sensitive. Every inch of her skin ached for his touch.

Julius must have read her mind for he began working on her clothes while she did her best to get him out of his. Her hands weren't cooperating in her haste to feel his naked skin. They were fumbling in excitement, and he had to take over. Holly watched as he unbuttoned his shirt before shrugging it off and tossing it to the floor. She put her hands on his chest, spreading her fingers over his pectoral muscles, her palms tickled by the light covering of masculine hair sprinkled over his chest.

He came down to her to caress her breasts with his lips and tongue, making her squirm and shiver with delight with every movement he made. He kissed his way from her breasts down over her stomach, dipping his tongue into the shallow cave of her belly button before going lower.

Holly sucked in a breath when he came to the heart of her. The feel of his lips separating her and the sexy rasp of his tongue against her sensitive flesh made her arch her spine like a well-pleasured cat. The ripples of an orgasm took her by surprise, taking over her body, shaking it, tossing it into a maelstrom of ecstasy that made her gasp out loud.

But even as the pleasure faded he was stirring her to new feelings, new sensations, new anticipations, as he sourced a condom and positioned himself between her thighs.

His mouth came back to hers as he entered her in a slick, deep thrust that made her whole body quake in response. His thrusts were slow and measured at first, allowing her time to get used to him. But then as she breathlessly urged him on he upped the pace, deeper, harder, faster, until she was rocking against him for that final push into paradise. He reached between their bodies to give her that extra bit of friction that pitched her over the edge. She cried out as the sensations tore through her in a rush, delicious wave upon delicious wave, roll upon roll. He waited until she was coming down from the spike before he let go. Holly felt him tense and then spill, his whole body shuddering until he finally went still.

It was a new thing for Holly to lie in a man's arms without wanting to push him off or rush off to the shower. It was a new thing her to not feel uncomfortable with the silence. Not to have regrets over what her body had done or had had done to it by a partner. Her body was in a delicious state of lassitude, every limb feeling boneless, her mind drifting like flotsam.

After a moment Julius propped himself up on his arms to look at her. 'Am I too heavy for you?'

Holly stroked her hands down to the dip in his spine. 'No.'

He brushed a fingertip over her lower lip, his expression thoughtful. 'I might've rushed you. It's been a while.'

'You didn't,' she said. 'It was…perfect. You were perfect.'

He kissed her on the mouth softly. Lightly. 'This is usually when I say I have work to do or head to the shower.'

'Classy.'

He gave a wry smile. 'If you give me a couple of minutes, I'll be ready for round two.'

Holly arched her brows. 'So this isn't a one-off then?'

His eyes darkened as they held hers. 'Is that all you want?'

She shrugged noncommittally and looked away. 'The itch has been scratched, hasn't it?'

He took her chin between his finger and thumb and made her look at him. 'This isn't the sort of itch that can be cured with one scratch.'

Holly kept her expression screened. 'What're you suggesting? A fling? A relationship? Not sure what your family would have to say about you and me hanging out as a couple. Or the press, for that matter.'

His frown pulled at his forehead like stitches beneath the skin. 'What I do in my private life is my business, no one else's, including my family.'

'What about Sophia?'

'What about her?'

Holly tiptoed her fingers up his spine to the back of his neck where his hair was curling. 'What's she going to say when she finds out we're sleeping together?'

'We won't tell her.'

Holly laughed. 'Like that's going to work. She'll know as soon as she comes back.'

He rolled away and got off the bed to dispense with the condom, a deep frown still dividing his forehead. He picked up his trousers and stepped into them, zipping them up with unnecessary force. 'What's your caseworker going to say when you tell her about us?'

'I'm not going to tell her,' Holly said. 'Why would I? It's none of her business.'

Julius scooped his shirt and thrust his arms into the sleeves. 'We can't continue this. It's wrong. I shouldn't have allowed it to happen. I'm sorry; I take full responsibility.'

Holly swung her legs over the edge of the bed and reached for her nearest article of clothing. 'Yeah, well, I guess it was just a pity thing on your part, huh?'

'What?' His tone was sharp, shocked...annoyed.

'You only slept with me because you felt sorry for me after I told you about my crappy childhood.'

His frown was so deep his eyebrows met over the bridge of his nose. 'That's not true.'

She gave him a direct look. 'Isn't it?'

He scraped a hand through his hair. 'No. Yes. Maybe. I don't know.'

Holly finished pulling on her clothes before she came over to him. 'It's fine, Julius. Stop stressing. I'm okay with a one-off. Doesn't make sense to get too cosy, since I'll be on my way in a couple of weeks.'

He looked at her for a long, pulsing moment. 'I suppose you got what you wanted.'

She arched a brow. 'That being?'

'From the moment you stepped into this place, you had your mind set on getting me to break, didn't you?' he said. 'It was your goal. Your mission. You did everything you could to prove I couldn't resist you. Well, you were right. I couldn't.'

Holly was a little ashamed of how close to the mark he was. But what was even more concerning was how she had ended up wanting him more than she had wanted anyone. She didn't know how to handle such want. Such longing. The need was still there. It was a sated beast that would all too soon wake again and be growling, prowling for sustenance. Even now she could feel her body stirring the longer she looked into Julius's dark navy eyes with their glittering cynicism.

'What will you do now you've achieved your goal?' he said. 'Give a tell-all interview to the press?'

Holly shifted her gaze from his in case he saw how hurt she felt. 'You have serious trust issues.'

He laughed. '*I* have trust issues?'

She swung back to glare at him. 'Do you really think I would share my body with you and then tell everyone about it? I'd be hurting myself more than you.'

'They pay big money for scandalous stories. Big money. You could set yourself up on this.'

Holly pressed her lips together as she went in hunt of her shoes but she could only find one. Frustration and hurt tangled in a tight knot in her chest, making it hard for her to breathe. She had given him every reason to think she would sell out to score points against him. The shaming truth was a few days ago she might well have done it. But something had changed. *She* had changed. His touch, his concern, his promise of protection had made something inside her shift. She couldn't find a way to reassemble herself. It was as if the puzzle pieces of her personality had been scattered and she didn't know how to get them back into order. The things she had wanted before were not what she wanted now.

It was disturbing—terrifying—to allow her nascent hopes and dreams to get a foothold. For the first time in her life, she'd caught a glimpse of what it would be like to be secure in a relationship. To be with a man who looked out for her, who wanted the best for her, who would help her reach her potential instead of sabotaging it. To be honoured and cherished. To be celebrated instead of ridiculed. To be accepted.

To be trusted.

To be loved.

Holly took a scalding breath and forced herself to look at him. 'I guess you'd better call Natalia and get her to take me away, then.'

Something passed over his features. 'No.'

'Why not?' Holly said, trying to squash the bubble of hope that bloomed in her chest. 'I'm nothing but trouble. I belong in jail, or so you said the other day.'

He let out a long breath and came back to where she was standing. He put his hands on her hunched shoulders, his touch as light as goose down but as hot as fire. 'You're not going anywhere.'

She ran the point of her tongue out over her paper-dry lips. 'I wouldn't have done it. I wouldn't have called the press.'

He gave her shoulders a light squeeze. 'I'm sorry.'

'It's okay. I get that you want to keep your privacy secure,' Holly said. 'I haven't exactly given you the impression I'm someone you could trust.'

He tipped up her chin with the tip of his finger. 'What am I going to do with you, Holly Perez?'

Holly looked into his sapphire-blue gaze. 'You could start by kissing me.'

He pressed a soft kiss to her mouth. 'Then what?'

She tilted her head as if thinking about it. 'You could put your hand on my breast.'

He cupped her breast through her clothes, his eyes glinting. 'And then what?'

She moved closer, letting her breath mingle with his as she slipped her hands around his neck. 'Figure it out,' she said, and his mouth came down and sealed hers.

CHAPTER TEN

A FEW DAYS later Holly watched as Julius slept. He was a quiet sleeper, not restless and fidgety like her. She could have watched him for hours, memorising his features, storing them in her mind for the time when she would be gone from his life. She had been playing a game of pretend with herself over the past few days, a silly little game where she wouldn't have to leave at the end of the time she had left.

She had even been so foolish as to picture her and Julius building a life together. Having a family together. Building a future together. Things she had never allowed herself to dream of before. She hadn't even realised she wanted those things until now. Every day she spent in his company she found herself wanting him more. Not just physically, although that had only got better and better. It was more of an intellectual connection, one she had never felt with anyone else. He inspired her, excited her, and challenged her.

Holly traced one of his eyebrows with her fingertip. 'Are you awake?'

'No.'

She smiled and traced the other eyebrow. That was the other thing she liked about him—he had a sense of humour underneath all that gruff starchiness. 'Are you dreaming?' she said.

'Yes, of this hot girl who's in my bed touching me with her clever little hands.'

Holly reached down and stroked his swollen length. 'Like this?'

'Mmm, just like that.'

'And in this dream did that same girl slide down your body like this?' She moved down his body, letting her breasts touch him from chest to groin.

'That's it,' he said in a low growl. 'I never want to wake up.'

She sent her tongue down the length of his shaft, then swirled it over the head and around the sensitive glans.

'Condom, *querida*.'

'I want to taste you.'

He muttered an expletive as she opened her mouth over him, drawing on him until he was breathing heavily. 'You don't have to…'

'I want to,' Holly said. 'You do it to me. Why shouldn't I do it to you?'

'I've never had someone do it in the raw before.'

'Lucky me to be the first.'

He frowned for a moment but it soon disappeared as Holly got to business. She watched him as she drew on him, her own excitement building as she saw the effect she was having on him. He pulled out just as he spilled, the erotic pumping of his essence thrilling her in a way she hadn't expected.

He threaded his fingers through her hair in long, soothing strokes that made her scalp tingle in delight. 'Holly…'

She looked up from where she had been resting her cheek against his stomach. 'What?'

He had one of his deep-in-thought frowns on his forehead. After a moment the frown relaxed as he smiled faintly. 'Just… Holly.'

She stroked his stubbly jaw. 'Not getting all sentimental on me, are you?'

The frown was back. 'What do you mean?'

Holly propped herself on one elbow as she trailed her fingers up and down his chest. 'This is just for now. Us, I mean. I'm going to England once I'm done here.'

He pushed her hand away and got off the bed. 'I know you are. I'm glad you are. It's the right thing to do.' He pulled on a bathrobe and tied the belt, his expression shuttered.

'You don't sound very happy about it.'

He threw her an irritated look. 'Why wouldn't I be happy about it?'

She gave a shrug. 'Thought you might miss me.'

'I will but that doesn't mean I want you to stay.'

Holly sat up and pulled her knees into her chest. 'I wouldn't stay if you asked me.'

'I'm not going to ask you.'

'Fine. Glad we got that settled.'

He went to the balcony doors and unlocked them. Holly stiffened. 'What are you doing?'

'I want some fresh air.'

Bitterness burned in her gullet. 'You're only doing that to get rid of me. It's cruel, Julius. You know how much it freaks me out. I thought you understood. I'll only come in here if those doors are closed.'

'It's just a balcony, for God's sake.'

Tears sprouted but Holly tried to blink them back.

'It's not just a bloody balcony!' She got off the bed, pull-ing the sheet with her to cover herself. 'I spent hours and hours—years—of my life frightened out of my wits, and now you're using that fear, *exploiting* that fear, to push me away because you're scared of how you feel about me leaving.'

He flung the doors wide open and stepped out on to the balcony, standing with his back to her as he looked out over the estate.

Holly felt a gnarled knot of emotion clog her throat. Her heart was beating too fast, too erratically. Her skin was icy-cold and then clammy-hot. Her vision blurred with tears. She tried to get away but the sheet wrapped around her halted her progress. She tripped, stumbled and then fell in an ungainly heap on the floor.

'Are you all right?' Julius was by her side in seconds.

Holly batted his hand away. 'No, of course I'm not all right. Close the freaking doors, will you?'

He gripped her chin between his finger and thumb. 'You're fine, Holly. Look at me. You're fine. No one's going to hurt you.'

She glared at him. 'You hurt me. You did. You shouldn't have done that.' Tears leaked out of her eyes in spite of all she did to try and stop them. She landed a punch on his arm but it glanced off as if she had hit stone. 'You sh-shouldn't have done that.'

'Hey…hey…hey…' He drew her against him, resting his chin on top of her head as he gently stroked her back in soothing circles. 'It's all right, *querida*. I'm sorry. I shouldn't have done it. I'm sorry. Shh, don't cry.'

'I'm not c-crying.'

'Of course you're not.' He kept stroking her, hold-ing her.

'I'm angry, that's all.'

'Of course you are. You have every right to be. I was being a jerk.'

'If you want me to leave the room or get out of your life just say so, okay?' she said against his chest. 'I can take a hint. I'm not stupid.'

There was a deep silence.

Holly listened to the sound of his breathing. Felt the steady rise and fall of his chest against her cheek and the slow beat of his heart. Felt his hand gently stroking her hair, his chin resting on top of her head. Felt her heart squeeze at the thought of how soon this was going to end.

Before she knew it, she would be on her way to a new life in England. The only contact she would have with him would be seeing articles about his family in the press. She wasn't falling in love with him. She wasn't. It was just that he was so…so different from all the men she had met in the past. He was impossibly strong, yet tender when he needed to be. He was a control freak but that showed he had discipline and self-control. He was a man with honour and standards. No one had ever taken the time to get to know her like he had done. He was interested in what made her the person she was and he inspired her to become who she was meant to be.

How could she not feel a little regret over her imminent departure? It was normal. It didn't mean she was falling in love with him. She had never been in love before and didn't intend to be now. She had seen first-hand the damage loving someone could do. You lost your power, your autonomy, your self-respect and your freedom. Love was a trap. A cage that, once you were in, you couldn't get out of. That wasn't what she had planned for her life.

Julius eased back to look down at her. 'I want you to do something for me.'

'What?'

He took her by the hands in a gentle hold. 'I want you to come out on the balcony with me.'

Holly tried to pull away but his grip tightened. 'No. *No*. Don't ask me to do that. I won't. I can't.'

He kept her imprisoned hands close to his chest. 'I'll be with you the whole time. I won't let go of you. Trust me, Holly.'

She felt the panic rise in her chest. Felt the bookcase flatten her lungs until she could barely inflate them enough to breathe. Could she do it? Could she trust him to stand by her and hold her, to help her confront her worst nightmare? Her skin crawled with dread. Her heart raced. Her stomach churned. 'I—I'm not sure I can do it… My stepfather used to drag me out there by the hair. He would lock me out there and then beat up my mum while I watched. Don't make me do it. I c-can't.'

Julius's expression flinched as she spoke but he kept hold of her hands, holding her gaze as he kissed her clenched knuckles one by one. 'Don't let him win any longer, *querida*. All this time he's had it over you by controlling you with fear. Give your fear to me. Trust me. I won't let you fall.'

I think I'm already falling, Holly thought. Feelings she had never expected to feel for anyone were slipping past the barriers she had erected around her heart. Her defences were no match for his tenderness, his concern, his steadiness and support. She couldn't allow herself to fall for him. This was a temporary arrangement that would end once her community service was over. She was a fool to imagine any other outcome. He was from a completely different world. He would have no place for her in it. She didn't belong. She was an outcast. A misfit. A nobody that nobody wanted.

'Okay…' Her voice came out scratchy as it squeezed past the strangulation of her fear.

He led her to the balcony doors. 'Okay so far?'

She nodded, swallowing another wave of panic. He opened the doors, and the fresh air wafted over her face. She gripped his hand so tightly she wondered why he didn't wince in pain.

'Good girl,' he said. 'Now, take one step at a time. We'll stop if it gets too much. It's your call.'

Holly took one step onto the balcony on legs as unsteady as a new-born foal's. The smell of freshly mown grass drifted past her nostrils. She tried to concentrate on the view, hoping it would distract her from thinking about the fear that chilled her to the bone.

'You're doing so well,' he said. 'Want to try a couple more steps?'

She took another thorny breath and moved one step forward. His hands squeezed hers in encouragement. She looked up at him and gave him a wobbly smile. 'Nice view from up here.'

'Yes,' he said but she noticed he wasn't looking at the view.

Holly looked at their joined hands. He wasn't letting her go. He wasn't pushing her beyond her limits. He had held true to his promise. The weight of fear began to lift off her chest. She could breathe. She could feel her heart rate gradually slowing. She wasn't cured by any means but she had made progress. She hadn't been anywhere near a balcony since she'd been a teenager. Years of terror had stalked her. Controlled her. She had taken two steps forward into a future without fear. Two steps. It wasn't much but it was enough to give her a glimmer of hope.

Holly looked up into his deep-blue gaze. 'Thank you...'

'I haven't done anything,' he said. 'I was just holding your hand. Next time will be easier. Soon you'll be doing it all by yourself.'

'I'm not so sure about that,' she said with a little shudder.

'You underestimate yourself,' he said. 'You can do anything if you try. You have so much potential. Don't let anyone take it away from you.'

Holly pulled away to go back inside. She hugged her elbows with her hands crossed over. It was all very well for him to talk about potential. He'd had a good education. Family money and opportunities she could only dream about. He might find his parents difficult but at least he had them.

She had no one.

Julius came up behind her and put his hands on her shoulders. 'Would you like to go out to dinner?'

Holly turned to look at him with a frown. 'In public?'

'That's where the restaurants tend to be.'

'Yes, and so are people with camera phones.'

'I know a quiet little place where we won't be disturbed,' he said. 'I know the guy who runs it. He'll let us have a private room.'

Holly hadn't quite let her frown go. 'Why are you doing this?'

'Doing what?'

'Acting like this is a normal relationship.'

A muscle moved near his mouth. 'You deserve a break from cooking, surely?'

'Then order takeaway.'

'It's just dinner,' he said. 'I sometimes take Sophia out for a meal.'

'I'd rather not.'

'Why not? You have the clothes to wear.'

Holly unwrapped her body from the sheet she was wearing and reached for a bathrobe. 'I'm happy to sleep with you, okay? But don't ask me to act like we're a proper couple. Date nights are out of the question.'

'Fine,' he said casually but it didn't fool her for a second. 'Forget I asked.'

Holly bit down on her lip as he strode into the en suite. He was upset with her for refusing but what else could she do? Dinner would have been nice but how could she control her emotions if he pressed her to do couple stuff? A romantic dinner for two was just plain wrong. She was not his romantic partner.

She never would be.

Julius knew he had no right to feel annoyed Holly had refused to go out in public with him. He knew they weren't in a relationship. It was just a fling. A convenient interlude that was going to end once her community service was up. He should, in principle, be in agreement about keeping their affair out of the public eye but he had wanted to spend time with her away from the villa where she felt like a member of his staff rather than his equal. He wanted them to be just two ordinary people who had an attraction for each other. He wanted to spoil her in a way she had never been spoilt before.

The very fact she didn't want to go public about their

involvement was a confirmation of the sort of person she was underneath all that 'junkyard dog' bluster. She was sensitive and easily hurt. She hid that vulnerability behind her don't-mess-with-me façade. The horror of her past sickened him. He wanted to make it up to her. To make her feel safe in a way she had never felt before. He needed time to do that. But how much time did he have? Not much. Not enough.

For some reason every time he thought of her leaving he got a pain below his ribs. A tight, cramping pain as if someone was jabbing him. What would happen to her when she went to England? She had no one. No family to watch out for her. She would be totally alone. His family annoyed the hell out of him most of the time but at least he knew they were there when he needed them. Who would Holly turn to if things went sour?

The way she had trusted him to take her out on the balcony had moved him deeply. He had seen the years of terror in her face. Felt it in her hands as they gripped his so tightly. And yet she had stood out there in his arms and given him a shaky smile, *trusting* him to keep her safe. Who would keep her safe once she left him?

Why the heck was he ruminating so much about her leaving? Of course she had to leave. It was what she wanted. A new start in her mother's homeland. A chance to get her life back on track, to pursue her dreams and put her past behind her. A past Julius would be part of. Would she ever think of him? Miss him?

He gave himself a mental shake and tried to refocus on the programme code in front of him. He wasn't supposed to be developing feelings for her. It was fine to care about someone, sure. It was fine to want to see her get on her feet and reach her potential. But caring so much he couldn't bear to think of letting her go was ridiculous. He hadn't wanted her to come here in the first place. How could he possibly want her to stay indefinitely?

He didn't do indefinitely.

Julius's mobile rang, and he was about to ignore it but changed his mind when he saw it was his sister, Miranda. Finally. 'Nice of you to get back to me.'

'I'm sorry but I didn't feel like talking to anyone,' Miranda said.

It was what his baby sister did when things got difficult. She went to ground. He knew she would call him eventually but it worried him she had left it so long. 'You okay?'

'God, it's just so embarrassing,' she said. 'Mum is beside herself and for once I can't blame her.'

'Have you met the girl yet?'

'No,' Miranda said. 'Dad's pushing for it. He wants a big family reunion. Can you believe it? Talk about lack of sensitivity. I just want to run away and hide some place until it all blows over.'

'Have the press hassled you for a comment?'

'Like, every day,' she said. 'The worse thing is they keep making comparisons. I'm now officially known as the ugly sister.'

'That's rubbish and you know it,' Julius said.

'Have you seen her, Julius?' Miranda asked. 'She's stunning. Like one of those lingerie supermodels. And guess what? She's an aspiring actor. Dad is so proud he finally produced a child with theatrical ambition. He keeps going on and on about it. It's nauseating.'

'What's she been in? I haven't heard of her before now.'

'She's only been in amateur things but now all she'll

have to do is name drop and the red carpet will be rolled out for her. You wait and see.'

'Connections will only get her so far,' Julius said. 'She'll need talent.'

Miranda gave a gusty sigh. 'I don't want to talk about it any more. So, how are you?'

'Fine. Been busy working.'

'Same old.'

He gave a rueful smile. 'Same old.'

'When are you coming over?' she said. 'Have you got any plans to visit?'

'Not right now.'

There was a short silence.

'Are you dating someone?' Miranda asked.

Julius tossed the question back even though he already knew the answer. 'Are you?'

'I know you think I'm wasting my life but I loved Mark,' Miranda said in her stock-standard defensive tone she used whenever the topic of her moving on with her life was brought up.

'I know you did, sweetheart,' Julius said gently. 'And he loved you. But if things were the other way around I reckon he would've moved on by now.'

'You obviously haven't been in love,' Miranda said. 'You don't know what it's like to lose the only person in the world you want to be with.'

Julius felt that sudden pang beneath his ribs again. He was going to lose Holly. In a matter of days, she would be gone. He would never see her again.

Which was how it should be, as she had a right to move on with her new life without him interfering.

Julius put his phone down after he'd finished listening to his little sister tell him a thousand reasons why she would never date another man. He let out a long sigh. There were times when he wondered if love was worth all the heartache. So far he had avoided it.

So far...

CHAPTER ELEVEN

A COUPLE OF days later Julius finished a tele-conference that had taken longer than he'd expected and went in search of Holly. She was out by the pool scooping out leaves with the net. 'One of the groundsmen can do that,' he said.

She turned around and smiled one of her cheeky smiles. 'Have you got something you'd rather me do indoors?'

He put his arms around her, bringing her bikini-clad body against his fully clothed one. 'Why are you always wandering around the place half-dressed?' he growled at her playfully.

'All the better to tempt you, my dear,' she said.

Julius brought his mouth down to hers. The heat of their mouths meeting always surprised him. Delighted him. She didn't kiss in half-measures. She kissed with her whole body. He drew her closer, his body responding to the slim, sun-kissed contours of hers. He kept on kissing her as he unhooked her bikini top so he could access her breasts. Her hands went to the buttons of his shirt, undoing each one with spine-tingling purpose.

He put his mouth to her breast, sucking, licking and teasing the engorged flesh until she was making breathless little sounds of need. He untied the strings of her bikini bottoms and cupped the pert curves of her bottom in his hands.

She tilted her head back to look at him. 'This is a little unfair. I'm completely naked and you're fully dressed.'

Julius swept his tongue over her pouting bottom lip. 'Let's take this indoors.'

She rubbed against him sensuously. 'Why not have a swim with me first?'

He couldn't resist her in this mood. She was so damn sexy he could barely hold himself in check. Within seconds he, too, had stripped off—apart from a quickly sheathed condom—and was in the pool with her, holding her against his aroused body as she smiled up at him with those dancing, caramel-brown eyes. He lowered his mouth to hers, his senses reeling as her tongue came into play with his. Her hands were around his waist, then caressing his chest, then going even lower to hold him until he was ready to explode. The water only heightened the sensations. The silky cool of it against their heated bodies made him all the more frantic for release.

He walked her backwards until she was up against the edge of the pool but, rather than have her back marked by the pool's edge, he turned her so her back was against the front of his body. He kissed his way from her earlobe to her neck and back again, trailing his tongue over her scented flesh, wondering how he was going to stop himself coming ahead of schedule with her bottom pressed up against his erection. She made a sound of encouragement, part whimper, part gasp, as he moved between legs.

He entered her deeply, barely able to control himself as her hot, wet body gripped him like a clamp. He kept thrusting, building a pace that had her hands gripping the edge of the pool for balance. He felt every delicious ripple of her inner flesh, the contraction of her around him as she came, triggering his own mind-blowing release.

He didn't want to move. He wanted to stand there on his still shaking legs and hold her against him.

She turned in his arms, looking up at him with a face glowing with the aftermath of pleasure. 'Ever done it in the pool before?'

'No.'

'Lucky me to be your first pool—'

Julius put his fingertip over her mouth to stop her saying the crude word he suspected she was going to say. 'Don't.'

She pushed his hand away. 'Don't be so squeamish, Julius. It's just sex.'

Just sex.

Was it? Was it just sex for him? Maybe for her it was but for him it didn't feel anything like the sex he'd had in the past. His whole body felt different with her. *He* felt different. Not just in his flesh but in his mind. Sex had gone from being a purely physical experience to a more cerebral—dared he admit it?—emotional one. He liked having Holly around. She was funny and playful, exciting and daring in a way that made him shift out of his comfort zone. But he had helped her out of her comfort zone, too. She had even allowed the balcony doors to be open in his suite when they made love the past few nights.

Made love.

The words jolted him. Maybe it wasn't 'just sex' after all. He made love to her. His body worshipped hers, pleasured hers and delighted in giving as well as receiving it. He had never wanted a woman more than her. She made him feel aroused by just looking at him. The scent of her was enough to make him hard. He only had to walk into a room she had been in earlier and his blood would be pumping. Her touch made his flesh tingle all over. The dancing tiptoe movements of her fingers made his pulse thunder and his heart race. Everything about her turned him on. He couldn't imagine another woman being as thrilling and satisfying as her.

But she was leaving in four days...

Which was fine. Just fine. She had her plans. He had his. He wasn't after anything serious. They'd had their fun. And it had been fun, much more fun than he'd realised a fling could be. She had taught him to loosen up. He had helped her confront her fears. She had revealed her past to him, which he hoped meant she was ready to move on from it. He wanted her to succeed. She had so much going for her. Her energy, passion and drive were wonderful qualities if channelled in the right direction.

Holly linked her arms around his neck. 'What's that big, old sober frown for?'

Julius forced a smile. 'Was I frowning?'

She put her fingertip between his brows. 'You get this deep ridge right here when you're thinking.'

He captured her finger and trailed his tongue the length of it. 'I'm thinking it might be good to go inside before we both get burned to a crisp.'

'Good point,' she said and walked up the steps of the pool.

Julius stood spellbound as she emerged from the

water like a nymph. She draped her wet hair over one shoulder as she squeezed the water out, reminding him of a mermaid. Her creamy skin was lightly tanned in spite of the sunscreen he'd seen her using. Her body was fit and toned yet utterly, irresistibly feminine.

She stepped into her bikini bottoms and tied the strings before she went in search of her top. Her smooth brow suddenly creased. 'Is that a car?' she asked, hurriedly covering herself.

Julius had been too focussed on her delectable body even to register anything but how gorgeous she looked. But now he could hear the scrabble of tyres over the gravel of the driveway.

'Are you expecting anyone?' Holly asked.

He vaulted out of the pool and reached for his trousers, not even stopping to dry himself. 'No,' he said. 'No one can get through the gates without the security code, unless it's one of the gardeners coming back in after mowing out front.'

'That doesn't sound like a ride-on mower,' she said, speaking Julius's thoughts out loud.

He shrugged on his shirt and quickly buttoned it. Under normal circumstances he would have got Sophia to answer the door. But with his housekeeper still away with her sister he could hardly send Holly dressed in nothing but a bikini. 'I'll see who it is,' he said. 'You stay here.'

Julius's heart sank when he saw the chauffeur-driven black limousine pull up in front of the villa. His mother. Dressed to the nines. There was no press entourage that he could see but he knew it wouldn't be long. His mother didn't go anywhere without the press documenting her every move.

'I'm coming to stay, Julius,' she said as her driver helped her alight from the car as if she were stepping out on the red carpet. 'I had to get away. The press haven't left me alone for a minute.'

'Have they followed you here?' he said.

'Not that I know of,' Elisabetta said. 'Why are you frowning? Aren't you pleased to see me? I cancelled the rest of my season on Broadway to spend time with you. This is the only place I'll be left alone. I was going to stay with Jake but he's always got some girl coming and going. And Miranda refuses to get involved. Not that I'd want to stay in her poky little flat.'

'Look, now's not a good time,' Julius said.

Elisabetta pouted. 'Don't give me your stupid work excuse. Your work can wait for your mother, surely? Don't you realise how desperate I am? Your father's ruined everything.' She paused long enough to narrow her gaze at him. 'Why are you all wet? And your shirt is buttoned up the wrong way.'

Julius gave himself a mental kick. 'I was having… er…a quick dip. You caught me by surprise.'

Elisabetta continued her tirade. 'I'm *so* furious. Do you know the girl's mother was a housemaid at the hotel he was staying in? A housemaid! How could he be so pathetic?'

Julius pushed back his wet hair with his hand. 'I really don't have time for this right now.'

'You never have time,' Elisabetta said, flouncing up the steps. 'All you have time for is work.'

'Mother, you can't stay,' Julius said. 'It's not…convenient. My housekeeper's away for a few days and I'm not prepared for visitors.'

Elisabetta turned with a theatrical swish of her designer skirt. 'Why do you always push me away? Can't you see I need you to support me right now?'

'I understand things are awful for you just now but you can't just dump yourself here without giving me notice,' Julius said. 'You could've at least called or texted first.'

Elisabetta's gaze narrowed again. 'Have you got someone with you? A lover? Who is it? You're such a dark horse. You never tell me anything. Even the press never knows what you're up to—unlike your brother.'

How could he explain his relationship with Holly to his mother? How could he explain it to himself? Was it even a relationship? Wasn't it just a fling? A temporary thing they both knew would come to an end at the end of the week? 'I like to keep my private life out of the news,' Julius said. 'Which is why you coming here is such a problem for me. You're a press magnet.'

'I hope you're not going to suddenly take your father's side in this,' Elisabetta said as if she hadn't heard a word he'd said.

'Why would I do that?' Julius said. 'What he did was unconscionable.'

'I blame that tramp who seduced him,' his mother said as she entered the front door of the villa. 'She betrayed him by not having the abortion he paid for. At least he offered to sort things out for her but what did she do? Went ahead and had the brat. The decent thing would've been to get rid of the mistake. Pretend it never happened. But no. Those ghastly little gold-diggers are all the same.'

His mother's logic—if he could call it that—had always been hard to follow. He was pretty certain Katherine Winwood would not like to be referred to as a 'mistake' or hear her deceased mother referred to as a 'ghastly little gold-digger'.

'If Kat's mother was such a gold-digger why did she wait until she was on her death bed to reveal her daughter's paternity?' he asked. 'Why not come forward years ago and line her pockets with silence money?'

Elisabetta threw him a fulminating look. 'How can you *defend* her? She was a housemaid, for God's sake.'

Just then Holly appeared dressed neatly in a skirt and blouse with her still-damp hair scraped back in a neat chignon. 'Welcome, Ms Albertini,' she said. 'Would you like me to take your things upstairs to your room?'

Elisabetta gave Holly an assessing look before turning to Julius. 'I thought you said your housekeeper was away?'

'She is,' he said. 'Holly's filling in for her.'

Elisabetta looked at Holly and then back at Julius, her expression tightening. 'So that's how it is, is it? You're sleeping with the hired help. Just like your father.'

Julius clenched his jaw. 'I won't have you insult Holly.'

His mother glared at Holly. 'I suppose you think you've got yourself a meal ticket by seducing my son.'

Holly hitched up her chin, her stance one of cool dignity. 'Would you like a drink brought up to your room? A bite to eat? Some fresh fruit?'

Elisabetta flattened her mouth. 'Did you hear what I said?'

'Yes, Ms Albertini, but I chose to ignore it on account of you being travel weary and upset over recent events,' Holly said. 'Now, if you'd like a drink or some other refreshment, I'll see to it, otherwise I'll leave Julius to show you to your room.'

His mother's brown eyes flashed as she turned to

Julius. 'Did you hear how she spoke to me? Get rid of her. Get her out of my sight. I won't be patronised as if I'm a child!'

'Then don't act like one,' Julius said. 'Holly might be acting as my housekeeper but that doesn't mean she isn't entitled to respect.'

'It's fine, Julius,' Holly chipped in. 'I can handle snobs like your mother.'

Elisabetta bristled. Her lips were pursed, her eyes blazing, her hands clenched. 'You disgusting little sow,' she threw at Holly. 'He can have anyone he wants. Why would he want *you*?'

'I'm great in bed,' Holly said. 'Plus, I cook an awesome meal. Oh, and did I mention I give great—?'

'That's enough,' Julius cut in quickly. 'Mother, you need to leave. Find a hotel somewhere. This is not the place for you right now.'

Elisabetta narrowed her eyes to slits. 'You'd choose *her* over your own mother? What sort of son are you? Anyone with eyes could see she's nothing but trailer trash.'

'Takes one to know one,' Holly said, calmly inspecting her cuticles.

Elisabetta's eyes bulged in outrage. 'What did you say?'

'Right. Time to go.' Julius took his mother's arm and led her back to the waiting car. His mother didn't like being reminded of her poverty-stricken background. It was mostly a well-kept secret, how she had grown up on the back streets of Florence, child of a single mother who had turned tricks to put food on the table. Elisabetta had reinvented herself when she'd moved to London to find a modelling job, which had then led to acting. Julius had never met his grandmother even though she had died three years after he and Jake were born. Not because he had been told of his grandmother's death. He had by chance come across the death certificate when he'd been a teenager sorting out things in the library down at Ravensdene. It was as if Elisabetta's past hadn't existed. It was erased from her memory.

But now, having got to know a little about Holly's desolate background, he wondered if his mother had had good reason to distance herself from it. Perhaps the memories, like Holly's, were too painful. Perhaps it wasn't a matter of pride and arrogance on his mother's part but shame. Was that why Elisabetta found it hard to be a mother herself? She hadn't been nurtured in the way most loving mothers nurtured their children. Elisabetta had pushed her children away unless she'd needed them to do something for her.

Like now, for instance. His mother would never come to visit him unless she'd wanted the visit to be all about her. She had never shown any interest in his work. He suspected she barely knew anything about his career. She had certainly never asked. He had always felt resentful towards her for her lack of interest but he wondered now if that was just the way life had shaped her.

Elisabetta got back in the car with a haughty flick of her Hermes scarf. 'I wouldn't demean myself by staying under the same roof as someone as common as that little tart. She'll bring you nothing but trouble. You mark my words.'

Julius closed the door and stepped back. 'I'll call you in a couple of days. Take care of yourself.'

His mother tightened her mouth as she looked straight

ahead. 'Drive me back to the airport,' she told the driver. 'It seems I'm not welcome here.'

Holly came down the steps to join him as he watched his mother's car disappear down the driveway. 'I might've overstepped the mark…just a little,' she said.

Julius put an arm around her shoulders and brought her close to him, kissing the top of her head. 'Only a little.'

She clasped his hand around her shoulder as she watched the dust stirred up by the car finally settle. 'Why did you defend me like that, anyway?'

He turned her in his arms to look at her. 'Why wouldn't I defend you? She was being rude and disrespectful.'

Holly's mouth twisted. 'No one's ever done that for me, or at least, not for a long time.'

Julius squeezed the tops of her shoulders. 'Then it's about time somebody did.'

Her eyes flicked away from his. 'It's nice of you and all that, but I'd hate for you to be estranged from your mother just because of me. It's not like I'm even going to be here much longer.'

Julius hated being reminded of the timeline. It was getting closer and closer to the end, and he knew he had to face it, but it was like facing a yawning chasm. Once Holly left, his life would go back to normal. Normal and ordered and…empty. 'What if you stayed a little longer?'

Her gaze was suddenly wary. Guarded. 'Why would I want to do that?'

Why indeed? he thought with a stab of disappointment. Clearly he was the one with the larger emotional investment in their relationship. *Emotional investment?* What the hell did that even mean? He wasn't in love with her. Was he? No. Of course he wasn't. He just had feelings for her. Feelings that were about care and concern for her welfare. Affection. She was a sweet girl underneath that façade. He'd come to respect her. To admire her. He'd come to enjoy their relationship.

Why was he persisting in calling it a relationship? It was a fling...wasn't it? Why had he been so convinced she was developing feelings for him? He'd fooled himself their love-making had made her fall in love with him. But sex was just sex for her. Hadn't she told him that repeatedly? The ironic thing was he'd said the same thing to women he'd dated in the past.

Julius shrugged. 'Just thought you might like to come out to the desert with me.'

Her brow wrinkled like crushed silk. 'The...*desert*?'

'I'm going on a trip to check on the software in the Atacama Desert,' he said. 'It's the highest and driest desert on the planet—that's why we do the infrared astronomy there, because of the absence of water vapour. I thought you might like to come with me.'

She pulled half of her bottom lip inside her mouth before releasing it. 'Look, it's a really nice offer, but I've already booked my air fare and I don't want to be charged a rebooking fee.'

'Don't worry about the money. I can help you with that.'

Her eyes met his with the kind of implacability and pride he had come to associate with her. And admire. 'It's not about the money. I've made up my mind, Julius. I'm leaving at the end of the week. I've waited years for this. You can't ask me to change my plans just because you want to have another week or two of sex.'

'It's not about the sex, damn it,' Julius said.

Her chin came up. 'Then what is it about?'

He framed her face in his hands. He felt as if he was stepping into mid-air off a vertiginous cliff. His stomach was pitching. Her eyes were giving nothing away but he could see a tiny muscle near her mouth moving like a pulse. 'It's about you. About wanting to be with you. Not because of the sex, although that's great. The best, in fact. But because I like you.'

Her eyes took on a cynical sheen. 'You *like* me.' She didn't frame it as a surprised question or a delighted statement. It sounded like she was mocking him for using such a trite word.

Julius brushed his thumbs over her creamy cheeks. 'I like how you make me feel.'

'How do I make you feel?' Her voice was toneless. As if she didn't really care how he answered.

'You make me feel alive.'

'Just…alive?' Was that a hint of delight he was hearing in her voice? Was that a sparkle of hope shining in her toffee-brown eyes?

Julius stepped off the cliff. He could no longer deny what he felt. 'I think I'm falling in love with you. No, strike that—I *am* in love with you. There's no thinking required. I know.'

Her eyes widened to the size of billiard balls. 'You're joking.'

'I'm not joking.'

'You're mad.'

'Mad? No. Madly in love? Yes.'

She opened and closed her mouth. Swallowed. 'But… but *why*?'

'Why?' Julius asked on the tail end of a laugh. 'Because you're the most fascinating, adorable, complicated and yet sweetest person I've ever met.'

Her forehead was lined again with worry. 'But your mother hates me.'

He smoothed away her frown. 'Only because she doesn't know you yet. She'll fall for you like I did once she gets to know how wonderful you are.'

She kept pulling at her lower lip with her teeth. 'Look, I really like you, Julius, but love? I'm not sure I even know what that word means.'

Julius tried not to be put off by her lack of enthusiasm. He understood her caution. She was used to people letting her down, exploiting her. She would be the last person to speak her feelings first. She would have to feel totally secure, trust that her heart was not going to be destroyed by someone who wasn't genuine. He could live with that. He loved her enough to be patient. He didn't need the words. He needed the action. The evidence. 'Love means wanting the best for someone,' he said. 'I want the best for you, *querida*. I want you to be happy. To feel safe and secure and loved.'

Her frown was back. 'I can't feel safe. Not here. Not in Argentina.'

'Because of your stepfather?'

She held her arms against her body, visibly shrinking her frame, as if trying to contain every bit of herself into the smallest package possible. 'You don't know the power he has. The reach he has. If he knew we were involved it could get ugly. Really ugly.'

'I can handle bullies like your stepfather,' Julius said. 'I survived English boarding school, after all!'

Her eyes showed her doubts in long, dark shadows

that went all the way back to her childhood. Julius could see the fear. He could sense it. It was like a presence.

She suddenly unpeeled her arm from around her body and held it wrist-up. 'This is what my stepfather did,' she said. 'He broke my arm in four places. He told me to lie to the doctors at the hospital or he would kill my mother or me or both.'

Julius looked at the white scar on her wrist, his gut boiling with rage at what she had suffered. 'The man is a criminal,' he said. 'He needs to be charged. He needs to be locked up and the key thrown away.'

Holly laughed but it wasn't with humour. It bordered on hysteria. 'He has friends in such high places he could wriggle his way out of any charge. He's done it numerous times. I know he's out there waiting for a chance to hurt me. I'm surprised he hasn't tracked me down yet. It's unusually slow for him.'

He took her in his arms and held her close. 'I won't let him hurt you,' he said. 'I won't let anyone hurt you.'

She pressed her cheek against his chest. 'You're the nicest man I've ever met.' Her voice was so soft he had to strain his ears to hear her. 'If I was going to fall in love it would be with someone like you.'

Julius rested his chin on top of her head, holding her in the circle of his arms. He swore he would do everything he could to make her feel safe. He would not settle until he had achieved that for her. Whatever it took, he would do.

Whatever it took.

CHAPTER TWELVE

HOLLY WOKE WELL before Julius the next morning. But then, she hadn't really been asleep. Even though Julius had made love to her with exquisite tenderness and had made her feel treasured and cherished, she had lain awake most of the night with a gnawing sense of unease. Sophia was returning today after extending her break with her sister. But it wasn't just about the housekeeper finding out about Holly's relationship with Julius. It was a sense the world outside—the world she had been pretending didn't exist—was coming for her. To seek her out. To make her pay the price for the bubble of happiness she had been in.

The fact that Julius had told her he loved her should have made her feel the most blessed person in the world but instead it made her feel the opposite. It was like tempting fate. Whenever things were going well for her, something always happened to ruin it. It was the script of her life. She had no control over it. She didn't dare to be happy. Happiness was for other people—for lucky people who didn't have horrible backgrounds they couldn't escape from.

Holly slipped out of bed and padded across the room, quietly opening the balcony doors and stepping outside.

It still amazed her how Julius had helped her overcome her crippling fear. But he was right. She had allowed her stepfather to control her through fear. She stood on the balcony and breathed in the fresh morning air. The sun was just peeping over the horizon, the red and gold and crimson streaks heralding a warm day ahead.

Julius's phone beeped on the bedside table, and Holly heard him grunt as he reached out to pick it up. She turned to look at him, all sexily tousled from a deep sleep after satisfying sex. He pushed his hair back off his forehead as he read the message. She saw his face blanch. Watched as his throat moved up and down in a convulsive swallow.

She stepped back into the room, pushing away the gauzy curtain that clung to her on the way past. 'What's wrong?'

He clicked off the phone but she noticed he didn't put it back on the bedside table. He was gripping it in his hand so tightly, she was sure the screen would crack. Every knuckle on his hand was white with tension. 'Nothing.'

Holly came over to him and sat on the edge of the bed beside him. 'It can't be nothing. You look like you just received horrible news. Is it your father? Your mother? One of your siblings?'

He pressed his mouth together so flatly his lips turned white. He swung his legs over the bed and stood, still gripping his phone. 'There's been a press leak.' He let out a hissing breath. 'About us.'

This time it was Holly's turn to swallow. 'What does it say?'

His expression was so rigid with anger, she could see

every muscle outlined as if carved in stone. 'It's not so much what it says as what it shows.'

Her stomach dropped. 'There are pictures? Of us?'

He scraped a hand through his hair. 'Yes.'

'Show me.'

'No.'

Holly got off the bed and held out her hand for his phone. 'Show me.'

He held the phone out of her reach, his face so tortured with anguish her heart squeezed. 'No, Holly. Please. It's best if you don't. I'll make it go away. I'll get my lawyer onto it.'

Her eyes widened. '*Your lawyer*? Surely they can't be that bad. How did anyone get photos of us? We haven't been out together in public.'

Julius was looking so ashen Holly felt sick to her stomach. She took the phone from him. This time he didn't fight her for it. It was like he was stunned. Shocked into inertia. She clicked on his most recent message. It was from his twin brother with a short message— WTF?—with a link to a press article with two pictures. They were erotic, almost pornographic shots of her and Julius making love in the pool.

Her mouth went dry. Dry as sandpaper. She couldn't get her voice to work. All she could think was how horrible this was for Julius. How shaming. How mortifying. Someone had captured them in their most intimate moments and splashed it all over the world's media. The media Julius did everything in his power to avoid. *This* was what she had brought to his life. *She* had done this to him. She knew exactly who was behind that long-range camera lens. This was how it was always going to be. She could never have a normal life. Not while her stepfather was alive. He would hunt her down. He would destroy her and anyone she dared to care about.

'I can make it go away,' Julius said into the canyon of silence.

Holly began collecting her things and stuffing them haphazardly into the backpack she had stored in his wardrobe.

'What are you doing?'

'I'm leaving.'

'You can't leave.'

She slung the straps of her backpack over one shoulder. 'I have to leave, Julius. I reckon I've caused enough trouble for you. I admit I wanted to when I first arrived, but even by my standards this is going too far.'

He frowned so hard his brows met over his eyes. 'You don't think I'm blaming *you* for this?'

'It's my fault,' Holly said. 'I've done this to you because I do this kind of stuff to the people I care about. I wreck their lives. I stuff up everything for them just by breathing.'

'You care about me?'

Holly mentally bit her tongue. 'I'm not in love with you, if that's what you're asking.'

'I don't believe you,' he said. 'You *do* love me. That's why you're running away like a spooked rabbit. You're too frightened to let me handle this. You want to trust me to keep you safe when no one's ever been able to do it before. But I *can* keep you safe, Holly. You have to trust me. I will *not* allow anyone to hurt you.'

Holly wanted to believe him. She ached to believe he cared enough to sacrifice his privacy, his reputation and even his family for her. But she wasn't worth it. She knew he would come to resent her for it. The press would never leave them alone. Her stepfather would see to it. Her stepfather would taint their relationship. He would sully it. Cheapen it.

And ultimately destroy it.

'I don't think you're listening to me, Julius,' Holly said. 'I don't *want* to stay. I wouldn't stay if you paid me to. I've got plans. I'm not changing them. My future is in England; it's not here with you.'

His mouth tightened. His hands clenched and unclenched by his sides. Holly got the feeling he was at war with himself. Fighting back the impulse to reach for her. 'Fine,' he said at last. 'Leave. I'll call Natalia and get her to pick you up. You won't be able to leave the country until your community service time is up.'

Holly knew it would be the longest three days of her life.

Julius stood in a stony silence as Holly was driven away by her caseworker. It felt as if his heart was tied to the rear of the car. The tugging, straining, gutting sensation took his breath away. He was sure she was lying and yet…and yet what if he was wrong? What if she had set him up from the start? She was a troublemaker. A rebel. She had openly admitted to wanting to make his life difficult. He thought back to the pool. Both times she had lured him out there…hadn't she? It had been her idea to make love out there. It wasn't something he would normally do. She was always poking fun at his conservative nature. Was that why? So she could set him up and shame him the in the most shocking way possible?

But then he thought of how she had trusted him enough to tell him about the horrible stuff that had happened to her as a child. That wasn't an act. She had the scars to prove it. Her stepfather was behind this photo scandal. He had to be. Julius just had to prove it.

If he could make Holly feel safe by seeing justice served then maybe, just maybe, she would trust him enough to admit to her feelings.

He reached for his phone and called a close friend, Leandro Allegretti. Leandro was a forensic accountant who occasionally did some work for Jake's business analysis company. They had gone to school together and Leandro had spent many a weekend or holiday at Ravensdene while they'd been growing up. If anyone could uncover secrets and lies, it was Leandro. He made it his business to uncover fraud, money laundering and other white-collar crime.

'Leandro?' Julius said. 'Yeah, it's me. Listen, I have a little project for you...'

Holly had finally made it to England. She had found a tiny flat in central London and even landed a job in a deli, which should have made her feel as if all her boxes were ticked, but she felt miserable. The weather was freezing, for one thing. And it never seemed to stop raining. She had spent years dreaming of the time when she would be here, doing normal stuff like normal people, and yet she felt lost. Empty. Hollow. As if something was missing. Even the shops didn't interest her. She hadn't heard from Julius, but then she didn't expect to, not really. She had cut him from her life in the only way she knew how. Bluntly. Permanently.

But she missed him. She missed everything about him. The security she felt when she was with him was only apparent to her now it had been taken away. She had felt *safe* with him. Now she was anchorless. Like a paper boat bobbing about in the middle of the ocean.

Holly was on a tea break in a nearby café when she

flicked through the day's newspaper and her eyes honed in on an article that was only a couple of paragraphs long about a recent criminal charge in Argentina. Her eyes widened in shock when she saw her stepfather's name cited as the man at the centre of the investigation that had uncovered a money-laundering and drug-running scheme that had gone on for over twenty years.

Holly sat back in her seat with a gasp of wonder. It had finally happened. Franco Morales's lawyer said his client had pleaded guilty and bail was denied. How had that come about? Who was behind it? Who had shone the light of suspicion on her stepfather?

A cramped space inside Holly's chest suddenly opened. *Julius.* Of course he would have gone after her stepfather. Hadn't he promised he would not allow anyone to hurt her? He had been true to his word. He had taken on one of Argentina's most notoriously elusive criminals and brought about justice. *For her.*

Holly shot out of her seat. She had to see him. She had to see him to thank him in person. To tell him… what? She sat back down in her seat. Huddled back into her coat. She didn't belong in his world. How could she? She worked in a deli. She had no qualifications. He was the son of London theatre royalty.

And his mother hated her.

'Is this seat taken?'

Holly looked up to see a woman standing next to the empty chair on the opposite side of the table. She looked vaguely familiar but Holly couldn't quite place her. Maybe she had served her in the shop in the past week or so. 'No; I'm leaving soon, in any case.'

The woman sat down. 'You don't recognise me, do you?'

Holly blinked as the woman took off her sunglasses. Why anyone would be wearing sunglasses on such a miserably wet day in London had occurred to her but then she figured it took all types. Now she realised it was all part of a disguise. A very clever one, too. No one would ever guess Elisabetta Albertini would frequent a humble little café in Soho dressed like a bag lady. 'No,' Holly said. 'Even your accent is different. But then, I guess you can do just about any accent.'

Elisabetta gave her a sly smile. 'So, how's London working out for you?'

'Great. Fine. Brilliant.'

'You'd better stick to your day job,' Elisabetta said. 'You're a terrible actor.'

Holly grimaced. 'Yeah, I know. But I hate my day job. I don't want to do this for the rest of my life. Nor do I want to be cleaning up after people.'

'What did you want to be when you were a little girl?'

'I wanted to be a kindergarten teacher—but why are you even asking me this after the way you spoke to me at Julius's? And how did you find me?'

'Julius told me.'

Holly frowned. 'But how does he know where I am?'

'He made it his business to find out,' Elisabetta said. 'Look, I was wrong to speak to you the way I did. Richard's parents did the same thing to me all those years ago when he brought me home to introduce me to them. They made me feel so worthless. I swore I would never treat any daughter-in-law of mine like that, but then I went and did it to you.'

'Daughter-in-law?' Holly said, frowning harder. 'No one said anything about marriage. We had a fling, that's all, and now it's over.'

'He loves you, Holly,' Elisabetta said. 'He'll want to marry you because that's his way. Jake would be another thing entirely. But with Julius you can be assured he'll always do the right thing.'

Holly narrowed her eyes. 'Did he *make* you come here to apologise to me?'

Elisabetta gave her a coy look. 'Does it matter? If he's going to marry you, then I'm going to have to accept it or lose him.'

Holly's frown deepened another notch. 'He shouldn't have done that. You're his mother. He's lucky to have you. I wish I had a mother. I have no one. No one at all.'

Elisabetta put her hand over Holly's and gave it a light squeeze. 'I'm not the best mother in the world. I know that, and it upsets me if I allow myself to think about it, so I don't think about it.' She pulled her hand away as if she had a time limit on touch and sat back in her seat. 'But who knows? Maybe I'll do a better job as a mother-in-law.'

'You mean you wouldn't...*mind*?'

Elisabetta gave a short but not very pleasant-sounding laugh. 'Of course I mind. But I'm an actor; I'll pretend I don't. But don't tell Julius. It can be our little secret.'

Holly gave her a telling look. 'You won't be able to fool him no matter how brilliant an actor you are.'

The older woman's gaze was suddenly very direct. 'Do you love my son?'

Holly gave a heartfelt sigh. 'So much it hurts to think I might never see him again.'

Elisabetta smiled a mercurial smile and popped her sunglasses back on as she got up to leave. 'I have a feeling you'll be seeing him very soon. *Ciao*.'

Holly gathered her things and made to get up but a tall

shadow fell over her. She looked up to see Julius standing there, beads of rain clinging to his cashmere coat, his hair and even to the ends of his eyelashes. 'I know my mother's a hard act to follow, but here I am. Did she apologise?'

'Yes…' Holly licked her suddenly dry lips. Maybe now wasn't the right time to talk about his mother's 'apology'. 'I can't believe what you did for me. It was… amazing. Unbelievable. I can never thank you enough.'

'There is one way,' he said. 'Will you do me the honour of becoming my wife?'

Holly thought her heart was going to burst out of her chest cavity with sheer joy. Could this really be happening? 'Why me? You could have anyone. I'm no one.'

He took her by the hands and gripped them tightly. 'You're everything to me. Everything. I love you, Holly. More than I can ever tell you. I know this isn't a dream proposal. In fact, I can't believe I'm proposing to you in a public place—but I can't bear another moment without knowing you'll agree to spend the rest of your life with me. You don't have to come back to Argentina if you don't want to. I can move back to England.'

Holly looked at him in stunned surprise. 'You'd do that for me?'

'Of course.'

She wrinkled her nose. 'But the weather's foul.'

'I know, but at least we could cuddle up in bed,' he said with a glint in his eyes.

Holly grinned back. 'I guess we could split the time between here and there. Summer here, winter there.'

'Sounds like a good plan to me,' he said, drawing her close. 'I missed you so much. I never realised what a boring life I've been living until you came into it.'

Holly felt the sting of happy tears at the back of her eyes. 'I was miserable from the moment I got on that plane. I'd planned that moment for years. I'd looked forward to it. Counted the days, the hours, even the minutes. But as soon as we took off I felt empty. As if I was leaving a part of myself behind.'

Julius blotted a tear that had escaped from her left eye. 'Do you love me or have I been deluding myself?'

Holly held his hand against her cheek. 'I love you. I'm not sure when I started. Maybe when you took me out on the balcony. You were so kind and patient. I didn't stand a chance after that.'

He smiled a tender smile. 'So will you marry me, my darling?'

Holly wanted to pinch herself to check she wasn't dreaming. 'No one's ever proposed to me before.'

'Lucky me to be the first.'

Holly put her arms around his waist and smiled as his mouth came down towards hers. 'Lucky us.'

* * * * *

If you've loved stepping into the world of
THE RAVENSDALE SCANDALS, *you won't want to miss the next sizzling instalment in this thrilling new quartet!*

AWAKENING THE RAVENSDALE HEIRESS
by Melanie Milburne—available January 2016

MILLS & BOON®

Why shop at millsandboon.co.uk?

Each year, thousands of romance readers find their perfect read at millsandboon.co.uk. That's because we're passionate about bringing you the very best romantic fiction. Here are some of the advantages of shopping at www.millsandboon.co.uk:

* **Get new books first**—you'll be able to buy your favourite books one month before they hit the shops

* **Get exclusive discounts**—you'll also be able to buy our specially created monthly collections, with up to 50% off the RRP

* **Find your favourite authors**—latest news, interviews and new releases for all your favourite authors and series on our website, plus ideas for what to try next

* **Join in**—once you've bought your favourite books, don't forget to register with us to rate, review and join in the discussions

Visit **www.millsandboon.co.uk**
for all this and more today!

a&b

Last Writes

A Collection of Short Stories

CATHERINE AIRD

Allison & Busby Limited
12 Fitzroy Mews
London W1T 6DW
www.allisonandbusby.com

First published in Great Britain by Allison & Busby in 2014.
This paperback edition published by Allison & Busby in 2015.

Copyright © 2014 by CATHERINE AIRD

10 9 8 7 6 5 4 3 2 1

ISBN 978-0-7490-1627-2

Typeset in 10.45/14.75 pt Sabon by
Allison & Busby Ltd.

The paper used for this Allison & Busby publication
has been produced from trees that have been legally sourced
from well-managed and credibly certified forests.

Printed and bound by
CPI Group (UK) Ltd, Croydon, CR0 4YY

For Eilidh Macmillan Watkin
with love

CONTENTS

LEFT, RIGHT, ATTENTION!

'That you, Wendy? It's Henry here. Look here, old girl, can I possibly come down to stay with you in Berebury for a few days?'

'Of course you can, dear,' said his sister, Wendy Witherington, without hesitation. 'The children will be delighted to see you and I know that Tim will enjoy hearing how things are these days in London.'

'Dire,' groaned her brother, who worked at the Foreign Office. 'Absolutely dire.'

'Then a few days in the country will be very good for you,' pronounced Wendy briskly. 'A complete break is what you need.'

'A complete break isn't what I shall be getting,' said Henry Tyler wryly. 'I'm afraid I shall have to bring some work down with me. No choice, worse luck.'

'Then don't expect to do it until the children

have gone to bed,' said his sister practically. 'They'll never forgive you if you don't spend some time with them.'

'All I can say, Wen, is that their company will be a great improvement on that of some of the people with whom I've had to spend my time with lately.' The upper echelons of the Foreign Office had no time these days for leisurely luncheons or even routine meetings. And hadn't had ever since Germany had seized the Rhineland.

'You do need a rest, don't you?' Wendy was his elder sister and thus felt able to comment freely. 'Come down whenever you like.'

'I'll come down whenever I can,' amended her brother in whom the pedantry of the Civil Service was deeply ingrained, even though civilised conversations with most of the ambassadors accredited to the Court of St James were now a thing of the past. 'But I warn you now, I'll have some work to do while I'm with you.'

'Dispatches from foreign parts?' said Wendy, who knew the term well enough but not what was really at stake in such diplomatic communications in the late 1930s – a notably tense time in European history.

'You could call them that,' agreed Henry, adding under his breath that it would be a great help if he could actually read and understand all

10

of them. A capacity to read between the lines went without saying in the Foreign Office but being a linguist was no help with those communications that involved code-breaking.

'Not Herr Hitler being difficult again?' asked Wendy, whose understanding of the European political scene was decidedly sketchy.

'I'm afraid so.' For one glorious moment Henry envisaged a world in which a young Adolf Hitler had been brought up by his sister, Wendy, and taught his Ps and Qs as firmly as his nephew and niece had been. Considerably sustained by this happy – but alas – imaginary vision he went on 'And my minister won't forgive me if I come back to the office without our current conundrum having been solved.'

As he packed his weekend case and tossed his homework into it that Thursday evening, Henry had second thoughts about having used the word 'conundrum'. 'Puzzle' might describe the copy of the typed sheet he was taking with him to Berebury better. Or even 'riddle'. That it, whatever it was called, was very important indeed there was no doubt whatsoever.

True, that piece of paper in his case did technically fall under the heading of 'Dispatches' and was so described at the Foreign Office but it had not arrived in any diplomatic bag. The

11

fact that the usual channels had not been used was only one of the things that underlined its importance.

Instead the message had reached London from continental Europe by a route so devious as to be unrecorded but known to involve a French abbé, a chorus girl coming home from a rather risqué engagement that had not met with the approval of the Third Reich and a somewhat hazardous exchange between anonymous patriots on fishing boats at sea.

The chorus girl had been already so scantily clad as to be considered not to merit further searching – as it happened a great mistake on the part of the authorities. And the soutane of the abbé had been similarly helpful in discouraging overenthusiastic rubbings-down. The fishermen smelt of fish and the sea and anyway no one knew that the message had reached them.

And now Henry had this precious piece of paper in his hands and could not read it.

Neither could the code-breakers at the Foreign Office, or even those at British Naval Intelligence's celebrated old Room 40 of the Great War. That their departments were about to be considerably beefed up was no immediate help to Henry. It was no consolation either that various other assorted patriots had probably also risked life and limb to get the piece of paper to him. All that meant was that the message was important. It wasn't something that he had ever doubted but it greatly added to his feeling of responsibility.

His sister, Wendy, duly met him at Berebury station and bore him off to a strenuous playtime with his nephew and niece. This was followed, after their bedtime, by a leisurely supper with his sister and her husband, Tim.

'Things not too good in London, eh?' surmised Tim Witherington, pouring Henry a generous nightcap.

'Not good at all,' admitted Henry. 'Damned tricky, in fact.'

'Not surprised,' said his brother-in-law, whose limp dated from the March Retreat of 1918. 'Even though you can't believe everything you read in the newspapers.'

'Of course, things are a bit different these days . . .' Speaking in generalities was taught at the same time as speaking in tongues at the Foreign Office.

Tim Witherington started to knock out his pipe on the hearth, caught his wife's eye and used an ashtray instead. 'I can see that. More undercover, I daresay.'

13

'More political, anyway,' said Henry vaguely. There were those in France – and some said in England, too – who held what his minister called 'doubtful views'. But who they all were in both countries was not always immediately clear – which was a big headache just now.

Wendy tactfully put an end to their conversation by putting her knitting down and getting out of her chair. 'You'll be wanting an early night, I'm sure, Henry. I've told the children to be extra careful not to wake you in the morning . . .'

It was an unnecessary warning. Henry had very little sleep anyway, having spent the night tossing and turning between bouts of staring at the scrap of paper and its short typewritten message. Bleary eyed, he stared at it once again in the morning and still made no sense of it.

NP AY YT FR BY LH WM RL BP QM LD
SS UD TO AS RT LO RP ER BY UT WJ
YO AD WA IY AR XY UP BS RT UD J

Henry Tyler didn't come downstairs that morning until after the children were safely at school and Tim Witherington well on his way to his office in the little market town.

'Coffee,' ordained Wendy, taking one look at his face. 'And toast.'

Wearily, Henry pulled a chair up to the table. 'Thanks, Wen. Has the newspaper come yet?'

She handed it to him and waited while he scanned the headlines. 'Nothing new,' he said, laying it down beside his plate.

'Is that good or bad?' she asked.

'You can't really tell these days,' he sighed. 'That's the trouble.' He couldn't remember when he'd last felt quite as tired as he did now.

'No,' she said. 'I can understand that but you're really worried this time, aren't you?'

'All I've got to do this weekend,' he responded lightly, 'is break a code.'

'That's all right, then,' she said calmly. 'It shouldn't be too difficult. The children won't be home from school until quarter past four.'

He laughed aloud for the first time in weeks. 'That's what you think, old girl.'

'You mean you can't do it?'

'I do indeed mean just that.' He was quite serious now. 'I've been working on it for quite a while already. And I'm not the only one to have had a go.'

'Can you actually read it? I mean, it's not in numbers like that funny thing from Russia, is it?'

'The Zimmermann Telegram and its threat

15

of "unrestricted submarine warfare"?' divined Henry without difficulty. 'No. That was a series of numbers and numbers and it usually means you need a code book before you can decipher anything.'

'Wasn't that a fake, anyway?'

'It was political,' said Henry with feeling.

Wendy frowned. 'So how do you know that what you've got isn't, too?'

'I don't,' said Henry. 'It's quite possible that it isn't a genuine message, which, were we then to act upon it, it would mean that we would all be deep in the mulligatawny.' He paused. 'And people might die.'

'And it's not in hieroglyphics or anything like that, is it?' said Wendy, ignoring this convolution.

'Nor in Cyrillic,' said Henry.

'What the children say to that is "Nice work, Cyril",' said their mother.

'Oh, I can read it all right,' said Henry, smiling at last. 'That's not the problem. It's typed.'

'Why?'

'Why what?'

'Why was your message typed? I mean, if it was urgent and private you'd think it would be handwritten. Typewriters make a fearful clatter. You can't really be private about it.' Before being swept off her feet by a young and handsome

16

Tim Witherington, his sister had worked as a secretary in the offices of Puckle, Puckle and Nunnery, solicitors of Berebury, and thus knew about such things.

'I'd never thought of that,' he confessed. 'I suppose it could actually have been written in an office if no one was watching what you were up to.'

Wendy knitted her eyebrows. 'Do you know who it's from? I mean, has it been written by one of those honest men sent to lie abroad for the good of their country?'

'An ambassador?' said Henry. Sir Henry Wotton's definition of an ambassador as such was famous. 'I doubt it. More likely, I'm afraid,' he added gloomily, 'it's been written by a good man sent to die abroad for the good of this country – or even perhaps his country, which might not be the same thing.'

'Current affairs aren't very good just now, are they?' she said quietly.

'No.' Henry shook his head. 'Especially in France.'

'*La belle France*,' said his sister, who'd honeymooned in Paris.

'The country is all right,' growled Henry. 'It's the politicians who aren't. You just don't know where you are with them.' Absently, he helped himself to some more coffee while he considered

17

the likely consequences of showing the message to his sister and thus breaking the Official Secrets Act. If he did and anyone found out that he had done he'd probably be sent to the Tower – or worse still, lose his pension.

'Politicians never are all right,' said Wendy Witherington, thus summing up world history in a nutshell.

'Look here, Wen,' he said impulsively, 'you were the confidential secretary to old Mr Nunnery, weren't you?'

'I was. For years. He was ever so upset when I got married . . .'

'I didn't mean that. I mean that you were used to handling very private matters in his office.'

'Naturally,' she said, bridling a little. 'Do you mean did I ever tell anyone anything I shouldn't? Because if so . . .'

'No, no,' he interrupted her hastily.

She gave a reminiscent smile. 'You wouldn't believe the number of people who tried to pump me about what was in old Mrs Wilkins' will. All three nephews and that young girl she was so fond of.'

'I do believe you, old thing. Where's there's a will, there's a relative.'

'And in the end when she died it all went to someone else.'

'Served 'em right,' said Henry.

'This message,' she said, deflecting him. 'I thought that since *e* is the commonest letter, that you had to look for that first.'

'You do if it's in English,' said Henry, who had been through this before in London.

'Will it be in English?' she asked.

'It should be,' he said carefully, 'because I am hoping that it's from an Englishman.'

'Were you expecting it?' asked Wendy Witherington intelligently.

'Yes and no,' he replied slowly. 'You see, we have a number of our people established in strange places.'

'What you call sleepers?'

'How do you know that?'

'Don't be silly, Henry. Everyone knows that.'

'And that's only all right if no one knows who they are . . .'

'And only if they are all right,' she said again.

'That's part of the trouble,' he admitted. 'If they aren't all right, then we're all in trouble.'

'Especially,' she said thoughtfully, 'if you don't know if they've been turned.'

'Who have you been talking to?'

'Me? No one, but I do read, you know.'

'There's something else,' he said. 'If they have been turned, we need to know exactly when.'

'I can see that. So you have tried looking for the commonest letter in other languages, too?'

'The one that's most likely to be their equivalent of *e*, you mean? Yes, that's all been done.'

'And?'

'There wasn't any letter that stood out as being used much more than any other.'

'That's quite odd.'

'That's what they said in the office, too.' Henry reached for the toast rack. 'Apparently it's the first thing the code-breakers look for.'

'What about every fourth letter or something like that?' she asked, automatically passing him the butter dish.

'We've all done every second, third and fifth letter as well until we're squiffy-eyed,' said Henry, 'and we still can't make any sense of it.'

'And put them in groups? Don't they do that, too?'

'They do,' said Henry wearily, 'and no, that didn't work.'

'What's the next most popular letter in English after *e*?' she asked.

'Probably *a*,' said Henry. 'And, no, that doesn't work either.'

'Marmalade, dear? It's home-made.'

'I'd better enjoy it while I can,' said Henry

gloomily, helping himself to a good spoonful. 'I doubt if you'll be getting any Seville oranges next year. And not only because of the rain in Spain falling mainly on the plain.'

'Poor Spain,' said Wendy. 'The news isn't good from there either, is it?'

'The news from nowhere is good,' said Henry, consciously parodying Samuel Butler. 'And Spain has its troubles, too.' That they tended to compound those of the United Kingdom he left unsaid.

But his sister wasn't listening. Instead a little smile was playing round her lips. 'You won't remember Mr Benomley, will you? He was the Chief Clerk at Puckle, Puckle and Nunnery . . .'

Henry shook his head, and gave his attention to the marmalade.

'He was ever so fierce. He really frightened all of us in the office. Wouldn't let us talk while we were working . . .'

'Quite right, too,' mumbled Henry, his mouth full of toast. 'Young girls need keeping in order.'

'So, when we wanted to say something to each other without him knowing, we would type the message in a code of our own and pass it over to the next typist.'

'You did, did you?' said Henry. 'What if he saw what you'd written?'

21

'We'd say it was only the office junior practising.'

'Adding lying to deception,' said Henry in mock solemnity. 'Girls will be girls, I suppose. And what was this great wheeze of yours?'

'We typed the next letter along to the one we meant.'

He stared at her, produced the message he'd been poring over most of the night and asked, half in fun, 'So what letters are next to *N* and *P*?'

She wrinkled her nose. 'From memory *M* and *N*?'

'That's no good then.'

'Wait a minute, wait a minute. If it was the last letter on the line that we wanted to use, we would go back to the beginning of the line. That would make *N* mean *M*.'

'And what about *P*?'

'Oh, dear, that's no good. That's the last letter on the top row so you'd have to come back to *Q* at the beginning. "MQ" doesn't mean anything.' Wendy Witherington looked quite crestfallen.

'Wait a minute, Wen. Suppose whoever typed this message knew this little game and was afraid other people might know it as well, what would he . . .'

'Or she.'

'Or she do to make it more secure?'

'Well, she could alternate right and left, I suppose . . .'

'Or left and right,' said Henry, seizing a pencil. 'Let's see . . . Left first would still give us *M*, right would give us *O*, then it's *A* and *Y*.'

'That would give you *S* and *T*,' said Wendy with growing interest.

'That's "most". . .' said Henry.

'Stay where you are, Henry, and I'll go and get my old typewriter.'

'At least that's an English word,' said Henry.

'Go on,' she urged, as soon as she came back with an elderly Imperial machine.

'*Y* and *T*,' he said.

'*U* and *R*,' said his sister, scanning the keyboard. 'I bet that's going to be "urgent".'

'Quick,' said Henry with mounting excitement. Forgetting all about the Official Secrets Act, he pushed the piece of paper in front of her. 'Do these letters, too.'

It did not take her long. 'Once a typist, always a typist,' she said, hitting the keys, first to the left and then to the right of the letters on the paper.

Henry stood behind her, looking over her shoulder as a message appeared. He read aloud.

MOST URGENT AGENT KNOWN AS DAISY IS A
TRAITOR ENTIRE HUISSELOT SECTION AT RISK

Henry pushed the marmalade to one side and made for the telephone in the hall.

He was back in minutes. 'Sorry, Wen, but I'll have to go straight back to London.'

She nodded her understanding.

'Tell the children it was a case of "Left right, left right, attention . . ." and that I'll be back as soon as I can.'

THE HARD LESSON

'That was Brenda Murgatroyd ringing from the hospital,' said Mrs Watson as she replaced the telephone receiver on its cradle. 'It's just as we thought. Poor Mrs Burrell has broken her wrist after all . . .'

The headmaster groaned aloud.

'She's been X-rayed and . . .' finished the school secretary, 'now she's waiting to have a plaster put on.'

'Go on,' he urged. 'Tell me how long . . .'

'Brenda said that the Accident and Emergency Department is particularly busy today . . .'

'How long?' he asked again, running his hands through what was left of his hair.

'Brenda reckoned they'd be at the hospital for another three hours at least for the plaster to be put on – let alone dry – and then she'll have to take Mrs Burrell home before she comes back into school.'

The headmaster groaned again and pulled a copy of the school timetable across his desk towards him. He studied it for the dozenth time. 'Mr Collins . . .'

'Leading a school party over at the Greatorex Museum,' said Mrs Watson. She cleared her throat and said, not for the first time, 'If you remember Mrs Martindale and Mr Legge are with him there, too.'

The headmaster roundly anathematised all school visits.

'Yes, headmaster,' said Mrs Watson kindly, aware that it was the absence of staff from the school and not the presence of their pupils at the Greatorex Museum that was causing the problem today.

'Mr Fletcher . . .' said the headmaster with the air of a man clutching at straws.

'Mr Fletcher is looking after all the lower forms which aren't at the Museum,' the secretary reminded him. 'I don't think there's anyone else left in the school who could do that.' She paused and added significantly, 'Or would.'

'Ms Dilnot?' He suggested tentatively.

'Certainly not, Headmaster.' Mrs Watson pursed her lips. 'Ms Dilnot would be a most unsuitable person to take Mrs Burrell's Relationships class at the present time. Not only is she herself in an advanced state of pregnancy but I understand that it is quite widely known both in and out of the staffroom that she is not prepared to name the father of her baby.'

'Really?' said the headmaster. 'She's very pretty, too, of course.'

Mrs Watson said distantly that she didn't see what that had to do with it and in any case that just left Miss Wilkins free to take Mrs Burrell's Relationships class, which she was sure the headmaster has known all along, hadn't he?

Miss Wilkins was the oldest member of his staff and quite the most strait-laced. It was a brave colleague who swore in the staffroom when she was there, let alone told a doubtful joke.

'For two pins,' he said wildly, 'I'd take it myself.'

'The governors would think there was something about their meeting that you wished to avoid, Headmaster,' the secretary said at once. She looked out of the window at the car park. 'And they're already arriving for it.'

'I'm afraid the governors would put an even worse construction on my absence than that,' said the headmaster realistically. 'They're a worldly-wise lot. All right, ask Miss Wilkins to come and see me, will you? Although heaven only knows what Mrs Burrell's class will say when they hear that it's Miss Wilkins who's going to take them for Relationships instead of her. If Miss Wilkins is prepared to do it, that is.'

'I understand,' said Mrs Watson astringently, 'that Mrs Burrell's class have already worked out that she's the only member of staff free to take them this afternoon.' Not being on the teaching staff gave the secretary better links with the politics of the playground than anyone else at the school except the caretaker.

'They're not slow at calculation when it suits them.' A lifetime in teaching had turned the headmaster into a cynic.

'I don't know how Miss Wilkins will feel about it,' went on the school secretary, 'but I am told that they are positively looking forward to her taking the class.'

'That must be a first,' said the headmaster, a bitter man, too, by virtue of his profession.

'Mathematics is not a subject that lends itself to popularity,' said Mrs Watson moderately. 'Not in the ordinary way – now "Relationships" is a different cup of tea altogether.'

'Let us just hope,' said the headmaster piously, 'that they don't try to teach Miss Wilkins anything that they know already and she doesn't.'

Miss Wilkins accepted the assignment in her customary calm, neutral way. 'Of course,

Headmaster. I can quite see the difficulty. Poor Mrs Burrell. Naturally, I don't know what she had in mind for today's lesson . . .'

'The prevention of teenage pregnancy seems high on everyone's agenda these days,' offered the headmaster, unusually tentative.

'I take it you mean its avoidance?'

'Yes, Miss Wilkins, of course I do.' The headmaster seldom welcomed the arrival of the Chairman of the Governors as he did then. 'Now, you must excuse me.'

If Miss Wilkins noticed the preternatural silence obtaining in the classroom as she entered she gave no sign of having done so. Nor did she react to the banana placed conspicuously on the desk before her. Instead, she regarded it for a long moment and then reached in silence for her handbag on the floor beside her. As she bent down, her head for a moment out of sight, a look of pure glee appeared on the face of he who had put the banana there, an unruly boy called Melvin. His boon companion, a gawky lad named Ivan, could not resist a titter. The girls remained quiet but watchful.

Miss Wilkins took something that was now in her hand and placed it on the desk beside the banana.

It was an apple.

'I trust the symbolism of the fruit I have brought with me will not be lost on the class,' she began in her usual hortatory manner. 'We will come back to it presently when we discuss the undesirability of teenage pregnancy.'

'And the banana, miss?' said Melvin cheekily.

'A valuable source of potassium,' said Miss Wilkins, failing to blush as Melvin had hoped. 'Now, there are two things I wish to say first – one to the boys and one to the girls.'

'Girls first, miss, please,' said Tracy, a precocious blonde. She twirled the ends of some strands of her hair across her face, peeping out behind them in a provocative manner somewhat beyond her years. 'We're more important now.'

'The most valuable thing, then, that all girls need to know and remember,' said Miss Wilkins, adjusting her glasses, and leaving aside the question of the improvement in women's rights for the time being, 'is that the human male is not a monogamous animal.' She swung round in her chair and pointed. 'Perhaps Ivan will tell us what the word "monogamous" means.'

Ivan stumbled with some inaudible words for a while before having to admit that he did not know.

'I have met very few men who do,' said Miss

Wilkins briskly. 'Perhaps Marion can tell us?'

Marion was a sentimental little girl, inclined to think well of everyone and everything. 'Like it says in the Marriage Service, miss, keeping only to each other.'

'Not having it off with anyone else,' amplified Melvin.

'Swans mate for life,' offered Harry, the class swot.

'It's the other sort of birds that we want to know about, Harry,' Melvin sniggered. 'The two-legged sort.'

'Swans only have two legs,' began Harry combatively.

'Swans have relationships, too, don't they, miss?' an earnest girl called Dorinda put in. 'We had that in Classical History. There was someone called Leda and she . . .'

'So it is said, Dorinda,' said Miss Wilkins firmly, 'but I am afraid we are not dealing with myth and legend this afternoon. We are talking about established fact.'

'I've had three fathers,' said a pert girl at the back of the class. She paused for a moment's thought and then added, 'That's up to now . . .'

'I saw *Swan Lake* at Christmas,' put in another girl. 'The swan died. It was ever so sad, but lovely if you know what I mean.'

31

'Ugh, that's ballet for you,' said a boy at the back.

'But then he turned into a prince.'

'A poofter . . .' said the same boy.

'No,' said the girl seriously. 'A prince.'

'What I myself have also noticed,' said Miss Wilkins, leaving aside the distinction, 'is something that you girls will find very hard to take when it happens to you in later life, as it probably will.'

'Middle-aged spread?' offered a plump girl called Maureen. 'My mum says it's having babies that does it.'

'Although,' proceeded Miss Wilkins as if the girl had not spoken, 'it is not what I could call a natural law in the sense that the human male not being monogamous is one.' She coughed. 'I think I should call it more of a personal observation, though I understand it has been recorded in cats, too.' Her head shot up. 'Yes, Melvin, I am well aware that some men and some alley cats have a lot in common. You don't have to tell us.'

'What is it that we'll find hard to take, miss?' asked Dorinda anxiously.

'That when your husband of many years leaves you for a younger woman . . .'

'My father called it trading Mummy in for a younger model,' said Charlene, 'like you do with cars. I don't like her. He sells them anyway.'

'Cars or models?' asked Melvin.

'Model cars, I expect,' chimed in Ivan.

'Cars, silly,' said Charlene with composure.

'When he does that,' continued Miss Wilkins smoothly, 'I think you will find that what you are pleased to call the newer model will also be a woman rather further down the social totem pole than the one whom he married.'

'That fits my father's new wife to a T,' said Charlene, looking up at Miss Wilkins, surprised and respectful. 'My mum says she's just a toerag.'

Miss Wilkins paused and said pedantically, 'I cannot explain this phenomenon except that it is also noticeable in the behaviour of tomcats. They will mate first with a pedigree queen, have a litter or two . . .'

'Or four . . .' put in a boy.

'And then mate with any old stray tabby cat,' said Miss Wilkins calmly. 'I understand that having this second string to your bow is to do with the preservation of the species on the grounds that the progeny from the lower-scale alliance is likely to be tougher than that of the pedigree match.'

'Survival of the fittest,' said Harry. 'We did that in biology.'

'Hybrid vigour,' said a boy at the back.

'Darwin and the descent of man,' said a girl.

'We did that in religious studies,' somebody contradicted her.

'The Creation and all that . . .'

'My dad hadn't better have any more children . . .' exploded Charlene suddenly, light dawning. 'We're poor enough as it is.'

'However,' said Miss Wilkins firmly, 'your desertion by your husbands is still in the far future. Today we are concerned with the more immediate . . .'

'What is it that boys need to know?' interrupted a copper-haired boy, known throughout the school as Eric the Red.

'You won't like it,' said Miss Wilkins.

'Go on, miss,' urged a tall youth, grinning. 'We can take it.'

'Very well.' Miss Wilkins swept the class with her steady gaze. 'Boys need to know that in the mating game, in spite of what they think to the contrary, it is the girls who choose them.'

'No, they don't.' Melvin cast a glance in the direction of Tracy. Eyes cast down behind her long blonde hair, she responded only with an enigmatic smile. He said, 'I choose the girls I want.'

Miss Wilkins smiled, too. 'You think you do, Melvin. That's all.'

'And then you try to get them in the club,' said Charlene, regarding the boy without affection.

Harry glanced anxiously at Miss Wilkins, but she was leaning forward, looking interested. 'So what do you do then, Melvin?' she asked. 'After you've chosen them?'

He pushed his chest forward and his shoulders back and opened his mouth to speak.

'He tries to have his own way,' muttered a girl in the class first. 'More's the pity.'

'You don't have to let anyone do that,' said Miss Wilkins. 'It's a free country.'

'I show them who's boss,' bragged Melvin.

'But if you have a baby,' said another girl, 'you can get a council flat.'

'And benefit . . .' said Marion.

'That is not enough to see you through twenty years of solitary motherhood,' said Miss Wilkins. 'Financially or emotionally.'

'But they can't make you marry the father, can they, miss?' asked Dorinda.

'Would you want to?' enquired Miss Wilkins with interest.

Charlene favoured Melvin with a cold stare. 'Me, I wouldn't.'

'And would the marriage last if you did?'

'Not with some people it wouldn't,' said Charlene with spirit.

'You could be right there,' agreed Miss Wilkins. 'A boy who would do that to a girl isn't likely to cherish her for long, is he?'

Tracy came out from behind her hair long enough to take a cool look at Melvin.

'So what about the baby then?' asked Miss Wilkins.

The plump girl called Maureen shrugged her shoulders. 'You get to keep it if you want to, though I don't want to get fat . . .'

'You can always have it adopted,' said Tracy nonchalantly.

Miss Wilkins picked up the apple between her two cupped hands and held it out in front of her. She looked down at it without speaking for so long that the class began to get a little uneasy. Then she said softly, 'What do you suppose happens to you, Tracy, if you have a baby and then have it adopted – not what happens to the baby – but to you?'

'Dunno, miss.'

'Think.'

'Well . . . nothing, miss.'

'Can anybody else think of what happens to a girl who has a baby and then never sees it again?' Miss Wilkins looked round expectantly.

'You can always get to see it if you want to,' said Charlene.

'No,' Miss Wilkins corrected her. 'He or she can get to see you but only if it is their wish. Not if you want to.'

'Not never?'

'Never,' said Miss Wilkins, trying to remember who it was on the staff had the misfortune to be trying to teach the English language to this class. 'So how do you imagine you are going to get through the years aware that your son or daughter is growing up without even knowing what you look like?'

'I read a book where that happened,' remarked Dorinda. 'It was ever so sad. When the lady said "Dead and never called me Mother", I cried.'

'And,' went on Miss Wilkins, 'not knowing what your child – your own child – is called afterwards either . . .'

'You can name it, miss,' said another girl. 'They can't stop you doing that.'

'Adoptive parents can give a baby a new name,' said Miss Wilkins. 'You may call your daughter Belinda but they can change it to whatever they like.'

'That's not fair,' said Dorinda. 'I'm going to call my first baby Heather.'

'We're not talking about the baby, Dorinda. We're talking about you and just how you're going to feel as that baby grows up without you.'

37

'I wouldn't feel nothing, miss,' said Tracy.

'Oh, yes, you would,' declared Miss Wilkins energetically. 'Let me tell you that your heart will ache forever over that child. You will celebrate her every birthday in secret because you won't be there and because you won't like to tell your husband or other children or friends about her.' There was a distinct catch in her voice when she added, 'You, of all people, won't be there to see her grow up. You won't be there when she first goes to school, when she wins a race on sports day, when she goes to her first disco . . .'

Dorinda looked uncomfortable. 'Wouldn't you get a photograph, miss?'

'Not even when she got married,' said Miss Wilkins brokenly, beginning to cry. 'And she was such a lovely baby . . .' She got out a handkerchief and blew her nose. 'I called her Belinda, you know, and I never saw her again after the day she was taken for adoption.'

'Not ever?' asked Dorinda, beginning to cry, too.

'Never,' sobbed Miss Wilkins, stooping to pick up her handbag as a clanging sound reached them. 'Is that the bell? I-I must go now . . .'

The headmaster encountered Miss Wilkins as he came out of the governors' meeting. 'How

38

went it?' he said, being a man well versed in asking open-ended questions.

'Quite well, I think, Headmaster, thank you,' said Miss Wilkins composedly.

'Good, good,' he said, no wiser, but still curious.

'Although, of course, in the nature of things one never knows with teaching what has stuck and what hasn't until much later.'

'True,' he said, adding delicately, 'Might I ask how you handled the subject – just out of interest, you understand?'

'If I had had a text,' mused Miss Wilkins, 'you might say it was that old nursery rhyme "Georgie Porgie, pudding and pie, kissed the girls and made them cry".'

CARE PLAN

'It may be something or nothing, Inspector.'

Since there was no sensible reply to this statement Detective Inspector Sloan waited in silence for his superior officer to continue.

'And it's a very delicate matter, too,' added his superior officer. Actually it was a very superior officer who had called Sloan to his office: the assistant chief constable to boot.

Detective Inspector Sloan assumed an expression designed to project at one and the same time dispassionate interest and total discretion.

'A family matter, actually,' vouchsafed the assistant chief constable.

If the expression on his face slipped Sloan hoped it didn't show. All police activities were family matters somewhere; what could be very difficult were cases when police matters and the family matters of those in the police force came together. As a rule, resolving these fell unhappily somewhere between averting a conflict of interest and not conspiring to pervert the course of justice.

'My family,' said the assistant chief constable heavily.

This, at least, explained Sloan's summons to an office with a carpet rather than one with the workaday linoleum that did duty as floor-covering in the rest of the police station.

'Ah,' he said.

'Exactly,' said the senior policeman eagerly. 'I knew you'd understand, Inspector.'

'When you say "family", sir . . .'

'My uncle, Kenneth Linaker.'

'I see.' Detective Inspector Sloan searched for the right way of putting his next question. 'He must be a good age – at least . . .' he ventured tentatively, since the assistant chief constable himself was pretty near the top of the promotion tree and his uncle obviously thus older still, 'that is, sir, he can't be young . . .'

'Just hit eighty,' said the assistant chief constable.

'Ah,' said Sloan again. Crime was definitely age-related, weighted to the young – older offenders usually growing either less able or more cunning. 'Some old gentlemen,' he said delicately,

41

'can become quite uninhibited – disinhibited, I think it's called – especially in the presence of younger members of the opposite sex.'

'Nobody at the residential home he's in has complained of that,' said the assistant chief constable, adding simply, 'yet.'

'Quite so,' said Sloan.

This was promptly undermined by Kenneth Linaker's nephew adding, 'But I expect the carers know how to handle that sort of behaviour in old gentlemen.'

'I'm sure they do,' agreed Sloan warmly. An experienced carer was worth her weight in gold – although the gold offered was usually nearer the minimum wage than not.

'They're very good there although to be quite fair, he himself does think he's not in his right mind any longer.'

'And you?'

'Oh, I'm all right still, I think, Sloan, thank you – oh, sorry.' He gave a wintry smile. 'I thought for a moment you meant . . .'

'My mistake, sir,' said Sloan hastily.

'Me, I think Uncle's not too bad mentally all things considered.'

Detective Inspector Sloan, no fool, decided against enquiring what the all things were that had to be considered.

The assistant chief constable leant back in his chair and went on judiciously, 'Mind you, Sloan, that's not to say he hasn't been difficult enough in his time. Petulant, I'd call him. And sometimes a little unwise.'

'Quite so, sir.' He coughed. 'I think that we can all say this about our relations at some time or other. Old and young.'

The assistant chief constable nodded absently, his attention apparently centred on a crumpled sheet of paper on his desk before him.

'This problem, then, sir, might I enquire its nature?' Sloan, not understanding anything, felt he was on safe ground there. There must be a problem in the offing or he wouldn't have been sent for. And the assistant chief constable wouldn't be regarding something written on a piece of paper in front of him in the anxious way he was, either.

'Not as easy to quantify as you might think, Sloan,' said the assistant chief constable. He waved a hand. 'Oh, I know that nowadays you people are taught to identify the problems first and then tackle them . . .'

This was not strictly the case. Identifying problems was not too difficult an exercise: nor, most of the time, was solving them. What was difficult was producing the evidence. But Sloan said none of this. Instead he concentrated on listening carefully to the assistant chief constable, leaning forward slightly towards him and displaying the attention proper to the very senior policeman.

'All we have to hand,' said that officer, picking up the sheet of paper on his desk, 'is this care plan that was found by my cousin Candida stuffed under a cushion on a chair in his room – she's his youngest daughter – when visiting her father in the Berebury Residential Home. And it worried her so much that she brought it to me.'

'I'm not sure that I know anything about care plans, sir . . .' He did know quite a lot about unsatisfactory homes for the elderly, though, and even a little about the outcome of so-called pillow fights with the obstreperous old. And of the prescribing of a liquid cosh by a compliant medical attendant when all other calming measures had failed.

'I understand,' said the assistant chief constable, stressing the words, 'that in theory care plans are documents purporting to incorporate the needs of the individual patient within the proper running of the residential home under its statutory provisions and are subject to meeting the requirements of the particular social worker who has done the original assessment of the patient.'

'The Berebury Residential Home does have quite a good reputation,' said Sloan, shamelessly hedging his bets by going on, 'as such places go.'

'I know,' said Kenneth Linaker's nephew. 'That's why they chose it.'

'This care plan, sir . . .'

'Worrying, Sloan, that's what it is.' The assistant chief constable passed the document across his desk to the inspector at last. It was headed 'K.L.' 'As you'll see, there's lots of information on it. Medical history, race, religion, relatives – that sort of thing, but at least it's only got his initials at the top, which is something these days when everybody knows everything about everyone.' He sighed. 'I'm afraid nothing's really confidential any more.'

Detective Inspector Sloan knew that this sentiment actually related to a recent leaking of information to the local newspaper by someone at the police station – which was misconduct in a public office for which the perpetrator could go to prison – and tactfully changed the subject.

'Is the medical history relevant?' he asked, being a man used to hearing it advanced in court by the defence more often than not. Relevant or not, too.

'I suppose so. He's on one of those feminising hormones for his prostate trouble – makes him a bit tearful and so forth, which he doesn't like. They've got him down on this care plan thing as rather inclined to bewail his fate. Quite embarrassing for the old chap.'

'Naturally,' said Sloan. Side effects were downplayed by the medical profession in much the same way as statistics were by politicians. When it suited them. In both cases.

'He thinks it's womanly . . .'

'This care plan – you said it worried your cousin,' suggested Sloan to hurry matters along.

'I'll say,' said the assistant chief constable. 'And not without reason.' He paused reflectively. 'Sensible girl, Candida, even though . . .'

'Though?' said Sloan into the little silence that had fallen.

'Though she upset the old fellow a bit when she wouldn't have him to stay with her.'

'A bit?'

'Well, a lot really.' The assistant chief constable looked uncomfortable. 'If you must know, Sloan, he cut her out of his will. And they've got all that down, too, in their wretched care plan. See, there, where it says "Execs", G and R. There's no mention of Candida at all.'

'I see.' As far as Sloan was concerned, where there was a will there was a relative. Or three. As well as executors.

'It was when he got too old to live alone. Frail and all that. His other two daughters – Geraldine and Rebecca . . .'

'G and R,' divined Sloan.

'That's right. Well, they tried looking after him in their own homes in turn . . .'

'But not Candida?'

'Not Candida. Said she would do her duty but that she wasn't cut out for that sort of thing.'

'I see.'

'But it got too much for the other two after a bit. He took to wandering, you know.'

'As they do,' said Sloan, who'd been on the beat in his day and thus knew quite a lot about the demented elderly who will stray in spite of everyone's best efforts to stop them.

'Frightened them by disappearing one night in the middle of a thunderstorm. That was the last straw as far as the two sisters were concerned.'

'I quite understand,' said Sloan. And he did. Unbiddable children were a sore trial to their parents but unbiddable parents, clinging to the last vestiges of their waning authority, could be an even sorer trial to their adult offspring. Role reversal, in his view, was only really acceptable at staff parties or in hospital on Christmas Day. 'Very worrying for you all.'

'That was when they thought he'd be better

off in a home. And it is a good one, although they do tend to have very young staff there from time to time. Girl students from the university in the vacation and so forth.'

'I'm sorry, sir, but I still don't see quite . . .'

'My cousins wouldn't contribute to his maintenance at first – at least, Geraldine and Rebecca wouldn't, even though he'd already given them half his kingdom so to speak.' He shook his head sadly and pointed to the care plan. 'That's all down there, too.'

'Not the sort of thing that should be put about in the home,' observed Sloan.

'It's causing no end of trouble in the family, I can tell you, because Uncle's not really rich any more and my wife and I have – er – a full quiver ourselves and can't really help, much as we would like to, of course.'

'Of course, sir. I quite understand.' Detective Inspector Sloan, with a wife and son and a mortgage to support, did not go into the question of what constituted 'really rich'. In his experience, to most people 'really rich' just meant someone with more money than they themselves had.

Instead, he cast his eye down the care plan and saw that 'family dissension, big time' had been duly listed. 'I can see that things must be difficult, sir,' he said. 'But, at least, all that that we're reading here seems to be true, so . . .'

'That's not all of it,' said the assistant chief constable hollowly. 'Go on.'

Detective Inspector Sloan took a firmer grip of the care plan and continued reading. 'Ah, I see what you mean, sir. There are what you might call – er – considerable complications.'

'I'd call them something else,' said the assistant chief constable forthrightly. 'And downright dangerous.'

'You mean this note about G and R being rather too attached to someone put down here as E.G.?' Sloan gave him an interrogative look.

'The Residential Home Manager,' said the assistant chief constable shortly. 'Must be. Name of Gwent. Edward Gwent. Personable chap. Very.'

'Both of them? G and R?'

'They've always been able to raise sibling rivalry to a fine art, those two,' sighed their cousin. 'I'm quite sorry for the fellow myself.'

'If it's him.'

'There's nobody else there with his initials,' said the assistant chief constable. 'I've checked. Quietly, of course.'

'Of course.'

'And having an affair is not a crime,' pointed out the older man.

'No, of course not.' Sloan didn't want to go into what it was. Not here and now.

He sighed. 'There's another complication, Sloan.'

'Sir?'

'Their husbands.'

'I can see that they would have a view . . .'

'A view!' snorted the assistant chief constable. 'You can say that again. Geraldine's husband is all right but I must say that Rebecca's is a bit of a pain.'

Detective Inspector Sloan, working policeman, wasn't listening. He'd just seen the last note on the care plan. It had been added in pencil. He read it aloud now. 'Sir, this says "G is going to kill R before the end".'

'I know. You do see why we're so worried, Sloan, don't you?'

'Yes, sir.' From force of habit he turned the page over. There was something written there, too.

'That, you see, Sloan, is the bit that's worrying us,' said the assistant chief constable. 'About G going to kill R.'

'Oh, I don't think you should worry too much, sir,' said Sloan easily. He handed back the care plan to his superior officer and leant back in his chair. 'I think you should see what's written on the back.'

Puzzled, the assistant chief constable said, 'I did earlier, Sloan, but I couldn't make anything of it.' He quoted it aloud. 'It says "We have seen the best of our time". Make a good motto for a residential care home, of course, but that's not what you mean, is it?'

'No, sir.' He frowned as a memory of some long-ago English literature homework came back to him. 'I don't think I can remember the rest of the quotation.'

'Quotation?' The assistant chief constable stared at him.

'I think it goes on "machinations, hollowness, treachery, and all ruinous disorders, follow us disquietly to our graves" but I can't be sure, sir.' He'd once heard a prosecution counsel quote it in a nasty case of fraud.

'That's from Shakespeare's *King Lear*,' said the assistant chief constable, sitting up. 'We did him.'

'So did we, sir. Not a good play for the young.' The unutterable sadness of the witless king had lasted with Sloan long after he'd left the classroom.

The assistant chief constable tapped the tattered care plan. 'A send-up, then. With K.L. standing for King Lear . . .'

'Not Kenneth Linaker,' Sloan reminded him. 'And no, not a send-up.'

51

'And C for Cordelia, G for Goneril and R for Regan,' said the other man, not listening. 'Not my uncle and cousins at all.'

'Not a send-up, sir,' he repeated. 'A precis.'

'By one of those students earning an honest penny there,' divined the assistant chief constable, slapping his thigh.

'Someone else's homework, I would say,' offered Sloan.

'But not ours,' said the assistant chief constable, suddenly jovial. 'Candida should just put this back where she found it and say no more. I'll tell her.'

'And the rest,' misquoted Detective Inspector Sloan, 'should be silence.'

SLEEPING DOGS, LYING

'Tickets, please.' The call resounded down the rocking railway carriage. 'Have your tickets ready . . . tickets, please.'

Alice Osgathorp reached for her handbag and got out two rail tickets. As she handed them over to the ticket collector she pointed further down the train and said, 'My husband's in the buffet car. You can't miss him. He's a little short man.'

The ticket collector nodded, punched both tickets and continued on his way. Alice settled back in her seat and began to relax and enjoy the passing scenery. It was a very real relief to be on her own now and she relished the peace. Nobody could have ever called home-life in Acacia Avenue, Berebury, peaceful. Not when Frank was around and constantly berating her for this or that – it didn't seem to matter what she did, he always found fault with it.

When, much later on that day, she proffered two tickets from Calais to Corbeaux, via Avignon, to the ticket collector on the French train she had much the same exchange with him as she had had on the English one.

But in French.

'*Mon mari est dans le wagon-restaurant, monsieur. C'est un homme peu grand.*' She realised too late that she should have said '*de petite taille*' – of small stature – rather than '*peu grand*', not that the French conductor seemed to have noticed. On reflection, though, she thought that although '*peu grand*' was a bit negative it described him much better than '*of small stature*'. Frank was a little man in every respect, but especially in the way in which he behaved. Small-minded, too.

She sighed and supposed she should have been more tolerant than she had been. The trouble was, like a lot of short men, he was always throwing his weight about, making her feel lower than a pig's trotter. And forever being critical about her lack of attention to detail. Well, he wasn't going to be able to say that again. She was pretty sure she'd thought of everything, absolutely everything.

As the train pulled out of Lille station she decided that 'Little Corporal' described him best of all. But small-minded, as well, she reminded herself as she settled comfortably back in her seat, prepared to enjoy the views of the French countryside and the unaccustomed pleasure of being on her own.

There was no doubt about the small-mindedness, or that her husband took a perverse pleasure in drawing attention to her shortcomings in public. That was what she found hardest to bear – and to forgive. She knew she wasn't as clever as he was even though she had held a job down all these years – but it didn't need trumpeting to all and sundry on every possible occasion.

It was his retirement that had driven her to take action: the thought of having him in the house whenever she came in was more than she could bear. 'I married him for better or worse,' she quoted to herself, 'but not for lunch.'

This long-planned French holiday had been to celebrate the beginning of that retirement of his. Well, in a way it was going to. She, of course, would have to go on working. Not that she minded. She quite enjoyed the companionship of her fellow workers and work was somewhere where she was properly appreciated.

At the Hotel Coq d'Or in the Rue Dr Jacques Colliard in Corbeaux she signed the register for

Frank and herself and said he would be along in a minute with the rest of the luggage. And, yes, please, she – they – would prefer to have their breakfast in their room every morning. It had been a very long journey. 'Dinner? No, I mean – *merci, madame,*' she said to the patronne, 'we will be eating out in the town tonight.'

Actually she didn't go out at all that evening but instead ate a picnic she had brought with her in her room. A light supper would help her eat two breakfasts the next morning. She spent the next day exploring the little town, having a cup of coffee here and a light lunch there, going into one church here and a *lanterne des morts* there and the little shops all the time.

In the late afternoon she came across a group of men playing pétanque in the shade of some lime trees. There was a seat for spectators set alongside the piste and she sat there as long as the play lasted, fascinated first by the glint of the steel balls and the balletic movements of the players, and then quite taken by the intricacies of the game itself.

The men taking part were not tall, either, but, unlike Frank, didn't seem to be given to cutting others down to size. It was the game that did that, of course, getting their boule nearer to the jack – *le cochonnet*, they called it – than anyone else's being no easy matter.

For the first week this became the pattern of her days and very agreeable she found it, too. A trip to the street market for fresh fruit, followed by a quiet sit alone by the piste, watching the games, suited her very well.

She could mull over the past without Frank standing over her, being critical, eternally finding fault. The name Hector would have suited him better than Frank but, oddly enough, she always thought of him as a latter-day Ahasuerus, the king who put his wife, Vashti, away because she would not display herself for the aggrandisement of himself and his court.

Most people, she thought idly, were all too ready to praise the king's second queen, Esther, for her good work, but Alice had always admired Vashti, Ahasuerus's first wife, all the more for refusing to bow to her husband's will. It was something that she, Alice Osgathorp, had always found difficult.

Until now, that is. At least Frank had never been able to fault her knowledge of the Old Testament and he hadn't known anything at all about her careful studies of plant poisons. Or of her purchase in the faraway town of Luston of the largest dog kennel she could find.

Only once was her reverie at the piste disturbed: this was when she had been joined by another Englishwoman, also on holiday.

'My husband says it's better than bowls,' Alice said to her, waving vaguely at the crowd of middle-aged men playing there. 'He always said he was going to take up bowls when he retired and now he has. French bowls.' She gave a light laugh. 'He's even taken to wearing a beret.'

'You're lucky,' said the other woman sourly. 'I can't get mine out of the bars, not nohow.'

'I must say my Frank likes his wine, too,' she said moderately. 'Especially the local ones – the ones that don't travel well. He says their Vin de Laboureur here is the best and we never ever see that in England.'

'I've always thought that they kept the best wines for themselves,' sniffed the other woman before taking herself off in search of her bibulous husband.

Actually Frank, Alice had to concede in his favour, wasn't a real drinker. Come to that he wasn't a real anything. Just as some men were just a bag of tools, so he was only a bag of grumbles for whom nothing was right – not ever. Unless, she amended the thought judiciously, he'd thought of it himself first. And then, of course, there was nothing ever wrong with it at all – ever. It was just as well that he'd been self-employed . . .

Alice had planned to stay at the Hotel Coq d'Or for at least another week but then luck provided an agreeable touch of verisimilitude. She had located the village cemetery and went there one morning with her camera. There must have been a recent death in Corbeaux because two men were digging a grave there.

Rightly deciding that any French workmen worthy of their salt would have an extended luncheon at midday, she stayed in the vicinity until they downed tools. Then she went back there with her camera and took some shots of the open grave.

She had a nasty moment when she got back to the hotel that evening and asked for the key of their bedroom.

The patronne gave her a keen look as she handed it over. 'Madame and monsieur are enjoying their *vacances*, I hope?' she said.

'Indeed, we are,' said Alice warmly. She patted her camera. 'It is so pretty here and I have taken many pictures already and as for my husband . . .' She let her voice trail away.

'Yes, madame?'

She gave a light laugh. 'He is enjoying playing pétanque and . . .' She hesitated and then said delicately, 'And what comes afterwards. You have so many bars here to choose from that he doesn't get back to the hotel as early as I would like. I have to stay awake to let him in our room.'

'I understand,' the woman flashed her teeth, a symphony of gold fillings, and smiled in quick sympathy. 'In the winter we call it *l'après-ski* but in the summer it is just the thirst from the heat of the day.'

'I do hope he doesn't disturb anyone when he gets back late,' she said.

'Nobody has complained, madame,' said the patronne, that being her measure of most things.

'That's a relief.' Alice looked suitably sorrowful as she added, 'I'm afraid he's got quite fond of drinking something here you can't get so easily in England.'

The hotel-keeper lifted her head in silent query.

'Pastis,' said Alice in a lowered voice. '*Sans eau.*' Édouard Manet's famous painting *Absinthe Drinker* was what had come to her mind but she didn't know if you could buy absinthe now. It had been different in 1858.

'Ah.' The woman drew in her breath in a sharp hiss. 'Pastis *sans eau.*'

'But,' said Alice bravely, 'I'm so enjoying exploring your lovely little town on my own.'

60

Actually there were one or two more pictures on her agenda still to be taken and she proposed to make her way to the cemetery to do so the very next day. It was strange, she noted subconsciously, how stilted her English became when talking to the French. 'We shall have many happy mementoes of our visit,' she added, again patting her camera. '*Très joli.*'

'It is indeed *très pittoresque* here,' said the patronne, flashing the improbable teeth again. 'Corbeaux is a famous old bastide town, you know.'

Alice returned to the cemetery the next morning and took several general views of the ornate gravestones there. The polished marble should come up very well in the photograph, she decided, before adding a couple of pictures of the views towards the mountains, taking care to include several cypress trees. 'Sad cypresses,' she murmured to herself, although she didn't feel sad. Only surprisingly exhilarated.

In the afternoon she found the local undertaker's shop and bought a couple of funeral vases – stout stone things – and an ornate creation of artificial flowers under glass known to the French as *éternelles*, but no longer permitted in an English graveyard. These she took to the cemetery, added some flowers, and photographed them on the base of a black marble tomb of a couple, long dead, called Henri Georges and Clothilde Marie, taking care, though, not include the headstone in her picture. She spent the rest of the day back at the pétanque piste, debating whether forging someone's death could be considered pseudocide: or, if not, what then?

Alice Osgathorp checked out of the hotel four days later. She did it in the middle of the afternoon – that secure hour when the little *femme de chambre* was taking the place of the patronne while the latter was, as usual, enjoying her postprandial doze.

'Monsieur will be bringing the luggage down soon,' she lied to the uninterested girl at the desk as she paid the bill for Frank and herself. At least money wasn't going to be one of her worries in future. Not only was everything in their joint names, but Frank had never believed in life assurance for the self-employed. She didn't suppose any government would mind if he didn't collect his old-age pension. 'Nothing to beat cash in hand,' he used to say, salting large notes away in biscuit boxes. 'The rats can't get at that and it always buys what you want.'

Two days after that, back home again, she telephoned the Berebury Pet Cemetery.

'I've just lost my dear old dog,' she quavered,

'and I would so like to have him buried properly.'

'No problem, madam,' the owner of Berebury's Pet Cemetery assured her. 'Here at what we like to think of the Elysian Fields we do everything properly.'

'The trouble is,' went on Alice tremulously, 'he was a very big dog.'

'That's not a problem,' said the man, adding rather too quickly, 'although it might cost a little bit more.'

'Of course, I quite understand that,' she hastened on, saying anxiously, 'but there is just one thing . . .'

'Yes?' said the cemetery owner. Nothing – but nothing – about the requests made by bereaved pet-owners had the power to surprise him any longer.

'I'd like him to be buried in his own kennel – at least,' she corrected herself swiftly, 'in a coffin made from the wood of his kennel. We thought he'd like that.'

'I'm sure he would,' said the man immediately, only glad she wasn't asking as some of his customers did for the canine equivalent of *pompe funèbre*. 'That's not a problem either, madam, although if it means a lot more digging that might come out a little more expensive, too.'

'Nothing's too good for him,' said Alice

brokenly. 'Besides with a Great Dane you have to get used to everything costing a bit more than you would with a Pekinese.'

The man, who had known owners almost bankrupt themselves over Pekes, said he quite understood, trying to work out the while how much he could charge for the burial – and then adding a bit. 'Would next Tuesday afternoon do you?' he asked. 'That'll give us time to dig the gr . . . get everything ready.'

'Tuesday will be fine,' said Alice. 'I'll arrange the minivan now.' She cleared her throat. 'You won't think me silly if I bring some flowers?'

'You can bring whatever you like, lady,' he said, mentally adding a little more still to the bill. They liked sentimental owners at the Berebury Pet Cemetery.

On the Tuesday, Alice wore black with touches of grey. She'd been doing that ever since she got home to lend a touch of mourning to her tale of Frank's sudden death abroad. The photographic views of the cemetery at Corbeaux had been shared with her friends at work and a generous employer had given her some compassionate leave 'while she sorted everything out'.

The minicab driver helped her with the dog kennel, now knocked into coffin-shape. Actually, that had been the most difficult part of the whole business, but eventually she'd found a sympathetic old carpenter in distant Calleford, to whom she had told her tale of losing her dog.

'Dog-lover, myself,' he'd said. 'How big was this old chap that's got to go in here?'

'Big. Eight stone and a bit. That was before he was ill, of course,' said Alice. This last at least was true even if – so to speak – the dog it was that didn't die. 'About, say, hundred and ten pounds, that is.' Kilograms were beyond her.

The cemetery owner received the coffin with practised compassion.

'And what about a stone?' Alice asked the man at the cemetery after the interment was complete. 'I should like him to have a stone.'

'No problem,' the man, pocketing her cheque. 'Just let me know what you want putting on it.'

'His name,' she sniffed.

'Which was?' He was a man inured to tears. Somewhere in his office, he'd even got a box of tissues.

'Hamlet, of course,' she said, sounding pained. 'I told you he was a Great Dane, remember.'

'Sorry.' He tried to make amends. 'And the inscription? A lot of people put "Thy servant, a dog". From Kipling, I think someone said it was. It's very popular.'

'I would like something from Shakespeare's *Hamlet*,' she said austerely.

'Fine.' In his time he'd had to put amateur verse on stones. 'We charge by the number of letters.'

'It's the words at the end of the play . . .'

'Which are?' He'd never liked doing English at school.

'"The rest is silence".'

She thought it would be, too.

QUICK ON THE DRAW

Jane steered their little car carefully into the car park of the Berebury Flying Club and switched off the engine.

Peter made no move to get out of the passenger seat. 'There's no hurry,' he said, leaning back. 'We're early anyway.'

'Better than being late,' said Jane briskly.

'I think we're actually the first here,' said Peter, looking round the empty car park and then over at the planes standing silent on the tarmac.

'All the more time to check your kit before you jump,' said Jane, turning her head to look at him.

He was still sitting in the passenger seat, his head sunk now between his hands. 'I can't go through with it, Jane,' he said and groaned. 'I just can't.'

'I don't see how you can very well change

your mind,' she said. 'Not now.' She sighed and added, 'Not without causing a lot of trouble all round.'

'It's never too late to change your mind,' he came back quickly.

Too quickly.

'And if you do?' she said not unreasonably. 'What then? Had you thought about what would happen next? It won't be any better tomorrow.' She turned her head as another car drove into the airport car park and came to a stop a little way away. 'Look, here comes the first arrival.'

A young man got out of the other car and gave them a casual wave as he walked off towards the Flying Club's hut. Peter gave the other driver a wan smile as he returned the wave. 'That's our pilot.'

'He's not very old, is he?' said Jane anxiously.

'Parachuting's a young man's sport,' said Peter.

'I suppose so,' she said doubtfully.

He gave her a little smile. 'And pilots are usually on the young side. Those that go in for sport, anyway.' He stopped speaking suddenly, a spasm crossing his face. His whole bearing changed and he sank his head back between his hands. 'Oh, God, Jane, I really don't think I can go through with it after all.'

'Yes, you can,' she said quietly. 'You must, in fact, or you'll always regret it.'

'There's no must about it . . .'

'There is,' she countered. 'Once you've said you will. Besides . . .'

'There's our instructor arriving.' He lifted his head briefly and pointed out a tousle-haired fellow, already kitted out in his flying suit, walking across the car park from a lively looking four-by-four. 'Hell of a nice fellow.'

'So's Mr Murgatroyd,' she remarked.

'I know, I know. Wouldn't hurt a fly,' he said with more than a touch of sarcasm. 'They always say that.'

'No need to be like that,' she said lightly, touching his shoulder as she spoke.

'Well, you know how I feel about him, don't you?'

She sighed. 'I do, but I'm sure there's no need. You've just got to be brave and screw yourself up to it.'

'It's all very well for you to sit there and say that,' he began heatedly, subsiding again suddenly, sinking his head back between his hands. 'Oh, God, I do feel awful.'

'It won't take a minute,' she said.

'That's got nothing to do with it,' he said.

'Yes, it has,' she came back at him. 'At least they

don't say that to you when you're having a baby.'

'I'm sorry,' he apologised. 'I'm being a bit of a baby myself, aren't I?'

'A lot of people do find it frightening,' she said. 'I know that. Especially the first time.'

'That does make it worse,' he agreed.

He waved at another arrival – a girl who was clambering at out of a snazzy red sports car. 'There's Shirley turning up as usual. She's the club's star performer.'

Jane gave the young woman a considering look. 'Got the figure for it, hasn't she?'

He smiled for the first time. 'They don't like you to be too heavy when you jump.'

'I can understand that.'

'She's done it dozens of times, of course.'

'Practice makes perfect,' said Jane. 'Come to think about it, Peter, Mr Murgatroyd must have done it hundreds of times.'

'Don't,' he groaned. 'I don't even like to think about it. Especially now.'

'Think how much better you'll feel when it's all over.'

'People always say that when it's not them who've got something nasty ahead of them.'

'That's true,' she admitted candidly, 'but then so is what they say about feeling better afterwards. It's true, too.'

'That doesn't help much though, does it, when you've still got to go through with it yourself,' he said.

'I suppose not,' she said, leaning over and nestling her head near his. 'My poor love, I hate to see you like this, I really do, but you've got to face up to it, you know. You can't go on like this.'

'It's not so bad some of the time,' he insisted.

'Darling, don't start that again. We've been over all that before.' She glanced across the airfield. 'Why don't you just go into the clubhouse and talk to somebody.'

'No one's all that chatty before a jump.'

'I'm not surprised.'

'Besides, you have to concentrate on checking your kit.'

'I should hope so, too,' she said sternly. 'Mistakes aren't going to get you anywhere at twenty thousand feet.'

Peter essayed a small smile for the first time. 'I agree. The penalties for failure are severe. Don't worry, I've checked my chute half a dozen times already.'

'And the reserve one?'

'And the reserve one.'

'But is anyone going to check that you've had no sleep for the last two nights?'

'No,' he said wearily, 'but perhaps I'll get some tonight.'

'Perhaps,' she said dryly. 'But only if . . .'

'Look, there's someone over there waving to me,' he said swiftly. 'That means it's time to go.' He opened the car door and slipped out, grabbing his parachute. 'They like you to check over all your kit in front of them before you take off.'

'Quite right, too.' She switched on the ignition as he closed the door behind him. 'I'll be on my way, then.'

'Better not kiss me . . .' he said.

'No, I understand.' She turned the engine on. 'Now, remember, I'll be back here to collect you at two-thirty.'

'I'm not likely to forget, am I?'

'Good,' she said firmly. 'Because you're Mr Murgatroyd's last patient and dentists don't like to be kept waiting – especially when it's for an extraction.'

1666 AND ALL THAT

Henry Tyler drifted, as was often his wont at lunchtime, across Green Park and then made his way into St James's Street. His destination, The Mordaunt Club, was discreetly tucked away behind the much more important buildings near there. It was well hidden. The club's nameplate was so unobtrusive as to deceive most casual passers-by into thinking it was in fact a commercial venture a little ashamed of having its being in such an august region of the country's capital.

'Morning, Mr Tyler, sir,' said the hall porter as he stepped through the door. The club itself was exclusive enough for the hall porter to recognise all its members at sight even though it was open to all those of a similar cast of mind to Sir John Mordaunt, fifth baronet, except, that is, for active politicians of any – or, indeed, of no – party. This reservation was because Sir John, (1643–1721), although an assiduous Member of Parliament himself in his day, had promised to vote in the House according to the promptings of reason and good sense.

The hall porter took a quick look at the pigeonholes ranked behind him. 'No messages for you today, sir.'

'Splendid,' said Henry warmly. In his line of country (he worked at the Foreign Office) and at this anxious time in European history (the late 1930s) the absence of messages could only be a good thing. Unfortunately most of those that he was receiving these days were exceedingly worrying ones for a man in his particular profession.

The porter went on to cast a swift glance down at the big diary open on his counter. 'Would you be expecting any guests today, sir? I don't think I've got a note . . .'

'Not today, Bill,' said Henry. 'Today I'm my own man.' With the numerous responsibilities attendant on Henry's present position in the Foreign Office, this was a rare treat and he intended to relish it.

'And shall you be lunching with any other members, sir?'

Henry shook his head. 'No, I'll be at the Long Table this morning.'

The Long Table at the Mordaunt Club was an old tradition. If any member didn't propose to eat at the club with other members by prearrangement or with guests, then – by a time-honoured convention – he sat at the Long Table at the far end of the dining room next to whomsoever happened to be sitting there already.

As a system it worked very well in that members often met other members whom they might not have otherwise encountered, but its greatest boon was that this encouraged courteous conversation rather than shop talk. Henry could do without shop talk.

'Oh, it's you, Tyler,' said the only other man sitting at the Long Table, his countenance brightening at once. 'Good to see you.'

'Morning, Ferguson,' responded Henry amiably. He knew Edward Ferguson slightly – he'd met him once or twice before at the club. If he remembered rightly, the man worked for another government department – the one so secret that none dared speak its name: hence its ironic nickname of "The Department of Invisible Men".' He said, 'And how's the world with you these days?'

'Just the man I wanted to see,' said Ferguson, ignoring this pleasantry. 'You're at the Foreign Office, aren't you, Tyler?'

Henry admitted to this with a certain amount of caution. Dealing with Herr Joachim von Ribbentrop was a full-time job these days. He didn't want to know about any extra problems, especially arcane ones from Ferguson's arcane department.

His fellow diner didn't hesitate for a moment. 'So you must be good at history then . . .'

'I don't think it follows,' Tyler temporised, although there were those in his ministry who were now regretting more than ever the activities of Lord North in relation to the American Colonies. It looked as though before long Britain was again going to need reinforcements from the other side of the Atlantic.

'What does 1666 mean to you?' asked Ferguson, pulling a piece of paper out of a waistcoat pocket.

'Fire of London,' responded Henry promptly. 'And to you?' he added politely.

'Incendiary bombs,' growled Ferguson.

'Ah . . .' said Henry, sighing. 'I'm afraid you could be right.'

'Although one of our people is a bit of an expert on the German Liquid Fire at Hooge – you know, when they sprayed jets of flame out of fire hoses in July '15.'

'As I remember,' mused Henry, whose own

ministry was regrettably full of old soldiers fighting old battles, 'the Fire of London was started by a careless baker in Pudding Lane.'

'I think this one's going to be started by a paper-hanger in Berlin,' said Ferguson, 'but the date 1666 – if it is a date, and we don't even know that yet – isn't the whole story. Unfortunately there's a bit of text that's a little less easy to pin down.'

'Codes and ciphers,' murmured Henry largely, 'are really getting out of hand these days.'

'If it had been all in numbers it would have been a mite easier for our code-breakers,' said Ferguson. 'You can do a lot with numbers and a decent cipher book.'

'I'm sure.' This was something that no member of the Foreign Office needed telling. Diplomatic bags were only theoretically secure and King's Messengers only safe couriers while actually alive. He helped himself to a bread roll from the basket on the table.

'Even with just numbers,' said Ferguson, 'and without a cipher book you can usually get somewhere if you put your mind to it.'

Henry Tyler nodded. They knew all about making bricks without straw at the Foreign Office, too.

'Besides, we were expecting this particular

message from our man in . . . never mind where –
to come in numbers,' went on Ferguson. 'It's two
particular numbers we want.' He grimaced. 'And,
Tyler, there's no need for me to tell you, we want
'em pretty badly. And the sooner the better.'

'So 1666 isn't one of them?' deduced Henry
intelligently.

'Our people think not.' Ferguson frowned.
'That's because the figures 1666 seem more of
a signature to the piece rather than part of the
story.'

'And that's not his – er – works number so to
speak?'

'It is not,' said Ferguson firmly. 'In spite of
what the general public may think our department
is not overmanned to the extent of having over
sixteen hundred employees.'

'Is this problem message of yours in English?'
enquired Henry idly. 'Ah, here's our waiter . . .'

Sir John Mordaunt had also put good food
high on his list of priorities, causing supplies
of game, pickled bacon, cheese and such-like
country fare to be dispatched to London from
his estate in the Midlands while Parliament was
sitting.

'I'll have the beef,' said Henry to the waiter,
eyeing the sirloin on the serving trolley. 'Medium
rare, please.'

Edward Ferguson opted for Barnsley lamb chops. 'English words,' he said when the waiter had departed, 'but it's just a meaningless list to anyone who reads them.'

'And meant to be meaningless to everybody except your department, I take it?' Henry Tyler knew he could ask this with impunity. There was a long tradition at the Mordaunt Club that that which was spoken there between members was as sacrosanct as the confessional. It was an unbroken history of total discretion that was implicit rather than having been enjoined upon the members, and very much in the tradition of the seventeenth-century country gentleman after whom the club was named.

'Exactly, but even our best brains can't get anywhere with it,' agreed Ferguson mournfully. 'All it seems to be is the names of some birds – our man was meant to be birdwatching, that was his cover – with a fox thrown in.'

Henry nodded. 'I heard that you'd snatched one or two of them from under our noses.'

'Birds?'

'Best brains,' said Henry.

'We trawl the colleges like everyone else,' said Edward Ferguson a trifle defensively.

'The women's colleges now, too, it seems,' said Henry. Women had never been admitted to the Mordaunt Club but he could see that at this rate it was going to be difficult to keep them out. If they were welcome in Edward Ferguson's department, let alone his own ministry, there ought to be a place for them at the Mordaunt Club too.

'You must admit that women perform this sort of work extraordinarily well, Tyler,' said Edward Ferguson, giving himself away by saying plaintively, 'Their minds do leap about so.'

'You mean that their minds make connections that don't occur to mere males,' agreed Henry sagely.

'So take this message then . . .' began Edward Ferguson again, waving his piece of paper in the air.

'Don't do that, Ferguson,' pleaded Henry, wincing. 'The Prime Minister's waving about of his famous piece of paper at Heston aerodrome is quite bad enough as it is. Go down in history, that will.'

'Sorry.' Ferguson glanced round. 'I'll read it out to you instead.' He placed the message on the table mat before him and read aloud, 'The first line goes "Ravens, widgeon, dotterel, collared dove", and the second line is "Mallard". . .'

'Beef,' said the waiter, appearing at Henry's elbow. 'With Yorkshire pudding, sir?'

Henry agreed to Yorkshire pudding. 'Go on, Ferguson.'

'There's just the fox with the mallard . . .'

'Funny, that,' mused Henry. 'Tell me, what sort of order of numbers are you waiting for?'

'Low thousands. At least,' he lowered his voice, 'I hope they're low. Otherwise . . .' He did not elaborate on this but opened his hands in an age-old gesture of despair and sighed deeply.

The man from the Foreign Office gave an understanding nod. Much was routinely left unsaid there, too.

'And I can assure you, Tyler, this isn't one of those so-called intelligence tests where you have to pick the odd one out in a sequence,' said Edward Ferguson with all the authority of one who knew that intelligence was not the only requirement of his department. Physical and mental sturdiness counted for more than brains in the Department of Invisible Men.

'But we do, don't we?' murmured Henry. 'Have to pick the odd one out, I mean.'

Ferguson looked anxious. 'You think that that's the only thing we've got to go on, do you?'

'One of the things,' said Henry.

Edward Ferguson sat up. 'There's something else, then? What have we missed?'

'I'm not sure,' said Henry slowly, 'but I think

there's something out of kilter about having a collared dove there.'

'It's a bird, isn't it?' said Ferguson, a touch of truculence creeping into his manner.

'It's a variety of bird,' said Henry, putting the truculence down to a combination of hunger and worry. 'What I would like to know is why it isn't just a plain dove?'

'There's a lot of symbolism attached to doves . . .' began Ferguson.

'It's a good deal too late now for ones bearing olive branches in their beaks,' growled Henry, upon whom even mention of the word 'appeasement' had begun to have a deleterious effect, 'if that's what you've got in mind.'

'No, I'm sure it's too late for anything like that,' assented Ferguson gloomily. He hitched a shoulder. 'One of your Foreign Office people was into birds, wasn't he?'

'Edward, Viscount Grey of Fallodon,' replied Henry promptly. 'Found them very restful after international diplomacy.'

'I don't find these birds at all restful,' said Ferguson pointedly.

'And a fox among the chickens is always dangerous in any shape or form,' said Henry absently. 'What is it about the word "fox" that makes it needed there, I wonder?'

'If he'd just wanted the letter *x* he could have said "waxwing",' said Ferguson, demonstrating that the message had already received quite a lot of attention in his own department, 'and kept to birds.'

'Your Barnsley chops, sir,' intervened the waiter, placing a plate in front of the member.

'What's that? Oh, thank you . . .' Ferguson's mind was clearly far away. 'So he must have wanted the *f* or the *o* to be in the message.'

'Or not wanted the rest of "waxwing",' said Henry. At the Foreign Office they always had to explore every possibility.

'That doesn't explain "collared", though,' said Edward Ferguson, applying himself to his chops with alacrity. 'He's got two *l*s in mallard already if that's what he wanted.'

'Back to your intelligence tests,' said Henry lightly. 'What is in "fox" and "collared" that isn't in "waxwing"?'

'I never was any good at riddles,' complained Ferguson.

'Or is in "waxwing" that isn't in "fox"?' said Henry, continuing the riddle theme.

'If *x* marks the spot, that is,' said Edward Ferguson, beginning at last to enter into the spirit of the chase. He was making short work of his chops.

'So why "fox" instead of "waxwing", if it was an *x* that was wanted?' mused Henry. 'There must be a reason.'

'Oh, yes,' said Ferguson, 'there'll be a reason, all right. Our man's a bright enough fellow. A Classical scholar, actually. We got him from . . . well, never mind where we got him from, except to say that they weren't at all pleased to lose him. Where he is now is what matters and in theory he's birdwatching somewhere in Eastern Europe, binoculars and all.'

'Which is why the message had to come *en clair*, I suppose,' divined Henry. 'Anything too obviously in code mightn't have got through.'

'Exactly.' Ferguson looked thoughtful. 'Besides, there's always the possibility that the fellow has had to dump his code book. As a last resort, of course, but sometimes the safest thing to do is to destroy it on the spot. We understand that.'

'Better than letting anyone else get their hands on it.' Henry chewed his beef for a while in thoughtful silence. 'Did your people find any other birds with two *l*s in them?' he asked presently.

Edward Ferguson looked uneasy and said with lowered voice, '"Swallow", but . . .' He looked round. 'We use that word for something else.

84

And only in extreme circumstances, of course.'

'So your man needed two *l*s for his message,' concluded Henry.

'Twice,' said Ferguson. 'Don't forget the mallard.'

'So both mentions are part of the message.' Henry suddenly sat up rather straight. 'The letter *l* does stand for something else, doesn't it? Have you forgotten?'

The other man still looked mystified.

'Give me a moment, Ferguson,' said Henry, putting his napkin on the table and getting out his pen. 'Now read the names of those birds out to me again while I try something.'

'Ravens . . .' said Ferguson, pushing his plate away.

'Five,' said Henry, scribbling on his napkin.

'Five what?'

'Five. Go on . . .'

'Widgeon.'

'One and five hundred,' murmured Henry.

'You're quite sure, Tyler,' Ferguson said acidly, 'that you don't mean the four and twenty blackbirds that were baked in a pie?'

'Quite sure,' said Henry. 'Next?'

'Dotterel.'

'Five hundred and fifty.'

'I've lost you,' said the man from the

department with no name. 'But if you insist . . .'

'I do,' said Henry.

'Then your "collared dove" comes next,' said Ferguson.

'One hundred and twice fifty,' said Henry.

'Twice fifty is a hundred,' objected Ferguson. 'Same thing.'

'No, it isn't,' said Henry, still scribbling. 'And five hundred.'

'You've still lost me,' complained Ferguson.

'Oh, and five hundred and five from the dove.'

'Then there's a full stop,' said Edward Ferguson, adding with more than a touch of irony, 'or isn't that important?'

'That's your first number then,' said Henry.

'I'm not with you,' said Ferguson.

'Your first number is the sum of all those I've already mentioned,' said Henry.

He scanned his eye down the figures. 'I don't know about you but I make that two thousand, two hundred and sixty-one.'

Edward Ferguson nodded. 'That would fit although it's a little higher than we were bargaining for.'

'Know thine enemy,' said Henry.

The man opposite leant over and said, 'And the mallard and the fox?' Ferguson gave a quick frown, lifted his hand to stay an answer, and said slowly. 'No, don't tell me. Would I be right in saying a thousand, two times fifty and five hundred for "mallard"?'

'You would,' said Henry. 'Good man.'

'Adding ten for "fox"?' Ferguson twitched the napkin out of Henry's hand. 'And our man couldn't use "waxwing" because it had got an *i* in it as well as the *x*. . . that right?'

'Which would have made it six instead of five,' agreed Henry. 'And therefore wrong.'

'The second number comes to sixteen hundred and ten,' said Edward Ferguson, pushing his chair back and getting to his feet. 'You'll have to excuse me, Tyler. I need to be getting back with these figures as soon as possible. They're important.'

'So was the 1666, if only we'd realised it,' said Henry. 'We were a bit slow there.'

'Slow? In what way?'

'Because 1666 is the only number which uses all the Roman numbers – MDCLXVI – and in declining order, too.' He sat back in his chair. 'That's what should have told us we were dealing with a chronogram – that and the fact that your chap is a Latinist.'

'A chronogram?'

'Chronograms,' pronounced Henry Tyler hortatively, 'usually combine an inscription and a date picked out to be read as Roman numerals, but you can do it with any words and numbers you like . . . oh, you're off, are you?' He turned his head as the waiter approached and said to the man, 'I'm sorry, Mr Ferguson is in a hurry and he's had to go. He didn't want a pudding today. Me? Oh, I think I'll have the apple pie . . . and while you're about it, would you bring me another napkin? I appear to have lost mine.'

GOING QUIETLY

He hadn't meant to kill Pearl. At least, that's what he told the police.

Afterwards, of course.

No, he insisted, he'd only meant to go along and see her for the last time.

Why? Because there were still one or two things left over from the divorce he wanted to clear up with her, that's why.

Big things?

No, not big things. Little ones.

Like what then?

Well, he'd have liked her to say sorry.

What for?

For walking out on him like she had.

In what way then had she walked out on him?

Without there being anyone else.

Ah . . .

On either side, he said pointedly, although he

supposed they'd be checking up on that.

They said they would. Routinely.

Although, he agreed readily enough, his solicitor had advised him not to go to see her but you know what solicitors are.

The police agreed that they knew what solicitors were.

Too careful by half, that's what they were, he sniffed. Besides, they didn't have feelings like normal men did.

Didn't lose their rag, he meant, did he? said the police. Like some men . . .

Yes, he supposed he did. What did that Simon Puckle, sitting behind his great big desk in his posh office, know about what made a man see red?

Solicitors, the police countered temperately, knew rather more about life than most men. Pity he hadn't listened to them, wasn't it?

Well, if they wanted to put it like that . . .

They said they didn't have to put anything in any way. All they had to do was remind him he didn't have to tell them anything without Mr Puckle being there. If it was Mr Puckle he wanted, of course . . .

He didn't need him now, he said.

The police said that in their view he needed a solicitor more than ever now.

He said it was too late, now Pearl was dead.

So was that all? they said, making a note. About this last visit? Just to get her to say she was sorry?

And to see where she'd settled after they'd split up. Not that she'd let him into the house. The back garden was all that he got to see of it.

Very wise, said the police, although not in the circumstances wise enough.

No, he agreed at once, it wasn't anything to do with him where she had gone but he wanted to do it.

And?

And it wasn't anything like their old house.

Naturally, said the police who knew rather more about one person families than most.

Nasty, poky little semi-detached place down by the river in Berebury, he sniffed. Half a garden and cheek-by-jowl with the people next door. When you think of the place they'd had before . . . before . . . there was no comparison. No comparison at all.

Was that where he was living now? asked the police. The old house?

No, it wasn't, he growled. He'd had to give up the old home when they'd broken up. That was another thing.

What was?

That she didn't seem to mind enough about losing the old home.

Ah.

She said she was quite happy here, where she was, thank you. The neighbours were pleasant people. There was a nice quiet old lady next door and some cheerful types across the road. They'd asked her over once or twice and there was another couple next door on the other side, out at work all day, but around at the weekend and they'd asked her in once or twice, too. That was what had got his goat . . .

What exactly?

That she preferred what she'd got to all that she'd had.

Including him?

If they liked to put it like that. Yes.

Ah, said one of the policemen, more toffee-nosed than the others. A touch of the Brownings, was it?

No, he shook his head. He hadn't shot her. He'd strangled her.

That, explained the toffee-nosed one, wasn't what he had meant. Robert Browning's 'Last Duchess' had a 'heart too soon made glad' and her husband hadn't liked it either. The Duke had given commands to have his wife murdered but he had taken matters into his own hands, hadn't he? Literally.

He didn't know she was going to provoke him

like she had, did he? he muttered defensively.

So why the ticket for the football match that he had set up to video?

He liked to see the game again. See where the ref had gone wrong and all that.

And the supporter's scarf with his name on that he'd dropped in one of the stands before leaving the ground at half-time?

Because, he snarled, he hadn't known that the little old lady was sitting just the other side of the garden fence and must have heard every word that passed between him and Pearl, had he?

True.

Otherwise he wouldn't have turned himself in. No, the old lady hadn't seen him but he'd said some very personal things to Pearl that only a wife could have known.

Loudly?

A man can't help shouting when he's worked up, can he? Not when a woman has made him see red.

Possibly not, said the police, deciding against telling him that the old lady next door was stone deaf and never wasted her hearing-aid battery when she was just sitting in the garden reading, and hadn't heard a thing.

LA PLUME DE MA TANTE

Rhuaraidh Macmillan, the Sheriff of Fearnshire, paced round his room in his house at Drummondreach for the umpteenth time that morning. He finished up – as he invariably did these days – looking out of the window and scanning the horizon for the hundredth time. In a more peaceful decade the sheriff might have taken time to congratulate himself on the beauty of the view across the Firth from Ardmeanach – the Black Isle – but not now, not in these so very troubled times.

True, looking towards the purple-headed mountain of Ben Wyvis presented a pretty sight to the discerning eye but these were not moments to be enjoying the beauty of the landscape. His problem was that the paths through the hills which led over to the west away from Fearnshire naturally enough led back from there too. There was the rub. That they could carry men from the opposite direction was his worry: men – armed men – from far away to the west back here to Fearnshire.

That those paths to and from the west were only one of the sheriff's problems he knew well enough. The trouble was that he couldn't actually see the other well-trodden ways – the ones that came from the south, the east and the north. Another problem was that it was near Candlemass – darkest February – when there were too few hours of daylight for comfort.

If he, Rhuaraidh Macmillan, had been able to crane his neck sufficiently far round to the left from the viewpoint of the ridge on which his house at Drummondreach was built, he would have been able to see the length of the Black Isle to the south and the paths that came from there, too, but he couldn't.

Those paths and what might be coming along them in his direction were another worry. Alas, the ways from Fortrose and Cromarty were out of his view altogether, which only added to the present discomfort of the Sheriff of Fearnshire. It was not for nothing that the promontory of Ardmeanach was known throughout Fearnshire as the Black Isle. It was because the whole was covered with dark pine trees. So now no one could say who was or was not approaching the back of Drummondreach through the woods. There was no view that way at all.

So that Sheriff Rhuaraidh Macmillan was a very anxious man went without saying in these greatly disturbed times in Scotland. He was, though, at the same time an unhappy man. And if the two conditions – the present unhappiness and the worried state – were not in themselves very closely connected, nevertheless there was no doubt that they had a common cause.

Rhuaraidh Macmillan went on pacing up and down in his house at Drummondreach and had to concede to himself that both his unhappiness and his worry stemmed from the arrival of Mary Stuart from France and her enthronement as Queen of Scots. As her father, James V, had put it so neatly on his deathbed, 'It began with a lass and it will end with a lass'.

It hadn't ended so far, but what man alive could say what the future held?

But it did mean that that second lassie – the one that it might end with: Mary, Queen of Scots – was now Queen of Fearnshire, too. And this – and here was the difficulty – this required the Sheriff of Fearnshire leaving his Highland home and going to Edinburgh to swear his fealty to her.

And if that was not bad enough it had also, alas, made Sheriff Rhuaraidh Macmillan feel he should acquire some little command of the French language before he made the journey south. The sheriff had the Gaelic and the English all right and some little Latin but not – so far – the French.

But 'Getting the French' so to speak in remote Fearnshire was not proving easy and the sheriff, no longer a young man, had been reduced to taking lessons from a youthful tutor recently engaged at neighbouring Pitcalnie Castle for the purpose of making the laird's daughters there fluent enough in the French language to be presented at the Queen's court.

The sheriff had with difficulty now accepted the principle that in the French language everything had a gender. His reluctance to do so had been compounded by certain illogicalities in this that he, Rhuaraidh Macmillan, had been inclined to cavil at.

Why, he had asked, should 'ship' be considered masculine – 'le bâtiment' – when every right thinking man – Scotsman, that is – knew that ships were always feminine? Every ship that the sheriff had ever known – and there had always been ships and plenty ploughing their way across the Firth – had invariably been addressed by all and sundry as 'she'. It even went for '*le rafiau*', the small sailing ships that could put into the little slipway at Balblair, not far from Drummondreach. Graceful line or no, they, too, were addressed as masculine in French.

The tutor from Pitcalnie had not attempted to explain this or any other Anglo-French anomaly the sheriff had latched on. Instead, he had merely counselled learning them by heart: worse, the man had added unhelpfully that that went for the irregular verbs, too. 'Learn them the hard way,' the teacher had said airily, being himself still young enough to do that with ease. 'You'll just have to commit them to memory.'

The irregular verbs had done nothing, either, to enhance the sheriff's already jaundiced view of the French language. Nor had he been exactly enchanted with some of their nouns. Why potatoes should be called '*pommes de terre*' or 'apples of the earth' defeated him. The word '*feu*', which he himself used often in his everyday speech, was a perfectly proper Scottish word for that ancient duty which was owed by a tenant to a landlord in whose fiefdom he lived. Why the French should use it for the word 'fire' he couldn't begin to imagine . . .

It was this struggle with a new language that accounted for the sheriff's present unhappiness.

The sheriff's real worry – admittedly a much more urgent one than becoming fluent in the French tongue – was a warring band of caterans that he had reason to believe was presently on its way to Fearnshire from somewhere else. That particular 'somewhere else' was almost certainly the west but not certainly enough for Rhuaraidh Macmillan – nobody's fool – not to maintain a keen watch on possible approaches from the other three points of the compass.

He smiled grimly to himself as he put his clerk to watch as well as he could in these directions. 'It's called *"placer une sentinelle"*,' he said to a bemused Dougal, 'although why the word *"sentinelle"* should always be feminine, I do not know.'

'All the sentries I've ever known have been men, my lord,' agreed Dougal hastily. 'Good men,' that worthy added somewhat ambiguously.

The sheriff sighed and took another turn round his room. Those who lived and had their being in the Highland fastnesses that comprised Fearnshire were usually quite unconcerned by what went on in faraway Edinburgh – but not now. It was a time of change in Scotland and as that clever young Italian, Niccolò Machiavelli, had pointed out, 'dramatic regime change' was always a dangerous time for any society. And dramatic regime change was undoubtedly what they had in Scotland just now.

Not everybody in Fearnshire liked it – Pitcalnie the Younger, for one, was known to be a rebel – and the sheriff did not blame them. The behaviour of she on the throne at the Palace of Holyrood was not meeting with favour in every other quarter either. And the county of Fearnshire was one of those quarters. In consequence, rebellion was raising its ugly head and, as is the way of such things, serious dissenters were being joined by a tatterdemalion collection of miscreants, ne'er-do-wells and landless clansmen disaffected by the toadying of their chieftains at that faraway court in Edinburgh.

One of these roving bands, he had been warned, was even now making its way towards Fearnshire on trouble bent. This was the cause of his worry and speaking to them in French wouldn't get him very far. While the unhappiness could wait, the worry couldn't and it was only a conscious effort of will that stopped him spending every minute of every day keeping his eye on the track that came down towards Dingwall from the west through the ancient settlement of Strathpeffer.

What he would do when he saw armed men approaching was a different matter and unfortunately time might well be of the essence. Mustering the forces of law and order was no easy matter in remote Fearnshire so the longer warning he had the better. Assistance against an armed band was not easily at hand at the best of times – even less so when it wasn't easy to know on whom to count for support.

This was because that well-known dictum 'he who isn't with me is against me' didn't hold when there were Fearnshire men unashamedly sitting on the fence, watching and waiting to see which way the tide of battle would go. The race would be to the swift, right enough, not to the loyal.

Appeals for loyalty to a distant monarch about whom little good had been heard were not likely to be entirely successful either. It would take time, too, and in some cases persuasion not far short of bribery, to get his nearest neighbours to rally to his side.

He mentally reviewed those on whom he could call for aid in upholding the rule of law while he once more drifted uneasily towards the point in his room where he could look to the west. One thing was certain and that was that it wouldn't be a collection of young Lochinvars coming out of the west and descending on Drummondreach.

On the contrary, in fact.

It was more likely that that it would be

a rabble led by Colum Mulchaich, ever a troublemaker, and it would be the sheriff's job to stop Mulchaich and his mob wreaking havoc on the countryside. The sheriff sincerely hoped that it wasn't also going to be his job to get Colum Mulchaich over to Crochair – more properly called 'the place of the hanging' – but if he had to do it, then duty demanded that he did just that.

He was about to take yet another turn round the room when the slightest of movements in the middle distance caught his eye. It was gone in a moment and he had to wait a full minute before he saw it again. He rubbed his eyes. He hadn't dreamt it. There was a small man clad in some tattered faded grey fustian creeping towards Drummondreach along the shelter of a faraway field wall down near the shore beyond.

The sheriff slipped out into his own front doorway and adjured the hall boy to keep his bagpipes silent at the approach of a visitor. 'Let the wee mannie come to the house any way he likes,' he said as the boy laid his chanter aside. 'He'll no want a fuss made.'

If he, Rhuaraidh Macmillan, was any judge of what the man wanted it was food and shelter. Even so the figure did not advance any further than the field wall nearest to Drummondreach. Instead, he just lay on the grass alongside the wall, making no more movement. It didn't take Rhuaraidh Macmillan long to work out why. The visitor – whoever he was – was waiting for darkness to fall.

The sheriff stopped his pacing up and down of his room and sat down to think instead. This could be good and bad. It might be that the man was a spy, an advance guard, watching and waiting to see that the sheriff was indeed in his home at Drummondreach. It might be that he felt in too much danger himself to advance any further in daylight. It might be that the stranger wanted the cover of darkness for some other fell purpose.

It was a full hour before the sheriff knew anything more. It was deep twilight before the man made a move and then it was only to the very edge of the sheriff's policies. He stood there for a moment and then raised his right arm and lofted something that looked heavy over a spot where the boundary wall looked at its lowest.

And then he was gone.

The sheriff stifled an impulse to go straight out to see what had been cast onto his land, his hand stayed by rumours of fatal explosions at faraway places in the south. Gunpowder, those had been. This, he decided after a long look, was a hefty round stone. Steeling himself and not seeing anything in the nature of a lighted fuse, he presently set out to examine it. It was indeed a round stone, and it was covered in skiver.

He brought it back inside the house and carefully unwound the piece of split sheepskin leather from the stone, full of hope that it might have a message written on it.

It had.

Calling for Dougal, his clerk, he started to read out the letters roughly scribbled on the skiver.

'Wait you, while I read it out,' he instructed him. Holding the skiver to the failing light he called out the words. 'It begins "MUCH, FRIENDS".
. . That's not very helpful. I doubt if it's any of our "friends" on the way.'

'So do I,' muttered Dougal under his breath, struggling with his quill.

'Then it has "BOOK, TOWNSHIP" . . . What does that mean, I wonder?'

'I canna' begin to say, my lord,' said Dougal, scratching the words down. 'All it does mean is that someone has his letters.'

'That's a good point,' said the sheriff fairly. Most of the insurgents wouldn't be able to read or write, although that didn't make them less good at the sword, but there would be one or two educated men among them. 'It goes on

"HARE, TREE" . . . Dougal, is there a somewhere near here with a special tree where hares meet?'

'Not to my knowledge, my lord,' said Dougal, literate but no countryman. 'Not until March, anyway.'

'Ah,' said the sheriff, 'this is better. The word "SECRET" comes next.'

'Secret,' echoed Dougal, obediently writing this down.

'And then there's "SHIP",' said the sheriff pensively. 'That's all. Now, read it back to me.'

The clerk said, 'Much, friends, book, township, hare, tree, secret, ship.'

'It disna mean a thing,' said Rhuaraidh Macmillan, dismissing his clerk and settling down to think. It still meant nothing after he'd called for candles to be brought, the better to see the written words, and that meant that if anyone else saw the message it wouldn't mean anything to them either, which might be important.

Searching for the place name he needed so badly – if, indeed, the message had been from a friend – he took the first letter of all the words but could make nothing of them however much he jumbled them about.

Even after he'd had the peat of the fire cast aside and logs brought in the better to warm his body on a cold night – and he hoped his brain, too – he couldn't fathom anything in the message. Together the words were meaningless no matter which way he looked at them. Separately they meant very little more.

Idly, he considered them one by one, pausing at 'township' since that was a word that did have connotations with all sheriffs. It had been the only English word which in French had also meant something to him. '*Banlieue*' that had been – and *banlieue* in French meant the extent within which the sheriffs could exercise their manorial rights and send out their proclamations – *banlieue* literally meant the place of a sheriff's jurisdiction. And this word he could understand – and remember.

He didn't need that clever young fellow from Castle Pitcalnie to remind him of the French for 'ship' either. It was '*bâtiment*' or . . . what was it for a small sailing ship? Dammit, he'd had the word on the tip of his tongue already today. He kicked a log on the fire back into the centre of the flames while he gave himself time to think. '*Radier*', that was it.

Pleased that he'd called two or three French words to mind he looked at the others on the list. If he couldn't do anything else, he'd see if he could translate them into French. The word for 'book' he knew was '*livre*' because that had been the first one the dominie had made him learn and the second was for 'hare' which he had to know because he hadn't got to confuse '*livre*' with '*lièvre*'.

Moderately pleased with himself, the sheriff settled back in his chair and decided to see if he could translate any of the other words. 'Friend' was easy – '*ami*'. The tutor at Pitcalnie Castle had adjured him to think of the English word 'amiable' and remember it that way. And so he had.

He'd remembered the French word for 'tree' all right – that was '*arbre*' – but not the one for 'much' or for 'secret'. He tried putting the French words that he knew in the same order as the English counterparts from the enigmatic message tossed onto his land.

(Much) *Ami, Livre, Banlieue, Lièvre, Arbre,* (Secret), *Bâtiment.*

Much good that did him.

What he needed, he decided, was whisky.

The whisky having been forthcoming, he settled back in his chair, feeling much better.

Much? Now he came to think of it, he did know the French for 'much'. It was '*beaucoup*' – as in '*beaucoup le whisky*'.

He sipped his whisky and slipped that in at the front of the list of French words and spelt

107

the first letters out – B A L B L A blank R. He frowned. Not 'bâtiment' at the end for ship but '*radier*' for sailing ship. That was better.

He sat up suddenly.

It didn't matter what the French word for 'secret' was – but the sheriff was prepared to wager that it began with the letter *I*, because those letters then spelt 'Balblair' which was where the jetty was.

So Colum Mulchaich was coming by sea. All Mulchaich had to do was to land boatloads of men by night until they were all safely and silently across the Firth ready to march on Drummondreach and take the sheriff by surprise.

That was all he needed to know.

Sheriff Rhuaraidh Macmillan set his whisky down while he summoned his piper to action. And toyed with a phrase he'd got his French-speaking dominie at Pitcalnie Castle to teach him: '*tous les rebelles furent pendus*' – the rebels were all hanged.

He'd remembered that all right.

THE LANGUAGE OF FLOWERS

'Friday of next week?' said Wendy Witherington. 'Of course, Henry, do come. We'll be delighted to see you. The countryside is looking absolutely lovely just now.'

Henry Tyler assured his sister that the view from his office in Whitehall was equally pleasant and that the sun was shining there, too. What wasn't so pleasant at this unhappy juncture in world history was the international situation where – metaphorically, at least – the sun was not shining at all and the clouds might well – metaphorically, anyway – be described as dark and gathering.

He did not say any of this to his sister but instead went on to talk about the ostensible reason for his visit to the little market town of Berebury. This was an evening engagement at Almstone College at the University of Calleshire.

'I do wish you didn't have so many things to do when you come down to stay,' said Wendy Witherington. 'It's such a shame that you always seem to be so busy while you're here.'

'I've only got to go to a dinner with old Toby Beddowes,' protested Henry Tyler. This was not strictly true but Henry was not in a position to explain the real reason for his coming down to Calleshire to stay with his sister and brother-in-law. 'That's on the Friday night. I'll be with you all for the whole weekend.'

'Good.' Wendy brightened. 'That means you'll have time to take the children to the zoo, then.'

'Well . . .' he temporised, 'I'll certainly do my best.'

Wendy Witherington played a mother's trump card. 'They'll be very disappointed if you don't.'

'And have you told them that their doting uncle is forsaking London entirely in the interests of family unity?' he said.

'I've told them that you're coming,' said Wendy neatly, 'but I'm not embarking on a lifetime of deception by telling them that you're coming down here just to see them.'

'Wise woman,' said Henry affectionately. 'Let them find out later that things are never what they seem.' In these dark days things were never what they seemed at the Foreign Office either.

It was a lesson he'd had to learn quite early on. The lessons that were being learnt after Herr Adolf Hitler's march into the Rhineland were something very different. And as for Italy and Spain and their leaders . . .

'And they're pretty excited already,' insisted his sister, ignoring this. 'Jennifer can hardly wait for you to get here so she can show you her new doll. It's called Shirley after Shirley Temple.'

Henry Tyler could hardly wait to get to Berebury, too, but for very different reasons.

'So,' went on his sister, 'I hope your friend Toby isn't going to take up all your time.'

'Oh, no,' said Henry airily. 'I'm just going to be his guest at High Table at Almstone College, that's all.' It wasn't all, of course, but there was no reason for his sister to know this.

If Toby Beddowes, Professor of Botanical Sciences at the University of Calleshire, had wondered why his old school friend, Henry Tyler, presently rather high up in the more rarefied echelons of the Civil Service, should have angled for an invitation to a High Table dinner at Almstone College he was much too discreet to say so. Instead when approached he had merely said, 'Of course, old chap. Any time.'

'No, Toby. Not any time. Friday next week.'

'Ah, I get you. Yes, of course. I'll book you in.'

111

He chuckled. 'You need to know that the meal starts when *Hemerocallis fulva* closes . . .'

Henry grinned. He knew that Toby Beddowes' famous Linnean Flower Clock was planted in a bed in the middle of the sacred turf of the college quad on the south side of the fountain. It was the botanist's pride and joy, as well as a splendid teaching aid about the great Carl Linnaeus of Uppsala and his *Philosophia Botanica* of 1751. The plants in it formed the clock by opening and closing at certain – and succeeding – fixed times by which the time of day could be known. He paused for thought. 'Let me see now, Toby, would that by any chance be anywhere near eight o'clock?'

'Got it in one, old boy.' Toby Beddowes sounded pleased. 'You could have mentioned the dandelion, of course, instead.'

'No, I couldn't,' responded Henry with spirit, 'because I didn't know that was one of your precious clock plants.'

'Any of the *Aequinoctales* would do,' said the Professor of Botany.

'One of them will do for Friday evening, thank you, Toby, whatever that long word means.'

'Right,' said Toby. 'I'll see you at moonflower time, then. That's when we foregather.'

'I'll look out for evening primroses, too,'

promised Henry, entering into the spirit of the thing.

'Seven-thirty in the Combination Room for sherry first,' said his old friend. 'That all right with you?'

'Thanks. I'll be there.'

Professor Beddowes, nobody's fool, said, 'Let me see now, where is it exactly you are working these days? Or can't you tell me?'

'The Foreign Office.'

'Ah, of course. By the way, we go in to dinner at *Hemerocallis fulva* closing time sharp.'

'I won't be late,' promised Henry.

And he wasn't.

'Master,' said Toby Beddowes on the Friday evening, 'may I present my guest, Henry Tyler, an old school friend?'

The Master of the College welcomed Henry with a civil handshake. 'I trust you'll enjoy your evening here,' he said, adding rather wistfully, 'Almstone isn't an Oxford or Cambridge college but sometimes the conversation at High Table can prove most interesting.'

'I'm looking forward to it,' said Henry truthfully. He'd come to listen and listen particularly to what was said by and to a certain Gustav Soderssonn, also due to be coming to the college as a guest that evening. Actually, realised Henry now, having cast an eye warily round the company beginning to assemble in the Combination Room, he could see that his quarry was already here.

The tall fair-haired scientist from Farnessnes Island was in the far corner of the Combination Room. He was being introduced to the little group round him by the member of the college who was presumably the man's host that evening. That, he had been told, would be Professor Marcus Holtby, a shortish man with smooth hair and a Clark Gable pencil-thin moustache.

Henry had been fully briefed on Professor Marcus Holtby before he had left London. The man held the Chair of Chemistry at the University of Calleshire but it was more the views he held that were of particular interest to Henry's department of state, which had categorised them in its usual understated way as 'doubtful'.

Taking the glass of sherry – a good amontillado – being offered to him from a passing tray, Henry revised his thinking. He had been fully briefed on Gustav Soderssonn, biologist, too, though the man couldn't really be called his quarry – Henry's role this evening could be more accurately said to be rather that of eavesdropper than hunter.

According to the appropriate attaché on the staff of the British Consul on Farnessnes Island the biologist was on a high-level tour of English universities seeking any very clever scientists who might consider emigrating to the presumed safety of Farnessnes Island ahead of the world war that was undoubtedly on its way. This Baltic island, not far from Sweden, and a rich source of both iron ore and diatomaceous earth, had for many years pursued a position of what Henry's boss called 'aggressive neutrality'.

'Like the Swiss?' hazarded Henry.

'Not like the Swiss,' the assistant secretary of Henry's department had replied swiftly. 'More like Pontius Pilate.'

'And are we talking treason?' asked Henry.

'More the enemy within, I would think,' the man had said. 'You must remember, Tyler, that "Treason doth never prosper" . . .'

Henry finished the quotation without difficulty. '"What's the reason? Why if it prosper, none dare call it treason".' He wondered if their minister was being got ready for his Sir Edward Grey moment, trying to improve on 'The lamps are going out all over Europe', which they certainly showed every sign of doing again now.

'Exactly,' said the man at the Ministry appreciatively. 'You can see the potential difficulty for us in having an island like that bang in the middle of the Baltic.'

'And with a good sea route to Danzig to boot,' pointed out Henry.

'I've never been quite sure about free ports myself,' murmured the other man with apparent inconsequence. He was old enough to have fought in the Great War – and to remember the Treaty of Versailles. He added, 'And territorial waters are always a problem. If I remember rightly Farnessnes Island is just outside a quite number of them.'

'Only just,' qualified Henry.

'And I don't think we're going to be saved by that whisker,' sighed the other Foreign Office man, his particular department of state having a long record of being saved by a whisker. 'The other thing we don't know about Soderssonn, by the way, is what sort of biology he's working on.'

The outcome of this conversation was that Henry had been detailed to keep a weather eye on Gustav Soderssonn during his proposed milk round of English seats of learning.

'A watching brief, you might say,' said the assistant secretary, who had been trained as a lawyer before he went into the Foreign Office. 'Probably no specific action called for at this stage.'

Henry had all but crossed his fingers as he left the assistant secretary's office.

'Anyone you particularly want to meet, Henry?' asked Toby Beddowes now, looking round the assembled company.

'Not really,' murmured Henry since it was true he didn't want to meet Soderssonn; only observe who he was talking to.

'Interesting bunch, of course, here. Almstone College has quite a reputation for science and philosophy.'

'A good mix those,' observed Henry sedately.

'What's that? Oh, quite,' said Toby Beddowes. 'Alan Walkinshaw's our really top man, though. Done a lot of good work on the mathematics of trajectories. The word is that he's in the running for a Nobel Prize. Odd that, considering that he's said to be a pacifist.'

'Money from old dynamite, you might say,' said Henry, relishing the irony.

'That reminds me, we've got a good geologist here, too. Name of Clifford, Malcolm Clifford.'

'Why the connection with dynamite?' asked Henry, mystified.

'Diatomaceous earth is a sort of sedimentary rock used in making the stuff. Malcolm Clifford knows all about that. Found in the Baltic. Off Denmark, anyway.'

'Really?' murmured Henry with a perfectly straight face.

'We've got some excellent historians here at Almstone, too, to say nothing of our new department.'

'Which is that?'

'Criminology.' Professor Beddowes pointed in the direction of a sharp-faced young man engaged in deep conversation with an elderly academic near the door. 'Peter Reynolds, said to be very highly thought of in his line.'

'Always a satisfactory state of affairs in an institution like this – to have good men on board, I mean,' said Henry Tyler hastily. 'You don't want the half-baked here.' He wished the same could be said of some of the incumbents of other institutions with which he had to deal. There were certain Mittel-European states whose behaviour at the present time could only be described as intransigent.

'He's just published a seminal work on motives for murder that was very well received,' Beddowes informed him. 'I'm told he has a tip-top reputation in his field, too, but I wouldn't know about the murder side myself.' He gave a self-deprecating smile. 'I'm only a botanist and plants don't kill – unless you eat the wrong ones, that is.'

'Always excepting the Venus flytrap, old boy,' said Henry as the dinner gong sounded and the group started to move towards the door. 'That captures and kills, you know.'

'Good point,' said Beddowes amiably.

As Henry had expected the food was good and the wine even better.

'Almstone has always prided itself on its battels,' said the large man with a booming voice sitting on Henry's left when he mentioned this to him and who introduced himself as Malcolm Clifford, the geologist. 'The inner man needs keeping happy. Most important.'

Henry said the same thing when turning to the man on his right-hand side, an untidily dressed fellow, his tie only just centred over his shirt, who said, 'The food's always been good at Almstone.' He put out a hand towards Henry. 'I'm Walkinshaw, by the way. Mathematics – and please don't tell me that all you know about figures is that two and two make four.'

'It's knowing how many beans make five that matters in my department,' countered Henry cheerfully.

'Ah,' said Walkinshaw, 'you probably need a philosopher for that one.' He crumbled a bread roll and then indicated a man sitting almost opposite them at the High Table. 'Or perhaps better still, a criminologist like Peter Reynolds over there.'

Henry followed his gaze. The young don was still talking urgently, this time to Gustav Soderssonn. His words floated across the table. 'Of course, my good sir, there are more reasons for murder than the layman might imagine.'

'Revenge, I would concede at once, your Shakespeare's *Hamlet* having spelt it out so well,' responded Soderssonn, smiling gently, with only a trace of an accent. 'And then there's gain, naturally.'

'I'm not sure why you think gain should be so natural,' put in Marcus Holtby, the Professor of Chemistry, across the table.

Malcolm Clifford whispered in Henry's ear, 'Holtby always tries to put a scientific slant on everything; and – which is worse – to think that everything – but everything – has a rational explanation. Doesn't make for popularity.'

Henry nodded and put this interesting thought at the back of his mind for further consideration at some unlikely point in the future when he had time to think.

'Gain is more natural selection than just natural, I would have thought,' observed a don on the other man's left. 'Survival of the species and all that, the winner taking all. That's gain for you.'

The others ignored him while the Professor of

English Literature murmured something about Shylock and *The Merchant of Venice* under his breath.

'Then there's jealousy,' continued Peter Reynolds, in full flight now. 'You know how it goes – "If I can't have what I want, I'll make sure you don't have it either".'

'Othello, The Moor,' said the man from Farnessnes Island promptly. 'Your national bard had that – how do you put it here? Sewn up?'

'Stitched,' murmured someone sotto voce.

'And there's always lust, too,' persisted the young don.

'Can't exclude that,' agreed Gustav Soderssonn, his smile still well to the fore. 'First-class motive, lust.'

'You can have lust for power, as well as women, can't you?' put in Alan Walkinshaw, looking round the all-male dinner table in a challenging fashion. 'We don't have too far to look for that, do we?'

Nobody mentioned Herr Hitler but the English literature don tactfully murmured *Macbeth*.

'There's the other sort of lust, Reynolds,' put in Henry's host, Toby Beddowes. 'Don't forget that.'

The criminologist looked up, pleased. 'I have got everyone talking, haven't I?'

'Come on, Beddowes, what's the other sort of lust?' said someone else. 'Tell us.'

'The lust for killing,' said the biologist.

'Blood lust,' remarked the young man thoughtfully. 'Of course . . .'

There was an awkward little silence and then someone coughed and said, 'There's murder for elimination, too.'

'We don't have to look too far for that, either, do we?' said Alan Walkinshaw.

'East,' said Toby Beddowes heavily.

'You're just talking about today, Beddowes,' said the history man reprovingly. 'I'd be counting Kings Henry Seven and Eight as masters of that art.'

Gustav Soderssonn leant forward and said, 'Gentlemen, aren't you forgetting that strange queen of yours, too? The one who was called after a drink. Or was it the other way round?'

'Bloody Mary,' said Malcolm Clifford, the large man with a patent interest in food and drink. 'Vodka in tomato juice.'

'With Worcestershire sauce and a dash of lemon,' added Marcus Holtby, the chemist, pedantically. He was a man who seemed to need to have the last word.

'Mary Tudor,' sighed the history don. 'A difficult woman.'

Gustav Soderssonn nodded. 'That's the girl. Didn't like disobedience and acted accordingly.'

Henry Tyler looked from one face to another, searching to see if anyone would speak about modern parallels with the current equivalent of an absolute monarch who daily ordered deaths with apparent impunity. 'Mary, Mary, quite contrary,' he murmured, almost to himself.

'There's judicial killing, too,' said another don. 'Don't they call that justifiable homicide?'

'That's only revenge wearing a different hat,' countered the criminologist.

'Don't you mean a black cap?' said Malcolm Clifford wittily.

'Society's revenge,' said Peter Reynolds, 'that's what that is.'

'Socrates,' remarked the philosophy don in a detached way, 'got murdered for asking awkward questions.'

'That reminds me,' said Henry's left-hand neighbour, 'where's the port got to?'

The decanter was rapidly located and passed to the left.

The history don advanced another thought. 'I suppose it's only a subsection of gain but what about the Terror during the French Revolution? Murdering everyone in sight in order to subdue the population by fright?'

At the mention of France Henry Tyler, civil servant at the Foreign Office, let his attention wander. France was very high on the list of worries there. When he brought his attention back to the High Table the conversation had moved on to the regrettable lowering of examination standards in the Western world in general and the University of Calleshire in particular.

It was not long, though, before the talk was turned to the putative delights of emigrating to Farnessnes Island. 'Complete intellectual freedom,' insisted Gustav Soderssonn expansively, 'and, of course, freedom from – well, anything that might happen on the international front.'

'Are you talking about physical safety?' asked the young criminologist pertinently.

'Of course, no one can guarantee anyone absolute safety these days . . .'

'I should think not,' put in the philosophy don.

'But naturally a totally neutral island should escape – what shall we say? undue interference – from any countries at war with each other.' Soderssonn looked round and said, 'And I do mean "any" countries.'

'What about your facilities?' enquired Toby Beddowes, eyebrows raised.

'I don't think you will find us stinting in any way,' said Soderssonn.

'Who's funding you?' asked Beddowes, quite brusquely for him.

'An international foundation,' said Soderssonn smoothly.

'And who's funding them?' enquired Beddowes.

'Various philanthropists and trusts.' Soderssonn waved a hand. 'You know the sort of thing.'

'I do indeed,' said Beddowes darkly.

At this point the Master intervened with a diplomatic enquiry about the wildlife on Farnessnes Island and the talk turned to other things.

At the end of the evening Henry thanked his old friend, Toby Beddowes, and made his way to his sister's house. It was late the following morning when he had a visit there from Detective Inspector Bewman of the Calleshire Constabulary.

The policeman did not beat about the bush. 'I understand, sir, you work at the Foreign Office.' It was a statement not a question. 'They have told me that you may be able to help us with our enquiries.'

Henry acknowledged that this might be so.

'We are interested in all those who were

dining at Almstone College last evening,' began Bewman.

'Ah . . .' So was Henry but he did not say so.

'And especially a small group who adjourned to the Senior Common Room afterwards and stayed up late.'

Henry said that he had not been one of them.

'We know that,' said the policeman calmly. He looked down at his notebook. 'There were four of them. Alan Walkinshaw, a very well-known mathematician, Malcolm Clifford who's a geologist and Marcus Holtby who I understand is a chemist.'

'That's right. The scientific sort – not your toothpaste and aspirin over the counter sort,' amplified Henry.

'And a Gustav Soderssonn, a guest who is also a scientist of some sort,' said Bewman, letting a little silence develop.

Then when Henry said nothing he went on, 'Apparently this gentleman spoke to them all about the advantages of emigrating to his part of the world at this particular moment in world history.'

'Farnessnes Island,' put in Henry.

'Soderssonn was staying at the college overnight and apparently said to them all that he would be in the quadrangle the next morning

126

if any of them wanted to come to see him and discuss the matter further.'

'And did any of them?' asked Henry with interest.

'Two of them.' Detective Inspector Bewman consulted his notebook. 'And they are all in agreement up to this point. At least, the three of them are – Holtby, Clifford and Soderssonn.'

'You have to start somewhere,' said Henry.

'Although, sir, I must say it seems to me to be rather a public spot for a quiet chat.'

'On the contrary, Inspector,' said Henry. 'You've got absolute privacy there in that you can't either be overheard or approached unobserved.'

'That's true. Anyway, after two of them had been to see him, Soderssonn said he made his way back to his own room and started to pack. He was due in Cambridge over the rest of the weekend.'

'And?' said Henry. What went on in Cambridge these days was someone else's problem.

'And that's when he says he heard that Alan Walkinshaw had just been found dead in his rooms.'

'Without ever coming to see him?' deduced Henry swiftly.

'That is so,' said the policeman. 'According

to the college servant who went in there to see to the room after breakfast, Professor Walkinshaw was alive and well then but he asked not to be disturbed again as he was checking some proofs for his new book.'

'And was he disturbed?' asked Henry. 'Or did natural causes overtake him?'

'What overtook him was a heavy blunt object applied to the back of his head,' said Bewman succinctly.

'When?'

'Ah, sir, now you've hit the nail on the head.'

A Foreign Office man to his fingertips, Henry let the inappropriate cliché pass.

'It would seem,' advanced Bewman cautiously, 'that the foreign gentleman went out into the quadrangle about nine o'clock this morning – or so he says – and sat on the seat between the fountain and that funny flower garden.'

'The Linnean clock.'

'Perhaps, sir, you'd be kind enough to spell that for me.' As Henry spoke Bewman conscientiously copied the word into his notebook.

'But Walkinshaw didn't ever come to see him?' said Henry.

'That's right, sir. Professor Holtby and Dr Clifford both came out to see this Mr Soderssonn but he says he waited by the fountain after they'd gone but the third man didn't turn up – naturally he couldn't on account of his being dead.' He stopped and said, 'He wasn't dead naturally, of course, if you understand me, sir. It was a very savage attack and unprovoked as far as we can see.'

Henry sat back. 'Gustav Soderssonn was trying to recruit him for his outfit on Farnessnes Island – the deceased was a world authority on the mathematics of trajectories.'

'Really, sir? Well, this Mr Gustav Soderssonn says he was sitting out in the quadrangle from about nine o'clock onwards and that was before his scout saw Professor Walkinshaw alive and well in his room.'

'And nobody else saw him out there then?'

'Not that we know about, it being a Saturday. The porter says no one came into the college this morning except the staff. I'm told most of the young gentlemen don't reckon to work at weekends and don't get up betimes while those who do are usually out on the river from early on.'

'Some of them don't reckon to work at any time,' murmured Henry.

'And the staff were all working inside the college,' said the policeman, whose own weekend was going to be a busy one too.

'Tell me, Inspector, is it a question of time being of the essence?'

He got an oblique answer. 'Professor Holtby and Dr Clifford were both with the Master at the material time, that is after the scout had seen Professor Walkinshaw alive and well. They were discussing with the Master how their going to Farnessnes Island would affect their careers at – how did they put it? "At this particular juncture in world history", I think was what they said.'

'Good point,' said Henry. 'But didn't they wonder why Walkinshaw wasn't with them?'

'No. He'd already told the pair of them that he might be a pacifist but that didn't mean he wasn't a patriot as well.'

'Bully for him,' said Henry absently, something from last night's talk beginning to come back to him. What was it that that young criminologist had said about jealousy? He frowned and murmured, 'If I can't have what I want then I'll make sure you can't have it either.'

Inspector Bewman said, 'Beg pardon, sir, I didn't quite catch that.'

'I think I might have been talking motive,' said Henry.

The police inspector brightened. 'I must say that any suggestion of a motive would be a help.

The deceased didn't appear to have any natural enemies.'

'We've all got natural enemies, Inspector. I think what poor Walkinshaw had were some unnatural ones.'

'Sir?'

'Yes, indeed – whatever powers that are really behind this scheme for Farnessnes Island staying neutral. A cock and bull story, if you ask me.'

Inspector Bewman said, 'What I am asking you, sir, is how, if this visitor from that island was sitting out there when he says he was, he could have had anything to do with killing our Mr Walkinshaw and,' the policeman drew breath and added what the Foreign Office would have called a rider, 'if he wasn't out there when he says he was how we are going to prove it.'

'Let me get this straight, Inspector. Walkinshaw was done to death sometime after nine o'clock while Holtby and Clifford were with the Master and Soderssonn says he was sitting in the quad . . .'

'That is correct, sir.'

Henry Tyler sat still, his gaze wandering through his sister's sitting-room window and out into the garden. 'Wait a minute, Inspector. Wait a minute. I've just had an idea.'

Inspector Bewman, wise man that he was, said nothing.

Henry got to his feet. 'I'll have to ring a friend first.' He reached for his diary and then made for the telephone in the hall, lifting the receiver and tapping the bar. 'Operator, can you get me this number?'

He called back to Bewman. 'They're ringing now.' He turned back to the earpiece. 'That you, Toby? Good, now listen carefully. This is important. Which flowers would have been open on your flower clock at nine o'clock this morning?' Henry fell silent, then said, 'You're sure? Sorry, of course you're sure. And at ten o'clock? Thank you and thank you for last night, too.' There was a pause, then Henry said, 'What's that? Do it again sometime? That would be good.'

Henry restored the receiver to its cradle and went back into the sitting room.

'Inspector, I suggest you invite Gustav Soderssonn to tell you exactly what flowers he saw open in the flower bed in front of him. He can't have failed to notice which they were. After all, he's a biologist when he's not acting on behalf of a foreign power.'

'Flowers, sir?'

'Flowers. If he doesn't mention the Californian

132

poppy and *Helichrysum* being out when he got there then he got out there much later than he said he did.'

'And so you mean he would have had time to kill Professor Walkinshaw while the others were safely with the Master,' concluded Inspector Bewman intelligently.

'Exactly.'

'But why?'

'Oh, that's easy, Inspector. If Alan Walkinshaw wasn't going to be one of them, then they had to make quite sure nobody else benefited from his research work. What he was working on is very important these days.' Henry waved his hand. 'His killing's just a variation of what a young criminologist was saying last night. I must remember to tell young Peter Reynolds how right he was.'

THE HEN PARTY

'He did what, Hamish?' exploded Sheriff Rhuaraidh Macmillan in disbelief. His temper had not been improved by his having been roused from his quiet time in the afternoon by the unexpected arrival at his door of three breathless young men. 'And why, may I ask?'

It wouldn't have been right to call his quiet time actual sleep – he was sure he'd done no more than close his eyes in deep thought for a minute or two. And hadn't he sat up straight enough – and as alert as ever – the very moment he heard the hall boy's bagpipes warning him that men were approaching his house at Drummondreach? A man of law needed to be alert right enough in these troubled times for Scotland.

Hamish Urquhart stood first on one foot and then on the other. 'It was only for a wager, Sheriff,' he said uneasily.

'Just a wee bet,' supplemented his friend, Malcolm, one of old Alcaig's sons.

'Nothing but a good hen,' chimed in the third man, Ian Macrae, Younger, of Cornton.

'There's no such thing as good hen,' countered Sheriff Macmillan sternly. Had he still been a young man himself the sheriff would have been a great deal more sympathetic to their sorry tale of dares and wagers than he found himself now.

'But . . .' began Hamish Urquhart.

'There's a man dead, you tell me,' he interrupted firmly. Loss of life and limb, common enough though it was in mid-sixteenth century Scotland, was still not something to be taken lightly by the law.

'Missing, anyway,' parried Hamish Urquhart.

'But deid all the same,' said Malcolm Alcaig flatly.

'Must be,' said Ian Macrae ineluctably. 'There.'

'Dead, then.' Rhuaraidh Macmillan's pardonable anger at the men was compounded by his having to accept that his dislike of wagers was yet another sign of his now being well and truly middle-aged. He liked the condition no more than did the next man but it was undeniable. And he had been made even more cross because the three men in front of him had just brought that uncomfortable realisation a little nearer.

'Aye, then,' conceded Hamish Urquhart. 'Dead.'

'From the hen?' The sheriff now knew for certain what he had been beginning to suspect for some time: that middle-age was most surely upon him.

There was a shuffling of feet.

'Just a simple bet, you say?' he thundered to the three young loons now standing in front of him at his house at Drummondreach, outraged by their sorry tale. Besides, like it or not, these days he needed his secure hour in the afternoon and resented being disturbed.

Hamish Urquhart hung his head.

'Dead where?' asked the sheriff bleakly. His writ ran throughout this part of Fearnshire and the deaths of all who died untimely there came within his jurisdiction. Those who died in their beds were outwith his remit: fever and old age had no need of the inquisition of Sheriff Rhuaraidh Macmillan.

Sudden death did.

Urquhart waved an arm and muttered 'Away to the west.'

'Stop havering, man,' commanded the sheriff. 'And tell me where.'

'Cnoc Fyrish,' answered Hamish Urquhart, jerking his shoulder in a more northerly direction.

'Cnoc an Deilignidh,' said Malcolm Alcaig.

'Meann Chnoc,' said Macrae of Cornton.

'The Big Burn?' asked the sheriff.

There was a pregnant silence.

'Well?' demanded the sheriff.

'Not the Big Burn,' admitted Hamish reluctantly.

'Where if not the Big Burn?'

'The Ugly Burn.'

'Strath Glass, then,' divined the sheriff. 'So where in Strath Glass?' he asked impatiently.

'Near Novar,' said Hamish Urquhart vaguely.

The sheriff said, suddenly struck by an unhappy thought, 'Where exactly at Novar?'

Urquhart stirred uncomfortably. 'The Black Rock.'

The sheriff said sharply, 'Places don't come more dangerous than the Black Rock at Novar.'

He meant it. The site was just a narrow fissure in the rock, high above the surrounding land and immeasurably deep. It was with good reason that that stretch of the River Glass at the bottom of the chasm was known as the Ugly Burn.

'And you all know that,' he said.

'Aye,' admitted Urquhart uneasily. 'We ken that, right enough.'

'That's what made it such a good hen,' said Ian Macrae naively. He quickly subsided into silence, though, when he caught sight of the sheriff's basilisk expression.

'This man that's either dead or missing . . .' began the sheriff sarcastically, motioning the hall boy to summon his clerk and get the little palfrey he used for rough terrain saddled.

'Both,' said Malcolm Alcaig, not a man noted for his intellect.

'Who is he?'

'Calum Farquharson of that ilk,' supplied Malcolm Alcaig.

'Ye'll ken him, maybe?' said Ian Macrae.

It wasn't so much a question as a statement. The sheriff was famous as a seannachie: the genealogy of the Highlands had been bred in his bones. Besides, Calum Farquharson had been a troublemaker since childhood.

'I know him fine,' said Rhuaraidh Macmillan dryly. A blackavised giant of a man, was Calum Farquharson, given to boasting, and with not half enough brain to go with his brawn. 'So what was the hen, then?' he asked crisply.

'The man was always so fu' of hisself,' put in Malcolm Alcaig obliquely. 'Farquharson had no modesty at all.'

'He thought he could do it,' shrugged Hamish Urquhart.

'Do what?' asked the sheriff.

'Clear it.'

'Clear it?' barked Rhuaraidh Macmillan. 'The Black Rock? Was he mad? It must be all of fifteen foot across at the narrowest.'

'Seventeen,' said Malcolm Alcaig.

'We measured it with a rope,' said Ian Macrae ingenuously.

'No man can clear that distance,' said the sheriff, turning as the hall boy led his little steed out of the steading, accompanied by his clerk. He swung himself into the saddle and motioned the others to follow him. 'And,' he added sourly, 'even Calum should have known that you can't cross a chasm in two stages.'

'Lachlan Leanaig bet him he couldn't clear it,' said Hamish, falling in behind the little steed. 'That was the hen.'

'And he couldna',' said Malcolm, looking round at the other two, 'could he?'

'No,' said Hamish.

'Yes,' said Ian Macrae suddenly.

'What!' exclaimed Hamish.

'He could,' insisted Ian Macrae.

They all stared at him.

'He could,' insisted Ian Macrae, 'but he didn't,' he added hastily. 'Not then, anyway.'

'But before?' barked the sheriff. His clerk was already busy making a note.

'Aye,' said Ian Macrae. 'He cleared it right enough before.'

'Before what?' demanded the sheriff.

'Before the hen.'

'He didn't tell us that,' said Hamish Urquhart, surprised. 'When?'

'Yesterday,' said Ian insouciantly. 'He cleared it all right yesterday.'

'We didn't know that, Macrae,' said Hamish Urquhart, turning on his friend. 'How did you?'

'I was in the wood and I saw him,' said Ian simply. 'He didn't see me, though.'

Hamish Urquhart stopped in his tracks and said indignantly, 'Then it wasn't a proper hen after all.'

'Highland gentlemen don't bet on certainties,' agreed the sheriff dryly, looking down on them from his mount, and leaving aside for the time being the more germane question of whether Lachlan Leanaig had also known Calum Farquharson had cleared the distance the day before. That could come later. 'So why didn't he clear it again today?'

That silenced them all.

'He had this pole . . .' began Hamish Urquhart eventually. 'But it slipped.'

'It was bendy enough, all right,' volunteered

Malcolm. 'We saw him test it before he made the leap.'

'And long enough,' offered Ian Macrae. 'He knew that, anyway, from yesterday.'

'And yet you watched him fall,' concluded the sheriff balefully.

'Och, we couldna' do anything else,' protested Hamish Urquhart. 'There was no stopping him once he'd taken the hen.'

'There was no stopping him once he started to fall,' observed Ian Macrae, Younger, of Cornton.

The sheriff glared at him. Ian Macrae wasn't any brighter than Calum Farquharson and that wasn't saying much for either of them.

Malcolm Alcaig said, 'And nobody knows how far it is to the bottom, do they?'

Nobody did know.

It was as deep as that.

'It's nothing but a wee cleft in the hill,' muttered Hamish Urquhart rebelliously. 'There's no width to it at all.'

'Maybe, but no one comes out alive at the foot of it,' said the sheriff. 'You all know that.' The cleft ran for a good few hundred yards between the rocks: the length had been measured time and again, right enough. It was the depth that hadn't.

'We tried to get in from below with a flare,' said Hamish Urquhart.

'Afterwards,' said Ian Macrae.

'But it blew out,' said Malcolm Alcaig, 'like it always does.'

'It was aye dark in there,' shivered Ian Macrae. 'You couldn't see your hand in front of your face.'

'And you were frightened,' finished the sheriff for them, digging his heels in to the palfrey's sides to urge it on.

'They say the Devil himself lives under the Black Rock,' said Hamish.

'I'll have no talk of diablerie, you understand,' said the sheriff firmly. 'You can't be blaming Himself for a bad hen.' He looked round. 'And where's Lachlan Leanaig now?'

'He's away to the Cloutie Well with Farquharson's coat,' Hamish Urquhart told him. 'The man took it off before he jumped and left it on the ground.'

'He'll no be needing it now anyway,' remarked Ian Macrae.

'A wishing well'll do no good to a man already lying dead,' said the sheriff. 'You should know that. All of you,' he added balefully, looking round at the sorry bunch before him. 'Even you. And that includes Lachlan Leanaig.'

'No harm in trying the Cloutie Well,' muttered Hamish Urquhart obstinately. 'No harm at all.'

'This hen . . .' began the sheriff on another tack, 'Was it for merks?'

Hamish Urquhart shook his head. 'No, no, Farquharson has no need of money.'

'Not now, anyway,' said Ian Macrae, Younger, of Cornton.

'Not then, either,' supplemented Malcolm Alcaig. 'He's got land enough and to spare.'

'So . . .' The sheriff was getting impatient, 'what was the stake then?'

The young bloods shuffled their feet, looking anywhere save at the Sheriff of Fearnshire, and kept silent.

'I'll have the three of you put in irons in an instant . . .' threatened Rhuaraidh Macmillan.

'Four,' said the incorrigible Ian Macrae of Cornton.

'So that's the way of it, is it?' deduced the sheriff, unsurprised. 'So what did Lachlan Leanaig bet Calum Farquharson, then?' Lachlan Leanaig was a wild man, too, if ever there was one.

'That Calum couldn't clear the Black Rock,' said Hamish.

'And the stake?' went on Sheriff Macmillan inexorably.

'Och, it was only a woman,' mumbled Hamish.

Sheriff Macmillan tightened his lips, prudently keeping his own counsel. It was only a woman ruling Scotland just now and there was not a lot to be said for her. And what there was, he thought to himself, was better not said aloud.

Malcolm Alcaig was more forthcoming. 'Jemima from Balblair,' he said.

'Big Jemima,' said Ian Macrae, waving an arm in the direction of the south-east. 'Lachlan's fancy woman, too.'

Rhuaraidh Macmillan made no answer to this, only partly because he had no breath left now with which to do so. Any doubt that the Sheriff of Fearnshire might have had about his growing older had definitely left him halfway up the climb to the top of the Black Rock. That had been very soon after the going had got too steep for his little mount and he had had to use his own two feet from then on.

But he kept silent partly, too, because from what he'd heard she who was known as Big Jemima from Balblair had much the same way with her as far as men were concerned as did Her Majesty at Holyrood. There had been the Queen's wee mannie, David Rizzio, and then the Earl of Darnley and now James Bothwell . . . No good would seem to have come to them either.

'Calum had got on the wrong side of Lachlan

144

over Big Jemima,' explained Hamish Urquhart. 'Lachlan said he'd forget the whole stushie if Calum cleared the Black Rock.'

'This hen,' said the sheriff acidly, 'when was it laid?'

'The day before yesterday,' replied Hamish Urquhart.

'And where, may I ask, was Lachlan Leanaig yesterday when Calum was practising his leap?' enquired the sheriff when he had got enough of his breath back to speak.

There was a silence, broken by the ineffable Ian Macrae. 'I saw him going down the path to Evanton. That was after I came out of the wood.'

'Was it, indeed?' said the sheriff slowly, motioning his clerk to write that down. No one in Edinburgh had been eager to write down what had happened to Rizzio and it seemed no one knew exactly what had happened to Henry Stuart, Lord Darnley at Kirk o'Field or, if they did, they weren't keen to write that down either. But Rhuaraidh Macmillan was Sheriff of Fearnshire and he would cause to be written that which he found, and all of which he found. Not for him the mockery that had been the trial of the Earl of Bothwell, he who was now married to the woman who was Mary, Queen of Scots.

'But I don't know if he'd seen Calum clear it,' offered Ian Macrae.

'Had Leanaig seen you?' asked the sheriff pertinently.

Ian Macrae shook his head. 'No, no, I was still in the wood then.'

'So you did see Calum leap and Lachlan might have done so, too,' concluded the sheriff. 'And neither of them knew you could have known anything.'

'Aye,' agreed Ian Macrae, nodding. 'That's the right of it.'

'If Calum knew he could clear it and Lachlan knew Calum could clear it,' objected Hamish Urquhart heatedly, 'then I still say it wasn't a proper hen at all.'

'That,' said the sheriff soberly, 'is something I am taking in to avizandum.'

Hamish Urquhart looked at the sheriff blankly, while Malcolm Alcaig poked his friend in the ribs and said, 'It means he's thinking.'

'Taking matters into consideration,' the sheriff translated for him as they reached the top of the Black Rock. What the sheriff was thinking about was a wager taken by a man – Calum Farquharson – who had already demonstrated that he could accomplish the feat concerned; and a wager made by a man – Lachlan Leanaig – who might very well already have known that it could be done. What the sheriff did know – had always known – was that two wrongs never did make a right.

'Wait you behind me, all of you,' he said, 'while I take a look for myself.' Sheriff Rhuaraidh Macmillan stepped delicately over the stony ground that had been the platform from which Calum Farquharson had taken his fatal leap, though keeping well back from the edge of the drop. 'Where were you all when Calum took his jump?'

'We three were over the other side, and Lachlan was with him this side,' said Hamish.

'Seeing him off,' said Ian Macrae.

'Aye, that he was,' agreed the sheriff dourly. 'With a vengeance.' He stooped and touched the ground in one place and then another. He brought his fingers up before his face to examine them more clearly and then asked, 'When did you all last take meat together?'

'The day before yesterday,' said Hamish, looking mystified.

'And where?' barked the sheriff.

'At Castle Balgalkin,' stammered Hamish. 'Lachlan's brother's place.'

'Then that's where Lachlan Leanaig can answer to a charge of murder,' said the sheriff, turning away from the Black Rock.

'Murder?' echoed Hamish Urquhart. 'But it was only a hen.'

'It was a calculated killing,' said the sheriff sternly. 'Why do you suppose you three were sent up the other side?'

'To catch Calum when he landed?' suggested Malcolm Alcaig.

'So that you couldn't see the fat on the stone that made his pole slip,' said the sheriff, advancing his sticky fingers for their inspection. 'And which is probably why Lachlan Leanaig is off to the Cloutie Well with Calum's coat. I daresay there was fat on that too, after Calum took it off and threw it on the ground just before he jumped.'

PLANE FARE

'I can't tell you how excited the children are, Henry.' Wendy Witherington had just met her brother off the London train at Berebury. 'They've been looking forward so much to your coming down.'

'Nothing like as much as I have to getting away from London, believe me.' Henry Tyler gave his sister a friendly kiss and heaved his Gladstone bag into the boot of the little car standing outside the railway station.

'You poor dear,' said Wendy. 'It must be hard going there for you just now.'

'Between the Stresa Conference,' said Henry, who worked at the Foreign Office, 'and the machinations of Herr Adolf Hitler, it is.'

'Well,' she said calmly, 'you know that nothing exciting ever happens here in Calleshire so you should get a little rest while you're with us.'

'My dear sister, what makes you think that taking young Edward to Sir Alan Cobham's Flying Circus isn't going to be exciting? If that isn't, then I don't know what is.'

'I know, I know,' she conceded. 'And I can assure you that you're not the only one to be excited. Edward's been talking about nothing except those magnificent men in their flying machines for weeks. He's been saving up for the flight ever since Christmas.'

'Good fellow.'

'Actually,' admitted Wendy, 'he's only got two shillings so far, but with the half a crown you've promised him, he's nearly there.' She steered the car out of the station forecourt. 'I understand he has high hopes of getting the last sixpence out of his father.'

'And what does Tim have to say about that?'

'I think,' said Tim's wife, 'that he hopes to negotiate a deal with Edward over removing some weeds in the lawn in exchange for that sixpence, but I'm keeping out of that one.'

'Wise woman,' declared Henry Tyler stoutly. 'If only some politicians could manage to keep their distance from some equally delicate negotiations, our life at the office would be much more manageable.'

'Treaty trouble?'

'It's not so much treaties that are the problem,' he answered her seriously, 'as hidden alliances.'

'Ah . . .' Wendy negotiated a blind corner with care. 'Secret promises.'

'You could say, Wen,' went on Henry, bruised from recent encounters with both Lord Halifax and Herr Joachim von Ribbentrop, 'that treaties are only written to be torn up . . .'

'I wouldn't say any such thing,' she protested.

'But at least,' he carried on regardless, 'with a treaty you can see what was and what wasn't agreed in the first place. Gives you somewhere to start.'

'Henry, you're getting cynical.'

'I can assure you, my dear, with the best will in the world, hidden alliances can undo a country completely.' Henry stared out of the passenger window as the car passed through the environs of the pleasant and peaceful little market town of Berebury and wondered how long it would remain both pleasant and peaceful. 'I'm glad Edward's happy, anyway. That's something to be grateful for at this sad juncture in world history.'

'Ecstatic would be a better way of describing his state of mind,' said Edward's mother frankly, 'even though at this very moment he might well be on his knees pulling out dandelions.'

'I'm glad to hear it,' said Henry Tyler.

'Aeroplanes are going to be the only way to travel one day and it's good for small boys to begin to learn that while they're young.'

Wendy Witherington shivered. 'There's a war coming, isn't there, Henry?'

'Edward'll be too young for it,' he replied obliquely. Obliqueness had been raised to a high art at the Foreign Office. 'Much too young.'

'Even so I still don't like the idea of him – or you, for that matter – going to a Flying Circus,' frowned Wendy. 'It doesn't sound very safe.'

'I don't think Alan Cobham wants it to sound safe,' said Henry Tyler who, by virtue of working where he did, knew all about the difference between what something sounded and what it actually was. 'He wants it to sound exciting even though it may be – will be – safe.'

Wendy shivered again. 'All I want is for everything to be safe,' she said.

'It isn't going to be "Peace for ever" old thing, or even "Peace for long",' he said, giving her a sideways glance, 'but I think you know that anyway, don't you?'

Wendy Witherington sighed. 'I do, and so does Tim.' She essayed a smile. 'At least Jennifer doesn't want to go up in an aeroplane. She says the noise keeps her dolls awake.'

'Good for Jennifer,' said her doting uncle

warmly, as Wendy slowed the car down for a pedestrian crossing. 'I say, not yet another Belisha beacon in Berebury, surely?'

'We shan't be able to move for them soon,' forecast Wendy. 'I don't know if Mr Hore-Belisha knows what he's started with his crossings for making pedestrians safe.'

'Probably not. Politicians seldom do realise what they've started and they've moved on before anyone finds out. There's just one thing though, Wendy,' Henry said, his mind still back at his office desk. 'I must warn you that if the Abyssinian Crisis gets any worse, I may have to go back to London in a hurry – or even to France.' He grimaced. 'I'm afraid the League of Nations isn't quite as resolute as the League of Gentlemen.'

'Henry, I beg of you not to mention Abyssinia while you're here.'

He looked up, puzzled. 'But Haile Selassie . . .'

'It's not him,' she said. 'It's Edward and his friend Frobisher.'

'Edward and Frobisher?'

'Edward and Frobisher and all the other boys in their class at school. They've started to say "Abyssinia" instead of "I'll be seeing you", and I just won't have it.' She turned her head. 'And it's no use your laughing, Henry. It's no laughing matter.'

'No,' he agreed soberly. 'Abyssinia is no laughing matter. The Lion of Judah is having a very hard time just now.'

'Poor little man,' she said compassionately. 'I felt so sorry for him when he walked out of that meeting.'

'He may be short in stature,' said Henry, 'but he's a great fellow all the same.'

'There's something else Edward and his friends are chanting all the time these days,' went on Wendy Witherington, the wife and mother in her triumphing over current affairs, 'so I'm warning you now.'

'Thank you,' he said and meant it. If only his political masters would give the Foreign Office more warning of what they were about to do and say before they did either life would be so much simpler for all concerned.

'You know that expression, Henry, "If pigs could fly . . ."'

'Of course.'

'They finish it with "you'd have to shoot your bacon".'

'So you would,' he said solemnly. Saving bacon – other people's bacon, that is – was what he had to do in his line of work. All the time.

'There's something else you should be prepared for,' she said lightly. 'Edward has decided he wants to work in the Foreign Office like you. He's going to ask you what he should study.'

'History and human nature,' grinned Henry, 'and a few dirty tricks on the side.'

'I'm not so sure that I like . . .'

'I know, tell him to start by learning to read upside down,' said Henry. 'That always comes in handy when you're sitting opposite a chap who's got his guidance notes on his desk in front of him.'

Wendy took a left turn and waved her hand in the direction of a big field on their right. 'That's Berebury aerodrome over there.'

'Airfield,' he corrected her. 'They don't call them aerodromes any more.'

'What about the sausage?' she pointed to something red waving in the breeze. 'Are they calling that something else now, too?'

'Windsock,' he said.

Young Edward used the right word for it, too, the next day when he and Henry reported to the little office at Berebury Airfield. 'And the wind's right for take-off, Uncle Henry,' he said jubilantly.

'Good.' Henry pointed to a plane on the runway, its propeller already turning. 'Is that ours?'

'No. That's a Heracles,' said Edward

knowledgeably. 'She goes to Le Touquet. Regular run every morning by the Calleshire Aviation Company.'

As the doors of the airport waiting room opened and a little clutch of travellers emerged, Henry realised that they were indeed genuine passengers not mere seekers of flying experience.

'Not many of them, though,' observed Henry. 'The plane'll be half empty.'

'I know. Frobisher's father says they won't be able to keep up the service much longer at this rate and he's very worried because he's got a lot of money invested in it.'

'Then what'll happen?' asked Henry. Thinking about what would happen in a given set of circumstances was something he did all the time – and only wished his political masters would do the same.

'Frobisher's father says if it goes on losing money it would have to close down,' said Edward. 'And then he'll be bankrupt.'

'I can see that it might have to shut up shop,' said Henry, a man who prized realism in others. 'And if he put all his eggs in one basket . . .'

Edward gulped. 'Frobisher says that would mean that they have to sell their house and move away. Frobisher wouldn't like that and neither would I.'

'Then what'll happen?' said Henry automatically. In the privacy of his own office in Whitehall he called his usual sequence of questions 'Consequences'.

'Dunno,' said Edward. 'Not after that. I'd miss him, though. A lot.'

'Edward,' asked Henry, 'do you and your friend Frobisher ever play the game of Consequences?'

'Sometimes,' said Edward. 'When we're bored.' Suddenly he tugged at Henry's sleeve. 'Look, Uncle, there's our plane. Over there.'

First, Henry watched as the Heracles took to the air, executed an elegant turn and set off over Calleshire towards the French coast, and then looked at where Edward was pointing. 'And is ours named after a Greek hero, too?'

'I don't think so,' said Edward uncertainly. 'We haven't started to do Greek yet. It's just an old biplane, anyway.'

'Don't tell your mother that, will you?' begged Henry. 'She's worried about us enough.'

'Nothing to worry about,' said the boy confidently, 'though I wish we were going up in that DH 84 over there. Lovely, isn't she?'

Henry looked across the airfield at yet another aeroplane.

'A De Havilland,' Edward informed him. 'They use those for the London–Paris run, too.'

'But you can't fly to Paris from here,' said Henry. His secretary had already ascertained in advance that if Henry were wanted in France he would have to fly from Berebury to Le Touquet where he would be met by a car and driver and hastened away to a conference at an unspecified location. To go back to Croydon, let alone Hendon, from Berebury and fly from there, would take much longer. Too long for his masters, anyway.

'No,' said Edward. 'That one goes to Le Touquet, too.'

'Why are there two services going to the same place?'

'I'm not sure,' said the boy. 'Frobisher's father thinks it's strange, too. But I can tell you one thing, Uncle Henry . . .'

'What's that?'

'People seem to prefer the De Havilland plane. Frobisher's father says that the Berebury Flying Company is doing very well and he can't understand why when the Calleshire Aviation Company isn't.'

'I wonder why, too,' said Henry idly, before putting the thought out of his mind as they were called to the departure lounge on the tannoy system. What exercised his thought processes after that was the exact position in the

158

stratosphere of the Seventh Heaven. Wherever it was, Edward at least reached it that morning.

He, himself, was brought heavily down to earth as soon as they got back to his sister's house.

'It's just too bad, Henry,' said Wendy, 'because you've really only just come, but you've got to go now . . .'

'London calling?'

'London calling,' she said, 'but it's France where you're wanted. You're booked on the four o'clock flight to Le Touquet.'

'That's the De Havilland,' said Edward before Henry could ask. 'Can Frobisher and me . . .'

'I,' his mother corrected him automatically. 'Not me.'

'Can both of us, then,' said Edward impatiently, 'come and see you off? Oh, please, Uncle Henry, please, Mummy.'

'Your secretary,' went on Wendy, 'said she was sorry it was so late in the afternoon but the earlier flight was fully booked.'

'Oh, please, Mummy,' persisted Edward, 'can we go to watch Uncle Henry take off?'

'If he doesn't mind,' said Wendy Witherington, passing the buck with practised maternal ease.

'The earlier one being the Calleshire Aviation Company's and the later one the Berebury Flying

Company's?' suggested Henry. 'Well, well . . .'

His sister frowned. 'I think that's what she said but it wasn't a very good line. Anyway, your tickets will be ready for you when you get to the aerodrome.'

'Airfield,' chimed Henry and Edward in unison.

'And,' said Wendy Witherington, rising above the correction, 'there will be a car waiting for you at Le Touquet.' She glanced down at a piece of paper in her hand. 'Your secretary thought you would like to know that your minister will be waiting at your destination.'

Henry bit back his immediate retort in the interests of childcare.

But he got back to the airfield early enough to drift into the offices of the Calleshire Aviation Company and enquire casually about a flight the next day.

'Very sorry, sir, but tomorrow's service to Le Touquet is fully booked,' said the booking office clerk, consulting a chart on the desk in front of him at some length.

'I really do need to get to France by tomorrow evening,' lied Henry. 'It's quite urgent.'

'I could only fit you in if there's a last-minute cancellation,' said the man. 'And we can't count on that. Very sorry, sir.'

'Is there any other service?' asked Henry.

'You could try the Berebury Aviation Company,' offered the man. 'They may be able to help you.'

'I'll do that,' said Henry.

In the event what he did was scribble a note, which he handed to Edward. 'Give that to your friend Frobisher,' he said.

'Frobisher?

'For his father,' said Henry. 'It might save him from going bankrupt.'

'But, Uncle . . .'

'For Frobisher's father,' said Henry Tyler. 'So that he knows his booking clerk's telling the customers that the planes are full when they aren't.'

Edward looked at him, wide-eyed. 'He was lying?'

'In his teeth,' said Henry. 'As I told your mother, learning to read upside down is very useful. That clerk wasn't looking at a booking list at all when he said the flight was full. It was just his own off-duty roster. My guess is that he's in league with the opposition.' He picked up his bag. 'There's quite a lot of it about.'

DEAF MAN TALKING

'Come down to stay? Of course you may, Henry. It'll be lovely to see you again.'

'Sorry it's such short notice, Wen,' said Henry Tyler, who was telephoning from his office in Whitehall, 'but needs must when the devil drives.'

'Henry, dear, you can always come at any time,' said his sister, Wendy Witherington, warmly. 'You know that. Besides, the children will be so pleased to see their favourite uncle again. You don't come back to Calleshire anything like often enough these days.'

'Life at the office has been quite busy lately,' he said mildly. It was the understatement of the year. The office at which Henry Tyler worked was the Foreign Office and his desk one of those situated in a room of its own with a large area of good carpet and it was very busy indeed.

'Then it will do you good to get away for a few days,' said his sister firmly.

'Tim will be pleased to see you, too. It's the Berebury Spring Meeting this week and it will be so nice to have you with us.' Tim Witherington was his sister's husband and a keen racegoer. 'You can help Tim cheer the horses on.'

'I've got to see a man about a dog as well, though,' insisted Henry. 'That's why I'm coming down.'

'You can do that, too,' said his sister placidly. 'All in good time.'

Henry didn't attempt to explain to her that what he – or the Foreign Office, either – didn't have was good time. World events were moving much too quickly for that, speeded by the activities of one Herr Joachim von Ribbentrop, presently German Ambassador to the Court of St James. Nobody there had yet decided whether the fact that the Prime Minister and Herr Adolf Hitler could only communicate through interpreters was a help or a hindrance. Henry, though, had written firmly in his latest precis that in his opinion 'Only bishops gained by translation'.

Actually, the man Henry had come to Berebury to see did have a dog but it wasn't about a liver-and-white spaniel called Raffles that Henry had come to see him. Henry found himself

163

standing beside the man and his dog, apparently by accident, when taking a walk in Berebury's public gardens.

Henry, armed with some pieces of bread, had been standing by the sailing pond there feeding the ducks when the other man, who had also been feeding the ducks but at a different point of the pond, casually drifted in his direction. He began speaking to Henry without looking at him, both looking out across the water, apparently unconnected.

'Briggs,' he said. 'Charles Briggs.'

'Thought so,' said Henry without turning his head. 'And our man?'

'He's the chap in the brown trilby over there,' said Briggs.

'Disguised as an Englishman, then,' said Henry ironically. The man in the brown trilby was moving his hand in an odd way between his hat and his shoulder.

'Sitting on the bench just to the left of that ghastly grotto,' said Briggs, ignoring this last.

'Very popular in eighteenth-century gardens, grottos,' said Henry. 'You used to keep a tame hermit in them to frighten the natives.'

'And now you have something nasty in the woodshed instead, I suppose,' growled Charles Briggs. 'Only our nasty piece of work isn't actually in the grotto. He's sitting out there in the open air.'

'Which you think he needs for his dirty work?'

'Well,' said Briggs frankly, 'he's signalling to someone but who or how we don't know. Except,' he added, 'he needs his arms to do it. Look at the way he's clenching his fists now.'

'And it's not by semaphore, you say.'

'First thing that we thought it might be because he was moving his arms so much, but as any Boy Scout could tell you, it isn't semaphore.'

'Or Morse?'

'We thought about that, too – you know, waving one arm for a dot and the other for a dash, but the code-breakers couldn't make anything of it. And before you ask, it's not your usual sign language.'

'Not a deaf man talking, then,' murmured Henry absently. 'But we do know that something is getting through to his masters, because we put some duff information in his way on purpose.'

'A test run,' agreed Briggs.

'Our people put it about that there was a secret arms dump behind Kinnisport and blow me if a couple of his friends didn't come noseying around four days later looking for it. It was the corporation tip, actually, so they couldn't tell if there was anything under it or not.'

'Doesn't surprise me at all.' Briggs tossed a handful of bread towards some noisy sheldrake. 'You let them go, I take it?'

'Oh, yes,' said Henry. 'We know all about them. But,' he added grimly, 'it won't always be dummy messages that your fellow sends and we must find out how he does it. And soon.'

Charles Briggs grunted. 'We've known that someone is picking up his messages but I'm blessed if we can work out how.'

'Pigeons?' suggested Henry.

'We checked that, too. Besides,' said Charles Briggs, 'we keep sparrowhawks on the strength, you know.' What might have been a grin passed over his face. 'Ever since the Duke of Wellington advised Queen Victoria to try sparrowhawks, ma'am, for a plague of sparrows.'

'Great man, the Iron Duke,' said Henry absently. That they could do with someone of his calibre in Downing Street today went without saying.

'Moreover,' said Briggs, tossing a handful of bread towards a flotilla of widgeon, 'someone's picking his messages up here, in this park.'

'Have you spotted who?'

'Not yet,' said Briggs under cover of the loud quacking of ducks struggling for the bread. 'There are quite a few people who come here every day, walking dogs and so forth. Men and women,' he

166

added darkly. 'Mata Hari didn't know what she was starting.'

'And the beauty of his method, whatever it is,' said Henry, 'is that he doesn't even need to know who he is signalling to.'

'Exactly,' said Briggs.

Henry Tyler cast his gaze round the pond. It was evidently a popular place in the middle of the afternoon. There were old men and women settled on the benches and several young women with prams strolling up and down in the early sunshine. The faces of one or two of those sitting on the benches were hidden behind newspapers and in the middle of one of the beds of tulips a gardener was engaged in weeding in a very desultory fashion. The desultoriness could have come from natural laziness or from keeping a keen eye on the man on the bench beside the grotto: Henry was unable to decide which. Unless he was very much mistaken, very soon able-bodied men would not be weeding flowerbeds but engaged on more active service elsewhere.

'Do be careful where you look,' urged Briggs. 'Remember, it's an old saying that if you can see them, then they can see you.'

Henry Tyler sighed. One of Whitehall's greatest fears at the present time was that the next war was going to be fought on the maxims of the last. He contented himself with saying 'Quite so,' and instead watched one child – a boy – who had caught Henry's eye. He was playing with a toy boat that was seemingly powered by a battery as it crossed the pond.

'Wireless?' he murmured to the man at his side, prompted by the sight.

'We can't pick up any signal.'

'Field telephone?'

'No wires in sight,' said Briggs, 'and his ordinary telephone's had a tap on it ever since Fritz moved here. Presumably he came to keep an eye on the new tank factory at Luston, to say nothing of the old aerodrome that's being refurbished with the speed of light. Oh, and the harbour over at Kinnisport.'

'Heliograph?' said Henry, who was renowned for sticking to the point at issue.

'In our weather?'

'We're not sufficiently grateful for the vagaries of the English climate,' conceded Henry.

'I don't think sunshine would be quite reliable enough,' said Briggs seriously, 'and anyway it would be relatively easy to spot and whatever this chap is doing it isn't obvious except for the arm movements. Look at him now – putting a hand to his ear.'

'As far as we can make out,' advanced Henry carefully, 'he's sending blocks of numbers.'

'Well, he would be, wouldn't he?' said Briggs. 'Only we don't know the code.'

'If we knew the numbers we might be able to work that out but what we really want to know is how he's getting them across to his contact,' persisted Henry, mindful of his obligations to one of the great offices of state.

'Which means you don't want him caught just yet?' deduced Briggs.

'Not until we know his working methods,' said Henry, adding lightly, 'After all, we might like to use them ourselves. You never know, do you?'

'Never,' said Charles Briggs, conspicuously emptying the last of his paper bag of bread over the water and preparing to walk away. He gave a loud whistle to his dog. 'Come along, Raffles. Good boy.' As the dog's tail waved excitedly he added, 'Shall I see you tomorrow, then?'

'Not tomorrow,' said Henry. 'Wouldn't do to be seen together too often. Besides, I've got to be somewhere else tomorrow. Let's say the day after.'

Henry lingered quite a while after Briggs had gone, from time to time tossing a handful of bread in the direction of a pair of ruddy ducks and glancing only once towards the grotto. The man there was definitely moving his arms about in a curious way. It was quite impossible to see which of the many people who were also about could be taking notes of what the movements meant.

'Casting his bread on the waters' would be the only way in which he would be properly able to describe his day's work to his superiors when he made his report that night.

The next day was different.

'Good to have you with us,' said Tim Witherington as they set out for the Berebury Races. 'Wen needs restraining once she's seen the jockeys.'

'I thought it was form that mattered,' said Henry.

'And the horses,' protested Wendy.

'That's true,' agreed her husband promptly. 'If it's a chestnut, she backs it.'

'What about the going?' enquired Henry. Just now the expression 'hard going' could be applied to places other than racecourses but he didn't say so. Days such as these must be enjoyed, indeed relished, come what may, because they might not come again for a very long time. If ever, he added to himself, a realist to the core. 'Surely the going matters, too?'

'It does,' said his brother-in-law jovially, 'but I swear Wen really goes by what the jockeys are wearing.'

'The colours are so lovely,' said Wendy Witherington dreamily. 'And the horses are beautiful always.'

'There – what did I say?' said Tim. 'That's women for you.'

'Time will tell,' said Henry. 'Now, which horse are you two going to put your shirts on in the first race?'

'That's the Perry Plate,' said his sister, consulting her race card. 'Me, I'm backing St Meast.'

'I like the look of Almstone,' said Tim Witherington. 'She ran well in her last race even though it was on ground that might have been too firm for her.'

'I'll remember that,' promised Henry. Firm ground was something they didn't have at the Foreign Office just now. In the event he plumped for a horse called Staple St James.

'You'll get long odds,' said Tom. 'She's never won much.'

'You've got to take some risks in this life,' he said idly, his mind still on the spy in the park.

'They're off,' said Wendy, jumping up and down in excitement. 'Oh, come on, do, St Meast.'

'It's no good, Wen, Almstone's way ahead,' said her husband smugly a few moments later. 'I'll just go and collect my winnings from Honest Joe over there.'

But Wendy Witherington had already turned her attention to the next race. 'Now, Henry, who do you think's going to win the Coronation Stakes?'

'Queen Elizabeth,' said Henry absently.

'I meant which horse, you silly,' she said affectionately, slipping her arm into his.

He backed the loser in that race, too.

'It's the Ornum Cup next,' said Wendy, peering at the owner's box, 'but I can't see the Duke anywhere.' She looked disappointed. 'The Duchess is there but he always comes, too. Always.'

Her husband gave a little cough. 'I heard that he was with his regiment,' he said quietly.

Wendy looked dismayed. 'Already?'

'Already,' said Tim Witherington. 'Now, who are you backing in the Jubilee Stakes?'

'Ryrie,' said Wendy. 'She looks a good goer and I've backed her at six to four. And you, Henry?'

'Cullingoak,' said Henry firmly.

'She's still a hundred to one,' said Tim.

'I have a weakness for outsiders,' said Henry truthfully. It was the insiders who were giving him trouble at the Foreign Office just now.

'Cullingoak's still running at a hundred to one,' said Tim, when he got back from the bookmaker. 'No hope, there, I'm afraid.'

'Never mind,' said Henry, suddenly alert. 'I

say, Tim, lend me your binoculars for a moment, will you?'

His brother-in-law handed them over with a laugh. 'Horses don't run any faster when you're watching them, you know.'

Henry didn't answer. He was concentrating his gaze on something that suddenly seemed familiar. There was a man standing beside Tim's bookmaker who was making gestures that he had seen before: odd movements of hand to shoulder. This man, too, had his arm bent at the elbow and was touching his hat and shoulder in rapid succession.

'You're meant to be watching the race, old boy,' said Tim, nudging him, 'not the tic-tac men.'

'So I am,' said Henry amiably. 'They're transmitting sets of numbers to other bookies, aren't they?'

Tom nodded. 'Only we don't know which ones. The bookies do, of course.'

'Of course. What you might call a racing certainty.' Henry handed Tim's binoculars back to him. 'I'm just off to make a telephone call but I'll be back in time for the Berebury Handicap.'

BENCHMARK

'I don't believe it,' said Detective Inspector Sloan.

'It's true, sir,' insisted Detective Constable Crosby.

'Tell me again what they said,' commanded Sloan.

'That they were thinking,' said the detective constable.

'That all?'

'Yes, sir.'

'You're joking.'

'No, I'm not, sir,' said Detective Constable Crosby earnestly.

'Then, Crosby, you might as well file the report under *T* for "Tall Order".'

'But that's what they said,' persisted the young constable. 'That they were still thinking.'

'Both of them?'

'Both of them. Larky Nolson and Melvin

Boness said exactly the same thing to me one after the other.'

Sloan said scornfully, 'Just that they were still thinking and it was no use interviewing either of them about last night's job at Bellamy's warehouse just yet?'

'That's right, sir, because they said they weren't going to say anything yet even if we tried to get them to all day.'

'I'm the one who decides when they're interviewed and for how long,' said Sloan, mindful of a whole raft of new requirements in connection with taking suspects into custody. 'And I'm certainly not going to try to all day. I've got better things to do.'

'Yes, sir.'

'Besides,' he added with some asperity, 'as you ought to know very well by now, Crosby, there are various procedures specifically designed to prevent the police trying to get anyone who is detained saying anything they don't want to. And I don't only mean torture,' he added, since this did seem to have been on the agenda of some less enlightened regimes.

'Yes, sir, I know that and so do they.'

'I'll bet they do.' Some criminals were better versed in police procedure than some policemen and Sloan for one knew that only too well. 'So where do we go from here? And, Crosby, I must remind you again that I haven't got all day.'

'I think, sir, what they mean is that they're not going to be saying anything at all to us about the raid on Bellamy's warehouse and what's happened to what they took – I mean,' the constable hastily amended this in the interests of political correctness, 'to what is said to have been taken from there – until they've finished thinking.'

'Finished!' snorted Sloan. 'They've never even started thinking. Not that pair.'

'No, sir.'

'If they had they wouldn't be in the police station in the first instance.'

'No, sir – I mean, yes, sir.'

'And I should also point out to you that if either of them could think any further then they wouldn't have been caught in such potentially compromising circumstances as they were at two o'clock in the morning.'

'No, sir.'

'Mind you, Crosby, on mature reflection, perhaps we should remember that stupid criminals are easier to catch than clever ones.' A clever villain was one of the reasons why Detective Inspector Sloan had other things to do that day; investigating transactional fraud not being for amateurs.

'Yes, sir, that's very true.'

'Anyway, why on earth should they ever think that we hadn't noticed the aforementioned circumstances at the break-in at Bellamy's last night? And the bolt-croppers they had with them and left behind them, come to that. What do they think we are? Blind?'

'No, sir. Actually "Going equipped" is one of the charges and "After the hours of darkness" is mentioned.'

'I trust,' growled Sloan, 'that you've made quite sure that they're being kept well apart.'

'Oh, yes, sir. They're definitely out of the hearing of each other.'

'And there's no way they can play games such as tapping the water pipes between cells with Morse code or whatever? Or, let us be realistic, mobile phones?'

'No, sir.' Crosby hesitated. 'But I think if they hadn't been separated they'd have decided between them what to say by now.'

'So do I, Crosby, so do I.' Inspector Sloan sighed. 'Then all I can say is that you'd better see that they don't get their act together while I have a word with him upstairs.'

Unfortunately him upstairs – actually his superior officer, Superintendent Leeyes – was not in a good mood. When appealed to for extra time he was more unbending than many a cricket umpire.

'I take it, Sloan, that applying for permission for extending their detention for further questioning is your idea of humour. Those two villains wouldn't begin to know how to think however long you gave them. Neither of them.'

'Very possibly, sir. And I can't even say in their favour that they're exactly cooperating with us either,' said Detective Inspector Sloan gloomily. Doctors, he knew, liked cooperative and optimistic patients. Policemen were happy to settle for cooperative interviewees, optimism not usually being called for in the circumstances.

'Cooperate with you, Sloan? Why on earth should they?' Leeyes sniffed. 'Remember, it's not incumbent on anyone who has been arrested to cooperate with the police. You should know that by now, man.'

'No, sir, but there can be advantages for the accused in doing so.' He frowned. 'Besides, there's something else. His present behaviour makes quite a change for Larky Nolson and that's something I can't understand. He usually croaks when he's been nicked, does our Larky. And pretty pronto, come to that. Something must be niggling him or else Melvin Boness has got some sort of hold over him.'

'Nothing to stop Larky rowing for the shore this time round if he wants to,' snorted Leeyes. The superintendent always liked an early admission of guilt, preferably accompanied by the prompt implication of any accomplices. It saved on the paperwork.

'I'm not so sure about that, sir,' said Sloan.

'What do you mean, Sloan? There's nothing stopping him admitting it, is there? It's a free country, isn't it? He can confess if he wants to.'

Since Superintendent Leeyes was in the habit of averring to all and sundry that it wasn't a free country any more, Sloan was careful what he said. 'Well, sir, if Larky were to confess and Melvin Boness kept his mouth shut, Larky'd probably get off and Boness'd get – what would you say – three years?'

'You never can tell with our Bench,' prevaricated Leeyes. 'That's the trouble with Hetty.'

Miss Henrietta Meadows was the chairman of the Berebury Bench of Magistrates and a stickler for the book.

'But . . .' began Sloan.

'Oh, all right then, three years, with luck,' agreed the superintendent. 'With luck on our side, that is,' he added, a man made bitter by light sentencing. 'I suppose you could say on the other hand Larky might get three years if Melvin Boness confessed and our Larky didn't.'

'But if they both sing and split on each other . . .' began Sloan.

'I reckon each of 'em would get two years or thereabouts,' pronounced the superintendent weightily. 'The Bench being what it is and Miss Meadows being what she is.'

'Exactly, sir. That's just what I mean because the other option is for them both to stay silent.'

'Ah! I get you.' Leeyes pounced. 'I doubt if they'd get more than a year then, not with our Hettie in the chair. She would argue that she hadn't got enough to go on and so it wouldn't be fair.'

'I daresay she would.'

'She calls it being punctilious,' went on the superintendent, carefully refraining from saying that wasn't what he called it.

'Advised by the Clerk, of course,' murmured Sloan.

'In my experience,' said Superintendent Leeyes loftily, ignoring this last, 'every Bench of Magistrates that I've ever known always gets cold feet when there's no defence put forward. They don't like it. Not cricket or something,' he said disdainfully.

'It takes two to tango,' said Sloan with seeming

irrelevance. It was true all the same, though, when it came to the law. Both the prosecution and the defence had to believe in the process – even if the accused didn't. Or the superintendent, he added piously to himself.

'Given half a chance,' growled the superintendent, misunderstanding him, 'either of 'em would lead us a pretty dance.'

'But,' Sloan pointed out, hoping he'd got it right, 'for each to act in the best interest of both is to run the risk of betrayal by the other.'

'As I have said time and time again,' trumpeted Leeyes, 'there is no such thing as honour among thieves.'

'No, sir – I mean, yes, sir.'

'Which is why you must keep them apart, Sloan. I don't like this idea of crime without punishment. Never have.' Actually, given half a chance, and with capital punishment still on the Statute Book, the superintendent would doubtless have favoured the ancient and customary ruling known as Gibbet Law which didn't trouble itself with trials.

'No, sir.' Detective Inspector Sloan drew breath and started on a different tack. 'The interesting thing is that if they both act selfishly . . .'

'I've never met an unselfish crook,' remarked Leeyes conversationally.

'. . . then it means that they do get some punishment but . . .'

'Although I daresay not as much as they should have done,' interrupted the superintendent robustly, 'and don't always get,' he added, mindful of the punctilious Miss Henrietta Meadows and the local Bench.

'But not as much punishment as they might have done if they hadn't both shopped each other,' finished Detective Inspector Sloan at last.

The superintendent sighed. 'So what you're saying, Sloan, is that if they both clam up, it's best for them.'

'That's right, sir.'

Leeyes said, 'Which series of theoretical propositions, Sloan, I may say is exactly what William Langland in his book *The Vision of William Concerning Piers the Plowman* called Do-Well, Do-Better and Do-Best.'

'Really, sir?' That must have come from the ill-fated evening course that the superintendent had attended on 'Early English Literature' – until, that is, he had fallen out with the lecturer over the matter of the lady fair in the traditional old ballad 'The Twa Corbies' who had ignored the body of her new-slain knight lying in the dyke and ta'en another mate. Criminal behaviour, the superintendent had called it, not prepared to hold that 'The Twa Corbies' was allegorical as well as poetic.

'Of course,' the superintendent went on thoughtfully, 'the pair of 'em might not know what's best for them.'

'Exactly, sir. The other thing they probably don't know is that the next best thing is for each of them to shop the other.'

'Well, they wouldn't, would they?' said Leeyes. 'Know that, I mean.'

'Not in the ordinary way – that is, unless they'd taken advice on the matter.'

Leeyes pounced like a cat on a mouse.

'Anyone who gave them that sort of advice would be in trouble.'

'I suppose, sir,' said Sloan hastily, 'they could have always agreed their best course of action beforehand.'

'In my experience,' said the superintendent loftily, 'the only thing crooks usually agree on beforehand is the division of the spoils and then they go and fall out over it afterwards.'

For one heady moment Detective Inspector Sloan considered bringing Geoffrey Chaucer's 'The Pardoner's Tale' into the discussion since that, too, was concerned with the criminal distribution of the spoils of crime but he dismissed the thought just as quickly. The superintendent might well have abandoned his study of Early English Literature before they'd got to *The Canterbury Tales*. 'I understand, sir,' he advanced cautiously instead, 'it's what the psychologists call the Prisoner's Dilemma.'

Sloan held his breath before he carried on since mention of psychologists was inclined to upset the superintendent. 'It's the paradox of a game between two contestants, sir,' he said hurriedly, 'in which one person's loss is not necessarily the other's gain.'

'Medal play in golf,' responded the superintendent immediately. 'It doesn't help your score if the man you're playing with shoots his ball into a water hazard. It's the course you're up against.'

'Er – quite so, sir,' said Sloan, not a golfer.

'Give me a "for instance",' ordered Leeyes, sounding unconvinced. 'And you needn't say the game of Rubber Bridge.'

'Roulette,' said Sloan on the spur of the moment.

'The banker always wins,' said Leeyes sourly.

'Yes, sir,' said Sloan, adding, 'They call it the non-zero-sum, by the way.'

'I call it a waste of time,' said the superintendent, 'and I'm too busy to go in to the ins and outs of it just now. Keep me in the picture though,

Sloan . . . and let me know who shops who.'

'If either of them does,' Sloan reminded him. 'Or both.'

'That might be the Prisoner's Dilemma, Sloan, but if neither of them sing, then I'm afraid it's ours.'

'Yes, sir.'

'And, Sloan . . .'

'Sir?'

'Make sure the best man wins.'

THE QUEEN OF HEARTS

'We must be very careful about what we do about this,' said the secretary of the Berebury Bridge Club. 'Very careful. Remember Tranby Croft.'

'Who was he?' asked the director.

'It wasn't a he,' said the secretary. 'It was a place. A house where a man was accused of cheating at cards. Baccarat, as it happens. It's a French game and it all ended in tears.' He pushed his glasses back up his nose. 'Well, in court, actually.'

'Don't like the sound of that,' said the club's chairman, edging his coffee cup to one side. The committee was meeting in his dining room.

'Moreover, it was with the Prince of Wales giving evidence,' said the secretary. 'The one who became Edward VII.'

'Tum Tum,' said the chairman.

The others stared at him.

'That's what they called him,' said the chairman, whose own corporation was on the generous side. 'Liked good food.' He picked up a plate and looked round. 'Another biscuit, anyone? I don't like the sound of court at all.'

'And I don't like the idea of anyone cheating here in our club in Berebury,' growled the director.

'And getting away with it,' chimed in the secretary.

'They haven't got away with it if we know about it,' pointed out the director.

'They have if we let them go on doing it,' said the secretary energetically.

'Get away with what, exactly?' asked the chairman. 'I need to know if I've got to take a view.'

'I've taken one,' said the director flatly.

The chairman suppressed a sigh. The director was inclined to take the football match view – the old-fashioned one, anyway – that the referee was right even when he was wrong and as far as the Berebury Bridge Club was concerned, the director was the referee.

'Suppose you give me the facts,' the chairman suggested. 'All I seem to remember is hearing that there had been a problem with a finesse at a match at the club last week. Is that what you're all talking about?'

'You weren't here at the time,' said the director pointedly. 'Holiday or business or something like that.'

The chairman ignored both his tone and the implied criticism and said, 'Go on.'

'It was someone . . .' began the director.

'Better just call them North,' advised the chairman cautiously, 'to be on the safe side.'

'Oh, all right, then, North it shall be,' acquiesced the director readily enough. 'It was like this, chairman. If he was North then it was East and West who were in a contract of four spades and I can tell you it was a bit iffy.'

'For one thing,' amplified the secretary, 'East had only given West, who was the dealer, a small raise on his opening bid of one spade. It was West who went on to a game contract in spite of that.'

'Not a lay-down then,' said the chairman, nodding his understanding.

'But West is a good player and knew what he was doing,' said the secretary.

'Such as finessing the Jack of Hearts,' said director. 'I know that because I was there.'

'So?' said the chairman, a man chosen for his eminent tact, discretion and good sense. 'I wasn't, so tell me.'

'I had told you that dummy wasn't all that wonderful, hadn't I?' said the director. 'Anyway, it was near the end of play. The Ace and Queen of Hearts were on the table – and the contract hung on either the Queen or the Jack making, all the trumps being out by then.'

'The lead was in West's hand at the time,' added the secretary, 'and he had the Jack of Hearts.'

'Not exactly a tenace, then,' nodded the chairman.

'What's that?' asked the secretary sharply.

'The combination in one hand of the cards next above and next below the other side's best in the suit,' explained the chairman. 'From the Spanish for pincers.'

'As I was trying to say,' interrupted the director, 'West leads the Jack of Hearts from his own hand up to the Ace and Queen on the table, naturally hoping that North will cover the Jack with his King.'

'Which he could only have done if he held it, though,' pointed out the chairman.

'Exactly,' said the secretary. 'That's the nub of the matter.'

'Which King of Hearts,' carried on the director, not deflected, 'could then be taken by the Ace, thus making dummy's Queen good.'

'Which Queen of Hearts West would subsequently play from dummy when it suited him,' finished the secretary.

'And thus making the contract,' said the director.

The chairman said, 'So if West played the Jack to dummy to finesse it and South and not North had the King and he puts it on the Jack and takes the trick, West loses the contract? That it?'

'It is. Although of course the Queen would be good after that, West doesn't make his contract and doesn't collect a lot of points. If my memory serves me right East/West were vulnerable at the time.'

'But not doubled,' said the director quickly. 'That would have made a big difference to the play in any finesse. West could have had some idea of where the King was if the contract had been doubled.'

'Only, that is,' pointed out the secretary pedantically, 'if the double had come from the stronger hand. Of course everyone knows that it's always better if it's the weaker hand that does the doubling.'

'And so,' said the chairman, never one to waste time, 'who did have the King of Hearts then?'

'That was the funny thing,' said the director. 'South had it and didn't put it on.'

'So West made his contract,' chimed in the secretary.

'Exactly,' said the director.

'Saving our bacon, if you ask me,' said the secretary, who hadn't liked the sound of Tranby Croft.

'Why on earth didn't South play his King?' asked the chairman. 'He gets the others down if he does.'

'I think,' said the director, choosing his words with some care, 'it was because he'd noticed that North hesitated before he played a low heart.'

'West must have noticed it, too,' said the chairman logically, 'which is presumably why he felt confident about going ahead with the finesse.'

'Exactly,' said the director, bringing his fist down on his other hand.

'And I say that's cheating,' insisted the secretary. 'On North's part, I mean.'

'Worse than that, he fingered a different card before he played a low one,' said the director, 'and South must have seen that as well as West.'

'That's cheating, too,' said the secretary.

'Misleading body language, that's what I say it was,' muttered the director, 'and it shouldn't be allowed.'

'I think you mean condoned but do go on,' said the chairman, who also served on the local Bench of Magistrates, and had learnt early on there not to pass judgement until he had heard the whole story, let alone both sides of it.

'And we – that is, I – think North did all that in order that West would think that he had the King even though he didn't and would therefore run the Jack through, leaving the Ace and the Queen on the table, thinking it safe to do so . . .'

'To be taken by South's King?' said the chairman intelligently.

'Which North must have known South was holding because he hadn't got it himself,' said the director.

'And if West had had it in his own hand he wouldn't have had to try a finesse?' said the chairman. 'That's so, too, isn't it?'

'Bingo,' said the secretary inappropriately.

'And thus make the contract fail,' concluded the director, 'and whatever you all say, I say that that's cheating.'

'I've always believed the best way to win at Bridge is never to say anything except "no bid" or "double", especially if there's drink on the table,' remarked the chairman inconsequentially.

The director's colour rose alarmingly. 'I would certainly not permit that, chairman. Not calling to your hand is quite reprehensible and certainly not cricket.'

'Same thing,' muttered the secretary under his breath. 'Reprehensible and not cricket, I mean.'

'I take it,' said the chairman, whose capacity not to rise to each and every provocation made him an excellent choice for this office, 'that after making the Jack in his own hand, West would then lead another Heart in order to repeat the finesse?'

'The attempted finesse,' insisted the secretary, whose pernickety ways made him such a good secretary.

'Not exactly,' said the director immediately, 'although obviously when he did so North simply played another low Heart.'

'Because he couldn't do anything else,' agreed the chairman, whom no one had ever thought to be slow on the uptake.

'Exactly,' said the director. 'But this time – and this is the beauty of it, chairman – I guess West doesn't have another Heart after that and so he plays the Ace from the table and . . . wait for it . . .'

'I am waiting,' said the chairman mildly. He had been working hard on establishing the principle in the club that one should only ever say one of two things to one's partner, whatever the provocation. They were 'Well done' or 'Bad luck' but he wasn't expecting this to be all in this case.

'South's King falls under it,' said the director

triumphantly, 'because he hadn't another Heart either and so he had to play his King. That makes the Queen of Hearts good, of course, and West makes his contract.'

'That's when the fun began,' said the secretary.

'Fun?' said the chairman with the raised eyebrows. Nothing was exactly fun on the Bench, either.

'North started storming at South for not putting his King on when he could and so getting their opponents down.'

'And?' said the chairman. There was always more to be said in the Magistrates' Court, too.

'And you'll never guess what South said,' grinned the secretary, 'when North asked him why he hadn't put his King on when he could have done.'

'Tell me,' said the chairman.

'He looked straight at North and said, "Because I thought you'd got it".'

'Lovely,' said chairman, rubbing his hands. 'Now that's what I call good endplay.'

IN THE FAMILY WAY

'I'll tell you two here one thing for sure,' said Martin, 'and that is that as far as I'm concerned Aunt Maude is not going into a care home. Ever.'

'It's all very well for you to say that,' objected his sister, Paula, 'but who on earth is going to look after her if she goes on staying at home alone?'

'Have you any idea what care homes cost?' said Martin.

'I have,' said Gerald morosely. He was the son of Aunt Maude's brother and thus cousin to Martin and Paula who were her sister's children. 'I come across it all the time at work and I know that it's a devil of a lot. The fees can eat up a family's capital in no time at all. And usually do.'

The three of them were having a family conclave – convened by Martin – about what to do about their childless old aunt who, notably self-reliant and independent until now, had begun to have falls and not remember yesterday. The bad winter of 1947 in very great detail, yes – but not yesterday. They had foregathered in the Calleshire village of Cullingoak and were now sitting round a table in The White Hart Inn having a pub lunch before going up the hill to Church Hill Cottage to visit their old aunt.

'Besides,' went on Martin, 'if she goes into a residential home she'll have to give away all those ghastly plants of hers first . . .'

'That wouldn't be easy,' shuddered Paula. 'I can't imagine anyone wanting them. They're absolutely awful.'

'I'm sure she wouldn't ever do it anyway,' said Martin. 'She's much too fond of them for that. Anyone want my onions? I think they spoil a Ploughman's Lunch and anyway I can't stand them.'

'Better than having a cat to leave behind, though,' said Gerald, withdrawing his own platter of bread and cheese a little: he didn't like pickled onions either. 'In my experience that can get really difficult. Or, come to that, a dog.'

'Plants must be easier to leave than either a cat or dog,' said Paula. 'No more onion for me, thanks, Martin. I've got plenty on my plate already.' She looked up and said seriously,

'Actually, I think we've all got quite enough on our plate, too, as far as Aunt Maude is concerned.'

Martin said, 'She's extremely attached to that wretched collection of hers although don't ask me why. And they'd never let her take them with her into a home. Nobody in their right mind would.'

Paula nodded. 'I agree they're enough to give anyone the heeby-jeebies, but she dotes on them.'

'If she was seventy years younger,' avowed Martin, 'I'd say she was an anorak about them.'

'I'd forgotten about all those funny things she grows,' admitted Gerald. 'Flycatchers or something, aren't they?'

'Flowers of Evil,' supplied Paula, 'that's what they're called. I don't like them.'

'You haven't visited her for a while, have you, Gerald?' said Martin rather pointedly. 'Well, I can tell you that there are more of them than ever in that precious garden room of hers. A specialised collection of the most revolting-looking plants you've ever seen but at least she can still get to them with her Zimmer frame. She doesn't go out in the garden alone any more, thank goodness. We don't want her to fall down and break her hip out there.'

'I think they're what are known as the insectivorous plants,' supplied Paula.

'Carnivorous, more like,' said Martin. 'Gardening can bring out the worst in some people. I shall never forget being with her once when I was little. We were in her greenhouse and she stood there in her brown Oxford shoes, pointed to the cucumbers with her umbrella, and said, "They're all right provided you nip out the male flowers". I was quite nervous at the time, I can tell you. I wanted to run away.'

His sister smiled and as was her wont, stuck to the subject. 'The hooded ones usually grow in poor soil and that's why they need the insects for nourishment.' Actually Paula had looked them up in a gardening book before she came but did not say so.

'I don't care what they're called or what their nasty little habits are,' said Martin strenuously, 'but I do know that they wouldn't want those in any care home that I've ever heard of and I must say I wouldn't want them in mine.'

'She does own her own house, after all, though,' pointed out Paula practically, again sticking to the point. She had travelled a long way to be there today and had to get back that night to her husband and three children and said so now. What she didn't tell them was that the aforementioned husband had taken to the whisky bottle and was slowly and surely ruining the family financially and emotionally as he descended into alcoholism. 'If it did come to a residential home,' she offered, 'Aunt Maude wouldn't be short of capital.'

'Oh, she's well minted, all right. I grant you that. And if it comes to the crunch, she's got a GSOH, too,' said Martin, giving a wicked grin. He turned to the others. 'In case you two don't know it, the letters GSOH stand for "Good Sense Of Humour" in all those advertisements for dating services for partners you see in the newspapers.'

'Really?' said Paula stiffly. Her brother Martin had just parted acrimoniously – and expensively – with his wife. This probably meant that he was now looking for another one – or a new companion, anyway. He must have been scanning the newspaper pages carrying advertisements for New Relationships headed 'Women Seeking Men' or even perhaps put one in himself in the 'Men Seeking Women' column.

'That's right,' said Martin. 'And for your information, sister dear, OHOC is their shorthand for having your own home and car.'

Paula had no doubt that Martin would be wanting to meet someone to whom that would apply since his former wife had decided that possession was nine points of the law and throughout the divorce proceedings had made it abundantly clear that she had no intention of moving out of the matrimonial home. And, moreover, hadn't done so.

'That would be a pretty dangerous thing to do,' put in their cousin Gerald. He was a cautious man, an accountant by profession, and certainly couldn't by any stretch of the imagination be said to have a Good Sense Of Humour. He owned his own home, though, and more than one car but was definitely not in search of a wife. He had one already although he didn't care to tell the other two about her notable extravagances and the delusions of social grandeur that he was finding it very hard to keep up with money-wise, qualified accountant or not.

'Never give anything away, especially information,' quoted Martin lightly. 'I agree – people should be much more careful in those advertisements.'

'Perhaps their own home and car is all they have to offer,' murmured Paula. She wondered idly if Martin himself was actually doing any advertising on his own behalf: if so, he was probably describing himself as 'Active, fun-loving and handsome'. She thought 'Broke, ex-divorcee with expensive tastes' would be nearer the mark but she did not say so. Instead she added her own credo: 'I expect a good sense of humour makes up for most things.' That it failed to do so when dealing with her husband's condition was something that was becoming more and more apparent.

'Well, Aunt Maude has got her own home anyway,' said Gerald prosaically. 'Thank God she was sensible enough to give up driving before driving gave her up. I know she hasn't got a car any longer because she told me she'd sold it and bought some more of those ghastly plants with the money.'

'It's a nice house, too,' said Paula, ignoring tempting conversational byways and still sticking resolutely to the matter in hand. 'She's always kept it in good condition.'

'And whatever you say it's not being sold for all the money to be spent on care home fees,' declared Martin firmly. He brightened and said, 'Perhaps we should send her off to a granny-grabbing party and let someone else look after her instead of us.'

'What on earth is . . .' began Paula. She subsided when she realised he was only pulling her leg.

'Are you sure we shouldn't be talking about a nursing home rather than a residential one?' said

Gerald, always a worrier. 'I mean if she's started to fall about already one of these fine days she's going to break something and they won't keep her in a care home if she does that.'

Paula groaned. 'And nursing homes are twice as expensive as residential ones.'

'What Aunt Maude needs,' pronounced Martin, 'is someone to come and live with her as a companion or something – all found, of course.'

'Then I WLTM them,' said Paula swiftly. When her cousin, Gerald, looked totally blank she explained, 'I think it stands in those advertisements for "Would Like To Meet". Martin's living in the past. People like that just don't exist any more. All the spinster nieces of the old days have gone the way of all flesh.'

'Not like you to go in for the double entendre, old girl,' murmured Martin sotto voce as Paula flushed.

'I would say that there would be plenty from the sale of the house to pay for care fees for a number of years,' said Gerald prosaically, not part of that exchange. 'I could do some sums, if you like.'

'She's not going into care whatever you come up with,' persisted Martin mulishly.

Gerald raised his eyebrows in much the same

way as he did when his clients finally confessed not only to having salted away their surplus funds in tax-free offshore islands but absent-mindedly also having forgotten to tell either him or the relevant authorities about them. He had his ready-made speech about rendering unto Caesar that which was Caesar's honed to a fine point when this happened but he had nothing to say now.

'That's all very well, Martin . . .' began Paula.

Gerald coughed. 'Although I do believe these days in some counties their social services visit people at home to keep them out of these care places. That can't cost as much, surely?'

'It doesn't,' said Martin flatly.

Paula stirred and said, 'The problem then is what happens when that's not enough. They can't stop people either falling down or wandering and that's when the real trouble begins.'

'Coffee, anyone?' said Martin, ducking the issue. 'Then I think we'd better get going. Brace yourselves for the cousinage having seedcake at Church Hill Cottage.'

Paula gave a little giggle. 'It ought to be Garibaldi biscuits.'

'Come again?' said Martin.

'Don't you remember? We used to call them squashed fly biscuits.'

Gerald gave an unexpected chortle. 'I'd forgotten those. Nasty chewy things.'

'You'll have to feed them to those awful flycatcher plants of Aunt Maude's, Martin,' said Paula, amused, 'and find out what they think of them.'

In the event Aunt Maude didn't offer them Garibaldi biscuits but there was a cake on the table when they arrived. Paula thought she caught a glimpse of mould at one edge of it, confirming what she had long suspected – that Aunt Maude's eyesight wasn't good any longer. There was more than one cobweb festooned across the corners of the room. Those, too, had clearly not been noticed by the old lady.

Martin had spotted them. 'It's a straight fight for any flies in the house between the spiders and the plants,' he hissed under his breath as Aunt Maude tottered out of the sitting room to make the tea. 'My money's on the spiders – quicker on the uptake.'

'Let me help you carry the teapot,' called out Paula after her.

'I'm quite all right, dear, thank you,' said their aunt firmly. 'I can manage quite well. There's plenty of life in the old girl yet, you know.'

Nevertheless Paula rose and held the door open behind her aunt, averting her eyes as

Aunt Maude came back into the sitting room with the heavy teapot swivelling about on a tea tray, the tea spilling out of the spout as it tilted dangerously to one side.

'Now then, my dears, tea first and then you must come and take a look at my little darlings,' said Aunt Maude, pointing to the open doors that led to the garden room and the several trestle tables beyond loaded with green, flowerless plants. She only got half the tea into the cups, the rest going either into the saucers or onto the tea tray as the teapot waved about uncertainly above them. 'Sugar, anyone?' she asked, quite oblivious of the fact that some of the tea had gone into the sugar bowl too.

'I'll help myself,' said Martin hastily, getting up and crossing over to the table. 'Let me cut the cake, Aunt, while you pour. I'm on my feet, anyway.'

The old lady did not demur at this and Martin, his back to the other two and his aunt, carefully cut four slices. He handed these round on plates, taking one himself and leaving one for his aunt. Maude insisted, though, on handing Paula her tea, the cup wobbling noisily in the saucer as she did so. The strain was too much for Gerald who nipped quickly behind her and collected his own cup and saucer before she could turn round again.

'Thank you,' said Paula, mentally debating whether she should emulate Queen Victoria, similarly caught in awkward circumstances, and drink from the saucer, (calling it an old-style 'dish of tea' the while), or simply toss the tea from the saucer back in the cup when her aunt wasn't looking. In the event she tipped the tea back into the cup from the saucer, slipping behind her aunt's back to do so while their hostess tottered towards her own chair. Paula examined her own slice of cake surreptitiously before she bit into it, hoping that Martin, too, had spotted the mouldy bits and cut the cake accordingly.

Aunt Maude sat down at last, peered short-sightedly round at them and said, 'How nice to see you all. Now, have you all got everything you need?'

'Everything, Aunt Maude, thank you,' said Paula politely.

'Yes, thank you,' said Gerald.

'Did you make the cake yourself?' asked Martin, looking innocent.

'Oh, yes, dear, although,' she said doubtfully, 'I'm afraid I mightn't have given it long enough in the oven. It's a bit undercooked in the middle.'

'I quite like sad cake,' said Paula gamely, the cake being definitely still very moist in the centre. Making conversation was proving much more difficult than she had expected and none of them liked to be the first to bring up the question of care of any sort.

In the event there was no need. Aunt Maude went back to her own chair and facing the three younger ones, took a sip of her tea and then, always a good trencher-woman, a couple of big bites out of her slice of the cake.

As Martin told Detective Inspector Sloan from 'F' Division of the Berebury Constabulary not very long afterwards, his aunt began to complain of pain in her throat and suddenly struggled to get her breath and then before she could speak again she had tumbled to the floor. 'And then, Inspector, she started to have convulsions. She was trying to talk but no words came.'

'We thought she'd had a stroke,' said Gerald, older than the other two and more experienced in both life and death. 'She had quite a high colour – her face went a sort of rose-pink.'

'Then she seemed to fall in to something like a coma,' volunteered Paula, still in something of a daze herself. 'And she died in no time at all.'

'We'd sent for an ambulance straightaway, of course,' said Gerald a trifle defensively.

'They were very quick in coming, thank goodness,' contributed Paula. She was sitting, pale-faced in her chair, her hands trembling slightly now and her eyes full of unshed tears.

The ambulance men had been very quick in sending for the police, too.

Very quick indeed.

'We wondered at first about getting her out into the fresh air,' said Martin to Inspector Sloan, 'but she died before we got her further than the garden room and the ambulance men wouldn't move her afterwards. They said we weren't to touch her either.'

'I see, sir.' The detective inspector made another note. He had already examined the garden room and noted that one of the trestle tables had been pushed roughly to one side. An amateur gardener himself, he had noted, too, the plant collection there with more than passing interest – and less revulsion than the deceased's relatives. He spotted several varieties of sundew with their hairy leaves designed to trap and digest insects. There was a group of Venus flytraps on another table and a whole assembly of pitcher plants, too, every one of them neatly labelled. Specialist was the word that came into his mind rather than anorak.

'And we didn't,' insisted Gerald firmly. 'Touch her, I mean.'

'And I also understand that none of you was alone with her here at any time,' said the inspector, looking round. There would be a better place to interview them all separately later but probably not a better time than here and now.

'That's right,' said Gerald, looking round at the others. 'Isn't it?'

Paula and Martin nodded in agreement. Martin said, 'All three of us arrived together and we hadn't any one of us left this room. There hadn't really been any time.'

'None at all, actually,' confirmed Gerald.

'We hadn't even got as far as her garden room until we carried her in there,' said Paula tremulously. Still choking back tears and searching for comfort, she added, Pollyanna-like, 'At least she died at home and among her precious plants. I know that's just what she would have wanted.'

What the police wanted was something quite different.

'And I don't mean just knowing the motive,' said Detective Inspector Sloan to Detective Constable Crosby when, after a lot of hard work, they came together the next day to review the case. 'There's means and opportunity as well.'

'No shortage of motive anyway, sir,' agreed Crosby readily. 'None at all, in fact. The deceased's solicitor confirms that they are each due to receive an equal proportion of her estate and from what I have established already they all three of them could do with getting their hands on their share as soon as possible.' The constable, who was unmarried, added, 'Matrimonial trouble, one way or another, the lot of them.'

'Potassium cyanide kills very quickly,' remarked Sloan, squinting down at one of the reports. 'That's why some of those defendants at the Nuremberg Trials had glass capsules of it parked in their mouths against a guilty verdict. It's highly soluble in almost anything liquid.'

'Forensics say that the cake was really moist in the middle – quite underdone, in fact – and that's what did the trick,' offered the constable. 'It was still a bit damp. Me, I like cakes that way. More filling.'

'Secret agents used to be given the poison, too, in case they were ever caught and tortured.' Sloan trawled through his memory. 'I think they were supposed to crush the glass with their teeth when danger threatened and it would dissolve in their saliva and kill them.'

'And she got it from the piece of cake,' reported Crosby. He pushed a piece of paper in Sloan's direction. 'At least that's what the forensic chemists say about what was in all those evidence bags we sent them.'

Sloan also read what the forensic chemists

had to say about the availability of one the most deadly of poisons. It seemed to turn up in a wide variety of places from metal-cleaning to apricot and almond stones. He flipped through the pages of his notebook. 'According to what each of the three of them who were there said . . .'

'And are prepared to swear to,' supplied Crosby, who had taken down the statements.

'. . . they all had a chance of doctoring her piece of cake without either of the others seeing them do it. Literally behind the old lady's back,' Sloan added gloomily.

The detective constable nodded and patted his notebook. 'That's right, sir. I've got it all written down here.'

'One at a time, too,' mused Sloan. 'First Martin cuts the cake out of sight of the others, then Gerald collects his tea from the tray himself and after that Paula goes behind the deceased's back to pour some of her tea back into her cup from the saucer. Or so she says,' he said, automatically adding the policeman's customary caveat. 'The two men don't seem to have bothered about there being tea in their saucers.'

The detective constable, who didn't trouble about tea that had slopped over in his saucer either, handed over a couple more documents to Sloan. 'Our famous specialised search team –

they're a cocky lot, aren't they, sir? Think they're God's gift to detectives, they do . . .'

'Never mind about that, Crosby,' Sloan said repressively.

'Well, they went through the sitting room and that garden room – thank goodness those awful plants haven't got flowers, my hayfever's been terrible this week – without finding anything at all that showed any sign of having held cyanide.' He had tried to write down something about a fine-tooth comb in his report but placing the hyphen had troubled him. 'They examined all the ground outside the windows, too, in case it – whatever it was – had been chucked out of one of them. Nothing there either.'

'No broken glass at all anywhere?' asked Sloan, still withholding comment on the Force's subsection devoted to leaving no stone unturned in their searches – and, of course, the furthering of their own reputation within the constabulary.

'Not a single shard, and they said to tell you that they were very sorry but that it didn't happen often that they didn't find anything at all.'

'There must have been something,' said Sloan irritably. 'Even those insect-eating plants couldn't have dissolved glass.'

Crosby turned over yet another report. 'The doctor said there was nothing like that in her mouth when he did the post-mortem.'

Sloan sniffed. 'Potassium cyanide, I would remind you, Crosby, is not the sort of substance you carry in your bare hands if you want to live.'

'No, sir.' The detective constable looked up and said, 'Although if it's for suicide and you can hide enough of it in a phial in your mouth without anyone seeing it's there, then you can't need a lot of it to do the trick.'

'Got it in one, Crosby. You don't.' Sloan waved one of the other reports in front of him. 'At least that's what Forensics say here.'

'So, sir,' he said slowly, 'is what we're looking for what the cyanide was in? The vehicle, you might say . . .'

'It is,' said Sloan weightily. 'We've got the motive and the opportunity. What we want now is the means of delivering justice to the culpable, otherwise known as hard evidence.'

The detective constable looked puzzled. 'How will it help if we find what the poison was in, sir?'

Sloan sighed. 'Because, Crosby, whoever poured the potassium cyanide onto the old lady's piece of cake will have had to handle the container him or herself. And drop the stuff on her slice from whatever it was in behind her back and out of sight of the other two.'

'Fingerprints, then,' offered the detective

constable, adding, 'and we've got those from all three of them.'

'They can hardly have worn gloves in the process, can they?' sighed Sloan. Detective Constable Crosby had never been considered the sharpest knife in the drawer: it was just the inspector's bad luck that there had been no one else on duty and available when the call to Church Hill Cottage had come in. 'Certainly not indoors on a warm afternoon. Even the old lady would have noticed those let alone the other two, unless that is they were all in it together, which I doubt.'

'Tricky,' agreed Crosby, 'because they wouldn't have had that long to operate.'

'No, and if they could have done that without leaving any traces of their DNA on whatever the cyanide was in – let alone fingerprints – then I'm a Dutchman.' He shrugged his shoulders. 'At least they couldn't very well have swallowed it, whatever it was. Even an empty container would have been too dangerous by half to do that.'

'And we know for sure that none of them had anything on their persons before we let them go because I was there,' agreed Crosby. 'They were all thoroughly searched from head to toe.'

'Thanks to Polly Perkins as well,' said Sloan piously, giving credit where credit was due.

Woman Police Sergeant Perkins had thoroughly examined a still-distraught Paula before she left her aunt's sitting room and was absolutely certain that there was nothing at all that could conceivably have had poison in it on or about her person.

Crosby shuffled the pile of papers that had accumulated on the desk between them and said wistfully, 'It'd be nice to catch out that team that searched the premises, sir, wouldn't it?'

'I would remind you, Crosby,' responded Detective Inspector Sloan stiffly, 'that the function of policing is to catch the perpetrator of a crime, not to undermine the work of one's colleagues.'

'It must be somewhere, all the same, that container that had the poison in it,' muttered Crosby.

'True, Crosby. Very true.' He sat back in his chair.

'A cup of tea, sir?'

'The best idea you've had so far, Crosby.'

The constable scraped his chair back and got to his feet. 'Back in a jiffy, sir,' he promised.

Sloan leant further back in his chair and considered the investigative trilogy of means, motive and opportunity once more. In this case motive and opportunity could be said to apply equally to all three cousins. The means of conveyance, though, still remained obscure and not yet associated with any one of them.

'Here we are, sir.' The constable arrived back with a tray of tea and a couple of buns. He set it down and then fished in his pocket for something. 'Time to take my hayfever stuff.'

Sloan helped himself to a cup of tea from the tray while Crosby opened a box and took out a capsule. 'Have a bun, too, sir. I'll just sink this and then I'll grab mine.'

'No, you won't Crosby,' said Sloan suddenly, rising to his feet and pushing his own cup of tea to one side. 'You'll put that teacup down and come with me. At once. I've just remembered something.'

'Yes, sir.' He scrambled up. 'Of course, sir. Where to, sir?'

'Church Hill Cottage, Cullingoak,' snapped Sloan. 'Now, stop talking and get moving. There's no time to lose. Oh, and pick up a murder bag.'

They were nearing the village before Crosby ventured to ask what it was that the detective inspector had remembered.

'That gelatine is a protein,' replied Sloan.

No wiser, the constable stayed silent until the police car was approaching Church Hill Cottage. 'Dynamic entry, sir?' he asked hopefully. Crosby enjoyed battering doors down.

'Certainly not,' said Sloan as the police car drew up in front of the cottage. 'Follow me, Crosby.'

'Where to now, sir?' he asked as Sloan undid a seal on the front door.

'The garden room. This way, Crosby.' Sloan pushed open the doors to the room and straightaway made for the serried ranks of insect-eating plants.

'What are you looking for, sir?' asked the constable uneasily.

'The *Nepenthes coccineas*,' said Sloan absently, his eyes roving up and down one of the trestle tables. 'Or perhaps the *Sarracenia drummondii*. You can ignore the others, Crosby.'

'Yes, sir,' said the constable, showing every sign of ignoring all the plants. 'Thank you, sir.'

Detective Inspector Sloan wasn't listening. He was walking up and down the garden room looking for the group he wanted. He stopped abruptly. 'Come over here, Crosby. This is where they are. The lidded pitcher plants. Dozens of them.'

Manifestly uninterested, the detective constable ambled over towards Sloan. 'Sir?'

'I think, Crosby, you might find the remains of a gelatine capsule in one of these little fellows. Lift its lid very gently and look inside. You begin looking in them here at this end of the bench and I'll start at the other end. Give me a shout if you see it.'

Crosby lifted the lid of the first plant and peered in. 'All there is in this one, sir, is some water.'

'Not water, Crosby. A solution of pepsin.'

'Really, sir,' he said, the yawn in his voice there if not openly expressed.

'For drowning the insects in,' said Sloan. 'Neat system, isn't it?'

'Yes, sir.' Crosby lifted the lid on the next plant, peered inside it and then let the lid fall back again.

'You see,' explained Sloan, 'pepsin is an enzyme that breaks down protein in slightly acid conditions and insects supply the protein the plant needs.'

'And gelatine is protein,' chanted Crosby, a lesson remembered.

'Exactly. Now, keep looking for the remains of a gelatine capsule in the pitcher part of the plant.'

In the event it was Sloan himself who peeped into a fine plant of the *Nepenthes coccinea* family and saw something there that was most definitely not insectivorous. Reaching for the murder bag, he picked out a pair of tweezers and retrieved two halves of an empty, clear capsule. Laying them carefully on some tissue, he said, 'That's good. No sign of any denaturing of the gelatine by the pepsin yet.' He looked up and grinned. 'There would have been if it had been in your stomach, Crosby, or we had left it in this plant too long. All we need now is to know whose fingerprints are on it and Bob's your uncle.' He lifted the lid of the pitcher plant and then very gently let it close again. 'An open and shut case, you might say.'

THESE FOR REMEMBRANCE

'Wendy, is that you? Henry here. Can you hear me all right? It's rather a bad line. Look, would it be all right if I came down to Berebury next Friday for the weekend? To see the children and so forth.'

'Of course, dear,' responded Henry Tyler's sister immediately. 'The children will be so pleased to see you again and all that's happening here is that Tim will be playing cricket on the Saturday afternoon.'

'Nothing changes, does it?' said Henry affectionately. Tim Witherington was Wendy's husband and village cricket on a Saturday afternoon was part of the very fabric of English society – an English society that Henry Tyler was labouring at his desk at the Foreign Office to preserve. That certain other forces were striving at this moment with equal determination to destroy it he left unsaid even though Herr Adolf Hitler's intentions in this respect were becoming clearer and clearer as time went by.

'I'll be coming down on the Friday afternoon,' he said to Wendy. 'That's if the plane from Cartainia gets back to London in time on Thursday evening for me to write my report before I catch the train.'

'Cartainia?' she said uncertainly. 'Henry, I don't like your flying to all these funny places – especially just now.'

'Don't worry, Wendy. Cartainia isn't the other side of the world. It's still in Europe, remember.'

'Only just and anyway that's really not a lot of consolation these days, is it?' she said dryly. 'It seems that it's Europe where all the trouble happens to be at the moment.'

'I agree Cartainia might properly be described as being on the very fringes of Continental Europe,' he conceded. This, although he did not tell his sister, was one of the emollient phrases he had briefed his minister to use when he accompanied him on his visit to its capital that week.

The trip there was ostensibly to lay a wreath on the Cartainia war memorial recording those lost in 1918 in one of the last battles of the Great War when a battalion from the Scottish Fearnshire Regiment had joined forces with the tiny Cartainian Army to fight off an invader. The Fearnshires had been thrown into the battle so commemorated at the last minute and thus sustained casualties too.

The fact that there were therefore many of their names on the memorial as well as Cartainian ones was the ostensible reason for Henry's Minster being there. In reality the visit was for the British government to garner as much information as possible about the future intentions of the Cartainian government and its people should a new war come.

Military historians, inured to bigger engagements, were inclined to describe the battle as a minor skirmish but to the Cartainians it had been a glorious victory and an occasion when they and the British had stood together side by side against a common enemy.

And won.

The situation was quite different now. Cartainia's delicate position on the extreme edge of Eastern Europe was less assured – but much more strategic. Certain hostile powers were eyeing its undefended little borders with the interest of a raptor, whilst Britain had more than a passing concern that it remained as neutral as possible for as long as possible at this important juncture in world history.

It was the current international detente that had led to Henry Tyler as well as his minister laying a wreath on the cenotaph commemorating the twentieth anniversary of the battle. The soldier who should have been doing so – the Colonel-in-Chief of the Fearnshire Regiment – was presently with his regiment and heavily engaged in training activities somewhere unspecified in Scotland and not available for any ceremonial duties farther afield than Edinburgh Castle. So Henry was standing in for him.

The Prime Minister of Cartainia was the first to place his wreath. This had been ceremonially handed to him by his Foreign Secretary, Stephan Kiste, a big fellow with prominent duelling scars on his cheeks, and a man said to be the prime minister's rival for power in the country.

Henry's minister had duly laid his wreath next to that already placed at the foot of the war memorial by the prime minister, an enigmatic politician sitting firmly – if warily – on the fence, watching and seemingly waiting to see which of the great powers would annexe Cartainia first and prepared to respond in the way which suited his own position best.

Henry's own minister had his wreath – a tasteful ring of Flanders poppies set in a base of laurel leaves – equally ceremonially handed to him by His Excellency the British Ambassador. Henry didn't need telling that 'Our Man in Cartainia' was a wily diplomat of great experience. The ambassador had already made the Foreign Office well aware that his every movement in Cartainia was being watched, his post intercepted, his conversations overheard by microphone and his telephone calls monitored. Not unnaturally, this absence of good communications was making getting reliable information out of the country and back to Whitehall extremely difficult.

The British minister, immaculately dressed in black jacket and spongebag trousers, had stepped forward, placed the wreath in exactly the right place, stood back, bowed his head in silent tribute for exactly the right length of time and even more cleverly managed to walk backwards to his allotted place beside the Prime Minister of Cartainia without looking round.

Next to come forward with his wreath paying tribute to the fallen soldiery of yesteryear was a much-bemedalled and grey-whiskered field marshal representing the Cartainian army, his wreath of entwined ivy leaves being handed to him by a uniformed cadet.

The last wreath of all – the one that had originally been intended to be laid by the Colonel-in-Chief of the Fearnshire Regiment –

was handed to Henry by an anonymous young man who emerged out of the little crowd round the cenotaph and pressed it into Henry's hand. The young man wasn't in uniform – something which seemed to surprise the field marshal who peered at him myopically. Indeed, the man looked rather as if he had got his best suit on and a somewhat crumpled one at that.

Henry himself did not recognise the man as coming from the Embassy and shot an enquiring glance at the ambassador. His Excellency, though, had had a rigorous education on the playing fields of Eton and his face betrayed no sign of a response whatsoever.

Henry took the wreath – a totally unexpected circlet of unusually colourful flowers – and proceeded towards the memorial with it. It crossed his mind that it might have been wired as a bomb to blow them all to perdition but nothing untoward happened when he propped it against the granite of the memorial. He, too, bowed, waited and then returned to his position while the prime minister stepped onto a podium, adjusted the microphone and began to deliver his speech.

Since this was delivered mainly in Cartainian, a language with which Henry was not familiar, and was almost certainly self-serving to a high degree, he turned his mind back to the curious wreath he himself had been given to place at the foot of the memorial. It stood out from the others, being a great mixture of flowers rather than leaves. It certainly didn't accord with Milton's poem 'Lycidas' and its famous lines 'Yet once more, O ye laurels, and once more / Ye myrtles brown, with ivy never sere'.

He continued to consider the wreath's curious composition while the prime minister droned on. It was comprised of a strange medley of flowers – some wild, some cultivated. He recognised a Guelder rose and next to it a harebell and then a shaft of goldenrod – not considered mourning plants any of them in his book. Perhaps such things were different in Cartainia. He would ask the ambassador, always supposing he got the opportunity to talk to him.

Henry stared down at the wreath for a long time, well aware that some of its flowers were far removed from those usually ordered by embassies the world over as suitable for a solemn occasion. Idly he started to list them in his mind, playing a sort of Kim's Game to himself as the prime minister spoke on. Some, he noted, must have been especially procured for the occasion since they were out of season and he would have thought not native to Cartainia anyway.

A civil servant to his fingertips, what crossed Henry's mind first of all about the wreath was the cost. He hoped there wouldn't be a Parliamentary Question on his return about what some Member of Parliament would be bound to describe as outrageous extravagance in these hard times. On second thoughts he decided that the expense of the wreath must have been sanctioned by the ambassador – or at the very least by one of his underlings – and nobody at the British Embassy in Cartainia was likely to make mistakes. Indeed, the staff on station there had been hand-picked for demanding duties at a difficult time in an uncertain posting.

His thoughts were briefly interrupted by an outburst of cheering from some of the crowd. Henry decided that the prime minister must have said something particularly martial – the British Ambassador's expression was too inscrutable to decode – and went back to thinking about the wreath and memorising what it contained.

Just as he did get a chance at the reception after the ceremony to start to ask the ambassador about the wreath, that most accomplished of diplomats appeared to spot someone else at the far side of the room with whom he positively must have a word. He politely excused himself before speeding off, saying softly over his shoulder as he went, 'There's rosemary, there's rue'. Henry, nobody's fool, did not repeat the question, merely placing the quotation as coming from *Hamlet*.

The incongruities of the wreath were still on his mind the next day when he got down to his sister's house in the little market town of Berebury in the county of Calleshire. After supper was over and the children had been packed off to bed Henry sat down with his sister and brother-in-law in their comfortable sitting room. Tim Witherington set about lighting his pipe, while Wendy got out a pile of mending.

'What on earth's that?' asked Henry as she produced from her work basket something wooden resembling a large toadstool.

'It's called a mushroom and it's for darning,' she said placidly, slipping it inside one of Tim's socks and picking up a long darning needle. 'I'm always mending the heels. I don't know what he does with his socks but they wear out in no time. Now tell me, Henry, how did your visit to Cartainia go?'

'That's if he's allowed to talk about it, dear,' her husband reminded her. 'The poor chap may be silenced by the Official Secrets Act or something.'

'Nothing like that, I promise you,' Henry assured her. 'In fact I would have said the entire

Cartainia press was there, together with at least one reporter from a Scottish newspaper.'

'Ah, yes, the Fearnshires,' said Henry's brother-in-law knowledgeably. He had been wounded in 1918 in the March Retreat and had a slight limp to prove it.

'The Flowers of the Forest,' murmured Wendy absently, selecting a skein of wool and holding it against the sock to match the colour.

'Indeed they "are a'wede awae"', said her husband, the old soldier, completing the melancholy quotation about the casualties of the Battle of Flodden Field.

'The Fearnshires lost a lot of men in the Cartainian action,' said Henry, coming back to the present, 'and I had to place their wreath for them.' He explained about the odd blooms of which it had been composed.

'Perhaps one of them was a regimental flower,' suggested Wendy. 'Something Scottish.'

Tim Witherington, a gunner in his day, shook his head. 'No, the regimental emblem of the Fearnshires is a bird – a capercaillie, I think. The one they call "the horse of the forest" or something like that, anyway.'

'This wreath,' said his sister. 'Tell me more.'

'There were all sorts of strange flowers in it. Amaranthus for starters . . .'

'That's "Love Lies Bleeding",' said Wendy promptly. 'What else?'

'Rudbeckia – oh, and a snowdrop – heaven only knows where they got that from in the summertime. High up somewhere, I expect,' said Henry. 'And I spotted veronica, too, but that's almost an any time of the year flower, isn't it?'

Wendy's lips twitched into a little smile as she threw a sly glance in her husband's direction. 'You haven't forgotten veronica and what it means, have you, Tim?'

'No.' Tim Witherington shook his head affectionately. 'Fidelity.'

'You won't remember, Henry,' Wendy explained, 'but I had it in my wedding bouquet.'

Actually, all Henry remembered about his sister's wedding was the agony of being Best Man and having to make a speech.

She gave a reminiscent sigh. 'And there was apple blossom in it, too – that was for good fortune – and arbutus. That meant "Thee only do I love".'

Her husband, with an unblemished record in this respect, stirred uneasily in his chair and began to tamp his pipe down while Henry started to recount the names of the other flowers he'd spotted in the wreath. 'There was something I'm pretty sure was helenium . . .'

Wendy put down her darning needle and said seriously, 'I was warned against putting any of those in my bouquet. They stand for tears.'

A thought was beginning to burgeon in Henry's mind. 'Wen, what does goldenrod stand for?'

She frowned. 'Precaution, I think. Yes, I'm sure. I used to know all the language of flowers when I was a girl.'

'And a yellow carnation?' said Henry, suddenly sitting up straight and taking notice.

'Ah, now that was something I was definitely told not to have on my wedding day which was a pity because my bridesmaids wore such pretty yellow dresses. Daphne looked lovely in hers – that reminds me, I must ring her for a chat. She's married now. To one of the ushers,' she added inconsequently.

'Why not yellow?' persisted Henry.

'Didn't you know, dear? It means rejection,' said his sister promptly. 'I know that because when one of my girl friends wanted to break off her engagement . . .'

'Monkshood?' he said rather quickly.

'I don't know about monkshood,' she replied with dignity. 'I only remember the nice flowers. I'd have to go and get my book and look it up.'

'Please do,' he said with some urgency. 'This

231

could be rather important.' As she got to her feet, he said, 'What about *Achillea millefolia*?' but she had gone before she could hear him.

'I can tell you that one,' said his brother-in-law quietly after Wendy had left the room. 'In the language of flowers it means war.' He puffed out some tobacco smoke. 'I remember that because one side used the name as an emblem in a training exercise we did in the Territorials in 1913.' He sucked on his pipe again, casting his memory back. 'The other side chose lobelia for malevolence. Our side lost.'

'There were some lobelia flowers in that wreath, too, you know,' said Henry soberly, ignoring the mock battles of men playing soldiers in peacetime.

'I reckon, Henry,' agreed Tim Witherington tacitly, 'that someone in Cartainia was trying to tell you something.'

'Monkshood,' said Wendy, coming back into the room with her finger keeping a page in a book open, 'means "Beware, a deadly foe is near".'

'And bilberry?' asked Henry, scribbling away now.

'Treachery,' she said.

'What about Guelder rose?' he asked.

Wendy's expression lightened. 'Oh, that's

easy. In the language of flowers that just means "winter".'

'I think,' said Henry, 'that in the language of flowers having it next to the *Achillea millefolia* might mean something.' Another thought besides 'war in winter' came into his mind. There had been unusual flowers either side of the bilberry. 'Tell me what betony stands for, Wen.'

'Surprise,' she said after consulting her book.

'And begonia?'

'Beware.'

Henry regarded his scribbled notes. 'A winter war following treachery. That's clear enough but who by, with or from? There must be a message here but what it means, I'm blessed if I know.'

'Have you told us all the flowers that were in the wreath?' asked his sister practically.

'I memorised them from the top,' said Henry, shutting his eyes and thinking back. 'Clockwise. I think I can remember them all. Oh, I didn't mention anemone did I?'

'Fading hope.'

'Or stephanotis. There was some of that there. Quite a lot, actually. It stuck out.'

'I don't need the book for that,' Wendy said, smiling. 'I can tell you without looking it up that it means "happiness in marriage".'

Tim Witherington waved his pipe in the air.

233

'Can't see where that fits in with the general tenor of the rest of the message, old chap. Odd man out in that lot, rather, happiness in marriage, wouldn't you think?'

'It is, Tim. And that's important.' Henry put his pencil away. 'I think I can place it now,' he said. 'I've just remembered the name of the Cartainian Foreign Secretary. He's called Stephan Kiste and I rather think we're heading for a war with him in the winter.' He got to his feet. 'Do you mind if I just telephone the Duty Officer at the Foreign Office?'

STARS IN THEIR COURSES

The waiter, Italian and dramatic, bounced into the restaurant kitchen. 'This man, he tells me that the table is booked in the name of Mr John Smith. Why, I ask you, not just say that he is Mr Smith?'

'Perhaps the lady is not Mrs Smith?' suggested the sous-chef helpfully.

'Perhaps he isn't Mr Smith at all,' said Danny, the kitchen boy, an aficionado of the wilder side of crime fiction.

'John Smith,' exclaimed the waiter scornfully. 'Everybody in England is called John Smith.'

The maître d'hôtel, more experienced, had come into the kitchen at this point, and overheard them all. 'He has the book in his pocket,' he said with indrawn breath. 'I could see it when I took his coat.'

There was no need for the maître d'hôtel to say which book was in the man's pocket. Its title was *The Good Cooks of Calleshire* and it had been striking terror into the heart of every restaurateur in the county ever since it had been published. The requirements for an entry in it were stringent indeed, its inspectors quite merciless in their judgements and, unlike the judicial system, there was no appeal. Appearance in the publication, though, guaranteed a steady stream of hungry customers throughout the year to every restaurant mentioned in it. The Ornum Arms restaurant in the little Calleshire village of Ornum had never achieved such a mention, something that had always rankled with them.

And cost.

'I've got the pair of them seated at table two in the window with the menu,' said the maître d'hôtel to the waiter. 'Give them half a moment, Giovanni, and then see what they want to drink. Don't be too pressing, and you, chef, be ready for anything.'

'As soon as I've seen to table seven,' said the chef pointedly. 'They were there first.'

'Oh, the old lady with the four young people,' said the waiter, who was young himself as well as Italian. 'They're drinking sherry – everything from sweet to dry. I heard the old lady tell them they should have an aperitif and like it. Stirred up the digestive juices or something. They've

236

ordered Vouvray and a Gaillac with their meal.'

'The party who came in early.' The chef liked diners who came in early so that he could get started.

'They've got to get back to their college tonight,' said Giovanni. 'The old lady told me that when they arrived.' She wasn't in fact old but the waiter was young and in the way of the young thought she was.

'They came in first,' repeated the chef, a stickler in these matters.

'And they all want something different for starters,' sighed Giovanni, 'except for the girl in the party and she doesn't know what she wants yet.'

'That may take a little longer,' said the chef sarcastically, knocking up a plate of prosciutto ham as he spoke.

'She still doesn't,' said Giovanni. 'She said she needed to think first.'

'All that students ever need to do is think, not work,' said the sous-chef richly. He had left school at the earliest possible opportunity and worked ever since. 'That's what they're supposed to do, isn't it? Think.'

'That girl had better make up her mind soon,' said the chef briskly, 'or she won't get a first course at all. I can't afford to hang about if there's a man from that book around checking up on us.'

The maître d'hôtel sighed, knowing better than to upset his chef by suggesting changing the order of serving at a crucial point in the evening's cooking. 'Right, then, just get on with the first job quickly so that we can get Mr and Mrs John Smith whatever they want.'

'With knobs on,' said the sous-chef who was English.

'And when they want it, too,' insisted the maître d'hôtel, who had his authority to maintain. He was a worried man. If Mr Smith was indeed an inspector from the Calleshire guide he, the maître d', was in for a hard time. The restaurant could expect unreasonable demands, undeserved criticism and – trickiest of all – uncertainty, all arising out of a visit from an anonymous inspector from the county eating-places guide. He corrected himself in his mind: an inspector who was meant to be anonymous. The maître d'hôtel though, like all his kind, was a man of the world and knew better than to believe that the letter of the law was always adhered to. Rules, in his well-thumbed book of life, might not have been made to be broken but in his experience they usually were.

'We'll know for sure if he's an inspector,' said Giovanni, 'if he and his wife . . .'

'If she is his wife,' said the sous-chef again.

'If they each want something different for every single course,' finished Giovanni. 'That's always a sign. And a different wine with each one.'

'When I began working,' reminisced the maître d'hôtel briefly, 'the woman always used to let the man chose the menu as well as the wine. That saved a lot of bother.'

Misogynists to a man, they all nodded in agreement with this good practice.

'This girl who can't decide what she wants to eat says she is a vegetarian,' Giovanni informed them, rolling his eyes.

'Didn't have many of them when I started either,' said the maître d'hôtel, 'let alone customers with allergies. I was told that in the old days if you had a food allergy you weren't expected to accept an invitation to a grand dinner in the first place or accept it and eat the dish and be ill afterwards.'

'It isn't like that any more, I can tell you,' muttered the chef, who had a shelf full of gluten-free flour. He sniffed. 'Mind you, they hadn't invented coeliac disease then.'

The maître d' considered saying that coeliac disease had been discovered not invented but thought better of it.

'And we would have to go and have not one but two vegetarian dishes for starters on the menu tonight, wouldn't we?' persisted Giovanni. 'All this girl has to do is choose between the honey-roasted shallots and the warm ratatouille tartlet with pesto dressing. I ask you, what could be easier than that?'

'I expect they taste much the same anyway,' said the kitchen boy, not often privy to eating such things after closing time.

'They do not,' said the chef, rising to the bait. 'You wait, Danny-boy, when I've got time I'll make you eat them both blindfold and . . .'

'And nobody's got any time for anything like that now,' said the maître d'hôtel briskly. 'Giovanni, you ask the Smiths about their drinks and I'll get that girl to make up her mind.' He added to himself, 'That's if she's got one.'

Miss Celia Sparrow certainly had got a mind and was exercising it now. 'You see,' she said, smiling winningly at the maître d', 'it all depends on what I'm going to have afterwards.'

'And what are you going to have afterwards?' he asked, carefully avoiding calling her either 'madam' or 'miss', aware that you never knew with young women of her age which was the better. Neither probably. Instead he flourished the main course menu in front of her. 'Let me see now – the vegetarian dish we have on the menu tonight is dolcelatte cheese and spinach risotto.'

'That's all, is it?' she asked.

'That's all,' he said firmly, forgetting all about calling her 'miss', and thinking her instead a right 'madam'. 'Unless,' he added, struck by a sudden thought, 'you would like the fish. Tonight it's supreme of halibut with a lime butter sauce.'

'Fish feel pain,' she said soulfully.

'How do you know that spinach doesn't, Celia?' asked one of the boys at the table. 'They say that cauliflowers cry out when they're cut down.'

'That's the trouble with people studying philosophy, Tristram,' said Miss Sparrow sweetly. 'They only ever ask the questions. They never answer them.'

The older woman at the table, clearly the hostess, smiled and said, 'That's a good question, Tristram. How are you going to answer that one?'

'I don't have to, Aunt Marjorie,' he replied, taking her seriously. 'It's quite wrong to suppose that philosophy has all the answers. You could say that realising that particular fact is lesson one.'

'Then why study it?' countered Celia Sparrow swiftly.

Suppressing a strong urge to inflict some pain on the girl, let alone on the fish or the spinach, the maître d' coughed and said that in this case madam only had to decide which starter went best with the risotto.

The girl ran a well-manicured fingernail down the first-course menu. It hovered for a moment over the shallots and then took a sudden dive towards the ratatouille tartlet. The maître d' snatched the menu back from her with unseemly haste and made for the kitchen at speed.

Giovanni, the waiter, was already there. 'That Mr Smith, he called for the wine list and,' he lowered his voice, 'now he is making notes from it.'

The maître d' muttered something profane under this breath. 'That clinches it. Stand by for them to inspect the plumbing before they go.'

'The plumbing's all right,' muttered the chef. 'It's the food I'm worried about.'

'Calm down,' said the maître d'. 'We can only do our best. Now get on with this girl's tartlet and that'll leave you free for doing Mr and Mrs Smith's starters.'

'They're not the only people who are going to be eating here tonight,' the chef began truculently, 'and if you think I'm going to . . .'

'I think you're going to do what you always

do,' said the maître d' in a dangerously calm voice, 'and cook very well indeed for everybody. Now get on with it.'

Two more couples came in after that and then a quartet of older diners. The four were obviously long-standing friends, not so much interested in the food as in what they each had to say to the others. One of the two couples only had eyes for each other, the other pair sounded as if they were spoiling for a fight.

The chef produced the starters for Miss Celia Sparrow and her friends and turned his attention to Mr and Mrs Smith's first-course requirements, juggling pan-fried duck foie gras in puff pastry with a sherry vinegar dressing for one of them alongside breadcrumbed goujons of lemon sole served with a Béarnaise sauce with tomato for the other.

'That'll keep them quiet for a bit,' he hissed at Giovanni as he handed them over.

'Don't you believe it' said the waiter. 'They're just making sure the white wine's properly chilled.'

'They've quizzed me about the pistachio nuts and wanted to know why we didn't have macadamia ones as well,' said the maître d', coming into the kitchen. 'And then they had the nerve to ask me where the olives had come from.'

'Tell them they grow on trees,' suggested the sous-chef, already deep in preparing the second course for the table of students. 'Anyway I've got Mr and Mrs Smith's roast rack of lamb in port wine and the fillet of venison in the oven as well for them when they're ready.'

'We mustn't rush them over their starters,' the maître d' warned the waiter. 'I'll just keep an eye on their plates and then I'll give you the OK when to serve their main course.'

'Righto,' said Giovanni, his Italian temporarily displaced by an English expression.

'And,' the chef reminded them, 'we mustn't forget those people on table seven who were here first. They all want something different, too. At least three of them do. The old lady and one of the boys both want the fillet of beef.'

'Her teeth are all right, then,' remarked Giovanni, whose own grandmother had lost hers.

'What do you mean?' demanded the chef combatively. 'There's nothing wrong with the beef. It's prime Scottish fillet with a special black peppercorn and garlic sauce.'

'All right, all right,' said the waiter pacifically. 'I'm going to serve their wine now. I bet you they won't ask if the Vouvray is properly chilled.'

They didn't. Miss Celia Sparrow took a sip of it from her glass and pronounced it excellent while Miss Marjorie Simmonds tasted the Gaillac and nodded her approval.

Meanwhile though, Mr Smith declared that his white burgundy had not been chilled long enough. As Giovanni restored it to the ice bucket without comment Mr Smith remarked that he had particularly wanted to drink it with his goujons of lemon sole. Giovanni offered to take the dish back to the kitchen. Mr Smith said that reheating would spoil it.

The maître d', sensing a stand-off, sailed up to the table and suggested more ice in the bucket.

Giovanni retreated to the kitchen, muttering that in Italy the craft of a waiter was held in high esteem. In a country as benighted as England a waiter was merely thought of as a postman delivering parcels of food to people too ignorant to know good food from bad.

The sous-chef offered to put sugar instead of salt on the man's venison.

'Or vinegar instead of that red wine jus you're always going about,' suggested the kitchen boy. 'He probably doesn't know the difference.'

Giovanni, remembering his heritage, drew himself up proudly and said, 'I would rather be like the Borgias and serve him poison.'

'That'll do,' said the maître d', coming back into the kitchen at that moment. 'Just get on with your work, all of you, while I see what everyone else wants. We're going to be busy tonight.'

'I'll say,' said Giovanni. 'The woman on table three is playing up because we haven't got any background music. I expect she wants it to cover up what she's saying to her husband. At it hammer and tongs already, they are.'

'And she's not going to have any music either,' said the maître d'. Music might be the food of love but at the Ornum Arms you had the food without it.

'At least that means that Mr and Mrs Smith can't complain that it's too loud,' said Giovanni.

'They'll find something else to moan about,' said the maître d', before resuming his professional smile when he left the kitchen. Table seven, he noted in passing, were now tucking in to their main course with all the gusto of hungry students.

'You should come over to Ornum more often, Aunt Marjorie,' he heard the one called Tristram say.

She beamed. 'It's not every day you win the Almstone Essay Prize, my boy. It calls for a celebration so you must all feel free to have exactly what you want to eat and drink.'

The maître d' smiled inwardly. The words were music to his ears and the only sort of music he liked to hear in any restaurant. What he heard next was not to give him so much pleasure. A peremptory wave of an arm called him back to the Smiths' table.

'My wife,' declared Mr Smith, 'says that her lamb is overcooked. That's right, dear, isn't it?'

'Lamb should be pink,' said the lady in question, pointing to her plate. 'Not too well done, like this one is.'

The maître d' looked down at a properly cooked rack of lamb, pink to exactly the right hue, took a deep breath and offered to supply one that was more undercooked.

'Not undercooked,' said Mrs Smith. 'Cooked just right.'

'Certainly, madam,' he said and shot back to the kitchen with the offending dish.

He was not well received there. 'All right, chef,' he said. 'You know it's perfect, I know it's perfect and I'm pretty sure the Smiths know it's perfect.'

'I'll eat it,' offered the kitchen boy, putting his hand out for the dish.

'No, you won't,' said the maître d', withdrawing it swiftly.

The chef reached for his Sabatier knife and waved it about in the direction of the door to the dining room in a gesture unmistakeable anywhere in the world.

'And you can put that away,' said the maître d'.

'It'll be pretty bloody next time round,' said the chef ambiguously.

'Look at it this way, lads,' pleaded the maître d', hoping that the chef was referring to the rack of lamb, 'think of it as being like life. It's not what happens to you that matters, it's how you behave when it does.'

'I know how I'd behave to the Smiths,' growled the chef.

'And me,' said the sous-chef.

The kitchen boy contented himself with drawing a finger across his throat while Giovanni muttered some Italian imprecation under his breath in which the word '*mafiosi*' was the only one distinguishable.

By way of a diversion the maître d' reported that the loving couple were feeding each other morsels of food.

'A waste,' pronounced the chef, a much-married man. 'That's no way to treat good cooking.'

Torn between the devil and the deep blue sea, the maître d' retreated to the dining room. The four old friends were tucking in to their meal but still talking nineteen to the dozen so, unwilling to disturb either the warring couple or the besotted one, he sailed up to table seven and enquired if all was well there, too.

Miss Marjorie Simmonds smiled benignly. 'It is,' she said, looking round at rapidly emptying plates. 'I'm sure they don't eat as well as this at college, poor things.'

'You can say that again,' said her nephew. 'I tell you we live on pasta and sardines there.'

'And baked beans on toast,' said Celia Sparrow.

'I'm not too sorry for them,' said Miss Simmonds, adding dryly, 'Of course, all this rich food may have taken their appetites for a dessert away.'

There was a chorus of dissent.

'I'll send the waiter when you're ready,' said the maître d'. He had already decided that he himself would handle Mr and Mrs Smith from now on. Collecting the barely cooked rack of lamb from the kitchen, he presented it to Mrs Smith, adding smoothly that he hoped it was now cooked to her satisfaction.

It was.

Giovanni, too, ignored both the warring and the loving couples – they behaved better in Italy – and contented himself instead with taking orders from table seven.

'Let me see now,' said Marjorie Simmonds, 'that's passion fruit and orange tart for you, Celia, isn't it?'

Miss Sparrow nodded. 'Yes, please,' she said, looking hard at Tristram. 'I adore passion fruit.'

'Cheese for me,' said Tristram gruffly.

The other two men, who looked as if they had gone to college for the rugby, settled for steamed chocolate and hazelnut sponge pudding and brioche bread and butter pudding.

Miss Simmonds regarded the dessert menu for a moment or two and opted for the coconut rice pudding with plum compote. Then she said to the waiter, 'Would you think me awfully awkward if I asked if we might take the menu home with us? It's been such a lovely evening.'

'Not at all,' said Giovanni, adding grandly, 'We change it every week.'

'I'm going to get them all to sign it, you see,' she said. 'It'll be a real memento of a happy evening.'

The waiter trotted back to the kitchen with the order. The maître d' joined him there a little later bearing the Smiths' dessert order in his hand. 'Madam,' he reported, now using the term pejoratively, 'would like the banana bavarois and sir is prepared to try our brioche bread and butter pudding.'

'Brave man,' said the sous-chef ironically. 'Who knows what goes in to that?'

'Snaps and snails and puppy-dogs' tails,'

chanted the kitchen-boy, the youngest there, ducking back in mock fear from an imaginary blow from the chef.

'And they want our best Sauternes with them,' said the maître d'.

It was after that when Mr Smith ordered liqueurs with their coffee that the maître d' was quite sure what was coming.

And he was right.

Much later, when all the other customers had left, the maître d' presented the bill to Mr Smith. The man cast his eye over it for a long moment and then murmured casually, 'Suppose we say, shall we, that tonight the drinks are on the house?'

Drawing himself up to his full height but in a voice that trembled slightly, the maître d' said, 'I'm very sorry, sir. I can't agree to that.'

'If you won't, then you won't, I suppose,' said Mr Smith, tossing his credit card on the table, 'but mark my words, man, you'll come to regret it.'

'Very possibly, sir,' said the maître d' with dignity.

'And naturally I shan't be adding anything on for service,' said Mr Smith.

'That, sir, is always entirely at the customer's discretion,' said the maître d' smoothly. 'Your coats . . .'

Mr Smith put his coat on so clumsily that *The Good Cooks of Calleshire* actually fell out of the pocket and onto the floor. The maître d' picked the book up and handed it back to him with the utmost civility and opened the restaurant door for the pair. 'A very good evening to you, sir . . . madam . . .' he said as he ushered them out, locking the door behind them.

'That's blown it,' he said, back in the kitchen. 'Get me a drink somebody. I need it.'

It hadn't blown it.

At that very moment Miss Marjorie Simmonds, a food writer of distinction, was penning a fulsome report to the editor of *The Good Cooks of Calleshire*, to which in due course, before posting it, she would attach the menu and the receipted bill.

A MANAGED RETREAT

Her father had been in the army and so Susan knew the difference – the important difference – between a retreat and a rout. 'A retreat,' the old soldier used to declare in the long, dull days of peace, 'is something you should manage positively and, incidentally, always refer to as a strategic withdrawal. A rout is something you can't manage at all.' He had been evacuated from Crete after the invasion and so used to add, 'You can't call a rout by any other name except a bloody shambles.'

Susan was determined that her own withdrawal from Oak Tree House in the village of Almstone – her house – their house – and now his house – should be a managed retreat and not a rout. She had therefore planned her last night there very carefully. She was alone in the house, of course, and had been for some time: all the while in fact since Norman had moved out and gone to live with his new ladylove. Susan had stayed on in the house, alone and sad, hoping against hope that she could go on living there.

It was not to be.

As her solicitor had pointed out, this was first and foremost because she would not be able to afford to do so until her divorce settlement came through. This fact had been reinforced after a time when the lighting and heating bills for the house had remained unpaid by Norman and supplies were cut off. She had found out the hard way, too, that Norman had cancelled their direct debits for all the other utilities.

'He's freezing me out,' she reported to her solicitor, waving a sheaf of bills in her hand. 'And in the middle of winter, too.'

'I'm afraid,' said the solicitor, a not unkindly young man, 'that unless you move out you may find yourself in court for non-payment.' He coughed. 'I must warn you that some of these undertakings can be notably unsympathetic. They cite the public interest and so forth.'

'What about my interest?' she demanded.

'I think,' he said, choosing his words with almost palpable care, 'that your best interest might be served by finding some less expensive accommodation until matters are – er – concluded.'

She had nearly broken down then and wailed. 'But it's my home. It's been my home ever since we got married.'

He shook his head. 'No, Mrs . . .'

She interrupted him. 'Please call me Susan . . . I don't like using my married name any more. It upsets me.'

'I understand. Right.' He gave a quick nod and resumed his discourse. 'No, Susan, I think you should appreciate that it's not your home any more. It's just a house in which you happen to have lived for a few years – something that will in due course form part of the value of the settlement that you will receive on your divorce. In my opinion . . .'

Susan drew breath to speak and then remembered that when solicitors used that expression it meant that they were charging for their time and so kept silent.

'In my opinion,' he repeated with some emphasis, 'you should in the meantime move out to somewhere you can afford as quickly as you can.'

'I thought possession was nine points of the law,' she said obstinately.

He pointed to the bills she had brought in with her. 'You could, of course, stay there and face eviction for non-payment of these accounts.

That in my view would be a worst case scenario. Bailiffs are not nice people.'

'I'm between a rock and a hard place, then, aren't I?'

He let a little silence develop before he murmured, 'These cases are never easy.'

She was going to challenge him on this but then realised that to him she was just another case: another sad case of a wife being deserted by her husband, a husband moreover who was determined to make life as difficult as possible for her. One of her friends had tried to explain this complex behaviour as demonstrating guilt on Norman's part but she hadn't gone along with that.

Now, instead, she asked the solicitor harshly, 'Then what's to stop my husba . . . Norman, that is – having our house instead as part of the settlement?'

'Technically there is nothing to stop him doing so provided that you are properly recompensed for your share.'

'So what's the difference?' The idea of Norman making Oak Tree House a love nest for the new woman was almost too repugnant for her to bear. What had made the situation even worse was that the new woman wasn't some young floozy – he hadn't even been trading Susan in for a new model. The creature was practically the same age as she was. As Susan had asked herself time and again, if the new woman didn't even have age on her side, then what did she have? Answer – even in the wee small hours – came there none.

The solicitor sighed. 'From what you have told me, Susan, your husband – your ex-husband, that is – would be in a position to be able to afford to live there and you aren't at the moment. Should you wish to keep the house at this point in time, you would have to buy him out and you aren't going to have the funds do that. Not until after everything is settled and maybe not then.'

'There's one law for the rich and one for the poor,' she said bitterly. 'Always has been.'

'I understand that he is a very successful businessman,' the solicitor responded obliquely. 'This, I may say, will ultimately be to your advantage – that is, when matters between you are finally settled. In the meantime . . .'

The meantime had amounted to Susan renting a small end-of-terrace cottage in the village of Larking. She was due to move there in the morning so tonight was her last in Oak Tree House. She might have spent it packing up her own things but these were all neatly boxed and awaiting Wetherspoon's, the removal people, in the morning. Or she could have had a farewell party for all the friends who had been so supportive in the dissolution of her marriage but she hadn't wanted that. It would have seemed like a wake. The following morning would have loomed like Banquo's ghost over them all and left them worrying what to say as they left.

So she hadn't wanted that either and yet she hadn't wanted to spend it wandering in a melancholy way from room to room, taking a last look at the remnants of her love and marriage. Instead she had thought of her father and decided to stage a managed retreat.

First, she planned to dine in style. Retrieving a pair of silver candlesticks – a wedding present from an aunt – from a packing case, she laid the table as carefully as if for a dinner party. The table was coming with her to the cottage but Sid Wetherspoon who was doing the removal for her had been very relaxed about leaving around what she needed until she actually left Oak Tree House.

'Larking's not far,' he'd said. 'Don't you worry, missus. Make yourself comfortable there until the morning.'

Comfortable wasn't exactly how she would have described the chilly echoing house, packing cases everywhere, but she wasn't going to let that spoil her last evening there. She'd chosen the meal with care. The food had to be cold – the camping stove was only really up to making hot drinks, not cooking. And the wine had to be white, the house being barely warm enough to make a red wine potable.

Fish was an obvious choice.

It was the fish that had given her the idea.

The prawns, actually.

Susan was very fond of shellfish and she decided to treat herself to prawns for her last meal in the house. She'd stood at the food counter in the shop for a while before deciding on a smoked mackerel salad to follow and then a sinful chocolate mousse.

She was quite surprised at the relish with which she ate it. A Barmecide feast, surely that was the proper name for a pretend banquet like this? More than once from sheer habit, she started to make some comment in the direction of the chair in which Norman had sat for so long and then stopped, realising at long last with some relief that she didn't really have anything to say to him any more.

The camping stove would run to coffee after that and then she would go to bed to keep warm.

Only she didn't, not straightaway.

Instead, cradling her mug of coffee between her hands for warmth as much as anything else, she sat on in the cold room, casting her eyes everywhere. She went out to the kitchen briefly but soon came back and resumed her seat. It was the chandelier over the dining table that drew her back there. She'd never liked it but Norman had been pleased with it, bringing it home in triumph from some auction sale or other. It was really too ornate for the house and being made of brass didn't go with the rest of the room but she had accepted it peaceably enough.

Now she contemplated with especial interest its octopus-like arms, some of which ended in sockets for candle-shaped electric light bulbs and others culminating in pieces of metal described in the catalogue as foliate. She had cleaned and polished it dutifully every spring since.

'And got to know its little ways,' she said to herself, going to the cupboard under the stairs and coming back with a pair of steps.

She had put a few prawns on one side to take with her for a snack lunch at Larking the next day but now she picked some of them up. Mounting the steps carefully, she unscrewed one of the foliate arms of the candelabra and inserted prawns into the hollow brass. Then she did the same thing again to another one. And another until the prawns had gone.

She clambered back down to the floor and

then had another thought. 'A bit of mackerel wouldn't do any harm either,' she murmured aloud and went up the steps again. 'Not too much, though.'

Susan left the house the next morning with an equanimity that surprised Sid Wetherspoon, an old hand at moving displaced wives. She settled down quite calmly in the cottage at Larking, too, professing little interest in the titbits of information that were fed to her by old friends about the house at Almstone.

'Norman's back living there,' reported one of them presently.

'Really?' she said. 'Not alone, I take it?'

'Doesn't look like it,' said her informant frankly. 'They've got two cars outside.'

It was several weeks later before someone else remarked to her that there had been a pest-control van parked outside Oak Tree House for a couple of days.

'Funny, that,' Susan said. 'I never had any trouble like that when I was there.' She was feeling quite cheerful since she'd just had the cheque for the final settlement from the break-up of her marriage to a man with money. This included a healthy chunk for her share of the going value of Oak Tree House at Almstone.

It was a considerable while after that when

an old neighbour, never a fan of Norman's, told her that there had been a surveyor looking over the house. 'He advised unblocking a couple of the old chimneys,' the neighbour said. 'I gather they've already had all the floorboards up.'

'My goodness,' exclaimed Susan. 'Whatever for?'

'The smell,' said the neighbour lugubriously. 'They don't know where it's coming from.'

'What smell?' Susan asked.

'That's just it,' said the neighbour. 'Nobody knows what it is but believe you me, Susan, it's awful. They had me in for a drink the other evening and it nearly made me sick. Norman's had the place practically torn apart looking for whatever's wrong but they can't find what it is.'

'Well, I never,' said Susan, adding with perfect truth, 'there was nothing like that when I was there.'

'I know that,' said the neighbour robustly. 'It was fine then.'

It was two months later when Susan spotted an advertisement for the house in the local paper.

'The agent's got a "For Sale" board up outside, too, not that anyone's going to buy it with that smell,' reported the same neighbour with that special satisfaction reserved for the trials and tribulations of unpopular others.

Going through the village herself a month or so later Susan noticed that the sale board was still there but that the house was now empty.

'The new woman announced she was going whether Norman came with her or not,' said another of the neighbours when Susan bumped into her. 'Couldn't stand the smell.'

Susan, reasonably comfortable in her little cottage at Larking, waited another couple of months before she took any action. It was when she saw Oak Tree House being advertised in the local paper by a different agent that she made an enquiry about the house. She got a guarded response from the agency.

'The property is on the market at a considerably reduced price,' said the agent with practised fluency.

'Really?' said Susan. 'Why would that be?'

'The owner has had to move for urgent domestic reasons,' said the agent.

'I see,' said Susan. 'Would it be possible to see over the house?'

'Of course, although we would need a little warning before we arranged a viewing.'

This came as no surprise to Susan. When she eventually arrived there with the agent she could sense that every window in the house must have been open hours beforehand. As she entered the front door she sniffed and said, 'Funny smell.'

The agent sighed but did not deny it.

'The house strikes one as cold, too,' she murmured.

'We opened it up earlier to give it a thorough airing,' said the agent. 'It's been empty and shut up for quite a while now.'

Susan wandered through the house, noting that nothing much had been done to it since she had left. Any inclination on the part of the new woman to expunge Susan's presence by redecoration had not been implemented.

'It is a terrible smell, isn't it?' she said to the agent at the end of her tour.

'Most unfortunate,' said the agent ambiguously.

'It must be much worse when the central heating's on,' said Susan, 'and the windows are closed.'

The agent did not attempt to deny this. He took a deep breath and said, 'I think, madam, you would find the owner willing to accept a considerably lower offer than the advertised one on account of the – er – drawbacks you've mentioned. Would you like me to ask him?'

'Please,' said Susan, although she waited a little while longer before she made her final – and even lower – offer for Oak Tree House. Even so, she was surprised at the alacrity with which it was accepted by Norman.

Her solicitor congratulated her on a really good deal, the contract to be signed as soon as a few details were settled.

'Details?' Susan asked, raising her eyebrows.

'Only the fixtures and fittings,' said the solicitor. 'Oh, and the vendor particularly wants to take the brass chandelier in the dining room with him. Apparently he's always liked it and technically it's not really a fitment. Is that all right with you?'

Susan paused before she answered him. 'I suppose so,' she said slowly. Then she smiled and added, 'Someone else can clean the brass.'

SPITE AND MALICE

Sheriff Macmillan received the news of the arrival of his visitor with a certain reluctance. Hector Leanaig, Laird of Balgalkin, was never really welcome at Sheriff Rhuaraidh Macmillan's home at Drummondreach.

This was because whilst the sheriff's writ ran throughout East Fearnshire he much preferred exercising his authority over those who lived at some little distance away from his home rather than those on his own doorstep. He had found that it made for better long-term relationships.

His current visitor was a case in point. The sheriff's home at Drummondreach was much too near for comfort to Balgalkin Castle and its stormy owner, Hector Leanaig.

'What is it anent now, Leanaig?' he said sternly when the man had been shown into the sheriff's study. It was not the first time Hector Leanaig had come to Rhuaraidh Macmillan's door with action in mind. Action against someone else, as a rule.

'More trouble down at Culloch Beg – Angus Mackenzie's place,' said Hector Leanaig hotly. 'The man's nothing but a common reiver.'

'Are you alleging,' said the sheriff, first and foremost a man of the law, 'that Mackenzie of Culloch Beg has stolen your cattle?'

'I'm not alleging anything,' retorted the Laird of Castle Balgalkin on the instant. 'I'm telling you that he has stolen them. And what I want to know is what you're going to do about it.' He shook his fist angrily at the sheriff. 'And aye soon, I hope.'

'When did this happen?' asked the sheriff, as unmoved by the shaking fist as by any other threat to his authority. The law was, after all, the law.

'The beasts were on Balgalkin's policies yestre'en right enough. I saw them myself. Today they're down at Culloch Beg's gang. Man, you've only got to go down there the day and take a look at Angus Mackenzie's demesne. Then you can see them for yourself.'

'Presently,' said the sheriff, not a man to be hassled either. 'And what does Angus Mackenzie have to say for himself?'

'Say?' snorted Hector Leanaig, his nostrils

flaring like those of one of his own bulls. 'Say! I'll have you know that I'm no' speaking to the man these six months and more.'

Aye, thought the sheriff to himself, there was the rub.

'He couldna' have some of my land as tocher, so he's taken my cattle as well as my daughter.'

'Dowry is the man's right, fair enough,' opined the sheriff mildly.

'Dowry!' spluttered Hector Leanaig. 'My daughter Cathie was carried away by that blackavised son of his.'

'Eloped is the word you're looking for,' said the sheriff. 'Not abducted.'

'She was gone in the night without telling anyone.'

'Eloped,' said the sheriff again.

'Taken,' insisted Hector Leanaig.

'She went willingly,' said the sheriff, adding cautiously, since he was indeed a man of the law, 'from all accounts.' He did not see fit to say that these accounts had come in the first instance from Elspeth, a kitchen maid in his own household, well in touch with the goings-on around her.

'That's just not so,' insisted Leanaig, jerking a burly shoulder. 'No lassie in her right mind would go willingly with a man like Angus Mackenzie of Culloch Beg's son. He's no more than a boy.'

'She's of full age,' pointed out Sheriff Macmillan. It was in all honesty all he could say about any lovers. Which maiden found which swain attractive was outwith his – or any man's – comprehension, let alone his jurisdiction.

And vice versa.

Especially vice versa.

'Sixteen! You call that old enough?' exploded the Laird.

'I don't,' responded the sheriff, a father himself, 'but custom and law does.'

Hector Leanaig breathed noisily through his flared nostrils. 'And as for that Callum Mackenzie . . .'

'He's of full age, too,' said the sheriff unhelpfully.

The Laird of Balgalkin gave an unseemly snort.

The sheriff carried on. 'Callum Mackenzie's a man now, Hector, and your daughter's a woman and there's nothing you can do about it. They plighted their troth, right enough.'

The man scowled. 'And if it's not bad enough to take my daughter in the night he goes and takes my kine, too.'

'And you want your kine back – is that it?' asked the sheriff, adding quizzically, 'Or your daughter?'

Hector Leanaig stared at the floor and growled, 'My daughter'll no' come back.'

'But you want your cattle?'

'That I do. I'm not having Angus Mackenzie getting a dowry for my daughter in that back-handed way. And it's a fine herd of beasts that are down at Culloch Beg just now. My beasts,' he added.

When appealed to, Angus Mackenzie did not dispute that they were Leanaig's beasts. 'Aye,' he said readily enough when the sheriff made his way later in the day to Mackenzie's land at Culloch Beg. 'They're Leanaig's right enough. They were down here on my gang the morn's morn and I sent a man up to tell him so.'

'You did, did you,' commented the sheriff dryly.

'Afore noon, that was, but no one's been down to drive them back.'

'Is that so?'

'Aye,' said Angus Mackenzie equably. He waved an arm over his land. 'And I hope they'll be quick at Balgalkin about coming for them. I don't have the pasture for that many head of cattle. You can see that for yourself.'

Sheriff Macmillan looked over Culloch Beg and nodded. 'He didn't tell me that.'

'So what would I be doing with them, anyway, Sheriff?' asked the man.

'Collecting the dowry for Leanaig's daughter, Cathie.'

A slow smile spread across Angus Mackenzie's weathered face. 'Ah, so that's the way of Leanaig's thinking, is it?'

'Of course,' suggested the sheriff slyly, 'the beasts might just have come down on their own accord for water.'

'After a dreich February like we had this year and when there's water and plenty up at Balgalkin?' responded Angus Mackenzie, waving an arm towards the heather-ringed hill. 'Why, even my own spring rises there.'

'So you'll be sending the beasts back then, will you?' said Sheriff Macmillan.

'I think,' said Angus Mackenzie, 'that Leanaig should be sending his own drover to take them back. Perhaps the same one,' he said, giving the sheriff a very straight look indeed, 'as drove them down in the night.'

'Even so, I trust you'll not be getting your Callum to take them back,' said the sheriff, who had quite enough legal work to be getting on with already and wanted no further trouble in the matter.

'That I won't because I can't.' Angus

Mackenzie jerked a horny thumb in the direction of the west. 'Callum's away over the hill just now bringing old Duart Urquhart's corp' back to the burying ground. His son's in Dingwall Gaol and canna' do it himself.'

The sheriff followed his gaze. Way beyond and above Castle Balgalkin the ancient coffin road could still be discerned across the heather. Since time immemorial it had been the way over from the west for horses, sheep, cattle and men – men that were dead or alive. The deer merely leapt where they wilt.

'I have the mortcloth here ready and waiting but it's hard work carrying a coffin so far over the hills and I think it'll be a day or two before they'll get back here,' said Angus Mackenzie.

'That's good,' said Rhuaraidh Macmillan, taking his leave and going back to Drummondreach.

It wasn't the last he heard of young Callum Mackenzie, though. Two days later an indignant Angus Mackenzie, his father, was on the sheriff's doorstep. 'The Laird of Balgalkin Castle'll no' let Duart's corp' through Balgalkin land and back down to the burying ground,' he said, his complexion an unhealthy red. 'Not all the time my Callum's in the burial party, that is.'

The Sheriff of Fearnshire considered this. Land

law in the Highlands was a matter of a complex mixture of inheritance and oral tradition. It wasn't like England where the Crown had held all land by right of conquest ever since William of Normandy had landed in 1066 and where all land was divided into holdings, some large and some small.

Scotland, on the other hand, had never been conquered and it would have been a brave man indeed who said Hector Leanaig had no right to Balgalkin and its castle, but it was surely an even braver owner of Balgalkin who defied the right of any Highlander the use of the old trackways, coffin carriers or no. Clan burial grounds and the paths back to them over the hills went a long way further back in history than any landholding.

'So what's happened?' asked the sheriff briskly, hoping it wasn't either violence or – worse still – violation.

'Callum's left Duart's coffin with the others to bring to the burying ground and is coming back himself through the haughland by the Firth.'

'Good,' said Sheriff Macmillan. The last thing he wanted to have to deal with that day was a fight over the right of way of a coffin. 'I'm glad to hear it.'

'It's no' good,' muttered Angus Mackenzie, going unhappily on his way and leaving the sheriff free to concentrate on the approach of the month of May and the annual celebration of Beltane. This time-honoured Celtic festival was when bonfires were lighted on the hills with much ceremony. Like some other ceremonies – and the sheriff always thought of weddings in this connection – after the solemnities the rite usually degenerated into something like an orgy.

This year it proved more – much more – than that. On the evening of the first day of May the hill behind Castle Balgalkin was in the long tradition of East Fearnshire lit with a ring of fires. Sheriff Macmillan watched at a distance as the hillside succumbed to more and more of the dancing flames. As darkness fell these were surrounded by more and more dancing figures, just as wild as the flames, Hector Leanaig undoubtedly among them.

What happened later was more obscure.

'Hector Leanaig says it was just a spark carried by the wind,' reported Angus Mackenzie to Rhuaraidh Macmillan the next morning, his face darkened with smoke and fatigue. 'Mind you, it was no' will-o'-the-wisp, that I can tell you.'

'The foolish fire,' mused the sheriff. '*Ignis fatuus.*'

'That's as maybe,' said Angus Mackenzie,

uncompromising now, 'but believe you me, Sheriff, it was no spark carried by the wind either that set fire to Culloch Beg.'

'What you are suggesting,' began Sheriff Rhuaraidh Macmillan carefully, 'is that the flame that got to Culloch Beg came from the Beltane fire on purpose.'

'There was no wind from there to my land,' said Angus steadily, 'and yet it is Culloch Beg that was burnt and burnt badly.'

'Wildfire?' offered the sheriff, more for form's sake than from conviction.

'Lightning without thunder?' said Angus Mackenzie sceptically.

'Perhaps not,' agreed the sheriff.

'So what about my buildings and my crops?' demanded Mackenzie, still irate. 'The law should be on my side, Sheriff.'

'There's the question of proof, Angus. The law requires proof.'

'There's the question of my cattle,' responded the man hotly. 'They didn't stand still at Culloch Beg to be burnt. They took to the hills and they'll be all over Fearnshire by now. And Hector Leanaig isn't going to come down and round them up for me either, is he?' He gave the sheriff a very straight look. 'I've a mind to go up to Balgalkin with Callum and . . .'

'You'll do no such thing, Angus Mackenzie,' ordered the sheriff at once. 'I tell you the law must be obeyed and no man's hand raised against another in violence.'

'No man's hand should be tied by the law. There's no justice in that.' Angus Mackenzie turned away, muttering under his breath something else that the sheriff did not quite catch. 'And it's my land that's burnt, remember. Not his. Or yours,' he added over his shoulder as Rhuaraidh Macmillan left Culloch Beg, promising to go and see Hector Leanaig the morn's morn.

The sheriff found the Laird of Castle Balgalkin in no mood for apology let alone regret. 'It was Beltane, Sheriff, and you know what that means.'

'Springtime,' said the sheriff shortly, grateful that the quarter-days of Candlemass and Hallowmass were winter ones and thus too cold for long outdoor jauntings, but still ready to believe that there was a connection between Beltane and the heathen god of high places, Baal. And to believe, too, that the devil's boots didn't squeak.

'The rising of the sap.' The laird gave him a wicked grin. 'A time when even a father feels young again.'

'Not a time when a man feels like revenge

for losing a daughter, eh, Hector? Or,' he added, 'guilty about a tocher unpaid?'

'A man who is wronged has his rights.' Hector Leanaig was quickly back to being as surly as usual.

'A man who is wrong has few rights,' countered the sheriff, a man of the law first and foremost.

'And a man canna' tell which way the wind will blow.'

'A man, Hector, can tell which way the wind has blown.'

'And it blew down to Culloch Beg and set the man's heather alight,' said Hector Leanaig, showing no visible sign of regret.

'Or which way the wind hadn't blown,' insisted the sheriff.

'His heather and his bothies all gone from what I've heard,' said Hector Leanaig, in no whit put out. 'And his cattle all over the place.' He gave a smirk. 'But as you'll remember well enough, Sheriff, the good book says "Man is born to trouble as sparks fly upwards".'

'These seem to have flown downwards,' observed Sheriff Macmillan acidly. From where he stood at the castle he could see the blackened stumps of heather on Angus Mackenzie's land below them. And, when the wind came from that quarter, smell the burnt outbuildings. There were none of Mackenzie's cattle in sight. 'Hector, this must not happen again.'

'We don't have fires at Lammastide,' said the Laird, wilfully misunderstanding him. 'You know full well it's too light by August to celebrate the first fruits of harvest with fire. You canna' do it in the long days.'

'I know full well it's too late for you to get your daughter back,' said the sheriff crisply, sticking to the point. 'But it's not too late to send her dowry after her.'

'Angus Mackenzie'll get nothing out of me!' Hector Leanaig flushed, turned on his heel and strode back inside his castle, while the sheriff made his way thoughtfully back to his home at Drummondreach. What was still on his mind was the legal phrase 'the burden of proof'. 'Burden' he decided was the right word, before putting the Laird of Balgalkin out of his mind for the time being.

Spring turned to a summer much sunnier than usual and February's rain dried out of the land, aided by high winds from the east. It was the sheriff's observant little kitchen maid, Elspeth, who told him one day that there seemed to be o'er much going on Balgalkin land.

'Ploughing, sir,' she said.

'Ploughing?' echoed Rhuaraidh Macmillan in disbelief. 'At this time? Never. Don't forget the man has right of feal and divot in the peat.'

Elspeth bobbed a curtsey. 'Turning the land, then, sir. They weren't using the tairsgeir at the peat hags . . .'

'But ploughing? Surely not just now.'

Thinking the girl was mistaken, the sheriff put this put of his mind, too.

That is until Angus Mackenzie was at his door again.

This was several days later. The owner of Culloch Beg had made his way once more to Drummondreach. This time he was crosser than ever, his face now a puce colour. 'The law's no good at all. Leanaig's still after his revenge for losing his Cathie, Sheriff.'

'What has he done now?' asked Rhuaraidh Macmillan cautiously. In his view the law and revenge should be kept well apart.

'My spring rises on his land and the water comes down to me from Balgalkin. Always has.'

'Go on.'

'Leanaig's torn up his ground caterways so it doesn't drain down the hill my way any more, and so cut off the burn. The whole of Culloch Beg's dry now – there's no' enough water in my stream for man or beast.'

Sheriff Rhuaraidh Macmillan considered this for a minute and then said, 'Angus, I'll have to take this in to avizandum.' Seeing the look of total bewilderment on the man's face he explained, 'That means to give the matter my earnest consideration – to think about it.'

'Thinking's no good to man or beast either, Sheriff. Thinking'll not get water back to Culloch Beg and I need it there.'

'Wait, ye . . .'

'And nor will the law.'

'The law is the law.' It was the sheriff's ultimate credo.

'The law'll no' get my water back but my Callum might,' insisted the man bitterly.

'Callum musn't try.'

'Leanaig says that a man can do what he likes on his own land,' countered a sorely tried Angus Mackenzie.

'No, he can't.'

'Yes, he can. He's boasting about it all over Fearnshire.'

'He can't do what he wants if that which he does is done deliberately and with malice against his neighbour,' responded Rhuaraidh Macmillan.

'Can't he just? This time,' repeated Angus Mackenzie spiritedly, 'I'm going to send Callum up there with some of my men and . . .'

'You'll do no such thing, Angus Mackenzie. You'll leave this to me. Now, away with you back to Culloch Beg.'

After the owner of Culloch Beg had reluctantly gone back to his own domain Sheriff Macmillan sat in his room for a long time thinking about Scottish law. He thought, too, and about that which wasn't either Scottish law or even strictly legal but might work.

Presently he stirred himself, sent for his clerk and his palfrey, and rode over to Castle Balgalkin in state. True enough, the land had indeed been turned, the furrows running laterally rather than downhill, thus turning water away from its natural way down the hill to Culloch Beg.

Hector Leanaig was unrepentant. 'I can do what I like on Balgalkin land. No man can gainsay that, Sheriff.'

'You have interfered with the natural run-off of the water, Hector.'

'What of it? It's Balgalkin's water.'

'Maybe, but it is a mark of civilisation, Hector, that the wronged party can be the party in the right.'

'And you call that the law?'

'I do. And Angus Mackenzie has been wronged by you, right enough.'

'It's my land,' said the laird carelessly, 'and I'll do what I will with it, whatever Mackenzie says. It's my daughter, too, that's away there,' he added, jerking his thumb down the hill.

'The law does not countenance such behaviour.'

The Laird of Balgalkin looked at the sheriff. 'The law has nothing to do with it.'

'The law, Hector Leanaig, is called *aemulatio vicini* and I'm charging you with a breach of it.'

Hector Leanaig shrugged his shoulders. 'I haven't the Latin.'

'It's an act towards a neighbour that is normally legally proper – such as your turning up your own land, Hector – which can be actionable if taken in malice and harmful to others.'

Hector Leanaig flushed. 'You'll no' get away with that, Sheriff, in any sort of court.'

'On the contrary, Hector, it's you who isn't going to get away with it. You'll answer to it, unless that is . . .'

The Laird of Balgalkin scowled. 'So it's got down to horse-trading, has it, this famous law of yours?'

'Only in a manner of speaking, Hector,' said the sheriff pleasantly.

'Well?'

'I think your behaviour calls for restitution

282

of all the wrongs you have done to Mackenzie, tocher and all.'

'So?'

'So,' said the sheriff in a steely voice, 'if this isn't done by the end of the week I shall have put you in Dingwall Gaol.'

Hector Leanaig shrugged his great shoulders. 'You've no grounds for doing that and you ken that well enough. It wouldn't be lawful and no court would agree to it.'

'That is so,' admitted the sheriff calmly, adding pedantically, 'On both counts.'

'Man, I'll be out the next morning and well you know it.'

'Maybe, but one night in there alongside Colin Urquhart'll be quite enough.'

'For what?' demanded Leanaig.

'To catch the smallpox from him. That's what he's got and what his father died from. Didn't you know?'

BUSINESS PLAN

'And they said that first of all we ought to have a business plan,' said the youngest among them, a lad who on happier ships might have been called the cabin boy, 'seeing as we could hardly advertise.'

'If that's all they said,' grumbled the one they thought of as the first mate, 'then we oughtn't to have sent you on the course in the first place. Cost a lot of dosh, it did.'

'Waste of good money,' said the third mate, who thought he ought to have been sent on it instead and said so. He would have been if he had been able to read and write.

'It wasn't a waste,' protested the lad indignantly, 'though they did complain that they were always sent junior staff on their course instead of senior management and they didn't like it.'

'What did I say?' The third mate looked round

challengingly at the others. 'I should have gone. Not him.'

'They said,' the lad carried on gamely, 'that even so there were all sorts of things we should be thinking about doing now trade was slackening off so badly.'

'Give me a for instance,' growled the first mate.

'Like having a mission statement.'

'I'm not having anything to do with missionaries.' The second mate sat up suddenly. 'Caused me no end of trouble did missionaries. Talking, talking, talking . . .'

'Mission statement,' repeated the cabin boy. 'It's nothing to do with missionaries.'

'That's good,' said the second mate, subsiding back onto his haunches on the deck.

'Tell us what it is, then,' said their leader, the tallest and the swarthiest among them.

'For starters,' said the lad, momentarily diverted from the subject of mission statements, 'he said we ought to be calling you Captain Hook.'

Their leader looked bewildered. 'Why?'

'He didn't say. He did ask though if you wore a black eyepatch and had a hook instead of a hand and I said no, you didn't, and there were thirteen hands on board.'

'And we don't fly the Jolly Roger either,' said

the oldest man there, the one they called the ancient mariner. 'I hope you told him that, too.' He thumped the deck. 'And about my wooden leg.'

The cabin boy kept going. 'And they said I ought to be called Little Billee – I don't know why.'

'Never you mind,' said the captain hastily. 'We aren't going to eat you.'

'Billy No-Mates,' crowed the second mate.

'Like I said,' the third mate, a man with a giant chip on his shoulder, reminded them, 'that course was a total waste of money.'

'We do use grappling hooks,' pointed out the captain thoughtfully. 'It's the only way to get onto some of the bigger ships. Them and hooked ladders.'

'Doesn't always get us over the side, though, does it?' said second mate, 'not now they've taken to covering the rails with barbed wire like they have.'

'Tell us what this mission statement thing is, then, boy,' said the captain. 'I'm interested.'

'It's supposed to set out what it is we're trying to do,' replied the cabin boy.

'We know what we're trying to do,' said the first mate briskly. 'Raise more funds.'

'And raise 'em more quickly,' added the second mate. 'Fuel's getting low.'

The cabin boy looked nervous. 'But they say we have to say what for.'

'I'll give you what for . . .' began the first mate, clenching his fists.

'Let him go on,' commanded the captain.

Before the lad could get a word in edgeways the second mate said simply, 'We take either ships or people hostage. That's all. Job done. Six words.'

'Seven,' said the third mate triumphantly.

'We have to tell everyone why we're doing what we are,' persisted the lad. 'That's the thing they were on about. Explaining.'

'I am the captain and that's what I do,' murmured the man, but under his breath.

'We do it for the money,' repeated the first mate heavily. 'You know that and everyone else ought to be able to work it out for themselves.'

The captain gave a short laugh. 'The shipowners can, right enough. And their insurers are even better at it. They know which side our bread is buttered, all right. Tankers are worth a lot of money.'

'But what do we actually want the money for?' squeaked the lad. 'They said that that's what they wanted to know in the first instance before they could advise us.'

'Equipment and overheads,' responded the

second officer promptly. 'Radar screens cost the earth these days and our stuff's going to need updating very soon.'

'So we don't have to shout "Ship Ahoy" every time we sight a vessel any more,' said the ancient mariner, who had done his turn in the crow's nest in days of yore.

'We very nearly missed that new liner out of Southampton the other day,' said the captain, nodding. 'I quite thought it was going to give us the slip. That would have been a pity because it was a whopper.'

'There was those good ladders, too, that we had to pitch overboard when that poncy frigate tried to come alongside us last week,' the first mate reminded them. He sucked his teeth. 'I must say the boys were a bit slow in getting out the fishing lines instead. And they asked what we'd caught.'

'Which wasn't a lot,' grimaced the captain.

'I didn't like it when they hailed us by saying "Avast, my hearties",' sniffed the first mate. 'Downright rude, if you ask me.'

'They get it from the pantomime,' said the captain. 'Not real life.'

'And we want money for running the ship, too,' said the first mate, still on track. 'Fuel doesn't come cheap, you know. And now that we have to go halfway round the island of Lasserta to get it, the cost mounts up something wicked.'

'They said on the course that that was what came of operating out of a failed state,' volunteered the cabin boy, his gaze going from one speaker to another like a devotee at Wimbledon, 'whatever that means.'

'If we put in anywhere else for it we'd be sunk,' said the second mate feelingly.

'Literally,' said the captain, 'and that's without anyone else on the high seas trying to do it. Which, I may say,' he added gloomily, 'they do. All the time.'

'There was that warship the other day . . .' began the third mate. 'They were itching to have a go. I could tell.'

'Then there's all those pesky mercenaries to be paid for,' cut in the first mate. 'And they don't come cheap. Ideas above their station, the lot of them, if you ask me.'

'Moreover,' said the second mate, 'they don't always obey orders. The other day when we were taking over that oil tanker from the Gulf one of them went down to the galley to nick some fresh meat. They only ever think of themselves, you know.'

'Victuals is always important at sea,' opined the ancient mariner. 'Always was, too.'

'Lucky not to have had a cleaver through his head,' growled the third mate.

'Or a knife in his chest,' muttered someone else. 'There's always knives down there in the galley. Downright dangerous if you ask me.'

That the man had a something approximating to a cutlass prominent in his own belt was ignored by them all.

'What about the cost of the upkeep of the hostages, too?' said the second officer, whose responsibility these had ipso facto become. 'Very picky, some of them are – especially the women. One of them wanted make-up. I ask you! Where do you suppose we could get her make-up in the middle of the ocean?'

The first mate stretched his arms above his head and said expansively, 'Easy. A luxury yacht. Time you lot started thinking outside the box.'

'Talking of hostages,' piped up the cabin boy quickly, 'they asked at the course if we had any experience of the Stockholm syndrome.'

The first mate scratched his head.

'There was that cruise ship out of Stockholm, last year, remember. Big one. Swedish. Didn't see any syndromes about. A lot of passengers, though. Quite upset they were. Rich, too, of course.'

The cabin boy looked anxiously from one face to another. 'They said,' he began tentatively, 'that the Stockholm syndrome was when hostages began to collude with their kidnappers.'

'That's good,' said the second mate richly. 'Them collude with us! It's us that colludes with them or else. Fetch and carry, that's all we do. That and post letters. Terrible some of them are for writing home. If they've got good homes, why do they leave them?'

'Don't forget we've got that prisoner to feed, too,' said the captain. 'You know, the one that called himself a negotiator and thought he could get us to accept peanuts in exchange for a container ship.'

'If you ask me keelhauling would have been too good for him,' sniffed the third mate. 'Too clever by half.'

The captain gave a short laugh.

'He kept on saying "Jaw, jaw is better than law, law". I don't know where he got that idea from since we're not in territorial waters in the first place. I had him put him in irons in the end to keep him quiet.'

The first mate turned back to the boy. 'Anything else, lad?'

'Yes, there was something else,' nodded the cabin boy in spite of all this. 'They said we ought to clarify our demands.'

The first mate gave a mocking laugh.

'"Your money or your life" being so yesterday,' he said. 'Is that it?'

'I've never killed anyone who didn't cough up,' said the second mate virtuously.

'But they don't know that you're not going to, do they?' pointed out the third mate.

'I could never see anything wrong with "Stand and deliver" myself,' remarked the ancient mariner reminiscently, 'except that it was what highwaymen used to say.'

'And midwives,' said a man who had gone to sea to escape a burgeoning family.

The captain stirred himself. 'That's what we are, though, isn't it? Highwaymen of the sea.'

The ancient mariner gave a sudden cackle and burst into song. '"'It's only me, from over the sea,' cried Barnacle Bill, 'the sailor and seadog'".'

The others ignored him. The third mate turned to the cabin boy. 'Here lad, what else did the man say?'

'That we shouldn't use words like ransom,' said the boy.

'And what, pray,' asked the third mate sarcastically, 'should we say instead? Please and thank you?'

'We should call it a release fee.' The cabin boy looked really frightened now. 'Not ransom.'

The third mate gave a great guffaw, while

the captain asked if there was anything else they should be thinking about.

'Subscribing to Lloyd's Register of Shipping,' said the lad. 'Or any website that tells you which ship is making for where.'

He was answered by a chorus from the others: 'Radar's better.'

'Even when they zigzag.'

'I was never very good at books.'

'We'd have to pay for it.'

'I get their drift, though.' The captain sounded quite pleased with his pun. 'But what we do need to know is how to get better prize money and more often.'

The cabin boy piped up again. 'That was another thing. They said we shouldn't call it prize money any longer.'

'If,' began the first mate hotly, 'they think I'm going to talk about bonuses with them being so unpopular now that it's what bankers get . . .'

'Variable pay,' said the cabin boy succinctly. 'That's the in word now.'

'Two words,' said the third mate.

'Anything else?' the captain asked the lad, not unkindly. 'Might as well hear it all while we're about it.'

'The competition . . .' said the lad, nervously looking round at them all.

The crew fell silent. Only the captain felt able to say something and that after a long pause when he murmured, 'The Shanty Gang.' Then he turned back to the cabin boy. 'Did you mention the Shanty Gang to them?'

The boy hung his head. 'Yes,' he nodded. 'At first they weren't sure what we could do about the competition.'

'Nor are we,' said the first mate crisply. 'Short of making the Shanties fly the Skull and Crossbones, that is, and they won't do that.'

'Then,' the boy piped up again, 'after they'd thought about it for a bit, they suggested what we should do was to warn other shipping about the Shanties. Their radio people will think the warning is coming from an official source and they'll move into our patch to get away from the Shanty Gang.'

'Nice,' said the first mate approvingly. 'I like it.'

'Why didn't we think of that?' asked the third mate. 'It'd have saved your course fees.'

The captain, sensing implied criticism, told the boy to go on.

The lad was struggling with an unfamiliar word. 'They said we should be mortising . . . no, amortising, that's it – amortising each year.'

'Sounds nasty,' said the first mate.

'Is it catching?'

'We haven't got a fever flag,' muttered the third mate. 'It got the moth.'

'It's putting some money aside each year to buy a new boat when this one gets old,' explained the boy.

'That proves that they don't really understand our business,' said he with the giant chip on his shoulder.

'No need for whatever it was you said, boy,' the captain came back swiftly. 'We just keep one of the ones we've captured.'

'There's a nice little schooner I've been keeping my eye on,' said the first mate. 'It does a regular run to Lasserta. We can pick it up whenever we want, can't we?'

The boy swallowed. 'Then they said we should be doing some projections.'

'That's just what I say.' The ancient mariner stirred. 'They should never have done away with bowsprits.'

'Not that sort of a projection, Grandpa,' said the first mate.

'Put him in the scuppers until he's sober,' began the third mate.

The boy hurried on. 'But most important of all they said we should have an exit strategy. You know, make a plan about what to do when the going gets nasty.'

'Scarper,' said the third mate.

'Scuttle,' said the first mate.

'Take to the boats,' the second mate chimed in. 'The little ones, I mean.'

The boy frowned. 'They did mention something about lifeboats but I don't think that's what they meant.'

'Not our sort of lifeboat,' said the captain, nodding. 'I've heard about them.'

The boy swallowed and then said in a voice scarcely above a murmur, 'They said there was something else we could always do if the going got tough.'

'When the going gets tough the tough get going,' chanted the second mate. 'Is that it?'

'Not exactly,' said the boy uneasily.

'Come on, tell us what it is.'

'Surrender,' the boy whispered.

Into the shocked silence which followed the word, the second mate eyed him up and down and then said, 'Never. What you've got to understand, pretty boy, is that whatever they told you on that course this is a rough trade . . .'

There was the slightest of squeaks as the lad hit the deck in a dead faint.

OPERATION VIRTUAL REALITY

The colonel had never dealt in such trifling matters as New Year Resolutions before but he'd taken one earlier this year and he had every intention of keeping it. It was never to spend a Christmas with his son and daughter-in-law ever again.

There was nothing wrong with his son except that he worked too hard and was given to doing his wife's bidding without complaint. The colonel's late wife, Mavis, had never ordered him about in the way that Peter's wife did. Of course he, the colonel, had naturally always done what Mavis wanted but that was different.

Quite different.

The festivities last Christmas at Peter and Helen's house had been a real penance. The noise and the confusion and the cold had been almost unbearable. The house itself was cold because his daughter-in-law, who was cold in other ways as well, was bent on saving the planet: the colonel suspected it was a way of cutting down on the heating bills. The food was awful, too, because Helen was a vegetarian and only served flesh and fowl with a visible repugnance as a concession to old established custom. The colonel, who had endured something only a mouthful short of starvation in a prisoner-of-war camp and had taken a resolution at the time never to go short of a good meal ever again, had tackled turkey cooked by an unpractised hand without pleasure.

Worse than the food and the cold though had been the parties given there: for friends on Christmas Eve and for neighbours on Boxing Day. Disparate groups as they were he still didn't know which collection of guests had been the least likeable. Both were noisy and comprised people he neither knew nor liked. Some of those there on both Christmas Eve and Boxing Day couldn't hold their drink. This was something the colonel had always viewed with displeasure in the mess and in civilian life afterwards.

True, he liked a whisky himself in the evenings but that was all. The colonel only ever drank in moderation and never swayed about like those people did, clutching their fourth drink, skin glistening, boasting to complete strangers about their latest successful deal or the defeat of a rival. Not that the colonel didn't know all about defeat. He did. He'd been in Crete in May, 1941, which had been a defeat all right and was when he'd been taken prisoner.

So once back in his own home he began to plan his strategy for next Christmas. The first thing he had been taught as a young subaltern was that strategy came well before tactics. His strategy now was that he was going to say that he was going away himself next Christmas and therefore couldn't go to his son's house for the festivities.

He wouldn't actually go away, of course, because all he really wanted to do was to stay in his own home in peace and quiet by his own fireside with a decent whisky within arm's reach.

He would pretend to go away.

That was it.

Reminding himself of the old army maxim that time spent in reconnaissance was seldom wasted, he set about deciding where he would say he was going. Marrakech was his first thought – the image of the souk there had always appealed – although Switzerland beckoned, too. In his mind he soon discarded both putative destinations – Marrakech because it would be pretty obvious that he was just going away to avoid Christmas with Peter and Helen, and Switzerland because everyone would be bound to insist that it would be too cold in winter for a man of his age. He toyed briefly with the idea of saying that he was visiting the West Indies but thought it would be too long a flight to seem plausible.

The ideal destination came into his mind one evening as he was going up to bed. Climbing the stairs took no little effort and a lot of concentration these days and he marvelled as he did so each evening how quickly he had scaled some high ground near the regiment's position near Rethymnon on Crete in 1941.

Not now.

Now every individual stair had to be negotiated separately, the physiotherapist's advice to put his feet on each tread as if it was new ground echoing in his mind as ever.

He often wondered how quickly he would scale his own staircase these days if he was being shot at as he was at Rethymnon. It would probably, he thought wryly, loosen up his arthritic hips better than anything the doctor gave him.

That was it, he thought, as he got to the upstairs landing, panting slightly. He would tell everyone he was going to go to Crete. And not for a holiday. He would say he was aiming for the military cemetery at Suda Bay to visit Peter's grave. That was the Peter after whom his son had been named; the Peter who had been killed at his side; the Peter who had been his best friend.

Nobody could argue with that.

Satisfied with his strategy, he went happily to bed. Tactics, which came a long way after strategy, could wait until the morning. Next day he started to scan the advertisements for holidays in Crete, noting the name of any firm who specialised in that destination. He found two or three and sent off for their brochures, enjoying a frisson of excitement that he hadn't felt in years.

He duly studied the options in glorious colour presented by the tour operators, finally selecting a tour that left on Christmas Eve and was scheduled to come back the day after New Year. That should do him nicely. He noted all the details carefully and committed them to memory, which was what he thought of as 'military precision' although for the life of him he couldn't see why the two words had ever come together. Not after the landings in Crete.

Then he left the brochure around in a conspicuous position should anyone call.

The first person to do so was the vicar. That cleric asked in his usual airy way if there was anything he could do for him, expecting the usual answer of 'Nothing, thank you'.

'There is, actually,' said the colonel this time. 'Could you get your son – he's computer literate, isn't he? – to find out the flight number of this tour for me?'

'Of course,' said Vicar readily. 'He'll enjoy doing that. Have a good trip, won't you? I take it you're quite sure you're really up to that sort of thing these days? The years take their toll, you know.'

Mrs Beddoes was not so easily convinced that he was. Mrs Beddoes came in and did for him twice a week, doing his shopping and washing. She checked up, too, on the home-delivery company which brought him a hot lunch every day. 'I'll cancel your order for the days you're away,' she said, giving him a dubious look. 'And the milkman.'

This was something he hadn't bargained for and, applying his mind to the problem, he started to secrete food in corners that Mrs Beddoes didn't clean too often. This brought the prisoner-of-war camp back to his mind very quickly. It was what they had done when a man was planning a break-out. The places, though, where little parcels of food could be secreted away in a camp regularly searched by hostile guards were different from those in a house only dusted intermittently. Nevertheless he gave his mind to the problem in proper military fashion and soon caches of food were being hidden away by him in improbable places.

'I'd better stop the newspapers, too,' Mrs

Beddoes said before bustling back to the washing machine.

The colonel's son was not easily converted to the thought of a journey to Crete in midwinter.

'Of course I understand, Dad,' Peter said when he was told, 'but are you quite sure you're fit enough?'

'Quite sure,' said the colonel firmly. 'And if I should happen to die over there, don't you worry.' His voice quivered a little. 'I shall be among friends if I do.'

'We'll miss you at Christmas,' said his son awkwardly. 'Helen will be really disappointed and so will I.'

'If I don't go now, it'll be too late,' mumbled the colonel. 'Your mother would never let me go there, you know. She was worried that it might bring it all back.' Mavis – his dear Mavis – had waited long years for him in war and would never have his peace of mind disturbed by revisiting the scene of that unhappy campaign.

'Fair enough,' conceded Peter in the end. 'Now, what about you letting me take you to the airport?'

'Not on Christmas Eve,' retorted the colonel crisply. 'Too many bad drivers about. Besides I've already fixed up a taxi. Both ways,' he added hurriedly.

'I'll have a note of the flight number, though, Dad, just in case.'

The colonel handed it over with an inward smirk. He'd always thought that they ought to have had him in Intelligence in the war and his masterminding of this little campaign proved it. He felt a warm glow of victory over his daughter-in-law who had somehow been subconsciously transmogrified into the enemy.

The person who wasn't at all sanguine about his going to Crete was his doctor.

The colonel, who had got used to a series of army doctors, (whom he had always mentally categorised as no good as soldiers in the army and no good as doctors in the civilian world), had been surprised by how well he had taken to the young woman who had looked after his Mavis so well when she was ill and dying.

'What's this I hear about your flying off somewhere without asking me?' she said when he went to the surgery for his routine check.

One of the things that being in action had taught the colonel was who to trust. He gave her a straight look and told her the whole truth, pledging her to secrecy.

'I'm very glad to hear it,' she smiled. 'Your heart's in no state for an air trip. Stay at home and keep warm. And don't worry, your secret's safe with me.'

He trotted home happily and went over his plan for the hundredth time, thinking it through for possible snags as he struggled upstairs every night. 'I'll fool 'em all,' he said to himself time and again.

It was a week later when he realised he had been basking in a false sense of security. He had forgotten all about Bob and Lorraine Steele. They were the good neighbours who lived opposite the colonel's house. They had a long-standing arrangement with him that unless his curtains were drawn back by nine o'clock in the morning that they would alert his doctor.

Reminding himself that the Duke of Wellington had also encountered unexpected reverses in his many campaigns and had not been daunted by them, the colonel applied himself to thinking of a way round this.

When he went away in the ordinary way to his son's house he left the curtains drawn together and the lights on a timer that switched them on when darkness fell. If the curtains remained open all the week – he could hardly draw them nightly if he wasn't supposed to be there – he would not be able to put a light on in the evening without being seen and that would never do either.

If the curtains remained closed all the time he was away – his usual practice – then he would have very little light in the day. He thought about this for a while and decided that creeping about inside the house in the half-dark in daytime and having electric light in the evening was the better option.

Breathing more easily again, he sat back and reviewed his plan. Logistics came some way after strategy and tactics but he thought he had that side of things properly buttoned up now. With some satisfaction he decided that he had covered all eventualities and that it would defeat the enemy nicely.

In the way of all military master plans he had given his a name. He was pleased with that, too. It was a phrase he'd picked up from the television: 'Operation Virtual Reality'.

It was three days into his seclusion that proper reality set in. One morning as he was coming down the stairs with only half the light he was used to, he stumbled and fell headlong to the floor, hitting his head hard.

And no one knew.

Not, that is, until the day after he had told everyone he was due back home.

And that was too late.

END MATTER

Miss Millicent Pevensey pushed her food about on her plate without enthusiasm. And, when she came to think about it, no wonder. A famous cookery writer had once declared in print that the first bite of a meal was taken with the eye and now she had found out for herself – the hard way – how right that particular author had been. The trouble was that these days she could no longer see the plate on which the food had been served, let alone the meal itself or even – sad to say – read cookery writers any more either.

Miss Pevensey was blind.

So she couldn't taste the first bite with her eye any longer. Either eye, actually.

The consultant ophthalmologist had been very kind when he broke the news that this was going to happen to her. 'You've got the wrong sort of macular degeneration,' he had said.

'Like the wrong sort of snow,' she had commented tightly at the time.

'I'm very much afraid so,' he said, grateful that she hadn't broken down.

So now she had physically to take her first bite of the food from the plate before she could even decide what it was she was eating – and that in spite of some officious carer announcing that it was Irish stew once again. Actually it was nearly always Irish stew. Before taking her first mouthful, though, Millicent Pevensey had to establish the whereabouts on her plate of each of the constituents of the meal. And, if the main one was meat, to locate the gravy as well as the vegetables.

Cutting the aforementioned meat could be a problem, too, which accounted for the frequency on the menu of Irish stew. When other cuts of meat did happen to be served, the helper on duty – usually the one whom Miss Pevensey most disliked – would, unbidden and unannounced, come up behind her and cut it up for her. This was before she could protest that meat tasted better if you had cut it up yourself. Not that there would have been any use in explaining this in atavistic, developmental terms to this particular woman.

The name which Miss Pevensey had privately bestowed on this least-liked member of staff was 'Magpie', although it was neither her nickname nor her official title. The latter was probably 'Carer' but this Miss Pevensey could never bring herself to call her because the woman patently didn't care. Magpies were, to say the least, unattractive birds, given to preying on the nests of smaller, defenceless members of the avian species and this was how Miss Pevensey had come to think of her.

'We'll have to wear a bib, won't we,' the Magpie had said the last time Miss Pevensey had unwittingly splashed gravy down her blouse. 'All those stains on your front . . .'

'Gravy stains are the medals of the kitchen,' Miss Pevensey had rejoined, but the woman had not understood.

'I'll get you one with a little drip tray at the bottom,' said the Magpie. 'That'll catch anything you let fall.'

And before Miss Pevensey could utter a protest a plastic breastplate with a little trough at the bottom had been hung round her neck.

She had conveyed her indignation, though, to her next visitor. 'I call it my albatross,' she said, adding wryly, 'and try to think of myself now as the Ancient Mariner.'

'Rotten,' agreed Meg Ponsonby, her one-time deputy at Ornum College at the University of Calleshire. 'Haven't they got any respect?'

'Not for what one once was, I'm afraid,' sighed Millicent Pevensey, sometime principal of that college. 'Of course, rationally it's not relevant. What one once was, I mean. We're all just the old, the blind and the infirm here. One's past doesn't matter in these places.'

'Well, then, it jolly well ought to be relevant,' said Meg stoutly. 'By the way, have you heard the latest about the vice chancellor?'

Millicent leant forward eagerly, Meg, dear Meg, being her only link with what she still thought of as the real world. 'No, I haven't. Do tell me . . .'

When Millicent Pevensey had first entered the Berebury Home for the Blind she had resolved to apply all the logic that had been so much part of her working life to her present situation and treat her time there as a new and different stage in her life. Unfortunately it hadn't proved easy to adapt to it and this was largely due to the effect on her of the carer whom she had dubbed the Magpie. Once the woman had found out that Millicent Pevensey had been connected with the world of education, she had been treated by the Magpie with a great deal less than respect.

It soon transpired that the Magpie had disliked school and everything to do with it. Not only that but that she hadn't done very well there either. Some primary-school teacher had once a long time ago failed this particular pupil – that much was evident – and Millicent Pevensey was paying the price now.

Defenceless as she now was she bore the petty slights the Magpie inflicted on her as best she could. But however patient and tolerant Millicent Pevensey was, the Magpie seemed to search out ways in which she could work out her latent dislike of teachers on the hapless resident. At least Millicent Pevensey hoped that this was the reason for her behaviour, the sinister Nurse Ratched in *One Flew over the Cuckoo's Nest* coming into her mind from time to time.

Whilst it had been agreed at the home that the blind woman should be addressed as Miss Pevensey, when no one else was in earshot – and only then – the Magpie always called her Millie. Miss Pevensey hadn't realised she could still feel such insensate anger. She hadn't been so cross since her young brother had broken her favourite doll and that had been very many years ago.

The Magpie's behaviour was not the only cross Miss Pevensey had to bear. There was old Angela Pullen. Angela Pullen was not only old but what was kindly called absent-minded. Miss Pevensey, who had to sit next to her at mealtimes, thought this was a serious understatement. The woman's mind was not so much absent as entirely missing. The last occasion on which she had asked Angela – who still had some little sight – what the time was she had been answered by a high cackle and the words 'Two freckles past a hare, eastern elbow time'.

Meg Ponsonby had frowned when told about this response, patently searching her memory. 'I think,' she said doubtfully, 'that one of the folklorists at the college might have noted that expression.'

'I would be very surprised if they had,' said Millicent Pevensey with spirit. 'The woman's lost her marbles.'

'I'm not so sure,' frowned Meg Ponsonby. 'In my experience you can never tell with folklorists.'

Then there had been the matter of Millicent Ponsonby's breviary. 'My little book. The one I keep by my bed,' she said to the Magpie one day. 'I can't put my hand on it.' This had been literally what she had wanted to do. Running her fingers over the little leather-bound volume as she went to sleep always brought the rubric back to her mind and soothed her.

'I put it on top of the wardrobe,' said the Magpie, 'seeing as you can't read it any more.'

The last straw – the one that led Millicent Pevensey to an entirely new course of action – had happened one morning when the Magpie had been called away in the act of helping her to dress.

'It was quite insupportable,' said Millicent, later that day to her friend, Meg. She was still palpably distressed. 'She left me standing there in my shift, saying she wouldn't be gone a minute. She'd been late coming in the first place – it was halfway through the morning – and when she came back – that is,' she corrected herself, 'when I thought it was she coming back it wasn't her at all.'

'Oh, dear,' said Meg Ponsonby, never slow on the uptake. 'And who was it then?'

'Arthur Maple.'

'Oh, dear,' said Meg again. 'I don't suppose our revered Professor of Moral Law at the University has ever seen a woman in a shift before, bachelor that he is. Didn't he knock?'

'Oh, yes, but the Magpie is supposed to knock, too. The worst of it was that he behaved as if everything was normal.'

'Good for him,' murmured Meg under her breath.

'As if,' went on Millicent Pevensey, unappeased, 'I always received visitors in a state of undress. I don't know if that was worse than if he'd run away like a frightened rabbit.' She trembled with anger at the memory. 'Quite insupportable.'

The words stayed with the blind woman. And so did the thought. Life really was beginning to be quite insupportable. And, now she came to think of it, there was no real reason why she should put up with life. She put her mind to what action to take as she walked round the indoor exercise room at the home – somewhere she always thought of as like a manège for schooling horses. There was a circular fence there with a rail at hand height for the blind to hold on to as they walked round and round.

She started on her plan the next time Meg came to call. 'Do you think you could you buy me some more paracetamol, please? I've run out.'

It worked once. When she asked Meg the same thing on her next visit she got a gentle 'No, Millie, I think not. You've got earth's work to do first.'

So she waited until she had a letter delivered to her room and then asked the Magpie if she could borrow a knife from the kitchen to slit it open.

'Not allowed,' said the Magpie at once. 'I'll open it for you and read it out if you like.'

'No, thank you,' said Millicent Pevensey firmly. 'My friend will do that for me.'

Clasping a glass of water while she swallowed her tablets one night put another thought into

Millicent Pevensey's still-agile mind. Blind she might be but she knew exactly where her wrists were – all she needed was some broken glass. This proved less easy than she had thought. Not only did the tumbler not break when cast with all her vigour to the floor but it rolled away and – without sight – she could not locate it.

Next she tried sending the Magpie away while she was having a bath but the Magpie would not be diverted. 'It's as much as my job's worth to leave anyone alone in the bath here,' the carer had declared. 'You might drown and I'd get the sack.'

'True,' agreed Millicent meekly. 'And that would never do,' she added in case the thought of suicide had crossed the Magpie's mind, too.

She tried to remember Dorothy Parker's litany of the ways in which one might kill oneself – razors that pained you, acids that stained you, guns that weren't lawful – none of which were accessible in the Berebury Home for the Blind. And now even North Sea gas didn't kill any more.

She toyed instead with the idea of electrocution as she plodded round the exercise room the next morning. 'It's like being in a prison yard except that we can't do it in pairs and talk,' she complained to Meg on her next visit. 'Bearing in mind,' she added pertinently, 'that prisoners can at least look forward to the end of their sentence.'

'Life must have a reason,' insisted Meg Ponsonby, an authority on Comparative Religions. 'Nothing makes sense if it doesn't.'

Millicent Pevensey, though, was undeterred in her search to end it. Electrocution had seemed simple enough at first thought – presumably one only had to take out an electric light bulb and stick one's fingers in the socket instead. The only snag was that there was no reading lamp beside her bed.

'No need, is there?' the Magpie had said when asked about this. 'Besides, there's a perfectly good light in the ceiling for those of us that have to work in the room.'

Millicent sighed when she reported this remark to Meg. 'That's all that one has become reduced to nowadays – work for someone else.'

'Cheer up,' said Meg briskly. 'One man's meat is another man's poison. And, anyway, the economists like people having work to do. Other people, that is.'

Millicent had managed a smile at this but had nevertheless gone on thinking. There was, she knew, a way of death popular in Balkan countries that could leave the general public unsure whether the victim – like Amy Robsart – had fallen or been pushed. Defenestration was the name of the game. That would be perfect.

The only snag was that the Berebury Home for the Blind was only one storey high.

Salvation, when it came, was unexpected.

There was to be an outing for the residents from the home to the seaside near Kinnisport. Above the town was a beauty spot on the cliffs looking over the Cunliffe Gap with the added attraction of a broad walk and tea shop, to say nothing of the even greater attraction of a free public car park.

'Doesn't a day like this make you glad to be alive, Millicent?' asked Angela Pullen as they tumbled out of their minibus into a pleasant breeze.

'I wouldn't go as far as that, Angela,' said Millicent dryly.

'I can feel the sun.'

'I can hear the sea,' said Millicent purposefully walking towards the sound. The grass was rough but springy as she strode over it, her white stick a great help on the turf.

'Millie, come back,' shouted the Magpie, spotting her and thus diverted from her task of helping the other inmates out of the home's minibus.

'The sea, the sea,' chanted Millicent Pevensey to herself, increasing her speed.

'Millie, you mustn't go any further,' the Magpie shouted after. 'Stop or you'll go over the cliff. Just stand still.'

Millicent stepped up her pace even more as she heard feet pounding after her.

'Don't move,' shouted the Magpie.

Millicent heard the woman panting behind her now and walked even more quickly over the grass in the direction of the sound of the sea, quite invigorated. She must be near the edge now. The sound of the sea was getting louder and louder. All she had to do was keep on walking as quickly as she could and keep ahead of the Magpie.

What was undeniable was that the Magpie had youth – and sight – on her side. She reached Millicent's side just as the blind woman sensed the upward rush of air denoting the very edge of the cliff. The Magpie grabbed at Millicent's arm but was caught off-balance by the white stick and it was she – not Miss Millicent Pevensey – who tumbled over the cliff edge.

The coroner was very kind when he heard that Miss Pevensey had really just been enjoying a stroll in the fresh air and had had no idea she had been so near the cliff's edge. He dismissed everything Angela Pullen said as unreliable but placed on record the devotion shown by the carer, which was to be highly commended.

To discover more great books and to
place an order visit our website at
www.allisonandbusby.com

Don't forget to sign up to our free newsletter at
www.allisonandbusby.com/newsletter
for latest releases, events and exclusive offers

Allison & Busby Books
@AllisonandBusby

You can also call us on
020 7580 1080
for orders, queries
and reading recommendations